The Speakeasy

EXTRA DIRTY

K. EVAN COLES AND BRIGHAM VAUGHN

Extra Dirty
ISBN # 978-1-913186-07-4
©Copyright K. Evan Coles and Brigham Vaughn 2019
Cover Art by Cherith Vaughan ©Copyright March 2019
Interior text design by Claire Siemaszkiewicz
Pride Publishing

EXTRA DIRTY

Dedication

Extra Dirty and the Speakeasy books came upon us out of the blue as we wrote the second book in the Tidal series. It wouldn't have been possible without the incredibly supportive people in our lives and some scene-stealing secondary characters.

For my husband, who is patient and encouraging of my endless scribbling.

For my son, who makes me laugh every single day.

For the people in and around my life who inspire me, let me be weird and make me feel brave.

And for Brigham Vaughn, who endures thousands of questions, listens to my rants, indulges my kooky humor and is nearly always willing to put pen to paper when our stars align.
— K. Evan Coles

This book is for my friends who were patient when I was too busy writing or editing to spend time with them. For the people who cheered me on and had faith in my writing long before I did. For my parents, who are the best patrons of the arts a writer could ask for.

And, mostly, for K. Evan Coles, who got me into reading and writing gay romance in the first place. I wouldn't be here without you! It's been a wonderful — and occasionally frustrating — journey. There's no one I would rather have done it with.
— Brigham Vaughn

K. and Brigham would also like to thank:

Their patient beta readers Shell Taylor, Rebecca Spence, Allison Hickman, Tracey Kemple and Sally Hopkinson. You helped us mold the story you see before you today. We could not have done it without you.

And the Speakeasy Crew who just won't stop talking — Jesse, Kyle, Will, Carter and Riley. Those boys have got a whole lot more company these days.

Chapter One

April 2015

Jesse Murtagh set down the packet of financial statements he'd been reviewing and smiled. He was seated in the back office of Under, a speakeasy in Morningside Heights, and life was good.

With Under approaching its one-year anniversary, the bar's earnings surpassed expectations each quarter. They boasted a full guest list every night, and Under appeared as a "must visit" on New York's fashionable lifestyle blogs and guides. Business was booming. And its success meant everything to Jesse and his business partner, Kyle McKee.

In addition to being Under's co-owner, Kyle also happened to be one of Jesse's favorite people in the world and one of his favorite partners in bed. Jesse would bet he'd find Kyle out in the speakeasy right now, too, readying the place for opening.

Jesse got to his feet. He locked the papers in the desk, then exited the office and moved toward the long bar that ran the length of the room. Under had a masculine, sophisticated vibe. Sleek leather seating areas dotted the room and open shelves lined the walls, backlit with amber lamps that cast a warm glow over bottles of rare and high-end liquors. On a typical evening, house music throbbed through the air by now, but Jesse and Kyle were holding a private party tonight, and silence reigned, save the sounds of Kyle at work.

"Hey, gorgeous," Jesse drawled. "When did you get here?"

Kyle glanced up at Jesse's approach. He smiled and the quirk of his full lips sent a ripple of heat through Jesse's body.

"About an hour ago." He shrugged easily. Kyle had dressed in black, as he always did for work, and rolled his shirtsleeves up to the elbow. His muscled forearms flexed as he polished a rocks glass. "I saw Matt upstairs when I came in. He told me you were here, but I figured you'd be busy counting the money. Thought I'd leave you to it."

Jesse rounded the bar with a laugh. "You know me too well."

Opening the speakeasy had been a departure from his usual business of running a growing regional media conglomerate with his family. Jesse had never even worked in a bar or restaurant, let alone owned one. But Kyle had mentioned the idea of opening a bar one night over dinner and drinks, and the way his dark eyes had shone had captured Jesse's fancy.

Jesse had mulled the idea over for several days, then brought it to his brother, Eric. He'd hoped Eric would talk him out of it and had thrown up his hands when Eric merely smiled.

'I'm not sure who you think you're fooling, Jes,' Eric had said. *'I can already tell you've made up your mind to do it.'*

And so, Jesse had found himself working with his accountants and his lawyer to create a business proposal. Within two weeks of that fateful dinner, he'd presented it to Kyle. They'd celebrated by screwing each other senseless, then started scouting for a location the very next day.

Jesse stepped up behind Kyle now and molded himself against his body. He wound his arms around Kyle's waist, careful to avoid the glass in his hands.

In many ways, Kyle appeared to be Jesse's opposite. His elegant, clean-shaven features and dark hair contrasted with Jesse's short beard and dark-blond, blue-eyed coloring. Jesse broadcasted his emotions, whereas Kyle was more reserved. Both men stood at six feet and were built long and lean, like runners. But where Jesse could be coltish in his movements, Kyle's were deliberate and graceful. Kyle, Jesse liked to say, had found his Zen.

Jesse nuzzled the side of Kyle's neck. "I take it last month's numbers are good?" Kyle's voice went low and throaty.

"Indeed." Jesse pulled him closer. He angled his hips and pressed his groin against Kyle's muscular ass, and his body paid immediate attention to that firm heat. "The numbers are so good, in fact, I think we should celebrate." He pressed a lingering kiss to Kyle's throat.

Kyle leaned back into him with a rumbling noise. He set the glass he'd been polishing on the bar. "What did you have in mind?"

"Next weekend off — Masen can handle things in your absence."

"Well, he'll like that."

Kyle sounded amused. They'd hired Masen Jones earlier in the year to help out, and he'd quickly become Kyle's right-hand man.

"A whole weekend, though... I don't know, Jes."

Jesse dropped one hand and palmed Kyle through his trousers, and, oh, yes, he was hard. Kyle let out a soft gasp.

"Friday and Saturday, then," Jesse bargained. He closed his eyes, heat flashing under his skin as Kyle pushed back and ground against him. "We'll go to that club in Chelsea you told me about."

"Oh, fine." Kyle turned in the circle of his arms. "I'll bring Jarrod and Gale as backup," he added, then looped his arms around Jesse's neck. "They can walk me home after you find someone to disappear with."

Jesse grinned. "You really do know me too well," he murmured and covered Kyle's mouth with his own.

The kiss deepened and Kyle groaned. Jesse palmed him again, his touch rough, and pressed Kyle backward hard into the bar. Kyle's cock twitched under Jesse's hand, and he broke away with a sharp inhale.

"Jesus."

"Jesse will do."

Jesse let Kyle go and leaned back enough to get his hands on Kyle's belt. Desire pulsed through him. Quickly, he opened Kyle's trousers and pushed the dark fabric down his legs. Kyle's eyes were wild when Jesse looked up again and a flush stained his cheeks and neck. He uttered a soft moan as Jesse sank to his knees.

Jesse kissed Kyle's thighs. He kneaded the soft, fair skin with his hands and dragged Kyle's boxer briefs down. Kyle sighed as his cock slipped free of the underwear and jutted up onto his abdomen.

Jesse pressed his face into the juncture between Kyle's thigh and groin and inhaled the smell of almond-scented soap and sweat and man. "Damn," he said, his voice low. "You always smell so good."

Kyle ran his hands over Jesse's head, then twined his fingers into his short hair. That possessive touch sent a jolt of lust zigzagging down Jesse's spine. He loved it when Kyle got rough.

Shifting, he held tight to Kyle's hips and opened his mouth at the base of his cock. He slowly dragged his tongue along its length.

"Oh, God." Kyle's low whisper set a fire in Jesse's belly.

He licked and teased the shaft before he ducked down and caught Kyle's balls with his tongue. He lavished them with attention until Kyle moaned steadily, then looked up and locked eyes with him. The dazed bliss on his face made Jesse's dick throb.

"Suck me," Kyle rasped out.

Jesse pulled back. He braced one arm across Kyle's abdomen and wrapped his free hand around his base. Very, very slowly, he slid his lips over Kyle, reveling in the bittersweet taste and weight of the hard, velvety flesh on his tongue.

He took Kyle deep and waited until his nose brushed the curls of hair on his groin before he swallowed. Kyle's eyes went wide. Jesse pinned him against the bar, and he bucked his hips forward, a strangled noise tearing out of him.

Kyle tipped his head back as Jesse sucked. He closed his eyes and swore, and his ragged tone went straight to Jesse's groin. Jesse dropped his free hand and palmed himself, past caring if he shot in his pants.

He worked Kyle hard with his mouth until a shudder racked his frame. Jesse moved the arm pinning Kyle's hips, which left him free to fuck Jesse's mouth. Kyle opened his eyes again and stared at Jesse, his gaze filled with fire. He started to thrust and desire rattled down Jesse's spine. He groaned with need and closed his eyes when Kyle gasped.

"Gonna come, Jes," Kyle said, his voice rough and desperate. He tensed at Jesse's moan. Then Jesse pressed the fingers of his free hand into the soft skin behind Kyle's balls, and Kyle fell apart with a cry.

He tightened his grip on Jesse's hair and his knees buckled. Jesse used his shoulder to hold Kyle up. His balls tightened as Kyle pulsed in his mouth, and he swallowed, tasting bitter and salt.

Kyle's panting breaths echoed through the silent bar. Jesse pulled off, his head swimming, and Kyle freed his shaking hands from Jesse's hair. He bent and hauled Jesse to his feet, and Jesse stumbled and clutched at Kyle.

"You okay?" Kyle asked with a smile.

"Dizzy. And I wanna fuck you right now," Jesse muttered. Jesus, he needed to come. He pulled Kyle in for a messy kiss and ground his erection against Kyle's thigh until Kyle broke away with a breathless laugh.

"I think we've violated enough health codes for now," Kyle said. "Besides, we don't have any lube or rubbers."

"There's some in the office."

"We used them up last weekend."

Jesse whined and rutted harder into Kyle. "Fuck."

"I said no," Kyle scolded, his tone playful and his brown eyes gleaming. He pulled his trousers up. No sooner were they buttoned than he sank to his knees and reached for Jesse's belt. "Lucky for you, there's time for me to suck you off and clean up."

Kyle worked Jesse's fly open and leaned in. He spread his palms over Jesse's thighs and mouthed him through his boxer briefs. Goosebumps rose along Jesse's arms at the press of damp heat and cotton against his erection. Leaning forward, he braced his hands against the gleaming bar, arrested by the sight of his friend. Kyle shut his eyes and nuzzled Jesse through his clothes. His long, dark lashes fanned over his fair skin, and his lips were parted and wet. He looked unbelievably erotic.

Jesse cupped his jaw. "Mmm, baby."

Kyle opened his eyes. He hooked his fingertips under the waistband of Jesse's boxer briefs, then pulled his trousers and briefs down. Jesse hissed. He bit his lip hard when his cock sprang free, and Kyle swallowed him down.

Jesse's world exploded in a roar of pleasure that wiped his mind clean.

Life was very good indeed.

* * * *

"What kind of poison are you mixing up?"

Jesse tossed a handful of Luxardo maraschino cherries in a Boston shaker and glanced up at his friend, Carter Hamilton.

"Red Moon over Manhattan," he replied as he muddled the fruit. "They're phenomenal."

Jesse counted Carter as another of his favorite people, though their days as lovers were over. Carter had spent much of his life believing himself to be straight, as had the man who'd become his partner, Riley Porter-Wright. Both men had been in their early thirties before they accepted their sexuality didn't fit the binary model, and when they'd come out, they'd turned their lives upside down.

Jesse and Kyle had met Carter during that chaotic time. Together, they'd helped him tap into a part of himself that had lain mostly dormant for decades, and the three formed a tight friendship that continued after Carter had committed himself to Riley.

"What are you and your man up to this weekend?" Jesse asked him. "And where is Riley, anyway?"

Carter's hazel eyes warmed at the mention of his partner's name. "He got hung up at the office — should be here soon. We've got the kids and dog this weekend while my ex is out of town, then Ri's going out of town, too. Oh, that reminds me. Sadie has a doctor's appointment on Wednesday, and I need someone to pick Dylan up from school. Any chance you can do it?"

"Sure," Jesse replied without hesitation. He enjoyed acting as babysitter to Carter's two children and rarely turned down Carter's occasional requests. "I can move a couple of things around on my schedule to make it happen." He added red wine to the shaker.

"Thanks — you're a lifesaver. I'll send a note with Dylan on Wednesday to give his teacher the heads-up." Carter smiled. "We'll be in Southampton the following weekend, by the way, to summerize the house. You and Kyle should come out."

Jesse furrowed his brow at his friend. He'd stayed at Riley's beach house on Long Island many times and knew they typically waited until mid-May to ready it for summer. "It's April tenth, Car. What's the rush?"

"I'm not sure." Carter raised his expressive brows. "I get the feeling Ri thinks Sadie and Dylan need more fresh air than they're getting here in the city. He keeps talking about grass and trees, like we don't have a garden out back at our place."

Jesse poured an ounce of bourbon into the shaker. "Riley grew up in this city, too. I'll lay bets he didn't have a yard as a kid."

"Of course he didn't. His mother would have let their rooftop garden go wild if not for their gardener." Carter laughed. "Ri did spend every summer out at the beach, though. He wants to pass the experience on to the kids."

Jesse huffed out a laugh. He didn't always recognize Carter's life these days, but he felt happy for him. He also made no secret of missing manhandling Carter's six-foot-five frame into bed. They'd had an amazing time learning how to please each other once, and their emotional attachment ran deep. Carter belonged with Riley, however, and Jesse knew it.

Carter wanted the big, romantic happily ever after with one partner and, while the notion made Jesse roll his eyes, he supported anyone's choice to make that life. So long as no one forced him into the same little box. He didn't believe in monogamy. He didn't much believe in the gender binary, either, because why would he limit himself to men or women, when he could have — and wanted — both?

Carter quirked a brow at him. "Something funny?"

"Just you and Ri," Jesse snarked. "You're so sweet I may barf."

"Please aim your vomit away from the booze." Kyle stepped up to join them. "Did I hear you say you're going out to Long Island next weekend?"

Carter nodded but didn't answer until Jessie finished rattling the shaker. "Yes. Want to come out? Kate will have the kids, so it'll be quiet and you guys can do something grossly domestic and uncool for a change."

Kyle grinned. "Jes is always uncool."

"Shut up, nerd. As it happens, we have free days next weekend," Jesse told Carter.

Kyle rolled his eyes. "I suppose we do. What can we bring? I mean, besides a selection from Jesse's extensive collection of sexual lubricants?"

* * * *

An hour later, Jesse walked out from behind Under's bar with a drink of his own. His body thrummed with satisfaction. It had been a trick coaxing Kyle into hosting these monthly parties because he'd hated the concept of losing an entire night's revenue. He'd relented after Jesse promised to fund the parties out of his own pocket but neither had expected anything more than the opportunity to enjoy their high-end man cave with friends.

They both looked forward to these Thursday nights, however, and Jesse in particular. Under meant a great deal to him and not because it generated steady revenue. He honestly loved the place. He re-invested his small salary back into the business and made every effort to ensure it thrived while Kyle ran the show from behind the bar. Because, within the speakeasy's walls, he didn't have to deal with his day job or his celebrity, or even the well-meaning expectations of his loving, supportive and redundantly heteronormative family.

Jesse sat on one of the low leather sofas and surveyed the scene around him. Riley and Carter were to his left, chatting with two of Carter's co-workers. Kyle stood at his station behind the bar, more out of habit than necessity, deep in conversation with their friends Will and David, who'd driven up from Long Island. Jesse's brother, Eric, was also present and entertaining clients at the far end of the room. His small smile told Jesse he had things well in hand.

A beautiful brunette in Carter's group stood then and stepped up beside Riley. She motioned at the space between him and Jesse. "Scoot over, handsome, so I can talk to Blondie here."

Jesse smirked at the laughter that rose up from the group. He'd been given the nickname by Astrid Larsen last fall. Their affair had lasted only a month, but they'd stayed friends and still saw each other regularly, both in and out of bed. And why not? Jesse admired Astrid's sharp mind and every inch of her five-foot-eight Finnish-Moroccan frame, and they always had fun together, whatever they got up to.

"I need a favor," she said and settled beside him. Astrid twined a long, dark curl of hair around her finger. "No, I need to gossip first. Isn't that tall slab of Asian man by the bar in politics?"

Jesse looked past Astrid to where David sat talking with Will and Kyle. "You've got a good eye. David also goes by Senator Mori," he confirmed. "He's Japanese-American, by the way, and represents District Eight on Long Island."

"I knew it. Unlikely I'd forget a face like his." Astrid's face took on a thoughtful expression. "I've got it now —

Mori is a Republican and his partner is the son of former Senator Martin, right? There were some pieces on them in the *Lifestyle* section of the paper. Martin and his son were estranged."

"That's right. Senator Martin introduced Will to David."

Will and David's story was more complicated than that, of course. Once upon a time, Will Martin had been Riley's boyfriend and held serious disdain for Carter, as well as Jesse and Kyle. After breaking things off with Riley, Will had become friends with their circle, and Jesse and the others had been there for him after his father had died last fall.

Astrid nodded. "Do you know if Carter's talked to Senator Mori about fundraising with us? LGBTQ-friendly Republicans aren't easy to come by. He's got potential to reach a whole new demographic of donors."

"Assuming David's not a self-loathing prick, right?" Jesse teased. He already knew David believed wholeheartedly in the work of the Corporate Equality Campaign's mission to protect the rights of LGBTQ employees in the workplace.

"I doubt you'd let him in the door if that were the case." Astrid's expression turned sly. She slid a finger along his jaw with a teasing touch. "Pretty sure you'd turn away an actual POTUS if they even breathed a word against someone you love."

"True," he conceded. "Talk to Carter, obviously, but I know he and David have discussed fundraising possibilities. Malcolm's already reached out to David's staff to set dates and times."

"Great—maybe I can get in on it, too. Malcolm's got a lot going on right now, and I'm sure he can use a hand."

Astrid dropped a hand on Jesse's thigh and squeezed slightly.

Oh, man.

He and Kyle had rules about keeping sexual relations out of the bar—unless the relations were with each other—but Astrid always pinged Jesse's buttons in the right ways. At this rate, he'd need to leave earlier than planned.

Jesse slapped a grin on his face and tried like hell to distract them both from his body's response. "You said you needed a favor?"

"Actually, I do." Astrid raised her brows. "I need a date for a cocktail reception and dinner next Wednesday. My parents are throwing an engagement party for my sister and I want some delicious arm candy to show off."

"I'd love to be your candy boy, but I've already got plans for Wednesday." Jesse turned in his seat to include the others. "Carter asked me to pick up Dylan after school and I promised I'd stay for dinner."

Carter pulled a face. "Sorry, Astrid. My ex is out of town next week, and so is Riley—he'll be at a conference in Tel Aviv."

"Oh goodness, don't apologize. Babysitting trumps engagement parties." Astrid's expression became impish. "I have to say the idea of one of New York's most sought-after bachelors on a school pickup list is precious."

Jesse rolled his eyes while Carter and Riley laughed. "Girl, no one cares about my bachelorhood. And it's not as if paparazzi hang outside the school, waiting for interesting people to show up."

"Like you're so interesting." Jesse stuck out his tongue and Astrid giggled. "I still need a date," she added, "or my family is going to be all over my case."

"What about Malcolm?" Jesse turned to the boyishly handsome man on Carter's right. "You got any plans for Wednesday evening, Maleficent?"

Astrid pressed her lips together to stifle another laugh, but Carter and Riley didn't bother hiding their amusement.

Malcolm Elliot raised a brow. "Who, now?"

"Maleficent," Jesse repeated, his tone sober. "She's one of my favorite evil queens, Malcolm, just like you." He lost the battle to keep a straight face after Malcolm threw a cherry from his drink that grazed the top of Jesse's head.

"I'm happy to be your arm candy," Malcolm told Astrid once they'd all stopped laughing. His smile lit his blue-gray eyes, and he appeared genuinely pleased when she clapped her hands.

Jesse watched him with interest. In addition to being whip-smart, Malcolm was younger than the men around him, in some cases by almost a decade. He stood six-foot-three and had a build like a brick shithouse and, while close to Carter, was far more reserved than the rest of their circle, almost closed-off. Jesse knew from past conversations that Malcolm liked baseball, sci-fi and sushi, but he didn't disclose much in the way of personal information.

Jesse smiled to himself. He didn't know which way Malcolm's bell swung, though he definitely rang gay in his mind. Maybe he could get the boy to loosen up this summer. He'd always enjoyed a project.

Chapter Two

"Late night?" Taryn asked. Her tone sounded sympathetic but laced with a hint of amusement.

"Uh-huh," Cameron Lewis muttered without lifting his head from his desk.

"Gig?"

"Yep."

"I thought you swore never to DJ on school nights again."

"I made bad choices." His voice was muffled.

"Well, you'd better pull yourself together. You have less than an hour to go until it's time to turn young people into future musicians!" She sounded disgustingly cheerful.

"How are you so damn perky?" he moaned, his head throbbing. The aspirin he'd taken before he'd left his apartment didn't seem to be kicking in.

"I made good choices!"

"Fuck off."

"You better be nice to me. One of those good choices was leaving early enough to go to Sufficient Grounds. I even brought you a tall, hot blonde."

Cam heard the quiet click of heels before the scent of coffee reached his nose. He lifted his head and stared blearily at his friend and fellow elementary school teacher at Midtown Academy, Taryn Guillory. "I take back everything terrible I ever said about you," he said, then reached for the to-go coffee cup she held out to him. The drink order began as a joke — Taryn had teased Cam about his preference for tall, hot, blond men, but he'd grown to like the lighter roast coffee. It was acidic but higher in caffeine — something he really needed today.

"Wait? When did you say anything terrible about me?" Taryn leaned her hip against his desk and mock scowled at him. Though she wasn't a natural ginger like Cam, her pale skin and hazel-green eyes made the bottled color stand out. Her look channeled Joan from *Mad Men* — though she was somewhat less curvy than the original — and made heads turn. Cam had watched her playful smirk turn students' parents, of both sexes, into flustered adolescents with crushes.

She poked at his forearm. "Cam. Focus. When did you say anything terrible about me?"

"Never, of course." He took a sip of the coffee and sighed with relief when it hit his tongue. Hopefully, the rush of caffeine would follow soon. "You're my favorite person in the whole wide world."

Taryn raised an eyebrow, her doubt obvious, but didn't comment. "So, tell me about these bad choices that led to you looking like roadkill this morning."

Cam leaned back in his chair, cradling the still-warm cup. "Jerry asked me to spin as a favor, and I couldn't turn him down."

"Jerry who? The owner of Club Ember?"

"Yeah. The DJ he'd lined up for the night canceled, and it was a private event. All the others were either booked or didn't want a Thursday gig either. He offered me a bit over what he normally pays me, and I owe him so…"

"I know he hired you to do regular gigs at Ember, but do you owe him that much?" Taryn shifted and perched on the edge of his desk.

Cam took another healthy swallow of coffee. "Yeah, I do. When I approached Jerry a few years ago, I was a no-name DJ with next to no club experience. I'd done house parties and a few small venues, but my résumé was shit. Ember was already a well-established nightclub in Chelsea. He took a chance on me. Besides, the gig isn't the reason I feel like death warmed over. Or, at least, not all of it."

"Do tell." Taryn's eyes brightened. "Oooh, was there a guy? I bet there was a guy."

"There was a guy. He's a bartender at Ember." Cam made a face. "I told you I made bad choices."

"Let me guess. Tall, hot and blond?"

Cam thought about the guy he'd gone home with the night before. Tall? Check. Hot? Check. Blond? Check and check. Damn it. He did have a type. "Nailed it."

Taryn snickered. "I think you nailed it, hon."

"That I did. Then he nailed me. Although, it's a bit hazy. There were shots involved. Many, many vodka shots."

"That's not like you. Especially on a school night. Did you at least have fun?"

He grinned. "Oh, I had a great time. I feel like hell right now, but great party, great drinks, great guy...yeah, no regrets. Other than doing it all on a Thursday night when I have classes on Friday."

"What's the guy's name, anyway?"

"Ben." Cam racked his brain. "Granger, I think."

"So are you planning to see Ben again?"

He shrugged. "We exchanged numbers. He said he'd text me. I told him I wasn't looking for anything serious but wouldn't be opposed to a semi-regular thing."

"Cool."

"At the very least, I'll see him at the club. Which could be awkward if it goes south, but it's not like we have to interact unless we want to."

"Yeah, true."

"What about you?" Cam drained the remainder of his coffee and tossed the empty cup in the trash next to his desk. "Anything exciting happen last night?"

"I scored the perfect dresser at Thrift Kingdom!" Taryn made a face. "Ugh. That sounds so much less exciting now that I say it aloud. Compared to you spinning at a private party and hooking up with a hot bartender, my life is lame."

Cam snorted. "My head is telling me I could use more lame. Besides, I know you've been looking for a dresser since you moved into the new place."

"It's so cute, too!" Taryn squealed.

Cam shot her a glare and she subsided.

"Sorry," she whispered. She pulled out her phone and, after a moment, held it up for him to see. "That's the dresser."

He nodded his approval. "Nice. Very mid-century mod. I'm surprised you found it. Stuff like that gets snatched up so quickly."

"Oh, I got lucky. I was there right when they put it out and I grabbed it."

"Awesome." Cam frowned. "Wait, how'd you get it home? You live on the fifth floor. What did you do, find big, burly men to carry it up for you?"

"Well..."

"Oh, no." He groaned. "I see where this is going, and I do not like it."

"Please? They said they'd hold it until Saturday. I'll pay for the Zipcar and buy you dinner after. Just think, you'll be able to skip the gym."

"But I'll be crippled by carrying a dresser up five fucking flights of stairs." He narrowed his eyes at her. "Now I see why you brought me coffee this morning."

"Guilty as charged. Look, I promise to round up my roommates to help you. And I'll buy coffee for you all next week."

"Ugh. Make it two weeks and you have a deal." He wouldn't have let his friend down for the world, but he wasn't above trying to wrangle a few perks out of her.

Taryn's phone buzzed in her hand. "Crap, that's my fifteen-minute warning. I should have been prepping." She hopped off his desk and brushed off her wool pencil skirt.

Cam looked at the clock and groaned. "You're telling me."

"Meh, have the kids hit stuff with sticks. That's all you music teachers do anyway, right?"

"And all you art teachers do is have kids throw paint on a canvas, right?"

"Touché." She paused in the doorway. "See you at lunch?"

"See ya."

Cam had noticed Taryn his first day at Midtown Academy. She'd been eating alone in the teachers' lounge and had given him a small, sincere smile when he'd asked if he could join her. He'd teased her about her wardrobe and asked if she was single-handedly trying to destroy all stereotypes about art teachers dressing like hippies. She'd primly told him that someone had to do it and why not her? Cam had cracked up, and they'd been friends ever since.

Taryn had been hired the year before Cam, but he'd observed she didn't have a lot of friends. It surprised him, given that she was smart, beautiful, an accomplished artist and great with the kids, but he eventually understood she intimidated a lot of people. Plus, she was an unapologetic flirt. Hell, she'd flirted with Cam until she realized she was barking up the wrong tree.

The Academy staff had never warmed up to Taryn, but the kids adored her. Cam watched her take kids who swore they hated art and turn them into enthusiastic artists. The staff liked Cam, and he made an effort to get to know them, but they could be a rather clique-y group and, since they were a bit stodgy for Cam's tastes, he didn't socialize with staff outside work. Being of a similar age, with interests in the arts and low tolerances for stodginess, Cam and Taryn had naturally gravitated toward each other.

Cam heard the chatter of kids' voices approaching and a cheerful-sounding, "Hi, Mr. Lewis!"

He glanced up from his desk and smiled at Sadie Hamilton, one of his first students to filter into the classroom.

"Good morning, Sadie."

"You look tired." She squinted at him. "Are you getting sick? My mom just got over a cold."

Cam found Sadie Hamilton to be bright, and she was one of his favorite students. "No, I don't think I'm sick. I didn't go to bed early enough," he explained. "That's why your mom and dads are always telling you to get enough rest. If you don't listen, you turn into a grown-up like me who forgets."

Sadie giggled, but before she could reply, her friend Emily arrived and pulled Sadie toward her seat, chattering about something her stepmom had done. Emily, along with Sadie and her brother Dylan, weren't Cam's only students with less than traditional family structures. The Hamiltons had one of the best functioning from what Cam could tell, though. Sadie's mother, Kate, and her partner, Robert, got along flawlessly with Sadie's father, Carter, and his partner, Riley. Or, flawlessly from Cam's perspective, at least.

He'd put together most of the pieces of the family's dynamics from what they'd told him, augmented by the gossip columns and the school's very active rumor mill. Apparently, Carter and Riley had been friends for years, but they didn't become a couple until after they were divorced. Of course, a lot of people believed they'd been having an affair behind their wives' backs the whole time. Cam figured it wasn't any of his business, but either way, they and Kate Hamilton were doing something right. Sadie and Dylan were happy, well-adjusted children.

The fact that Kate remained civil with Carter and Riley, much less parented with them, was in itself a minor miracle. And one for which Cam felt deeply grateful. Teaching could be a difficult job under the best of circumstances, but warring parents made it a nightmare.

The remainder of the students arriving reminded Cam he needed to focus on his job and he looked down at his day planner. Time to figure out which lecture from next week he could substitute for today's. Preferably one that was quiet.

* * * *

Cam was ready to face-plant onto his bed after he unlocked the door to his loft apartment in Brooklyn. His typical forty-five-minute commute from Midtown East where he worked had taken over an hour and a half, thanks to delays at the East River ferry. Freezing rain made for a miserable bike ride to his DUMBO neighborhood, and he felt tired, cold and grumpy.

He kicked off his boots near the door and added them to the pile. Five people living in one apartment meant a mountain of discarded footwear at any given moment. "It looks like a centipede lives here," Cam could hear his mom muttering to herself. Not that he or his four siblings had ever listened, but every so often, her voice urged him to at least cull his contribution to the pile.

With rain dripping from his boots and no motivation to do a damn thing about it, he left them to dry.

He spread out his hat, gloves and scarf, too, then hung his jacket on the slightly listing coat rack he'd picked up on a thrifting trip with Taryn. The white-painted cinder block walls were a pain in the ass to hang anything from, so he'd gone with the freestanding option. It beat the pile of jackets they'd had before.

Cam trudged down the hall, debating if he should grab a quick bite before he passed out.

"Hey, man." Myron walked by the open-concept kitchen, his words muffled by a mouthful of peanut butter and marshmallow fluff sandwich. He ate one every single day, and Cam shuddered every time.

"Hey."

Myron swallowed. "You look bushed."

"I'm dead," Cam agreed. He pulled open the refrigerator door and stared at the meager offerings on his portion of the shelf. They'd had a pizza party at the school the other day, and Cam had taken home the leftovers. Thank goodness because he didn't have the ambition for anything more involved.

"Cold pizza it is," he muttered. He retrieved the box and tossed it onto the counter.

"Are you coming down with something?" Myron was a bit of a hypochondriac, and he eyed Cam with suspicion.

"No." Cam yawned. "I had a gig last night and worked today. I'm running on two hours of sleep."

"Ah." Myron nodded. "I'm getting ready to go to work now."

Myron Goodman worked as a jazz pianist at a local lounge and had a side business selling refurbished phones online. He brought in a decent amount of money, and Cam thought it was all legit. Well, most of it anyway. He paid his rent on time, so Cam didn't ask questions.

Cam grabbed a slice and took a bite of Hawaiian pizza. "Anyone else home?"

Myron shook his head. "I haven't seen Louise in a couple of days, and Bernice and Kevin are out."

Louise Hicks and Bernice Weber were the only other names on the lease with Cam's and Myron's. But Bernice and her boyfriend, Kevin Dolan, were usually joined at the hip and, for all practical purposes, Cam had four roommates instead of three.

Since Kevin chipped in on rent, no one argued. Although Cam was sick of finding Kevin's beard hairs in the shower. He hoped they were beard hairs, anyway.

"I'm gonna crash when I finish eating then," Cam said.

"I'm heading out in fifteen, so you should be good."

Cam wasn't a light sleeper — especially when this tired — but the more roommates home, the noisier the place got, and he wouldn't turn down a few hours of uninterrupted sleep.

"Thanks, man." Cam ripped paper towel off the roll, tossed another slice of pizza on top of it and jammed the box back in the refrigerator.

Cam trudged to his bedroom and stuffed pizza in his face along the way. His room was the size of a shoebox, with just enough room for a bed, a narrow dresser he could only open with the bedroom door closed, and a makeshift clothing rack. Because the building was a former industrial space, and since they'd framed the bedrooms with the apparent goal of cramming as many in as possible, it had no closets. The bedroom walls were nine feet tall but open to the ceiling. He couldn't count the number of times he'd heard his roommates having sex.

Still, the rest of the place was pretty nice. He liked the cinder block walls, concrete floors and huge windows. True industrial spaces in the neighborhood were getting harder and harder to come by. They were hard to come by in the entire Tri-State area, according to Cam's dad, who was an electrician in New Jersey.

Cam finished his pizza, tossed the paper towel in the trash and sank onto the bed with a grateful groan. He should brush his teeth, but he could barely keep his eyes open. As he stripped down to his boxers, his phone tumbled onto the bed. That reminded him he hadn't called his mother. They spoke once a week, on Thursdays, but he had missed her call last night.

"I'll call when I get up," he muttered under his breath, knowing that if he didn't, he'd have concerned-sounding voicemail messages saying, "I know you're a grown-up, honey, but I'm your mom. I still worry."

Cam set an alarm on his phone, plugged it in to charge and crawled under the covers with a grateful sigh.

I should text the bartender from last night, too. But his eyelids were too heavy to lift, and he was out before he could reach for his phone again.

* * * *

"Hey, Cam." Ben smiled brightly at him and slid a bottle of water across the bar. Ember was hopping tonight.

"Hey." Cam smiled back. He raised his voice over the mix he'd queued up to play during his break. "And thanks. Good to see you again."

"You too." Ben leaned on the bar. "I'm about to take my break. Wanna go out back with me while I have a smoke?"

"Sure." Cam didn't smoke, but he'd enjoy talking to Ben again. After his nap yesterday, he'd forgotten to text Ben—he had called his mother, thankfully—and was glad he didn't seem upset.

Ben grabbed his own bottle of water and a hoodie, then came out from behind the bar. He brushed his fingers against Cam's waist when he passed. "You want your coat? I don't think it's raining anymore, but it's fucking freezing out."

"Yeah, let me grab it."

"Meet you out by the dumpsters?" Ben flashed a grin at him. "Wow, if that isn't the worst pickup line ever, I don't know what is."

Cam laughed. "I'll be out in a minute."

It didn't take him long to retrieve his jacket from the DJ booth then make his way through the maze of back hallways in the club to the rear exit.

Ben was smoking a cigarette when Cam pushed open the door and stepped into the cold April night. He wedged a piece of wood between the door and frame to prevent them from getting locked out. The alley smelled faintly of garbage and cigarette smoke, but the cold air kept it from being too unpleasant. July and August were unbearable.

"Good call on the coat." A shiver hit Cam. The DJ booth had been sweltering earlier and now the sweat froze on him. He tucked his hands in the pockets of his black wool jacket.

Ben nodded. "Yeah, it's fucking cold, even for April. I'll try to make it quick."

"Sure, no problem."

"So, how hungover were you yesterday morning?" Ben flicked ash off the cigarette, and the cherry on the end glowed red in the dim alley.

Cam groaned and burrowed his hands deeper into the coat pockets. "Ugh. Class was rough."

"You're a teacher, right?" Ben sounded a touch guilty. "I think I remember you saying that, anyway."

"Yeah. I teach elementary music at Midtown Academy."

"Fancy."

Cam smiled. "It's a private school, but it's not one of the crazy exclusive ones where parents have to sign their kids up the moment they give birth. We're well funded, especially compared to the public schools, but not super pretentious."

"Cool. You like teaching there, then?"

"Absolutely, although I did not enjoy it on a Friday with a hangover. I'm not going to lie. I changed my lesson plan and went with lectures about music theory and composers instead of having the kids play instruments. My head couldn't take it."

"Whoa, that seems advanced for little kids."

Cam shrugged. "I'm not getting into complex theory or making first graders write long essays or anything. But we start with the basics and build from there. My fifth graders recently wrote a short paper about their favorite composer. That kind of thing."

"Huh." Ben stubbed out his cigarette and dropped it in a nearby empty tin. "I don't remember having music classes like that back from where I'm from."

"Where is that?"

"Indiana." He grimaced and reached in his pocket. He popped something—a mint maybe—into his mouth. "It was nothing but cornfields and American flags. I came to New York with dreams of being an actor, and I wound up bartending."

"Not an uncommon story in New York."

"Nope. We're a dime a dozen here." Ben stepped closer.

Cam smiled at him again. "I think you're a bit above average. I haven't seen you act, but your bartending is top-notch, and you're no slouch in bed."

"Yeah? Glad to hear it." Ben slid a hand into Cam's back pocket. "I wasn't sure when I didn't hear from you today. You don't seem like the kind of guy to wait a few days just to play it cool."

Cam winced. "No, I'm not. And I'm sorry. Today was nuts. It's not that I wasn't interested."

"No pressure."

"I would like to hook up again," Cam admitted. He grasped the front of Ben's hoodie and tugged him closer. "As long as you're still up for the casual thing."

Ben's breath—minty with a hint of smoke—wafted across his lips. "I'm up for that."

Cam closed the distance between their mouths. The kiss sent a satisfying hum through his body before he pulled away. Good to know his memories of the night with Ben—while slightly foggy from too many vodka shots—were accurate.

A shiver racked Ben's body, and he pulled away from Cam. "How about we take this someplace warmer? I'm freezing my balls off here."

Chapter Three

Jesse took pains to be outside Midtown Academy on East 27th Street by two-twenty p.m. on the following Wednesday, phone in one hand and a bag of snacks for Dylan in the other. He read his messages and email and glanced up from time to time at the other adults gathering around him on the tree-lined sidewalk. Several attractive faces caught his eye. Hot damn, this was a good-looking bunch of caregivers. Mostly parents, he guessed, with non-parents mixed in. Nannies and babysitters, and people like Jesse. Okay, maybe no one else quite like him, but surely there were other non-parents on the pickup lists, too.

He tore his eyes away from a sexy brunette in riding boots who kept smiling at him and stared at the school's elegant façade instead. He admired the variations in the six interconnected brownstone buildings, though he could almost feel the brunette's eyes on the side of his face. Jesse didn't plan to do anything about it—he preferred not to get involved with the parents of small children. Families were more baggage than he liked to handle.

No problem with extra baggage when you were fooling around with Carter, an annoying voice in his brain murmured. That was because Carter hadn't made more of their stint as friends with benefits or pressured him to be anything other than an overgrown playmate to Sadie and Dylan. Jesse was immensely fond of the Hamilton kids. They were quirky and hilarious, but, most importantly, they weren't his, and Jesse could hand them back to their parents anytime things got too complicated. In his opinion, complicated relationships took the fun out of life and sex.

The school bells rang, and Jesse pocketed his phone in his leather coat. At two-thirty-three, the doors of the main entrance swung open, and the first wave of children emerged. Jesse knew from previous pickups that the academy dismissed rooms by number and floor. Dylan's and Sadie's classrooms were located on the second floor toward the back of the school, and it often took a while for them to make it outside, so he didn't think it odd when ten minutes passed without Dylan making an appearance. He straightened after he caught sight of a petite woman with golden brown skin and a pixie haircut wearing a red pea coat. He recognized her as Dylan's homeroom teacher, but he didn't see Dylan with the group of students behind her.

Stepping up with the crowd of other caregivers, Jesse focused on catching her eye. Despite the flurry of activity involved in handling twelve second graders, she met his gaze quickly. Recognition crossed her face, and she raised a finger in a "please hold" kind of signal. After her last charge had walked off — with the flirty brunette in the riding boots, no less — Dylan's teacher stepped forward.

"Mr. Murtagh, right? I'm Miss Danvers."

"Yes, hello. We met last fall. I'm here to pick up Dylan."

"Yes, Mr. Hamilton told me to expect you for pickup today. As did Dylan," she added with a smile. "Repeatedly, at regular intervals during the day."

A warm feeling spread in Jesse's chest. "I see. Dylan's just excited he didn't have to tag along to the doctor's office with his father and Sadie. Anything I should know before I take him home? I mean, besides knowing where Dylan is?" Miss Danvers' cheeks turned pink, and Jesse pushed down thoughts about her level of attractiveness. Which was really high, not that he could do anything about it.

"Dylan forgot his recorder in the music lab," Miss Danvers replied. "I let him go back to get it rather than waiting for tomorrow and Mr. Lewis should be walking him out in a moment."

Jesse furrowed his brow. "Recorder? As in the musical instrument?"

"That's right." Miss Danvers nodded. "The second grade is learning to read music this year to prep for more formal musical training next year. The children practice with the recorders every day to further their memorization techniques."

Before Jesse could respond, Dylan's voice rang out.

"Hey, Jesse!"

Miss Danvers stepped back and was replaced by a man Jesse guessed to be Mr. Lewis, the music teacher. Jesse didn't pay him much mind and instead focused his attention on the little boy in the blue parka looking up at him with a big smile. Dylan Hamilton exuded boyish energy. He had a strong will and a wicked sense of humor and was as quick to laugh as to argue with his older sister, Sadie, over almost anything at all.

"Dyl Pickle!" Jesse exclaimed, raising a hand to meet Dylan's in a cracking high-five. Dylan had inherited his mother's blonde hair and blue eyes, but he'd recently sprouted up tall and rangy, signaling he might take after his father.

"It's about time you got your lazy tuchus out here, kid. I've waited fifteen whole minutes since the bell rang!" Jesse put his hands on his hips in a show of mock anger and Dylan rolled his eyes, but before they could carry on with their playful sniping, Mr. Lewis cleared his throat.

"That's my fault, and I apologize."

Jesse turned his attention to the music teacher, and a prickle of sudden awareness fell over him.

Damn.

He'd expected Mr. Lewis to be…well, he didn't know what he'd expected. Someone middle-aged, perhaps, maybe on the mousy side. Certainly not the young and very attractive man standing in front of him with auburn hair peeking out from beneath a gray ski cap.

"I left my recorder in the music lab," Dylan piped up. He smiled at Jesse and Mr. Lewis, then took hold of Jesse's hand.

Jesse grinned. He also tried not to notice the Cute Music Teacher's lovely light brown eyes and the freckles sprayed over the bridge of his nose, but, oops, too late.

"Miss Danvers told me about your music program," he said to Dylan instead. "Pretty cool you're already learning to read music."

Dylan shrugged. "I guess. It's not like it's hard. And Mr. Lewis is a good teacher."

Jesse bit back a laugh. Like so many children his age, Dylan shared every thought and feeling regardless of time or place, something Jesse admired very much. He shifted his attention to the man in front of him. "Hi, I'm Jesse. Dylan's with me today."

Mr. Lewis nodded. "He mentioned someone different would pick him up today. Dylan seemed concerned about making the extra trip back to my room, but I assured him you wouldn't mind waiting a few extra minutes."

Jesse studied the concern flitting over Dylan's face and gave him a smile. "Of course I didn't mind, silly. Besides, what would your dad and Sadie say if I turned up at your place tonight without you?" He angled his head and studied a giggling Dylan. "So, do we have everything now? Books, assignments, bagpipes, drums?"

"I don't play bagpipes, Jesse!"

"Oh, too bad—they're one of my favorite instruments. Looks like you didn't forget your head back in Mr. Lewis' classroom, so at least we don't have to worry about that."

Dylan laughed. "My head doesn't come off, der-r-r."

"Dylan should have everything," Mr. Lewis said with a chuckle. "I even put new copies of his sheet music in his folder. The originals were looking a little ragged, and I know how much he enjoys practicing. That's what took us so long to get out here."

Jesse raised his brows at Dylan. "Nice! What songs will I be hearing today?"

"Um, I have *Au Claire de la Lune* and *Sailor, Sailor on the Sea*." Jesse blinked at the unfamiliar song titles, but Dylan continued on blithely. "Mr. Lewis gave me new songs to try because I learned the other ones already."

"Dylan and a few of the other students were quick to pick up music reading and I've moved them ahead in the song workbooks," Mr. Lewis said. "Playing *Hot*

Cross Buns for four weeks in a row can be kind of demoralizing when you're ready to learn new songs."

"I'll take your word for it," Jesse replied. "That last one sounds more like a dance club name than a song title, so clearly I am out of my depth." He watched, charmed as Mr. Lewis blushed, and pink stained the fair, freckled skin of his cheeks and throat.

Interesting.

Cute Mr. Lewis almost looked like he'd been caught out, but doing what? Jesse wanted to know more about that blush and how far the color traveled beneath the collar of his gray parka.

He suppressed a sigh as Dylan shifted beside him. *Damn it.* Flirting with Dylan's music teacher was a bad idea. They'd lingered long enough for most of the crowds around them to clear, and Dylan seemed antsy to end his school day.

Jesse made big eyes at his charge. "You ready to go, big guy? We need to pick up a few things on the way back to your dad's so we can make dinner for him and Lady Sadie."

Dylan snapped to attention. "Ready! What are we making?"

"Your sister requested bugs again, and I thought I'd dress up some mac 'n' cheese." Jesse caught the music teacher's bewildered expression and chuckled. "I'm talking an inside joke about seafood here, Mr. Lewis — Sadie and Dylan think shrimp look like bugs. It's disgusting, I know, but please don't call CPS."

Mr. Lewis laughed outright and the sound did funny things to Jesse's insides.

"Well, that clears things up without making any sense." Mr. Lewis waved at Dylan. "I can see you're in good hands, Dylan. I'll see you tomorrow!" He exchanged nods with Jesse, eyes sparkling beautifully, then turned back toward the school.

Jesse and Dylan moved off, joining the stream of foot traffic. The cloudless sky over them allowed the sun to warm the spring air, so they skipped the subway and headed back to Carter and Riley's townhouse in Murray Hill on foot. They chatted about Dylan's day while Jesse did his best not to think about Mr. Lewis. However, thoughts of the music teacher continued to return to him, like the way the corners of his eyes crinkled when he smiled.

He and Dylan were in a market near Dylan's home buying shrimp and lump crabmeat when Jesse's curiosity got the better of him. "How do you like learning the recorder?" he asked. They were waiting at the seafood counter and Dylan took a bite of the fig bar he'd chosen to snack on.

"It's good," Dylan said through the mouthful. "I told Mr. Lewis I want to play percussion next, and he said he'd talk to my mom and dad and Riley about it."

"What'll you play in percussion?"

"Bells and drums," Dylan replied.

"Bells?"

"Orchestra bells. The real name is glockenspale. No, wait. Glockenspiel! They're like a metal xylophone. They're wicked loud," Dylan added with obvious glee.

Jesse chuckled. He could guess at the mixed feelings Dylan's decision had inspired in all three of his parents. "Sadie plays piano, right? You don't want to learn that?"

Dylan scoffed. "Nah. I mean, if I can't play drums, I guess I'll play guitar."

The defiant gleam in his eye warmed Jesse's heart. He appreciated the kid's rebellious tendencies, even knowing they'd someday drive his parents crazy.

"I'm sure your mom and dad and Ri will figure it out with Mr. Lewis, buddy," he said. "Besides, playing guitar is pretty awesome, too."

"That's what Mr. Lewis said."

Jesse raised his brows. "Did he now?"

"Yep." Dylan nodded. "Mr. Lewis plays piano, guitar and the thing that kind of looks like a guitar but it's round?"

"The banjo?" Jesse guessed. That figured. Any hipster musician worth his salt owned one.

"Yeah! He brought it to class at the beginning of the year and played a bunch of songs. It was silver and shiny and loud, too. And Mr. Lewis can play really fast!" Dylan crumpled up the fig bar wrapper and shoved it in his coat pocket. "I think he plays other things, but I don't know what they are."

"What makes you say that?"

"He said he plays music after school, too. Which means he makes music almost all day long! Cool, huh?"

The admiration writ large in Dylan's expression made Jesse smile. "Cool, Dyl."

After they'd dropped Dylan's backpack and the groceries at the townhouse, they walked Leo, the family's Border collie. Then Jesse helped Dylan with his homework and Carter and Sadie turned up while Dylan practiced songs and Jesse heated water for the pasta. For the next several hours, he and the Hamiltons settled into the cheerful chaos that marked life with young children.

Sadie and Dylan were sticking spoons to their noses when Carter caught Jesse's eye over the table. "Thanks again for helping out today. I know you could be wining and dining Astrid right now."

"I can wine and dine Astrid anytime," Jesse scoffed. "Seafood mac 'n' cheese with you and the rugrats, on the other hand, is a much rarer affair. Besides, you've been with these monsters for five days already, so I figured you could use some form of adult conversation over dinner tonight."

"Is that what we're doing?"

Jesse narrowed his eyes at Carter. "Don't be mean or you won't get any of the cookies Dylan and I picked up at the bakery counter."

"They look so good," Dylan cut in, cheese sauce dotting the bridge of his nose. "Jesse wanted to get a fruit salad, but I told him the cookies looked way tastier."

Carter held up both hands in surrender, his expression almost comically pleading. "Okay, you win. I take back anything snotty that's come out of my mouth for the last two hours."

Jesse broke up laughing. "Jesus, your face. I always forget your kids got the big puppy dog eyes from you and not your ex."

"Hah, it's true." Carter looked a bit frazzled and there were cheesy fingerprints on his shirt, but he appeared content. "Did Dylan use them on you today?"

"A bit, yes. He went back to the music lab after dismissal and it took him a while to get outside. He gave me the face after the music teacher mentioned Dylan said I might leave without him."

"Oh?" Carter glanced at his son, who'd been helping Sadie get sauce all over her face. "He actually said those words? That you wouldn't wait?"

"I'm not sure. I'm more paraphrasing what his teacher said than Dyl himself." Jesse sipped his wine. "Speaking of Mr. Lewis, is he even old enough to be teaching? He and the adorable Miss Danvers could pass for college students."

Carter leveled a knowing look at him. "What did you do?"

"Nothing at all." Jesse made puppy dog eyes of his own at his friend. "I simply realized how very young they seem to be and wondered about the dearth of cozy-looking, middle-aged schoolmarms at that school."

"The schoolmarms seem to be aging out of the system," Carter replied and lifted his glass. "I think I told you Kate and I went to an open house at the school last summer and couldn't believe how many new, young faces there were. I swear, I almost had an existential crisis."

Jesse stared at him for a moment. "Oh, I remember this conversation from your housewarming. Something about the music teacher being a fetus with two first names."

Carter inhaled wine at the non sequitur, and several moments passed before either of them could stop coughing or laughing to speak again. The kids joined in, even though neither knew what amused the adults so much, and Sadie handed her father a napkin to dab his eyes.

"You're a wreck, Daddy," she told him. On top of inheriting her father's dark-brown hair and hazel eyes, Sadie also frequently channeled Carter's serene demeanor, as she did now.

"Yes," he croaked out. "Yes, I am. Thanks, honey." Sadie leaned over and hoovered up a piece of fallen macaroni from the table with her mouth and Dylan looked on, clearly impressed. Carter wrinkled his nose. "We use utensils at this table, Sadie, c'mon."

Jesse covered another laugh with one hand.

"I told you the teachers were practically fetuses," Carter clarified then, his focus back on Jesse. "And that the music teacher had two first names and therefore could not be trusted. His first name is Cameron, in case you didn't manage to worm it out of him."

"I didn't, thanks, and you hit the nail right on the head." Jesse reached for the bottle of wine to top off his glass. "Cameron Lewis is two first names, and he and his colleagues are practically babies."

Carter waved off his offer of a refill. "They know what they're doing and the kids like them. Age and wisdom don't always go hand in hand, you know."

"Oh, God, you sound like Yoda."

"I feel about as old as Yoda right now. But don't mind me. I just need to sleep over the weekend and I'll be fine. Speaking of which, you and Kyle are still coming up on Saturday, right?"

"Absolutely. Kyle's taking me to a club Friday night, and we'll probably crash at my place for a few hours afterward, then meet up with you guys Saturday afternoon." Jesse rubbed a hand over his head. "Then again, we could leave Manhattan after the club and drive straight down to your place, too. We'll bring breakfast if that happens."

Carter grimaced. "Ugh, my brain is crying even thinking about that level of sleep deprivation. You sure Kyle's going to be able to stand being away from the bar two nights in a row?"

"Eh, we'll see." Jesse shook his head, his smile fond. "I know he can—it's a matter of making sure he does. The guy deserves a couple of nights off, so we have to do our best to force him to relax."

"Says the guy who never relaxes." Carter smiled as Jesse raised his hands in mock outrage. "What club is he taking you to?"

"Club Ember. It's under one of the boutique hotels in Chelsea. One of Kyle's friends curates the bar menu."

Carter's eyes shone with amusement. "You're taking a night off from your underground bar to go to an underground nightclub to check out the competition?"

Jesse laughed. "Busted. It won't be all work, no play, however. I can't speak for Kyle, but I plan to do what I always do best—check out the beautiful people of Manhattan and find someone fun to play with for a couple of hours."

Chapter Four

The last three times Cam had glanced up, he'd caught someone staring at him. Someone very attractive with a beard. The distance made it hard to be sure, but Cam had a nagging feeling he should recognize him. He seemed familiar, but Cam couldn't place him. Actor, maybe? He reminded Cam of Captain Kirk in the new *Star Trek* movies. The one both better-looking and far less annoying than the actor from the original TV series, at least as far as Cam was concerned. He'd had that argument with his roommate Myron more than once.

They did get some famous names in the club, but since this guy was accompanied only by a second hot guy with darker hair and no entourage, Cam guessed it wasn't him.

Cam watched him surreptitiously during his set. He was a good dancer and he'd put on a nice show with the dark-haired guy. They moved together well, like they'd done it many times before. Partners? Fuck buddies? Cam couldn't tell. They seemed comfortable with each other, but the bearded guy spent a lot of time eyeing Cam, too. There was no mistaking the fact that Cam was being eye-fucked.

Not that he minded.

Threesome? he wondered. He didn't make a habit of them, but they could be fun. There were worse thoughts than being sandwiched between those two. Blood rushed to his groin at the idea.

Cam looked away and focused on the music, but his attention was drawn back to them. When the bearded guy pressed a kiss on his dance partner's cheek and made a beeline for Cam, he wasn't surprised. He lowered his headphones so they hung around his neck and smiled.

"Great set," the man shouted.

"Thanks! Glad you're enjoying it."

"Jesse Murtagh." He held out a hand. "We met the other day."

Cam narrowed his eyes. "That's how I know you! I knew you looked familiar. You picked up Dylan Hamilton at school. You're friends with his father, right?"

"Guilty as charged." Jesse grinned. "And you're Dylan's music teacher, Mr. Lewis, right?"

"Cameron. But you can call me Cam."

"So, you're a music teacher by day, secret DJ by night, Cam?"

Cam laughed. "It's not a secret. I mean, the school knows about my side gig."

"Still, it's kinda sexy." Jesse's gaze raked over him and Cam's blood heated. "I like it."

"Thanks." Cam felt flustered all of a sudden. God, the man's charm was potent. He'd been intrigued after they'd met at the school, but he'd also been working and he'd tried hard to maintain a professional demeanor. Technically, he was working now, too, but no one cared if he flirted with the club's patrons.

"Do you have a break coming up at some point?"

Cam glanced at the time on his laptop. "In about an hour."

"Excellent." Jesse flashed him a brilliant smile. "Then I'll meet you back here in an hour. I'm buying you a drink."

"Pretty sure of yourself, huh?" Cam grinned. Jesse clearly assumed he was gay or bi. Cam hadn't been subtle about checking him and his friend out earlier.

Jesse grasped Cam's upper arm and leaned in. His hand was warm on Cam's skin, and his beard tickled his cheek and ear. "One thing you should know about me, Mr. Lewis, is that I am always sure of myself. And I usually get what I want."

I believe it, Cam thought. But he pulled back so he could look Jesse in the eye and kept his expression neutral. "That's two things."

Jesse tipped his head back and laughed. "You are correct."

Cam decided to string him along a little further. He was interested, but he liked the idea of making Jesse squirm a little. "Meet me back here in an hour and we'll talk about a drink. No promises."

"Done." Jesse squeezed his arm again. He'd sailed right past the part where Cam hadn't actually agreed to have a drink with him. "I'm looking forward to it."

Cam spent the next hour in a bit of a daze, trying not to sneak glances over at Jesse, hyper-aware that he'd taken a seat with a direct view of Cam's booth and hadn't taken his eyes off Cam. The attention was flattering—if overwhelming. After meeting Jesse at the school, Cam had checked the pickup roster and recognized his name. Some googling had brought a wealth of information to his fingertips.

Jesse Murtagh was a force to be reckoned with. He had a well-documented reputation as a bisexual playboy—complete with pictures of various beautiful people on his arm—and was equally well known for being an integral part of his family's media company. Murtagh Media had begun a venture to acquire Radio Clash, a popular internet radio platform, with Jesse spearheading the project. He appeared to be every bit as accomplished as he was attractive.

And, for some unfathomable reason, Cam had caught his attention. Cam didn't consider himself a slouch in the looks department. Sure, some guys weren't into redheads, but he'd never had any shortage of attention. The DJ gig didn't hurt, either, and most guys seemed impressed by his work as a music teacher, too. But in the end, Cam was an attractive, middle-class—at best—dude from Jersey. Which put him in a different league from Jesse.

Even with those thoughts swirling through his head, Cam switched over to the pre-planned playlist and took off his headphones when Jesse walked toward his booth with a purposeful stride—precisely when he'd promised to arrive. He handed Cam a rocks glass with clear liquid and ice.

Cam raised his eyebrows but took it.

"I promised you a drink," Jesse said. "Vodka. On the rocks. Your favorite, right?"

Cam blinked at him. "How do you know what I drink?"

"I quizzed the bartenders. I like to do my research."

"Apparently." Cam sniffed the glass and took a cautious sip. The vodka was smooth and flavorful, with very little bite. "What is this?"

"Christiania. It's a potato vodka from Norway."

And top shelf, Cam knew. He was familiar with the brand. He'd just never splurged on booze that nice. "Well, thank you. It's delicious."

"Want to come meet my friend?"

"Uh, sure." Cam took another sip of his drink to cover his surprise. He'd half-expected Jesse's suggestion to be a lot more salacious. But as they wove through the club together, he realized that didn't fit with what he'd seen of the man at all. Despite his phenomenal charm, he seemed too polished to take such a crude approach.

"Cam, this is my friend and business partner Kyle McKee. Kyle, this is Cameron Lewis. He teaches music to Sadie and Dylan and lives a double life as a DJ."

"Nice to meet you." Kyle's dark eyes and handsome face were intense-looking, but his smile and handshake were friendly.

"You too," Cam said. Jesse gestured to the low-slung black leather couches. Once they were seated and Cam had taken another sip of his drink—damn, it was good—he looked at Kyle. "You work for Murtagh Media, too?"

Kyle shook his head. "No. Jesse and I own a speakeasy called Under Lock & Key. Under, for short."

"Huh." He'd seen that name in his Google search.

Jesse grinned at him. "You're familiar with my work?"

"Yes. Well, I have to admit, after we met at the school the other day, I googled you. There's a wealth of information about you out there. Your reputation precedes you, Mr. Murtagh," Cam said drily. "Which is why I'm not convinced having a drink with you is a good idea."

Kyle laughed. "I told you that was bound to happen one of these days, Jes."

"I'm not saying it's a bad thing," Cam said in an earnest tone. "A little daunting maybe. We hardly run in the same circles. I mean, I saw a picture of you palling around with a senator and his boyfriend. I hang out with school teachers, bartenders and bouncers."

"Hey, what's wrong with bartenders?" Kyle said.

"Nothing!" Cam protested. "That's not what I meant at all."

"Good. Since that's what I am."

Cam gave him a puzzled frown. "But you said you owned part of the speakeasy?"

"I do. But I still think of myself as a bartender." Kyle leaned forward and rested his elbows on his knees. "I get what you mean, though. The guys I hang out with feel out of my league sometimes. But you know what? They're also some of the nicest, most genuine men out there — Jesse being a notable exception of course."

"Hey!"

Cam grinned.

"You know I love you, Jes."

"Humph." Jesse sounded unconvinced.

"And as far as your reputation," Kyle continued.

"Watch it, buddy." Jesse shot him a glare.

"Well, there's a reason you cast your net wide. If you stuck to your own pond, you'd run out of fish," Kyle said with a smirk.

Jesse gave him the finger and Cam laughed.

Okay, so maybe they weren't quite the intimidating men Cam had expected. He liked their banter. They seemed relaxed and comfortable together, and other than Cam's momentary panic about insulting Kyle's profession, he found them surprisingly easy to talk to.

"How long have you been spinning?" Kyle said.

"Since high school. I made friends with a DJ, and he taught me what he knew and introduced me to other people in the business. I practiced, volunteered to do some house parties until I built a decent reputation. During college, I got paid to do house parties. After I got some more experience under my belt, I talked the club owner here into giving me a trial run. He was impressed enough to let me spin on occasion, and after a slot opened up for a regular Friday night gig, I got it. I do shows on Saturdays and the odd weekday when they need someone."

"Impressive," Jesse said.

"But you also teach at Midtown Academy?" Kyle asked.

"I do. I love teaching. That's my passion. Spinning is more of a…side gig to keep things interesting."

Kyle nodded. "So, if you suddenly became famous and in high demand, you wouldn't quit teaching?"

"Hell no. Why? Would associating with you be a boost to my career?" Cam joked.

Jesse and Kyle exchanged glances. A flicker of some emotion Cam couldn't identify crossed Jesse's face. "It's been known to boost the careers of others."

Cam stared at him, open-mouthed, for a moment. "I was *kidding*," he said.

"Yes, well, I wasn't." Jesse wrapped his long fingers around the glass in his hand. "People sometimes get involved with me in order to get attention for their business or brand needs."

Cam grimaced. "That's horrible. But, yeah, I can see that happening."

"Well, I mean, it could be worse. At least they have good taste."

Kyle chuckled. "And Jesse's ego survives, unscathed."

"Well, I promise the thought never crossed my mind," Cam said in a firm tone. "That's not why I'm having a drink with you."

Jesse seemed to relax and he rested his arm on the back of the sofa, letting his fingertips graze Cam's shoulder. "I didn't think so, honestly."

"That's my cue to go see how Gale and Jarrod are doing, then find myself some company for the evening," Kyle said. "Nice to meet you, Cam."

"You too," Cam said sincerely.

Kyle stood, then leaned in and brushed his lips across Jesse's cheek. "Please behave."

Jesse looked affronted. "Do I ever?"

"No." Kyle smiled, his affection obvious. "But Cam seems like a nice boy. Be gentle."

"Oh, fine."

Kyle disappeared and Cam turned to look at Jesse. "You two seem...close." He took a sip of the vodka.

"We are. We fuck around a lot."

Cam choked on his drink.

Jesse angled his body toward Cam and leaned in. Cam mirrored his actions. "Does that bother you?"

Cam coughed a few times to clear his throat, then shook his head. "Why would it? I don't care who you're involved with."

"Oh, you know. Not everyone is comfortable with my friendship with Kyle. They get jealous knowing I like to bend Kyle over my desk. And that I like to go behind the bar, drop to my knees and blow him."

Cam coughed again, but this time, it had nothing to do with the vodka he'd inhaled. That was a surprisingly hot mental image. He slid closer to Jesse. "Hey, I fooled around with one of the bartenders here in the broom closet the other night, so I'm not in a place to judge. Besides, it's not like I'm in any position to be jealous."

"Some people I've gotten involved with have been quite judgmental."

"Oh? Are we involved?" Cam asked. "Because I kind of missed the part where I agreed to that."

Jesse laughed. "Touché." His blue eyes sparkled at Cam. "I want to make it clear I am interested, though."

"Noted." Cam dropped a hand on Jesse's thigh and lightly squeezed.

"I like you, Cam. You're capable of holding your own against Kyle and me in conversation, and Carter and his kids tell me you're a fantastic teacher. You're also a stellar DJ, and"—Jesse brushed his fingers across Cam's short hair—"I am a big fan of gingers."

Cam pulled back. The reminder that the Hamilton kids were his students had the effect of an icy bucket of water to his interest. He cleared his throat. "I'll be honest. The offer is very tempting, but I don't think getting involved is such a great idea."

Jesse frowned at him. "Why is that?"

"The situation is just too complicated. You're friends with my students' parent, you're close with Dylan and Sadie... There's a lot of potential for it to get ugly."

He couldn't deny being attracted to Jesse, but he wasn't about to get involved with a student's de facto uncle. No matter how hot and charming.

Too bad. Cam excused himself with a wistful smile and walked away a few minutes later. It could have been a hell of a lot of fun.

* * * *

Within an hour of Cam returning to his booth, Jesse and Kyle left separately. Kyle with a gorgeous Latin-looking guy and Jesse alone, though Cam doubted he would have had to. A small part of him regretted turning Jesse down, but a larger part was relieved he hadn't crossed that line.

Dylan and Sadie were great kids and Cam hated the idea of upsetting the delicate dynamic he'd worked out with their parents. Safer to keep his sex life as far from work as possible. *I don't have quite the same qualms about getting involved with people at the club*, he admitted to himself as Ben walked toward him.

"Hey, how was your night?" Cam asked Ben with a smile. Last call had been a while ago and people were filtering out of the club in pairs and small groups.

"Long, but I made good tips. Yours? Did you strike out with that guy or what?" Cam gave him a puzzled frown, and he shrugged. "He asked me about your drink of choice."

"Ah. And, no, I didn't strike out," Cam admitted. "It's complicated."

"Hmm. So, how did you like the Christiana?"

"It's amazing. Well out of my usual budget, but it was a nice gesture."

"Yeah, smooth move there," Ben said, his tone admiring. "Looks like it didn't work."

"He's a friend of the dad of two of my students, and it seemed like a bad idea," Cam explained. He slipped his laptop into his bag and secured it.

"Makes sense." Ben leaned in. "Well, at the risk of sounding like I'm offering myself as a consolation prize, what do you think about coming home with me tonight?"

"I'd love to," Cam said, "but I'm spent. Another time?"

"Sure thing." Ben flashed him a crooked grin. "Guess it's two for two for you tonight."

"At least you know not to take it personally." He zipped his jacket and slung the bag over his shoulder. He didn't mention that the other reason he didn't want to go home with Ben was because he didn't want Ben getting attached. Cam wanted a quick fuck, not a relationship. Maybe it was better if they let things cool down before they hooked up again so there was no confusion about what they were doing.

"No kidding. I mean, it'd be a nice boost to the ego to have you go home with me after you turned down Jesse Murtagh, but I'll console myself with the fact that at least you turned both of us down."

"You know who he is?"

Ben shrugged again. "Doesn't everyone?"

Chapter Five

As they'd agreed, Jesse met Kyle at his building in Chelsea at ten a.m. on Saturday morning. Kyle opened the Range Rover's passenger door and greeted Jesse cheerfully, but he grimaced after placing his bags on the backseat. Kyle also didn't remove his sunglasses after he'd settled into his seat and his quiet sigh upon buckling his seatbelt provided the final giveaway.

Jesse gave Kyle a once-over and grinned at his battered jeans and soft gray hoodie. He had a red and black plaid jacket in his lap. Seeing Kyle out of his usual blacks never failed to tickle Jesse's fancy as well as turn him on—Kyle looked delicious no matter what he wore—but he decided he'd tease him about his lumbersexual ensemble later.

"How hungover are you?" he asked instead.

"Maybe a little," Kyle replied with a sniff. "Honestly, I think it's more lack of sleep hurting me this time than an overload of booze."

"Ah, I see." Jesse put the SUV into gear and eased it out into traffic. "Who are we blaming for keeping you up?"

"Jakob. He's a cop with the 10th Precinct."

Jesse rolled his eyes. "You're such a slut for a uniform."

"I so am. He wasn't in uniform last night, though."

"Shame. You could have asked him to cuff you."

"I would never!" Kyle laughed. "Okay, maybe I would. I kind of like this one. He does yoga so he's very flexible."

"Oh, man, I want in on that!" Jesse exclaimed over more laughter. "At least hook me up before you two get all monogamous and forget how to have fun in a group setting."

"Quit it. I met the man less than twelve hours ago! The only things I know we have in common right now are a shared love of frozen pizza and gaming."

"Ah." Video games were one of Kyle's few personal indulgences and he didn't play lightly. "What did you play and for how long?"

"*Fallout*, until about two hours ago."

Jesse caught Kyle's pained grin and barked out another laugh. "Wrecked. You are officially ridiculous."

Kyle flapped a hand at him. "Yeah, well, you should know I'm taking time off when *Fallout 4* is released."

"Noted. I can't believe you wore yourself out gaming with the sexy cop instead of fucking."

"Hey, we had sex first!" Kyle smothered a yawn behind his flappy hand. "More than once, thank you very much. Not everyone is as single-minded as you," he chided. "How is it you're so bright-eyed and bushy-tailed this morning, anyway? Did you and the delicious music teacher manage to leave the club early last night?"

"We didn't, or at least not together," Jesse replied, his tone light. "He turned me down." He could practically hear Kyle's jaw drop.

"You're shitting me."

"I shit you not. He gave me a line about things being too complicated because I'm friends with Carter and his kids." A line of total bullshit, Jesse thought. He glanced at Kyle, who took off his sunglasses.

Kyle furrowed his brow. "How is that complicated?"

"I don't know."

"And that was it?"

"Essentially. Cam finished his drink and toddled off back to the DJ booth. Some girls stopped by the table and we had a round of drinks, but they were more interested in dropping Molly than anything else, and you know that's not my scene." Jesse glanced at the traffic in his rearview mirror. "I left the club around three a.m."

"Huh." Kyle ran a hand over his hair. "Well, this is unprecedented."

"Hardly. I do sometimes leave a venue on my own."

"Yeah, and when? Because I don't remember the last time we went out on the pull and you left alone."

"Actually, I feel it prudent to clarify some details at this juncture. I left Ember alone, true. But my solitude only lasted as long as it took to get to Astrid's." Jesse smiled at Kyle's chuckling.

"I love that your backup plan is a former beauty queen."

"Don't be bitchy." Carefully, Jesse stretched out a hand and booped the tip of Kyle's nose with his finger. "Astrid is smart and beautiful."

"I know. And fond of you."

"Well, duh. I gave her a rain check last week when I had to pick up Dylan," Jesse explained. "She called me yesterday, wanting to meet up, but—"

"You laid eyes on Cam at the club and decided to take a detour first," Kyle finished. "Interesting that you ended up back on the first track anyway. What time did you get home this morning?"

"Around the same time you and the cop hung up your game controllers, I'd bet. I'm sad that's not a euphemism for anything sexual, by the way." Jesse laughed as Kyle gave his arm a light slap.

"Shut up, you."

"Oh, get some sleep, Crankella." Jesse used the SUV's controls to seal off the city's noise behind the windows. "We've got at least a couple of hours for you to get over your bitchery, and I'll wake you up when we get close to Southampton."

Kyle slid his sunglasses back on. "Okay. You sure you don't mind?"

"Of course not."

"You don't wanna talk about the music teacher?"

Jesse pressed his lips together. Then Kyle placed one broad palm against Jesse's hip, and his irritation at recalling Cam's dismissal faded. "No, I'm good. There's nothing to talk about." He frowned at Kyle's grunt.

"Oh, hell."

"What?"

"I'm not buying this 'live and let live' act you've got going, babe. I saw the way you looked at that kid and I know you. You're being way too agreeable about getting shot down, and it's not like you at all." Kyle exhaled loudly. "You're going back to the club to see him again, aren't you?"

"It may have crossed my mind," Jesse allowed. And that was another line of total bullshit because he planned to pay Cam another visit.

"Can I ask why?"

"Because I enjoy a challenge, Kyle. Plus, as you said, the kid is delicious." He smiled when Kyle chuckled.

"Ugh, I suppose he is." Kyle patted his hip and settled back farther into the seat. "I know it's none of my business, but be careful, okay?"

Jesse switched lanes. "What are you talking about?"

"Maybe the kid has a point about your connections to the Hamiltons. If you two hook up and things go bad, it could make things weird for you all."

"Dude, come on." Jesse shook his head as if to clear it. "I'm looking to have sex with the cute redhead, not start a romance. You know me better than that."

"Okay, fine." Kyle crossed his arms over his chest and yawned. "What about Carter and Riley?"

"What about them?" Jesse shrugged off Kyle's concern. "Riley's never weird about the people I get involved with, and I used to fool around with his boyfriend. And you and I both know Carter's way more open-minded than people give him credit for. Hell, he recruited Astrid to work at the CEC despite the fact she and I were seeing each other."

Kyle hummed thoughtfully. "True, true."

Jesse leaned over and squeezed his knee. "I know what I'm doing."

"That's what I'm afraid of," Kyle grumbled. "You and your plots, always up to no good." His voice had lowered, however, and the next sound out of him was a soft snore.

Jesse settled into the drive to Long Island. Kyle had a point—he didn't like the way things had gone down at Ember. However, his dissatisfaction didn't hinge on whether he and Cam had hooked up or not.

While Jesse's reputation as a hedonist might be well earned, it captured only part of his nature. More accurately, he was a non-conformist. With few exceptions, he did what he felt in the moment, in business and in the bedroom. Sometimes, that meant spending the night with multiple partners, but occasionally, it meant he wasn't in the mood for company at all.

He'd wanted company the night before, and specifically Cam's. Jesse's interest in him after their exchange at Midtown Academy had increased once he'd gotten a good look at Cam outside of his conservative educator vibe. Cam matched Jesse's height, and the cut of his stylish T-shirt and jeans hinted at a toned, fit body. The slim silver ring in his left nostril suited his DJ alter ego, but Cam didn't play the brooding starving artist type one might expect. His smiles came easily and made his eyes sparkle and were touched with exactly the right amount of insouciance to be tempting.

All that said, Cam had hooked Jesse's interest by walking away without a backward glance.

Jesse frowned. Sure, he recognized Cam's reluctance to get involved with friends of Midtown Academy or parents of the school's students. But he was neither of those things, and only an occasional babysitter for the Hamilton kids.

No. Jesse suspected the blow off stemmed from other reasons. He just needed to figure out what those reasons were and work a way around them.

* * * *

Two and a half hours later and after a quick stop at a local bakery, Jesse and Kyle stepped over the threshold of Riley and Carter's second home. A chorus of greetings rang out over the excited noises of David and Will's dog, Mabel, a sweet-tempered Inu-Husky mix.

"We wondered if you'd follow through on the breakfast threat," Riley teased. He took their overnight bags.

"We didn't leave the city until after ten, so we brought gooey things for dessert instead." Jesse handed off the bakery box to David and squatted down to say hello to Mabel.

"From the seat marks on Kyle's face, I'd say you boys were up a lot later than you expected." Riley smirked and headed upstairs to stow their things.

"Hey, don't look at me," Jesse protested. "He fell asleep before we even left Chelsea, but I had nothing to do with it."

Kyle's ears turned red. "We went to the club last night as planned," he explained and moved toward the kitchen with David and Will. "Jes says he slept somewhere in between leaving and meeting up this morning, but I can't say how much I slept myself."

After letting Mabel love all over him, Jesse joined the crowd in the kitchen, the dog at his heels. His friends clustered around the kitchen island while Carter and Malcolm carefully constructed spring rolls and Kyle unpacked the weekender bag he used to carry bottles of specialty booze.

"Riley mentioned you and Kyle were checking out the competition last night," Will said. "I guess I assumed you'd be going to another speakeasy rather than a nightclub, however. What's the name?"

"Club Ember," Jesse replied.

"What did you think? Did you learn any new tricks?" Malcolm eyed the bottles Kyle set out. "And what's all this?"

"The clear bottle is pear vodka. The yellow is a sour mix, and the blue and purple are schnapps." Kyle pointed at the bottles while Malcolm raised his brows. "I put the vodka up at Christmas and the schnapps at the end of last summer when blueberries and blackberries were in season. I figured they'd be perfect for spring cocktails."

"He's not making anything we drank last night, by the way," Jesse said. Riley walked in and joined them. "Kyle started scheming over recipes last week when Carter mentioned coming out here. To answer your question, Mal, the drinks at the club were good, but nothing rocked my world."

Jesse told the others more about Ember while Kyle filled rocks glasses with ice and measured out ingredients.

"It's been an embarrassingly long time since I went to a club, especially since moving out here," David said. "I stick to the smaller places closer to Freeport out of laziness. I'm not even sure they qualify as nightclubs."

Jesse stared at David. "Well, that's just bad form, Senator Sexy." He chuckled at David's scowl — he hated that nickname with a passion. "You don't seem to have any problem showing your face at Under, so why not a nightclub?"

"Well, for one, you keep letting me into the speakeasy, which is a point in Under's favor." David smiled at the others' laughter. "Plus, with my job, I need to be careful about appearances — too much partying isn't healthy PR for a politician."

"Okay, but what does that mean?" Jesse asked. "You're not allowed to set foot in a nightclub ever again?"

"You sound oddly offended, Jes," Riley said.

"I believe I am. The idea of being forbidden to enjoy myself so as to avoid negative appearances is horrifying."

He could tell from his friends' expressions his comment had struck a nerve. For good reason, most of them erred on the side of conservatism and caution, protecting their careers and their families in the process. In direct contrast, Jesse did what he wanted and his family was long accustomed to dealing with any wrinkles his actions might cause in the court of public opinion.

"It's not a matter of being forbidden," David said, a pensive expression on his face. "It's more being smart about where I'm seen and with whom."

Jesse grimaced. "That sounds like being forbidden by slow degrees." He accepted a glass of brilliant blue something-or-other from Kyle, and the others murmured in agreement. "Regardless, you and Will should make a point of coming with us the next time. I'll be dragging Malcolm out, too, and Carter and Riley, whether they like it or not."

Carter frowned. "Wait, what? What did I do?"

With a fond grin, Kyle handed Carter a glass and rose up on his toes so he could press a kiss to the corner of his mouth. "Pouting is hereby forbidden while I enjoy the rest of my time off, babe. I'd much rather eat, drink and be merry." Kyle held up his glass in salute.

"Hear, hear," Jesse chimed in and the others followed suit.

The conversation paused as everyone tasted their cocktails and an outburst of compliments followed. Jesse caught Kyle's eye. Hot damn, the man knew how to mix up magic.

"This is fantastic," Riley declared, his eyes on his glass. "I have no idea what I'm drinking, of course, but it's delicious! What's it called?"

"It's a Dick Sucker." Riley's mouth fell open and Kyle's dark eyes glowed with mischief and delight. "And that's exactly how I want you to look every time you taste one, Ri."

Once Carter and Malcolm finished the spring rolls, everyone grabbed their jackets and trooped out onto the beach for a walk. Kyle and Malcolm took the lead, followed by Riley, Will, and David. Carter and Jesse brought up the rear while Mabel ran back and forth among the three groups.

"You feel like running tomorrow morning?" Carter asked.

"Yes, as long as it's not before eight a.m." Jesse raised his brows at Carter's aggrieved expression. "I'm taking time off, Car, and I'd like to actually sleep in for a change."

"Okay, I get you."

"You gonna wrangle anyone else to join us?"

"Riley and David said they'd be up for it," Carter replied. "Will rejected me and Malcolm's on the fence, but I think it's got more to do with Kyle's cocktails than anything else—they're giving people delusions of grandeur." They laughed together, then fell silent for a minute before he spoke again, his tone more tentative.

"Are you really going to force me to go to a nightclub with you?"

Jesse chuckled. "Of course not. I'd be happy if you and Riley wanted to come out with me, but I'd never force you to do anything you didn't want to." He looked askance at his friend, whose eyes were focused on a faraway point farther up the beach.

"What's going on in that brain of yours, Car? You've been strangely quiet for someone with a house full of people."

Carter drew in a noisy breath through his nose. "My mother's been calling me. She wants increased visitations with Sadie and Dylan."

Jesse looped his arm through Carter's. He ached for his friend, whose parents had all but cut ties with him after he'd come out of the closet. Even after nearly two years, Bradley and Eleanor Hamilton continued to voice their disapproval of Carter and Riley's relationship, and Kate Hamilton supervised any time the kids spent with their grandparents.

"That's promising, isn't it?" Jesse asked. "I mean, at least your mother's talking to you—that's more than you could say six months ago."

"True. She's decent to me when we talk. Of course, I can't tell if she actually wants to speak to me or if being pleasant is a means to an end for her." Carter shook his head. "I feel ridiculous because I know I'm acting like a child who wants his mom's attention instead of a grown man. The whole thing makes me want to throw myself out a window."

"Ugh, you're so dramatic." Jesse gripped his arm more tightly. "You need a night out with me. Will's already said he and David are up for it, so don't you and Ri be the old guys who stay home to binge watch Netflix."

Carter rolled his eyes. "Okay, enough with the guilt trip, jeez. If we don't have the kids the next time you and Kyle go to this nightclub of yours, we'll come, too."

"Excellent." Jesse licked his lips, a frisson of nerves rolling over him. "This seems like the right time to tell you I ran into someone you know at the club, by the way."

"Someone I know? Not Malcolm, obviously."

"No, though I can imagine him at Ember. It was your kids' music teacher."

Carter made an O with his lips. "You're kidding!"

"Nope. Cam spins records there as a side gig, and he's a decent DJ."

Carter blinked, then abruptly narrowed his eyes at him. "Cam, huh?"

"That's what he told me to call him when I bought him a drink." Jesse smiled at Carter's despairing sound. "Relax, that's all I did — buy the kid a drink and talk to him about music."

Unfortunately.

Jesse still didn't know how things with Cam had gone from "foregone conclusion" to "sorry, but fuck off". Cam had clearly been interested in him. His gaze had crawled all over Jesse while they sat together, scanning the breadth of his chest and lingering over his eyes and mouth. After Kyle had left, they'd huddled together on the black leather sofa, faces separated by mere inches. Cam had put his hand on Jesse's thigh and squeezed, and Jesse's cock had stirred. He'd considered winding his fingers into Cam's hair and tugging to expose the long, pale column of Cam's neck.

But then some kind of switch had been thrown and things screeched to a halt.

"We both know drinks and talking aren't all you plan to do," Carter observed. "If it were, we wouldn't be having this conversation in the first place."

"That's fair." Heat crawled up the back of Jesse's neck. He sometimes forgot how well Carter could read him. "Kyle's already told me it's not a good idea to start up with Cam."

"And you ignored him because you don't agree." Carter grunted softly. "Well, for what it's worth, Kyle's got a point. Cam Lewis works with Sadie and Dylan a couple of times a week. You don't care about your work and personal lives overlapping, but not everyone has the same gift for compartmentalization."

Jesse smirked. "I promise to treat him with kid gloves."

Carter nodded but drew his brows together. "Whatever happens, try to leave the kids out of it, okay?"

"Hey." A chill settled over Jesse at his friend's words. He stopped walking and looked Carter square in the face. "Of course, Car. Anything that happens between Cam and me is our business, not Sadie's or Dylan's. You know me better than that, right?"

Carter's expression softened. "I do know you, and I believe you mean what you're saying. I also know you're a force of nature and by that I'm talking tornado-strength winds. I don't want either of you to get wrecked if you decide to sweep the music teacher up, Jes."

Jesse studied his friend's expression for a long moment, arrested by the concern he read there. He felt oddly touched to understand Carter's concern wasn't just for Cam but for Jesse, too, and he exhaled a quiet breath. Jesse didn't know what he'd done to deserve his friends, but he was supremely thankful to have them in his life.

"I'm telling Cam you compared him to an old barn in your storm metaphor," he said at last. He laughed and ducked when Carter aimed a whack at his head.

Chapter Six

The sound of a throat clearing made Cam look up from his laptop screen. Carter Hamilton stood in the doorway, looking handsome in a navy-blue suit.

"Do you have a moment?" he asked.

Cam stood and smiled at him. "Of course. How can I help you, Mr. Hamilton? Is everything okay with Sadie and Dylan?"

He offered Cam a warm smile in return. "Everything's great. My ex-wife and I were here for parent–teacher conferences with the kids' teachers and I thought I'd pop in. What I wanted to discuss has nothing to do with Sadie or Dylan, however. Or at least not directly."

Frowning, Cam tilted his head. "I'm not sure I follow."

"I'm rambling, aren't I?" Carter leaned against the doorframe. "My point is I'm aware of what happened with you and my friend Jesse."

A chill slithered down Cam's spine. *Shit.* This was exactly why he'd turned Jesse down. It had been a difficult decision, but this confirmed he'd made the right one. "Please allow me to explain," he croaked.

Carter straightened and held up his hands. "Oh, God, no. I didn't mean to scare you. I wanted to tell you not to worry. To not hold back on our account if you're interested in Jesse."

Cam blinked at him. This conversation was the opposite of what he'd expected. "Err. Say what now?"

"Jesse and I discussed it. I think it's admirable you're concerned about the impact it could have on Sadie and Dylan. But unless you think your interactions with the kids or Riley and me will change if things don't go well with Jesse, I don't see how it would be a problem."

Cam considered Carter's words for a moment, then shook his head. "I wouldn't dream of treating your kids differently, and, at worst, it might be awkward between you and me for a while. But I would never take anything out on anyone in your family. I can separate my work and personal lives."

"What you do is your decision, of course, but as far as I'm concerned, if you're into him, go for it."

"You've totally taken me by surprise," Cam admitted. "But I'll be sure to think about it."

Carter gave him a speculative look. "Do you have plans Thursday night?"

Cam mentally reviewed his schedule. "I don't think so."

"Because I'd like to invite you to come to Under."

"Jesse's bar?"

"Technically, it's a speakeasy, but yes."

"I…um." Cam cleared his throat. "Are you sure he wants me there? After all, I did shoot him down."

Carter grinned. "That doesn't happen to Jesse very often. If anything, he's even more intrigued by you now that you've done it. He's still considering his next move, so the ball's in your court. If you want to see Jesse again, come to Under on Thursday. The worst that happens is you have some great drinks and make a few new friends."

"Sounds good. Unless I've forgotten about plans I already made, I'll be there."

"Fantastic. I'm glad to hear it." Carter held out a hand and a business card to Cam. "If you do decide to come, shoot me an email. You'll need a passphrase to get into the speakeasy."

"Thanks." Cam accepted the card and shook his hand, still slightly dazed by the turn the conversation had taken. "Have a good evening."

"You too."

Carter walked toward the door and Cam resumed his seat.

"One thing." Cam glanced up with a quizzical expression. "Jesse's not the monogamous type, so if you're thinking—"

Cam cut him off. "Trust me, I'm not looking to get involved with anyone seriously." *Much less a guy with a reputation like Jesse's.*

* * * *

On Thursday night, Cam stood in front of the mirror in his bedroom and frowned at his reflection.

He'd filled Taryn in on the situation with Jesse and she'd agreed that Cam worried too much about the conflict of interest.

'He's not Dylan's father,' she'd pointed out. 'Or even a family member. Jesse's their friend, right? There are no rules about that. And you're going to turn down a chance to hook

up with one of Manhattan's most notorious playboys? How are you not all over that?'

He'd snorted. 'Because that's never been my thing and you know it. I'm not a fame whore.'

'Yeah, but think how amazing he must be in bed.' Taryn had gotten a dreamy expression on her face. 'Ugh. He's so good-looking I can't stand it.'

'Want me to give him your number?' Cam had asked, amused. 'Because he swings both ways.'

'Don't tempt me.' She'd glared at him. 'Now, you're going to that speakeasy and you're going to hook up with that absurdly beautiful man.'

'Yes, ma'am.'

He scrutinized the outfit he'd put together and sighed. "Nope, looks ridiculous." He snapped a quick picture and sent it to Taryn with a message.

HELP! What do I wear to a speakeasy??

A minute later, his phone pinged and he scanned Taryn's response.

Not that! You look like you're trying too hard. Black pants, black button-down and the gray leather jacket you bought at Thrift Kingdom earlier this winter.

Cam quickly stripped out of his outfit and threw on the one Taryn suggested. He snapped another picture and sent it to her.

Better?

HAWT was her prompt response followed by *Go get 'em, Tiger!*

He replied with *Thanx*. He couldn't resist poking fun at Taryn's ridiculous spelling of 'hot'.

Cam slipped on a silver bracelet, grabbed his phone and wallet and left the apartment. He took the train to Morningside Heights. Lock & Key was a short walk from the subway station and he arrived with ten minutes to spare. Carter had given him the passphrase of 'Cork Total Abstinence Society' but also promised to meet Cam at the pub.

Cam strolled in, figuring he'd have to wait a few minutes until Carter arrived. He spotted Jesse at once, leaning on the bar and talking with the female bartender behind it.

"Hey, Jesse," he said.

Jesse turned. His face lit up when he saw Cam. "Hey there. You made it."

Nerves washed over Cam and he cleared his throat. "Yep. I take it Carter told you I was coming?"

"He mentioned it." Jesse bade the bartender goodbye, then crossed the room to Cam. He wore a simple and exquisitely tailored gray flannel suit with a crisp white shirt, open at the collar. His eyes were so blue it hurt to look at them.

Cam took a deep breath to hide the fact that his heart had sped up at seeing Jesse. But damn, he was even hotter than Cam had remembered. "Are you the welcoming committee?"

"I do like to greet new people," Jesse said. He reached out and grasped Cam's biceps and squeezed. "But I looked forward to seeing you."

"Yeah?" A weird flutter filled Cam's chest.

"Mm-hm. You intrigue me, Cam."

"You probably don't get turned down every day."

Jesse gave him a half-smile. "It's more than that."

"I want to apologize," Cam said. "I got spooked by the idea of awkward situations with the Hamiltons."

"I understand. I'm glad Carter changed your mind."

"Me too."

"I don't know if he told you, but Carter and I had a discussion, too. There were metaphors comparing me to a storm and dire threats if I wasn't careful about how I treat you." His tone sounded wry.

"I'm a big boy," Cam said. "I appreciate Carter's concern and his invitation tonight, but I make my own decisions about whom I get involved with."

Jesse's gaze flicked over him. "I have no doubt."

"Good."

They stared at each other for a few long beats until Jesse cleared his throat.

"Let me take you downstairs and introduce you to everyone." He turned and placed his hand on Cam's lower back. He guided Cam toward an unmarked door next to the bar. Being even that close to him made every nerve in Cam's body light up. He felt hyper-aware of Jesse's heat next to him and the subtle richness of his cologne. They paused at the end of the hallway by an old-fashioned phone mounted on the wall. Jesse opened another unmarked door, and they traveled down one more long hallway followed by a set of stairs.

At their foot, he brushed against Cam and pushed open a third nondescript door and revealed a gorgeous, sleek club. Under was filled with gleaming wood, rich leather and a number of stunningly attractive people. Impressed, Cam glanced at Jesse. He felt so out of his depth.

"This place is incredible. You and Kyle have done something amazing here."

A wide smile transformed Jesse's face. "Thank you. I'll be sure to tell Kyle you said that. I love my work at the media company, but this place feels like home."

He nodded to a well-built man stationed by the door. "Thanks, Jim."

Jim appeared to be a bouncer of some kind and he nodded back with a small grin. "A pleasure, Jesse."

Once inside, Jesse gestured toward the far wall. "We recently hired a DJ to spin here a few times a week. What do you think?"

Cam squinted at the woman behind the turntables for a moment before he recognized the signature pigtails of Mary-Alice. He didn't know her personally, but he knew her by reputation. "Mmm, she's pretty good, if you don't have high expectations."

Jesse's laugh drew the attention of a small group of people who glanced over at them, their curiosity obvious. "I enjoy your bluntness, Cam. Come on, I'll introduce you to a few new people and some I know you'll recognize."

Cam followed him over to the group, which included Carter and Riley.

"Hey," Cam said, lifting his hand in greeting. "Thanks for inviting me tonight, Carter."

He gave Cam a warm smile. "Glad you could make it."

Riley shook Cam's hand and echoed the sentiment.

"I'd like you to meet my sister, Audrey, and her husband, Max. Aud, Max, this is Sadie's and Dylan's teacher, Cameron Lewis," Carter said.

Cam tried to hide his wince and Carter gave him a serious look. "In the interest of keeping everything separate, I have a suggestion. How about you and I stick to honorifics and last names for school-related things and first names everywhere else?"

"Yeah, I'd like that," Cam said with a relieved smile. A little mental separation was a good thing. He juggled distinct personas as teacher and DJ. This would be no different. "And please call me Cam."

Audrey looked back and forth between them. "I feel like I'm missing something here, but it's lovely to meet you, Cam." Her emphasis on his name made Cam laugh.

"It's nice to meet you, too, Audrey."

"So, how did you end up here?" Audrey asked. "I'm all for the guys bringing in new attractive men, but are you trolling the New York school system for teachers now?" She glanced at her brother.

Carter grimaced. "Ugh, no. Well, Jesse was apparently trolling, but that's nothing new."

"Oh, I'm not here for Jesse," Cam said. "Carter promised good drinks. That's what I'm here for."

"Oooh. Ouch." Jesse chuckled, then squeezed Cam's waist. It occurred to Cam he'd stood with Jesse's arm around him since they walked up. It had felt so natural Cam hadn't even noticed. "Well, if Cam is only here for the drinks, I'd better play the good host! Come on. Let's see Kyle about getting you a cocktail."

Jesse guided him to the bar where several guys stood talking, including Kyle, who was stationed behind it.

"Glad you could make it tonight, Cam," he said with a big smile.

"Thanks."

Cam went through another round of introductions. He caught the names Malcolm, Gale and Jarrod but quickly lost track of which name belonged to which guy.

"My brother, Eric, comes in regularly, too," Jesse said after the trio excused themselves and moved to a seating area. "But he couldn't make it tonight."

"It's nice that you're so close," Cam said, although he was relieved not to see Jesse's brother. He didn't think he was up for meeting a good chunk of his friends and his family in one night.

"What can I get you to drink?" Kyle said. "Since you liked the Christiana, Jes made sure I had a couple of bottles on hand, but I may have an even better suggestion. Industry City Distillery is nearby, and they produce incredible artisanal vodka from sugar beets. It's the only vodka made here in New York City. It's not as smooth as the Christiana, but the flavor is amazing."

"Sounds great," Cam said. He couldn't believe Jesse remembered the pricey liquor he'd liked and made sure it was on hand in the event Cam showed up. It occurred to him that Jesse had made a sincere effort toward getting to know him despite Cam blowing him off, and Cam hadn't reciprocated at all.

Some flirting couldn't hurt. He shifted, letting the side of his body rest against Jesse's. Jesse glanced at him out of the corner of his eye like he'd heard Cam's signal loud and clear. *Good.*

Kyle handed Cam a glass filled with clear liquid.

"No ice?" Cam raised an eyebrow at him. "I like vodkas, but I don't drink them neat."

"Give it a try," Kyle coaxed. "It brings out the flavor to drink it this way."

Cam took a hesitant sniff of the liquor. "Huh. It's almost sweet. Kind of like vanilla."

The first sip had a remarkable smoothness, followed by a peppery bite and a clean finish. It tasted completely different from the Christiana, yet was every bit as delicious. "I like this a lot."

Kyle grinned at him. "I'm glad to hear it."

Cam set the glass on the bar and patted his back pocket. "Should I start a tab?"

Kyle shook his head. "We don't charge for the private parties."

"Wow." Cam glanced between them. "That's, uh, generous. To say the least."

"That's Jesse," Kyle said.

Jesse rolled his eyes. "It's just a party, babe."

A chorus of greetings came from behind them, and Cam turned to see a tall man with glossy black hair and handsome features step through the door. Another equally handsome man followed, his hair a light brown. Cam had seen pictures of Senator Mori and his boyfriend, Will Martin, with Jesse, as well as after they'd announced their relationship last fall. Cam didn't pay much attention to politics, but news articles about a mixed-race, gay Republican senator and his liberal partner were hard to miss.

Cam couldn't believe he was in a bar with these men. As a guest and not the hired help.

"I'll introduce you, Cam," Jesse said.

Cam picked up his drink with a nod of thanks to Kyle and followed. A flutter of nerves vied with the vodka-fueled warmth in his stomach.

"Will! David! Glad you could make it," Jesse said.

Will smiled and embraced him. "You know we try not to miss it."

"Let me introduce you to someone new. Will, this is Cameron Lewis. He teaches music and lives a double life as a DJ. Cam, this is Will Martin. Law professor, writer and currently shacked up with the illustrious senator here."

Cam held out his hand. "Nice to meet you."

"You too."

Jesse gestured toward the senator. "David Mori, but he answers to Senator Sexy."

David held out his hand and laughed. "Nice to meet you, Cam. Jesse is the only one who calls me that, by the way. I prefer David."

Jesse's eyes gleamed. "So he says, but I think he secretly enjoys it."

David grinned. "You see the kind of people at this bar? I have one piece of advice for you, Cam. Run while you still can."

* * * *

A few hours later, Cam sat beside Malcolm on a sofa, both of them chatting with Riley. Malcolm worked with Carter, and he was quiet but friendly. A couple of drinks allowed Cam to relax at the surreal experience of socializing with some of New York's most powerful and attractive people. With a few exceptions, the group tended toward gay or bi. Everyone welcomed him, and despite the fact that many of the people in attendance were over five years older than Cam—except maybe Malcolm—and quite a bit more famous, he was enjoying himself.

"Carter said you were hesitant to get involved with Jesse," Riley said.

Cam nodded. "I didn't want to create any awkwardness because of the kids."

"I understand," Riley said. "I assumed maybe it was because he and Carter dated."

Cam glanced at him, his eyes wide. "They did?"

Riley made a small O with his mouth, then glared at Malcolm, who appeared to be chuckling behind one hand. "Hush, you."

"I didn't say a word," Malcolm protested, his eyes shining with amusement.

"Not with your mouth, you didn't," Riley muttered, though he smiled, too. He glanced back to Cam. "It's a very long story, but Carter dated both Jesse and Kyle for a while before he and I got together."

"I thought you and Carter started dating right after you got divorced." Now Cam was thoroughly confused. "At least, that's the impression I got."

"Like I said, long story," Riley said with a dry chuckle. "I'll tell you about it sometime. The short answer is that it was a while after our divorces before we started seeing each other and we were both involved with other people first."

"Oh, sure. I'm sorry. I don't mean to pry."

Riley waved off his apology. "It's fine. The connections within this group get complicated as hell. Carter, Jesse, and Kyle were a thing, and I dated Will. Carter and I were involved with our friend Natalie, who's over there with her boyfriend." He shook his head. "Again, part of the story of how we got where we are now."

"I have a spreadsheet listing all of the pairings and connections if you need a reference guide," Malcolm said. His deadpan expression cracked at Riley's bark of laughter.

"He probably does," Riley agreed. The merry gleam in his eyes made Cam grin.

"It's impressive everyone's managed to remain friends," he said.

"I think a lot of it is due to Jesse," Riley mused. "He sets the tone for this group. He's so open about his sexuality and involvements, and it — pardon the pun — rubs off on all of us."

"I can see that." He didn't know Jesse well, but seeing him interact with his friends had given Cam a much clearer picture of the kind of man he was.

Cam went to sip his drink and noticed he'd emptied his glass. He excused himself. "I think I'll get a refill."

"You should let Kyle mix you up one of his crazy juices," Malcolm said. "He does an amazing job with mixed drinks."

"I will." Cam smiled at him. "Thanks for the suggestion."

Cam made a beeline for the bar and leaned his elbows on it. Kyle gave him an expectant look.

"Malcolm suggested I let you whip me up a drink."

"I'm glad to hear it. Because I came up with one in your honor."

Cam laughed, surprised and taken aback. "I don't even know what to say."

"Well, I hope you'll say you enjoy it." Kyle winked at him.

While Kyle mixed the drink, Cam watched the crowd. He found his focus drawn to Jesse. He stood across the room, talking to Carter and either Gale or Jarrod. He laughed at what someone said and pressed a smacking kiss on Carter's cheek. The sight made Cam smile. Jesse glanced up and caught Cam watching him. The wink he threw at Cam sent a pleasant shiver down Cam's spine.

He had no idea what he'd done to attract Jesse's attention, but he'd begun to appreciate it.

"Here you go." Kyle nudged his elbow and Cam turned back to face him. "One Brooklyn Ginger for the Brooklyn ginger."

"What's in it?"

"Ginger syrup, vodka, grapefruit and peppercorns."

Cam took a sip. It was sweet and tart with a lingering bite. "Whoa, that's good."

Kyle looked smug. "I'm good at what I do."

"Yes, yes, you are," Cam said with a laugh.

"Are you having a good time tonight?" Kyle asked, his expression growing serious again.

Cam nodded. "I am, yeah."

"Was I right?"

"About?" Cam gave him a quizzical look.

"About what I said when we met at Ember. How great the speakeasy crew is?"

"You refer to yourselves as the speakeasy crew?" Cam asked, amused.

Kyle ducked his head and looked sheepish. "Yeah, I think either Will or David started it, and it kinda stuck."

David. It blew Cam away to be socializing with a state senator and to hear other people refer to him casually. Although he'd been nothing but friendly and welcoming, so maybe Cam was putting him on an unnecessary pedestal. "You were right about the group. They're great guys."

"We all need this place," Kyle said, resting his elbows on the bar. "For one reason or another. Riley and Carter lost their families when they came out. So we're their family. David needs a place he doesn't have to be a senator for a few hours. We give him that."

"And Jesse?" Cam asked, very curious to learn more about him. "He helped you build this place. Does he need it?"

"He needs it more than any of us," Kyle said. "That's why he helped create it."

Cam's brow furrowed. Why would a charming, successful man like Jesse need an underground hangout? Then the pieces clicked. "He needs it because he trusts the people here," Cam said, his voice growing more and more sure the longer he spoke. "He needs to know the ones he gets close to aren't using him for fame or social connection or anything else."

"You're very astute. Not many people see past his surface."

"He doesn't let them," Cam countered. "The charm deflects everything."

"You saw through it."

"I think I've barely scratched the surface," Cam admitted.

* * * *

Cam was still mulling over his conversation with Kyle when Jesse sauntered over. "I hope you're enjoying yourself."

"I am," Cam said. "Unfortunately, I'm going to have to call it a night soon. I have school in the morning."

Jesse touched his forearm. "Well, as much as I'd like to talk more, I'll let you get home. We can't have the man molding young, impressionable minds too tired to do his job tomorrow."

"Thanks." Cam sipped his drink. "Oh! Have you tried the cocktail Kyle made for me?"

Jesse's hand lingered. "The Brooklyn Ginger? No, I haven't had the pleasure."

"Want to?" Cam injected a flirtatious note into his voice.

Jesse's full lips turned up at the corners. "I'd love to."

Cam handed him the drink. Jesse took a sip, his stare never leaving Cam's. There was something pornographic in the way he licked his lips. Jesse handed back the glass. "Delicious."

Lust shot straight to Cam's groin. He gulped down the final sip of the cocktail and cleared his throat.

"I guess I should head out now."

"Why don't you say your goodbyes to the guys, then I'll walk you out?"

"Afraid I'll get lost?" Cam asked.

"No." Jesse's gaze was intense, his eyes startlingly blue.

"Oh." Cam wet his lips and watched Jesse track his movements. "Sure, just give me a moment."

Cam said goodbye to Riley, Carter and Malcolm, a strange feeling buzzing through him. He shook David's and Will's hands and got a nod and a knowing smile from Kyle.

Shit.

He was really doing this. If he gave the go-ahead, he didn't think Jesse would hold back at all. Which meant things were about to get very, very interesting.

He followed Jesse out of the speakeasy and through the unmarked doors. He half-expected Jesse to reach for him the moment they were alone, but he didn't stop until they reached the sidewalk in front of Lock & Key.

Jesse faced him, and Cam took a deep breath. The streetlight illuminated Jesse's face, and his intent expression made a shiver run down Cam's spine.

"What do you think?" Jesse asked.

"Of?" Cam couldn't stop staring at his mouth. There was a hint of silver in his dark blond beard, and Cam wondered what it would feel like against his skin.

"The speakeasy."

"It's phenomenal. I'm glad I came tonight."

Jesse leaned forward until their lips were less than an inch apart. "Cam, tell me if I'm out of line here."

Cam couldn't think of a single objection, so he answered by pressing his lips to Jesse's.

Jesse let out a quiet sound and brought a hand up to cup the back of Cam's head. Cam teased at the seam of Jesse's mouth with his tongue and he opened, allowing Cam inside. Cam groaned.

Jesse stepped closer and embraced him, their bodies coming together full-length.

The kiss was slow and deliberate. Skillful. Not Cam's hurried fumbling with Ben or any other guy he'd kissed in the past. Jesse took his time.

This kiss Cam felt down to his toes.

He gripped the back of Jesse's suit jacket and let him take the lead. The soft prickle of Jesse's beard against his jaw made his cock fill, and Jesse let out a low, appreciative sound in the back of his throat when Cam pushed against him.

Jesse deepened the kiss. He dropped a hand to Cam's back and pressed their lower halves together more tightly. Jesse was hard, too.

They pulled apart, more to catch their breaths than anything, and Cam swallowed hard, his lips still tingling from the kiss.

"I'm glad you came tonight." Jesse brushed his thumb across Cam's lower lip and sent a shiver through his body. "And I'm glad you gave this another chance."

"Me too," he said, his voice faint.

Jesse leaned in for another kiss, and Cam welcomed it. After a deep, thorough kiss, Jesse drew back but only far enough to place a peck to the corner of his mouth.

He worked his way across Cam's jaw to his ear. Cam closed his eyes and enjoyed the slow exploration.

"I want to ask you to come home with me," Jesse said in his ear. The warmth of his breath made Cam shudder.

He slid a hand lower and gripped Cam's ass. "I want to find out if you're ginger everywhere. And I want to know if you taste as good as that cocktail Kyle made for you."

All Cam could manage was a little groan.

"As much as I want to ask you to come back to my place, it is a school night. So I guess I'll have to let you go." Jesse pulled away, his voice husky. "For the sake of the children's education."

"That's a good idea," Cam said, straightening. His tone sounded breathy and reluctant, even to his own ears. "For the children."

Jesse gave him a faint smile and leaned in for a final brief but thorough kiss. He drew back when a car pulled up. "There's your ride."

Cam gave him a puzzled look. "You called a car for me?"

Jesse shrugged. "Less chance of me changing my mind about letting you go home alone."

"Thanks." Cam was strangely touched by the gesture. He reached for his wallet and searched through it. Jesse made sounds of protest.

"You don't need to pay me back."

Cam pressed his business card into Jesse's palm. "My number's on there. Text me."

Jesse closed his fingers around it and nodded. "I will."

Cam gave him a final hard, quick kiss before he jogged to the vehicle and got in.

The car pulled away from the curb, and Cam had the sudden sense he'd gotten in way, way over his head. Involving himself with Jesse was the craziest idea he'd ever had, but there was no chance of stopping now.

And he couldn't wait to see what it led to.

Chapter Seven

Jesse let himself into his brother's condo, hauling his briefcase and two bags of groceries with him. "I'm here, guys! Please, put your fucking clothes on!"

"Words I never thought I'd hear you utter."

Jesse grinned at his sister-in-law, Sara, who made a beeline through the space toward him, her big brown eyes gleaming. "Honey, I may be a rake, but I have no desire to see Eric's hairy ass. You, of course, are welcome to disrobe at any time."

A smile lit her lovely face. "You're just jealous he has nicer legs."

"Bullshit." Jesse set the bags down. "I know you're biased, but nothing about that big lug's body is nicer than mine, including his legs. Don't tell him I said that, though — I don't want to hurt his feelings." He looked Sara up and down and admired the swell of her belly under her black sweater dress. He drew her into a hug.

"Hey, beautiful."

"Hey, yourself." Sara pulled him close. "I'm glad to see you."

"Me too." He dropped a kiss on the top of her head before letting her loose. "Where is Eric, anyway? Clothing aforementioned hairy ass?"

"He ran down the street to the pharmacy." Sara ran a hand through her short dark hair. "We're leaving for Vermont on Friday after work, and he wanted to stock up on his migraine meds."

"Isn't the whole point of going to your country house to avoid stress and, by association, migraines?"

"Yes, but your brother likes to be prepared." Sara moved to help him with the bags, but Jesse waved her off.

"I've got it."

"I'm pregnant, Jes, not incapable of carrying freaking groceries."

"Ooh, big scary feminist." Jesse puffed out his chest. "Now move your ass, please. I have to cook dinner like a properly emasculated modern man."

Sara laughed. "What are you making tonight?" she asked and led the way to the kitchen.

"Spicy Orange Beef." He set everything on the counter. "You're still off chicken, right?"

Sara grimaced. "Yeah. I can't describe why, but it tastes so very wrong right now."

"Meh." Jesse began unpacking the bags. "There are other things to eat. At least you haven't had any morning sickness."

"True." Sara pulled wineglasses from a cabinet and noises from the front door echoed down the hall. "Still, I feel kind of bad. Eric's missing some of the things we used to eat."

"Are we discussing the Great Chicken Ban of 2015?" Eric walked into the kitchen and joined them. He had more brown in his hair and more gray in his eyes than his brother, but he shared the incandescent Murtagh grin. "I told you, honey, I get plenty during the week when Jes and I go out for lunch."

Sara glanced at Eric. "So you say. I still find it hard to believe."

"There's a place near the office and everything's fried," he replied. "It's a wonderland of bad foods."

"Eric stuffs himself with whole buckets of chicken," Jesse added. "It's utterly debauched and I'm so proud." He squawked when Sara pinched his waist.

"I hate you both right now. Not fair you look like this when you eat junk." Sara set a glass in front of Jesse and pouted until he eyed her askance. "Oh, don't mind me. I'm just cranky because I'm four months along and already the size of a house."

"You are not the size of anything," Eric scolded. He moved closer and slipped an arm around her. "Half the people we meet don't even know you're pregnant, honey."

"That means they think I'm the one who's eating buckets of chicken, but they're too polite to mention it."

"You may be right." Jesse dug into his briefcase for what he and Kyle had fondly dubbed the Pregnant Lady Mocktails. "C'mere, girl, and let me pour you a drink."

"Ooh, yay." Sara's eyes gleamed and she stepped up beside him. "What have you got?"

"Agua fresca with hibiscus, blood orange and vanilla. Kyle brews up stuff like this for Carter and he sent me the recipe last night." He handed her the jug he'd stored in his office refrigerator all day.

Sara uncapped the jug and sniffed. "Man, that smells delicious. Almost makes me feel less shitty about my expanding waistline."

Jesse filled a tumbler with ice, then set it down and picked up a lime. "If you think it'll help, I'll buy you one of those Baby on Board T-shirts."

"Ugh, no thanks." Sara wrinkled her nose. "I don't need to be reminded that I'm basically a spacecraft for what may be a hostile life form."

Eric's eyes shone with amusement when Jesse turned to him, dumbfounded. "Sara's got it in her head that pregnancy is essentially hosting an alien being. I blame all those sci-fi movies she watches."

"You guys are so weird," Jesse mused. "Promise me that'll never change."

"Says the weirdest of us all," Eric retorted. "Don't worry. From what I've seen, raising a family is only going to make us weirder with time." He aimed a significant look at his brother. "You could try it, you know. Maybe change your mind about this professional bachelor thing you've got going."

Jesse barked out a laugh. Eric had fallen head over heels for Sara on their very first date, and they were so happy together. They'd built a great life between their Rose Hill condo and Vermont farmhouse and were embarking on parenthood with unabashed joy. Eric wanted the same kind of happiness and contentment for his brother.

The idea of easing into a lifestyle like Eric's made Jesse's chest tighten, however, and not in an enjoyable way. He didn't know how to live a life so quiet and, well, stifling. His spirit thrived on being unorthodox. To him, Eric's picturesque, very staid existence was inconceivable.

"You know me better than that, bro." He garnished the glass of agua fresca with a slice of lime and handed it to Sara. "I'm having way too much fun in this city to settle into anything deep. Training for a second marathon with Carter is the most serious commitment you'll get from me."

"Better you than me, man. I thought my knees were going to fall off last year."

Sara hummed into her drink. "I think I'm in love."

Jesse and Eric laughed. "Now you sound like my brother," Eric said.

"Hey, I have never fallen in love with a drink." Jesse pressed his lips together over another laugh at Eric and Sara's twin expressions of disbelief.

"You fall in love with people and inanimate objects every week," Eric said.

Sara nodded. "That's kind of your thing, babe."

"Okay, fine." Jesse turned his attention back to preparing dinner. "I don't fall in love, however. It's more a super-deep and short-lasting infatuation."

Eric chuckled. "True. Like the club in Chelsea you told me about. You're definitely infatuated with it, or something in it."

Jesse's movements came to a standstill for a moment before Sara's voice caught his attention.

"What club is this?" she asked.

"Club Ember." Eric gestured at Jesse with his wineglass. "He and Kyle checked it out and Jes has gone back, what, three or four times since then? Which means either the music and booze are phenomenal or there's another draw, as in someone gorgeous owns the place."

"The owner is Dad's age and working on his third wife," Jesse replied. He peeled a piece of ginger. "He's attractive but not my type. I told you, I like the place and I've gotten friendly with one of the DJs."

"Looking to hire him for Under?" Sara asked.

"I considered asking him," Jesse admitted. "But the kid lives in Brooklyn, and he has a day job—I doubt he'd care to make the trip that far uptown, no matter how good the pay is. He's been out to the bar, though, and met the guys."

Of course, Jesse had zero business interest in Cam. For all he knew, Cam could very well be interested in spinning at Under. He'd never brought it up, however, and Jesse didn't plan to, either.

He turned the bulk of his attention back on the food while Eric and Sara discussed transportation from Brooklyn to the Upper East Side. He felt oddly tense. He always shared details about his partners with Eric and Sara, and it was out of character for him not to disclose the extent of his friendship with Cam. Specifically, that he and Cam exchanged messages every day. And that each time Jesse went to Ember, he and Cam spent Cam's breaks making out in dark corners of the club.

Jesse dusted a steak with baking soda. He didn't know what held him back from talking about Cam, especially as he didn't have much to tell. So far, Cam was still being cagey about going on an actual date. Cam had been busy most weekends and Jesse in London every few weeks to oversee the internet radio venture, too. Just kissing Cam was hot, though, and Jesse enjoyed hanging out with him. He wanted more—a lot more—from Cam, and he wanted it soon.

A flush of heat worked its way up under his shirt collar. Damned if his body didn't respond to the memory of Cam pressed up against him. He frowned and carried the plate of steak to the refrigerator to chill. Cam's path would intersect with Eric's and Sara's sooner or later. Jesse needed to get his head in order before that happened.

* * * *

Jesse checked his messages during his walk home that night and found a couple from Cam. They'd discussed favorite foods earlier in the day, and Cam's varied tastes pleased his adventurous palate.

I have a gnocchi problem, Cam's last text read. *I straight out love them. They're like little pillows of potato goodness from God.*

I happen to agree, Jesse replied. *Further evidence we should have dinner. I even know a place that serves fantastic gnocchi, and I'll bet you've never been.*

Cam didn't reply straight away, but Jesse didn't fret. It was late and Cam no doubt had lesson plans to work on and an extensive collection of vinyl to catalog. Jesse was stretched out in bed reviewing documents for the internet radio project on his tablet when his phone pinged again.

Showing off is rude, Cam wrote. *I'm free Friday night, Big Money. Wanna put your wallet where your mouth is?*

Jesse smiled down at his phone. He could think of plenty of places he'd like to put his mouth, and damn Kyle for telling Cam about that ridiculous nickname. Quickly, he checked a few things online, then turned his attention to a reply.

I'll pick you up outside the school at 3:00, Red. Bring a jacket.

* * * *

Two days later, Jesse met Cam near the main entrance of Midtown Academy. Cam had his gray leather jacket slung over his shoulder and still wore a school-appropriate blue Oxford shirt and khaki trousers rather than the edgy pieces he wore to spin at Ember. He looked good enough to eat.

The afternoon sun lit up Cam's fair skin and made the reds in his hair burn bright. For a split second, the sight struck Jesse, leaving him almost transfixed. Cam smiled widely when he saw Jesse, and cast an appreciative glance at his slate wool suit.

"I didn't expect to see you on foot," he called as Jesse got closer. "I thought for sure I'd get a ride in the mystical Range Rover you keep talking about."

"Hey, I'm not ashamed to admit I love my car, but she won't be much help where we're going tonight." Jesse held out his hand. If they were anywhere else in Manhattan, he'd be kissing the shit out of Cam. But here, in front of Cam's workplace, he could play innocent, at least for a moment, and shake hands.

"Where's your nose ring?" he asked.

"At home," Cam replied. "Visible piercings outside of the ears are against academic dress code."

Jesse fought back a leer. He'd look forward to checking Cam for not-visible piercings then. "Are you ready to go?"

"Sure," Cam let go of his hand. "Are you going to tell me where we're going at three in the afternoon?"

"All in good time." Jesse made an "after you" gesture and the two fell into step. "We're not walking far. We've got one stop to make before we get going, and I'd like to buy you a drink."

Cam looked at him askance. "Are you playing hooky to get tipsy?"

"Maybe." Jesse winked. "But my brother's covering for me at the office. He's owed me favors since he and Sara got stuck in Boston during one of those crazy storms in February. We didn't see them for almost four days."

Cam winced. "Four days?"

"He and I cover for each other any time it's necessary," Jesse replied. They turned left on Third Avenue. "That said, Eric being out of town made my life a pain in the ass, and I feel no guilt calling in a favor today."

They chatted and made their way east, and Cam glanced around, his curiosity plain. Jesse knew he was trying to figure out their destination without asking. He looked dumbfounded when Jesse led him under FDR Drive and toward the waterfront, and finally caught hold of his arm. He pulled Jesse around to face him.

"Okay, I give up. I can't take it another minute."

"What are you talking about?" Jesse feigned bewilderment.

"Where are we going?"

"Out to dinner."

"Where? On the banks of the East River? Because eww."

"I thought we'd go farther north." Jesse pressed his lips together to keep a straight face, and Cam pinned him with a glare.

"Then what are we doing here?"

"I told you—we need to make a stop first, and I want to buy you a drink."

Cam balked. "We can't get a drink around here," he insisted with a wave at their surroundings.

"Says who? This is New York, Cam, there's always a bar nearby."

"Okay, but—"

"You'd be surprised by how many wee watering holes there are if you'd take a minute to look around."

Cam groaned and the last of his composure slipped away. "Hail Mary and all the saints. Will you quit being such a pain in the ass and tell me where the fuck we're going already?"

Jesse laughed so hard his eyes watered. "Fucking A, Cam!"

Cam's cheeks flushed a deep red and covered his mouth with one hand. "Oh, my God. I'm sorry. I didn't mean to yell at you."

"Yes, you did." Jesse held out a hand to prevent him from bolting. "I didn't know you were even capable of losing your shit in such spectacular fashion. You were doing so well playing cool!"

Cam's expression shifted and became defensive and unhappy, and Jesse's heart gave a little squeeze. Cam slid his eyes away.

"Aw, come on." Jesse tugged him in closer and waited until Cam met his gaze. "I was only trying to wind you up."

"I know." Cam cleared his throat. "I'm, um, not always great with surprises."

"Well, that's good to know. Does that mean you're going to yell at me again when I tell you where we're going for dinner?"

A smile crept back onto Cam's face. "I hope not, but I guess that depends on where we're going."

Jesse jerked his head toward the waterfront. "Let's go." He rolled his eyes when Cam hesitated. "Get your ass in gear, Red, before you make us late with all this pissing around. I promise to tell you everything once you've got a drink in your hand."

They continued bickering, but Cam's efforts to give Jesse a hard time left him distracted, and he didn't notice the Skyport Marina signs at first. When he quit bitching, he took a good look around and raised his brows at the luxury yachts.

"Are we going on a cruise?"

"Close." Jesse's stomach gave a funny flip.

What the fuck? Why did he suddenly feel nervous?

He checked his watch, more to give himself something to do than to know the time, and when he focused on Cam again, he felt settled. He led Cam toward the entrance of the Blade Aqua Lounge.

"Despite your foot dragging, we're right on time. Our flight doesn't leave for another thirty minutes, which gives us time for the drink I mentioned."

Cameron crashed to a stop and stared, his eyes huge. "Our flight—?"

"Leaves at four p.m.," Jesse finished. Delight unfurled in his chest at Cameron's undisguised shock. He didn't react as Cam opened and closed his mouth a couple of times. He and Cam liked to tease each other, but he sensed Cam's composure was shaky in that moment.

"Where are we going?" Cam finally asked. His grip tightened when Jesse urged him back into motion.

"Out to dinner, silly. You told me about your gnocchi problem, and I remembered this place on Nantucket

Island. Makes some of the best I've ever eaten on the East Coast."

Cam blinked. "Nantucket, Massachusetts?"

"That's right." Jesse smiled. "The quickest way there from New York is to fly, of course, so I booked us seats on a seaplane. I thought that'd be nicer than a helicopter." He reached for the lounge door. "I mean, helicopters are fucking cool, but super noisy, and I feel like talking tonight. We can do a helo another time, if you like."

Cam stood before the open door for a long moment. His cheeks were flushed again, and his eyes sparkled with what Jesse hoped was excitement.

"Is this the part where you yell at me again?" he asked gently.

"No. But you sure are a special kind of crazy." Cam's lips turned up in a slow, wide smile that warmed Jesse's insides.

He shoved the feeling aside and opened the door. "Girl, please — you ain't seen nothing yet."

The date went off beautifully. After the short flight, Jesse and Cam rode a taxi downtown and spent time sightseeing. Cam didn't say much during their stroll through the picturesque streets, and Jesse wondered more than once if he'd miscalculated the whole evening. However, the pretty town piqued Cam's curiosity and he soon opened back up. By the time Jesse suggested having a drink before dinner, Cam had become his lively, flirty self again and started teasing Jesse with his sly grin.

They touched back down in Manhattan after ten p.m., following a fantastic meal that included the gnocchi Cam so loved. Cam agreed every bite had been worth the trip. He and Jesse slid into one of the Murtagh family's cars outside the marina, but before Jesse could ask if they should drop Cam at home, Cam put a hand on Jesse's thigh. That wordless gesture sent a bolt of heat straight to Jesse's gut, and he told the driver to take them to his place near Madison Square Park.

Cam said little during the short ride, but his lips curved in a smile when Jesse covered the hand on his thigh with his own. His placid demeanor broke after they'd stepped into the elevator in Jesse's building, and suddenly, Jesse had an armful of warm, lithe, fucking beautiful man.

Cam groaned loudly. His cock pressed hard against Jesse's hip, and Jesse pushed him backward. He relished Cam's grunt as he made contact with the elevator's wall. Jesse pinned Cam there with his body. Neither was gentle as they pulled at each other, their kisses hungry and biting.

Cam gasped. "Jesus, Jes."

Jesse hummed. "I know."

He kissed Cam deeply, heat thrumming through him. Their tongues slid together, and Jesse dropped a hand and palmed Cam through his trousers. He felt a little drunk, though they'd only had one cocktail on the return flight. He just liked touching so much. Cam growled at Jesse's groping, but they both went still when the elevator chimed. The doors slid open and Jesse stepped back with a chuckle.

"We're lucky no one else got on," he mused. He and Cam stepped out of the car. "Not that I would have stopped."

"Not that I would have noticed," Cam countered with a snigger. He moved aside to allow Jesse to open the door, but quickly stepped up behind him. He moved his hands up under the hem of Jesse's suit jacket and grasped his waist, his touch hot through Jesse's shirt. Jesse bit back a groan.

He hustled Cam inside. Jesse punched in the alarm code as Cam let out a low whistle. He stared at the loft with wide eyes.

"Holy hell. This place is fantastic."

"Thanks." Jesse turned away from the keypad and cupped Cam's jaw with one hand. Fire raced under his skin at the lust he glimpsed in Cam's face. "I'll show you around sometime."

He pulled Cam into a scorching kiss. They fumbled with each other's clothes, leaving a trail of discarded garments and shoes on the way to the master bedroom.

They staggered through the open doorway, Cam's fingers pressed into the muscles of Jesse's upper back. Jesse reached blindly for the light switch, muttering in between kisses.

"Shit. Mmm. I want you." His chest ached at Cam's dark chuckle.

"Want you, too. So much, Jes, you have no idea."

Jesse slid his hands under the waistband of Cam's boxer briefs. God, he loved the feel of a man's skin under his fingers. He walked Cam backward until his calves hit the bed, then pushed Cam down with both hands. Cam bounced onto the mattress with a laugh, but the merry noise faded into a sigh as Jesse bent to pull off Cam's boxer briefs.

With Cam naked, Jesse disrobed, too, then crawled onto the bed and settled over him. Even that small distance seemed too much for Cam. He dragged Jesse down for another kiss. This kiss was more languid and sensual but no less heated, and the longer it went on, the more it set Jesse's whole body on fire. He met Cam's stare when they broke apart, and the world ground to a halt around them.

Jesse bit his lip. He'd known Cam would be fantastic in bed, but this… He couldn't remember the last time he'd been so turned on simply from the touch of another person's bare skin.

Cam reached up and ran his fingers over Jesse's lips. "Need you in me," he said. His breath caught when Jesse dipped his head and took Cam's first two fingers into his mouth.

Jesse sucked hard, flexing his tongue over the sensitive pads of Cam's fingertips, and his cock throbbed at Cam's groan. He forced himself to pull away after Cam squirmed, and pushed up onto his knees, admiring the toned body laid out before him, all flushed pink skin and lean muscles. Cam propped himself up onto his elbows, his cock rigid against the rusty curls of hair on his groin. Simply looking at the pearl of pre-cum on its tip made Jesse's mouth water.

"Fuck," he breathed.

He stretched toward the nightstand for a condom and lube, aware of Cam moving, too. Cam was kneeling in front of Jesse when he straightened back up, fire in his eyes. He dropped a hand and stroked himself, and his mouth fell slightly open. Jesse stared, unmoving, until Cam reached for him.

"Not so fast, Red." Jesse went still at Cam's next words.

"I've been tested and I'm negative." Cam gave him a small smile. "If that's what you're worried about, I mean."

Jesse grinned. "I wasn't, but thank you for being forthright. I'm negative, too." He flipped open the bottle of lube and wet his fingers. "Now be a good boy and let me open you up."

Jesse tossed the bottle and condom down on the mattress. He nudged Cam's legs open a bit wider with one knee, then reached for Cam's cock. Their fingers slid alongside each other's and goosebumps rose up on his skin when Cam moaned outright.

Cam shuddered hard and let go of himself. He reached his hands up and grabbed hold of Jesse's hair, then pulled him into a deep kiss. The sting of pain melted into pleasure and Jesse groaned into Cam's mouth. He moved his other hand and rubbed at the sensitive skin behind Cam's balls.

Cam broke away with a gasp as Jesse worked a finger inside him. "Oh, fuck."

He let go of Jesse's hair but didn't turn him loose. Cam slid his hands around the back of his neck instead, then pressed their foreheads together. Cam pushed down against the finger inside him and Jesse let out his own groan.

"God, Cam."

Their panting breaths mixed as Jesse worked Cam open. Cam sealed his mouth over Jesse's again and kissed him hungrily. Cam unlocked his hands from behind Jesse's neck and ran them over his chest, the touch sending sensation zinging through him. Sweat sheened their skins.

Cam broke the kiss and mouthed his way over Jesse's jaw and neck, his sharp, nipping kisses sending almost painful jolts right to Jesse's cock. Jesse pulled his fingers free and rested his hands on Cam's ass while Cam licked Jesse's chest. He swore as that wicked mouth closed over his nipple.

"Cam." Jesse grunted and squeezed the flesh in his hands at Cam's chuckle. "Cameron."

"Oh! Okay, okay."

Cam straightened up, panting. He gripped Jesse's shoulders tightly and guided him backward, pushing until he'd settled with his back against the headboard. Jesse laughed at being manhandled, but the laughter faded when Cam swung one long leg up and over and straddled him.

Cam stared at Jesse, his gaze rapt. "Gorgeous," he murmured, his voice so low Jesse thought maybe he hadn't meant to speak. Jesse stroked Cam's flanks and held the stare until Cam turned away for the abandoned condom and lube.

Jesse fought not to react as Cam prepared him but lost the battle the moment Cam took him in both hands, his touch firm and wet and, oh, so fucking good. Jesse groaned. He was so hard. Even those few strokes set his body shaking. Jesse closed his eyes. He leaned back against the headboard as Cam worked the condom over him, and his toes curled with pleasure.

Cam shifted his weight and Jesse forced his eyes open again. He grasped Cam's waist, holding him steady, and Cam guided Jesse inside him. Cam's eyes glazed over as the cockhead breached the tight ring of muscle and he sank slowly down, his face gone slack. Jesse lost himself in the heat and pressure of the body around his, his every nerve pulling tight. He gasped as Cam rolled his hips.

Jesse stroked the skin over Cam's torso with his hands. Cam's eyelids fluttered and he pushed back when Jesse thrust up. That changed the angle, punching Cam's prostate, and Cam jolted. He yelped and tightened his grip, pressing his fingers with bruising force into Jesse's skin. Jesse savored the throb of pain. His vision narrowed as he and Cam found their rhythm, the orgasm gathering power in his groin.

Cam dropped one hand and fisted himself. He whispered encouragement as Jesse raised a hand and joined him, pumping in tandem, their grips overlapping. They watched each other, the breaths loud in the otherwise silent room, until Cam's eyes clenched shut. He arched his back and cried out, and Jesse bit his lip hard. His balls drew up tight.

"Oh, God," Cam whined. "So good. So good, Jes!"

"Fuck, yes." He set a punishing pace and thrust hard, over and over, until Cam fell apart.

Cam's voice broke on Jesse's name. His face twisted and his cock pulsed, and Jesse's laugh of sheer relief cut off into a moan as his own orgasm crashed over him. His world spun down in a haze of sight and sound, and he surged forward. He pulled Cam close, needing his touch. The moment stretched and lengthened, and his body shook.

They rocked together, riding out the high, until Cam slumped bonelessly into him, oblivious of the mess between them. "Holy shit," he slurred.

"My thoughts exactly." Jesse nuzzled his face against Cam's throat. "You okay there?"

"I'm fantastic." Cam sounded dazed and amused. "I can't move and my whole body feels like jelly. It's awesome."

Jesse snorted. "Radical, dude." He shifted, easing Cam and himself deeper into the bed until they were lying down. Cam's eyes were glazed when he picked up his head and a goofy grin crossed his face.

Jesse laughed. "You're a human disaster."

"Mmm-hmm. I'm leveled." Cam inclined his head and dropped a kiss on Jesse's chest. "You know you love it."

Jesse did love it. He couldn't remember the last time anyone had ridden him so well, particularly a man. And while they were both still loopy with hormones, he wanted to turn the tables as soon as possible. Moving quickly, he reached down and grabbed Cam's ass, then swallowed his whine with a kiss.

No time like the present.

Chapter Eight

"Water please," Cam said to Emily.

She grinned and slid a bottle across the bar. "I saw you coming and had it ready!"

"Am I that predictable?"

"A little bit, yeah." She winked at him and Cam laughed. She was right. He stopped by the bar for water at least once a night. And Emily had worked at Ember longer than Cam had been doing gigs there.

Someone gently bumped his shoulder. Cam craned his neck and found Ben smiling at him. "Hey there."

"Oh, hey," Cam said. "How are you?"

A vague sense of guilt washed over him. In all the excitement of his hookups and date with Jesse, Cam hadn't thought much about Ben. Of course, he found it hard to think about much of anything else with Jesse around. Christ, Cam daydreamed about him instead of focusing on prepping for class and even while he spun records. Thinking of the way Jesse's mouth tasted or the sounds he made when he came. The warmth of his smile or his unreserved laugh when he was amused.

Jesse was a ridiculous, beautiful distraction that would only get worse. They'd fucking flown to Nantucket on Friday afternoon for some of the best damn gnocchi he'd ever had. Not to mention the sex. *Jesus.* Cam couldn't remember the last time sex had left him so wrung-out and satisfied. His head was still spinning like one of his records when he'd finally gone home the next morning.

Jesse had made an impression Cam couldn't deny.

"Cam?"

He blinked and focused on Ben. Cam cleared his throat, his cheeks warming with embarrassment. "Yeah, sorry. What did you say?"

Ben slid a hand along Cam's back. "I asked if you want to come out back with me?"

"Uh, sure." Cam followed Ben through the crowds to the back hallway.

"What have you been up to?" Ben asked.

Cam shrugged, although Ben couldn't see him. "Work, mostly. I went to a friend's dinner party last night. Nothing too exciting."

Okay, that was a lie. His date with Jesse had been exciting as fuck, but it didn't seem prudent to bring that up with Ben.

"What about you?" he asked, changing the subject.

"Same. Work. Hanging out with friends. Nothing earth-shattering."

And that concludes this conversation, Cam thought. He stepped through the back door of the club after an uncomfortable silence. That was the problem with Ben. While a nice enough guy, he and Cam didn't have a ton to talk about. He lacked Jesse's zeal for life. But it was grossly unfair of Cam to compare them, too.

113

Cam jammed the board between the door and frame before he faced Ben. The minute Cam straightened, Ben kissed him. Cam let out a muffled sound against Ben's mouth but kissed him back. *Okay, I guess I should have seen that coming. After all, we're not out here for the conversation,* he thought ruefully.

Cam raked a hand through Ben's thick hair and tilted his head, giving Ben better access to his mouth. Ben groaned and pressed full-length against Cam, tugging his shirt from his jeans. His hands were hot and eager on Cam's waist, roaming across his skin. Cam staggered backward a bit, stunned by Ben's eagerness. His head bumped against the door and he grabbed Ben's hips to steady himself. Cam wanted to be enthusiastic about kissing Ben, but everything felt strangely flat.

Cam deepened the kiss, chasing the elusive high he'd shared with Jesse, but where there had been heat and desperation with Jesse, this was all just lukewarm. He pulled back and Ben let out a small, disappointed sound. He stared at Cam with a quizzical look.

"What's wrong?"

"Uh. Look." Cam licked his lips. "I'm not sure I..." He fumbled to find the words. "I'm not really feeling this."

A line appeared between Ben's eyebrows. "Feeling what?"

"Um. You and me."

The line deepened. "Tonight or...?"

"In general."

Ben stepped back. "Does this have to do with Jesse Murtagh?"

"Sort of?" Cam hedged. He cleared his throat. "He and I have been fooling around lately."

"Yeah, I've seen you making out with him all over the club," Ben snapped.

Cam bit back an apology. While he felt shitty he'd upset Ben, his annoyance seemed out of proportion. He'd never promised Ben anything. "We agreed this would be casual," Cam pointed out.

An annoyed look crossed Ben's face. "Right."

"I'm sorry, Ben. I'm not trying to be an asshole here."

"I get it. Whatever." He glanced at his phone. "My break is almost up anyway. See ya around."

Ben walked toward the door. He disappeared through it without a backward glance, and the board propping it open tumbled out. Cam grabbed the door and replaced the board, then leaned against the brick wall. *Fuck.*

That hadn't gone well.

Cam didn't have a clue if or when Ben's feelings had changed. There were no strings between them. Or there weren't supposed to be, anyway. He'd had no indication Ben thought this was anything more than a fun fling to pass the time.

Ben had no right to be jealous about Cam getting involved with someone else. Maybe it had more to do with Ben feeling miffed about being blown off for someone like Jesse.

Shit. Jesse.

He was...*fuck.* Cam didn't know what he was. But Ben couldn't hold a candle to him.

Cam had never encountered anyone like Jesse. Funny, charming, absurdly handsome and rich didn't begin to cover it. He was also smart as hell and one of the most interesting people Cam had ever met. He liked Jesse's passion for life and the way he approached everything with no apology.

Of course, Cam had been impressed by the trip for his favorite food. Who wouldn't? It had been an amazing touch, but Cam hadn't been impressed so much that Jesse shelled out a shitload of money. When Cam called him 'Big Money', it was a nod to the joke Kyle had started, not to urge Jesse to do something outlandish.

No, Cam felt quite sure he'd arranged the trip and meal to put a smile on Cam's face more than wow him with his wealth. It had worked, too. Cam couldn't remember a date he'd enjoyed so much. And he'd thought about little else since.

"Cam?"

Cam looked up and found Jerry, Ember's owner, staring at him with a concerned expression.

He straightened and cleared his throat. "Hi, Jerry."

"Everything okay?"

"Yeah, I came out here for fresh air."

Jerry frowned and glanced at his watch. "You've gone way over your break time, which isn't like you at all. I came looking for you to talk about an unrelated topic."

Cam grimaced and strode toward the door Jerry held open. "I am so sorry. I got lost in my thoughts." He glanced at the time on his phone while he hurried down the hall. "At least the playlist I cued should still be up. This shouldn't have happened and it won't again."

Jerry nodded and fell into step beside him. "Well, you've never made a habit of taking too long of a break, Cam, so I'm not concerned," he said.

"Thanks." Cam managed a tight smile. "What did you want to talk to me about?"

"Oh, I have a special event coming up next fall I thought you might be interested in taking part in. It's a fundraiser."

* * * *

An hour later, Cam was still kicking himself for losing track of time. Jerry hadn't seemed concerned, and the crowd hadn't noticed, but Cam had always promised himself never to let his personal life get in the way of his job and he'd done exactly that. Maybe not directly, but the situation with Ben and Jesse had distracted him. Cam wasn't okay with that at all.

To make up for it, Cam put more showmanship into his set than usual and worked the crowd. They ate it up. Twice, phone numbers were slipped to him, although he didn't know if he'd act on them or not. Cam didn't need any more complications at the moment, but he didn't want to totally rule them out, either.

He scanned the crowd again, pleased that people appeared to be enjoying themselves. Cam loved the feedback from the crowd and the flow of energy between them and him. It was one of his favorite parts of spinning and never failed to put a smile on his face.

Cam groaned when he spied Kyle through the crowd, though. Where Kyle was, Jesse could usually be found nearby. And the last thing Cam wanted to deal with tonight was his biggest distraction. In person.

Cam forced his eyes away, but his attention drifted to Kyle again. He was easy to spot, his height and coloring making him stand out in the crowd. He shifted and Cam caught a glimpse of a head of lighter hair. A moment later, the crowd parted and revealed Jesse standing beside a brunette woman in a slinky black dress. They were all laughing.

God damn it. Why tonight of all nights? Cam thought with a groan. Still, a part of him was glad to see Jesse, despite the possible distraction.

When their gazes met, Jesse's face lit up. Even in the swirling lights of the dance floor, Cam saw him wink and grin. Warm pleasure surged through Cam, and its intensity took him by surprise.

Cam grinned back. For a moment, they stood there staring at each other across the club floor. Jesse was the lone still point in the surging, dancing bodies around him as the colored lights glinted off his hair. As usual, beautiful people packed the club, but Cam couldn't take his eyes off him.

After Jesse turned back to his friends, Cam continued observing him surreptitiously. He leaned in and spoke to the woman in the black dress, and she gave him a playful swat him on the arm. It looked like an affectionate gesture and the way their bodies moved together spoke of familiarity.

Cam watched them dance and flirt and understood what made Jesse so successful. His charm was genuine. When he showed interest in someone, the rest of the world disappeared. In that moment, no one else existed but the person in front of him. His attention wasn't faked. Despite the fact that Kyle stood some feet away, and Cam on the other side of the club, no one seemed to exist to Jesse but the woman in front of him.

Cam knew from personal experience what it felt like to be Jesse's sole focus. He had no doubt anyone involved with Jesse was dazzled by the attention, too. It had to feel very cold once the attention turned away. Cam felt a bit of that at the moment, actually.

The thought and unfamiliar emotion that followed made Cam's chest ache. He forced his gaze away again.

Whatever Cam might be feeling, this wasn't the time or the place to analyze it.

He tried to focus on his work but, after a while, caught a glimpse of Jesse heading toward him with Kyle and the woman in the black dress in tow. Jesse raised an eyebrow in question when they reached Cam's booth, and Cam gestured for them to come back. He lowered his headphones and smiled.

"Fancy seeing you here," he said, raising his voice over the music.

Jesse gave him a quick, but more than friendly, kiss on the lips. "Hope it's not unwelcome. You looked kind of scowly earlier."

Cam made a dismissive motion with his hand, not wanting to get into it at the moment. "Work stuff," he said. "Nothing major, but thanks for asking."

He held the hand out to Kyle, who'd been observing them with a speculative expression. "Great to see you, Kyle."

"Yeah, you too. Fantastic set." Rather than settle for a handshake, Kyle pulled him into a warm hug.

"Oh, thanks." Cam hugged him back, his smile genuine when they parted. "The energy is good tonight. Hope you're all having fun."

"We are." Jesse put his hand on Cam's shoulder. "Cam, this is Astrid Larsen. She works for the CEC with Carter. Astrid, Cam Lewis."

"Jesse's been raving about this gorgeous ginger DJ from Brooklyn and I had to see for myself," she said, her face aglow. Cam had zero sexual interest in women, but he thought she was stunning. Some combination of genetics had left her with dark hair and eyes, richly tanned skin and a Scandinavian name. "It's nice to meet you, Cam."

"It's nice to meet you, too," Cam said. "I hope you're enjoying yourself."

Astrid nodded. "Oh, I am. But it's hard to have a bad time with Blondie around."

Her voice held a flirtatious note as she glanced at Jesse. His answering smile and their earlier interactions made Cam wonder if they were former or current lovers. With Jesse, one never knew.

"True enough," Cam answered, his tone dry. "Hey, give me one second, okay?"

He slipped his headphones on and cued up the playlist again, switching from vinyl to digital to allow himself a few more minutes of hands-off play. "Okay. All set," he said, turning back.

"You have great taste in music," Astrid said, her tone admiring. "It's so refreshing to be somewhere that isn't playing the exact same handful of songs every time."

"Thanks. Variety is a big priority for me," Cam explained.

"Me too," Jesse joked. They all laughed, but he sobered quickly. "Anyway, we don't want to distract from your work any further, but I wanted to introduce you to Astrid and say hi."

"Hi. And I'm glad you did," Cam said. A part of him wanted to ask Jesse what his plans were for the night, but Cam didn't want to monopolize his time or attention.

Astrid said goodbye and disappeared, followed by Kyle, but Jesse lingered for a moment. "Are you free tonight after you're done with your set?"

"I'd planned to go home and crash, but I'm open to suggestions."

"Too tired to come home with me for a drink? I figured I'd invite Astrid and Kyle back and you could stay after. If you like, of course."

"I could do that," Cam said with a smile. "With some caffeine in me, I can go for a few more hours. I'll sleep in late tomorrow."

"That's what I like to hear." Jesse grinned and glanced around. "Damn, I wish we had a bit more privacy back here."

Cam pictured himself spinning while Jesse sucked his dick, hidden from the crowd by the front of his booth, and bit back a groan. "Me too."

Despite the lack of privacy, he tugged Jesse toward a semi-enclosed corner. Jesse didn't waste any time and, the moment their lips touched, arousal surged through Cam. God, yes, this was what he'd missed earlier. He'd been right putting Ben off. Why settle for lukewarm?

Jesse was anything but.

* * * *

"Want another?" Kyle asked.

Cam glanced at his empty glass. "Sure. I feel bad about you playing bartender in your off time."

Kyle laughed. "You worry too much, Cam. I'm a total nerd about cocktails. I enjoy this."

He took the glass Cam held out and their fingers brushed, lingering for a moment longer than necessary. The warm light in Kyle's brown eyes made Cam hyper-aware of his intense attractiveness. Not Cam's usual type, but damned good-looking.

Cam glanced over at Jesse, who watched them with a small smile. "It seems like the caffeine worked," he said. He looked relaxed, sprawled on the couch beside

Cam with his sleeves rolled up and his shirt unbuttoned to reveal a thin undershirt that molded to every inch of his torso.

"It has," Cam agreed. His mouth felt dry, and he didn't know if his head was spinning from the drinks Kyle had mixed, the proximity to Jesse or the energy flowing among the three of them.

Cam, Jesse and Kyle had left together after Cam's gig finished. Astrid had begged off due to brunch plans the following morning and said goodbye at the club. They'd gone straight back to Jesse's absurdly spacious and stylish loft. A few drinks later, Cam was feeling relaxed but alert. And struggling to keep his hands off Jesse.

"I'll be back in a few," Kyle said.

"C'mere," Jesse urged with a crooked grin after Kyle left. As if he could read Cam's thoughts.

Cam complied. He'd ached to touch him since they'd kissed earlier, and they'd have a few minutes while Kyle worked his magic with liquor and mixers. Cam straddled Jesse and threaded his fingers through his thick hair, leaning in to seal their mouths together. He tasted of spiced rum and let out a low, contented sound in the back of his throat when Cam deepened the kiss.

Jesse gripped Cam's ass and kneaded the muscles.

"I've wanted this all night," he whispered against Cam's mouth.

"Me too," Cam managed before he dove in again, kissing Jesse deeper and harder. He wanted to rip his clothes off just to feel all that warm skin against his own. Ice clinking in glasses made him reluctantly lift his head. He'd forgotten about Kyle for a minute.

Kyle sat on the other end of the couch, watching them over a drink. "Sorry," Cam said, his cheeks heating. He scrambled off Jesse's lap and onto the couch between them. "I—"

"Oh, don't stop because of me." A small smile played at the corners of Kyle's mouth. "I enjoyed watching." He'd been flirting with Cam all night. Subtly, but unmistakably. A definite shift had taken place in their interactions, and Cam had questions about where it was headed.

Well, that was a lie. Cam thought the whole evening had been a low-pressure hint that Kyle would be open to joining him and Jesse in bed. Given Jesse's involvement with Kyle and his general approach to life, Cam had no doubt he'd be on board with anything Cam was up for.

Cam was the one who was apprehensive. He'd had a few threesomes before—mostly in college, but one as recent as six months ago. Cam enjoyed them, but he was unsure about the idea of one happening right now with Jesse and Kyle.

"Drink?" Kyle offered Cam a glass, and he took it with a smile. In deference to Cam's earlier tiredness, he'd mixed up a fancier version of Cuba Libres using small batch cola, spiced rum and lime. Several had already gone down easily, and Cam felt great.

Jesse stood and excused himself for a moment, disappearing down the hall toward the bathroom.

"I hope I'm not intruding tonight," Kyle said.

Cam shook his head. "No. I enjoy hanging out with you. Even without your bartending skills."

Kyle looked pleased. "Good."

"Anything new with you?" Cam asked.

"Not particularly. Trying to find someone I can play *Fallout* with. I had a fun thing going with a sexy cop for a while — great sex and gaming in the downtime, but it turned out he was married." Kyle scowled.

Cam took a moment to digest his words. "That sucks."

"Mm-hm." Kyle's scowl deepened. "I don't appreciate being lied to."

"If you're looking for someone to game with, I'd be up for that," Cam offered. "I don't play much — mostly with my roommate Kevin — but I do enjoy it."

"Yeah?" Kyle's expression brightened. "Sounds great. I'm looking forward to playing with you."

"It sounds like the conversation has taken an interesting turn." Jesse strolled into the room with a grin on his face.

Kyle chuckled. "We were discussing *Fallout*. Your boy here and I are going to play sometime."

Jesse wrinkled his nose and sat beside Cam. "That's much less exciting than I'd hoped for."

"It's not always about sex," Kyle teased.

"It should be," he answered with a huff, draping an arm over Cam's shoulders.

Cam smiled. "I'm amazed you get anything else done."

"And yet I play a major part in two very successful businesses," Jesse stated. "It's called multitasking."

"With you it should be 'multi-multi-tasking'."

"I'm not sure I like you two ganging up on me," Jesse said.

"Bullshit," Kyle countered with a grin.

"Physically, yes. Gang up on me all you want." Jesse winked. "This two of you teasing Jesse together thing is what's bullshit."

Cam laughed and took another healthy sip of his drink. He enjoyed the banter the two of them shared, and whatever happened later tonight, Cam was having fun now.

"Mmm, I love your laugh," Jesse said. "It makes me want to kiss the shit out of you."

Cam smirked. "So, what's stopping you?"

Jesse raised an eyebrow but didn't respond verbally. Instead, he leaned forward and pressed his lips against Cam's. They kissed for a while, and Cam became aware of the heat of Kyle's body on his other side and the sensation of being watched.

After a few minutes, Kyle's large, warm hand landed on Cam's knee. He jumped a little. "This okay?" Kyle asked in an undertone, almost in his ear.

"Yeah, yeah, it's good," Cam said against Jesse's mouth. He shivered at the feel of Kyle's breath against his neck.

"Good." Kyle moved his hand higher, and Cam shifted, spreading his legs apart. He groaned when Kyle reached his crotch and rubbed the hardness there. Jesse explored Cam's chest with one hand and brushed a thumb across Cam's nipples.

"Fuck," Cam muttered. It was sensory overload to have both of them touching him at once.

"I want to fuck you while Kyle sucks your cock," Jesse murmured. "Would you like that, Cam?"

Cam's entire body tensed, half-turned on, half-overwhelmed by the idea. Did he want it? Yeah, a part of him did. But this was all going faster than he felt prepared for.

"Wait. Hang on a sec." Cam eased away from Jesse and Kyle and licked his lips. "I'm not sure I can do this tonight."

Kyle and Jesse both sat back, and Cam glanced between them. "I'm not saying never, and believe me, it's no reflection on you, Kyle. I'm just not sure I'm..." He struggled to put the words together. Between worrying about what happened with Jerry and the bullshit with Ben earlier, Cam didn't know if he was in a place where he could jump into a threesome and enjoy it. Or maybe he wasn't spontaneous enough to jump into it without prior thought.

"Hey, it's cool." Kyle patted his thigh and there was no hint of annoyance on his face. "If you're not one hundred percent on board, I respect that. And trust me, I'm not trying to horn in on what you have going on with Jes."

To be honest, Cam had no idea what he had with Jesse, but he appreciated Kyle's understanding.

"Thanks," Cam said with a grateful smile. "Jesse already knows I'm not always great at spontaneous." He glanced over at Jesse, hoping he wasn't annoyed. Thankfully, his smile was understanding.

"I'm gonna head out then." Kyle gave them a small wave.

Jesse stood and kissed Kyle, who then leaned down and gave Cam another kiss. Cam returned it with enthusiasm. "If you do change your mind, Cam, you know how to find me. If not, no worries. I'll see you around anyway. I'm looking forward to gaming with you."

"Great," Cam said, relieved Kyle's feathers weren't ruffled. He almost regretted not going through with the scene they'd had in mind tonight, but not quite enough to change his mind.

"Have fun, boys," Kyle called out before he shut the door.

When they were alone, Cam turned to Jesse, feeling oddly shy.

"C'mere," Jesse said in a soft tone. He sat back on the sofa and tugged Cam down with him. Cam went willingly. "You okay?"

"Yeah," Cam said. "My head's in a weird place tonight."

"Yeah, I got that," Jesse said. He ran a hand up and down Cam's back. "You said so at the club earlier. What's going on? Work?"

"Sort of?"

"Talk to me," Jesse coaxed. "I'm not just trying to get in your pants here, Cam. I do care about what's going on with you."

"I know," Cam said. He traced his fingertips across Jesse's firm chest, wishing there wasn't fabric between them. "I hooked up with one of the bartenders a couple of times, and I'm not feeling it anymore. He got pissy about it, then I got distracted and took such a long break, the club owner hunted me down."

Jesse made a face. "Ah, yes, the overly clingy types. I'm familiar with them."

Cam could imagine he was. "Well, if I'm ever being that way, let me know."

Jesse smiled at him, but the look in his eyes was quite serious. He brushed Cam's cheek with his thumb. "I will. But you have nothing to worry about, Cam. I'd like to see more of you, not less."

The weird knot of worry that had sat in Cam's chest since the encounter with Ben loosened. Cam leaned in and kissed him. "You're okay with me not being up for Kyle joining us?"

"Of course. It would have been fun, but I don't want you to feel pressured to do anything you're not sure you want to do."

"Give me time to think about it," Cam said. "I don't know. Like I said, I'm not feeling it tonight. Going to bed with you and Kyle sounds fun, but I have to be sure about it. And with the mess in my head right now, I can't be sure I'd still feel good about it in the morning."

"That's fine." Jesse expression relaxed. "I'm not going anywhere, Cam."

"Good." Cam leaned in and kissed him.

"Bedroom?" Jesse asked when he pulled back. Cam nodded.

They stripped as soon as they were in the bedroom and it didn't take long for them to pick up where they'd left off. Cam crawled over Jesse's reclined body and took his cock in his mouth. Cam teased him for a long time. He took great delight in drawing it out, making Jesse pant and squirm while Cam worked him over.

He pushed Cam away with a desperate groan and fumbled for the stash of condoms nearby. "You're going to be lucky if I last longer than two seconds," he said with a shaky sounding laugh. "But I'll try."

Cam made a move for the lube, but Jesse gently batted his hand away. "Let me. If I watch you prep yourself, I will lose it now."

"How do you want me?" Cam asked.

"Every way I can get you." Jesse's smile was lascivious.

Cam grinned back. "I'm up for that, but I meant now."

"On your back."

Cam shifted onto the bed beside him and settled onto his back. He thrilled as Jesse rolled on the latex with trembling fingers. He loved that he could get Jesse so worked up.

Jesse stretched out over him and slipped two slick fingers between Cam's legs. Cam parted them farther and groaned when Jesse teased his rim. Jesse used slow, firm pressure to push his fingers inside. "Yesss," Cam hissed, his hips rising and falling to meet the probing touch. "Oh, God, Jes. Feels so good."

Jesse nipped at Cam's chest with his teeth. "You need more?"

"I need your cock." Cam clutched his shoulders. "Just fuck me. Now."

"Greedy." Jesse withdrew his fingers, leaving Cam feeling empty. "I like it."

With another slick of lube on his cock, he settled back over Cam and aligned himself. Cam urged him on, gripping his ass to encourage him to go deeper.

"Give me a minute," Jesse said with a gasp. He slid a hand under Cam's shoulders and threaded his fingers into Cam's hair.

They paused and Cam looked up, barely able to keep his eyes open or his hips still. Cam's whole body was tight with tension and want, and when Jesse groaned and plunged deeper into him, Cam sobbed with relief. They grasped and bit at each other, grappling and searching for more. The rhythm of their fucking grew erratic and desperate, Cam holding on to Jesse as he encouraged him to go harder, letting out wordless sounds of need.

"Cam," Jesse cried out and the broken sound made Cam clench around him. They came, one after the other, and not until his shaking slowed did Cam realize he'd clutched Jesse so hard his fingers ached.

Jesse kissed him, the gesture surprisingly tender after the force of their orgasms. He withdrew long enough to remove the condom, then stretched out next to Cam.

A sheen of sweat covered Cam's body and the air cooled his skin. He pressed a kiss to Jesse's shoulder. "Fuck, Jesse," he said a short while later, his voice low. He still felt shaky.

"You can fuck Jesse later. He's going to need a couple minutes to recover first."

Cam laughed and pulled him even closer, despite the sweat. Jesse held on tighter, too, and for a short while, they lay quiet, their breathing gradually slowing.

"Damn we're good at that," Jesse said.

"I'd have to agree." He craned his neck and looked at Jesse. "I hope you aren't too disappointed it was just the two of us."

Jesse stayed silent long enough that doubts began to creep in, but eventually, he answered. "No, I'm not disappointed at all." His voice held a note Cam couldn't begin to identify.

"That's good."

Jesse sifted his fingers through Cam's hair for a moment before he replied. "Yeah. Yeah, it is."

Cam turned his head and kissed Jesse's chest again. A strange feeling that he'd never experienced before bubbled up in him. He had no idea what it meant and no desire to analyze it at all. Maybe he should enjoy the moment for what it was and leave it at that.

His lids were heavy all of a sudden, and he reached down with a groan, fumbling for the bed covers. Jesse helped pull them up and Cam settled on his side. Jesse clicked off the light and curved around him, settling an arm around Cam's waist.

In no time at all, he fell asleep.

Chapter Nine

Jesse ignored the dull throb behind his eyes and settled into his seat on the jet that would fly him back to New York. This was his fifth day waking up in London, and the summer sun brightened the skies outside the first-class cabin.

"May I offer you a glass of champagne, Mr. Murtagh?"

Jesse glanced up at Charlotte, a flight attendant with whom he'd flown before, and met her dark-blue eyes.

"Yes, thank you. The Grand Siècle will be fine."

"Of course."

Charlotte set a tulip glass on the panel by the window and filled it with pale gold wine. She showed him a serene smile as he tasted the champagne — which was, as always, delicious — and waited for his nod.

"We'll begin takeoff in about twenty minutes." Charlotte placed an amenity kit including pajamas and travel bag on the ottoman across from Jesse's seat. "Is there anything else I can do for you in the meantime?"

He set his glass down. "I've got a bit of a headache, actually. I'd love a coffee once we're airborne."

Charlotte gave him a gentle frown. "No need to wait for takeoff, sir. I'll bring your coffee in a moment."

"Thank you, Charlotte."

Jesse turned back to the window after she'd moved away. He enjoyed traveling both for pleasure and for business, and he felt a genuine affinity for the bustling metropolis of London. However, the past week had put heavy demands on his business and social schedules, and he needed time off. He wouldn't get much for a while yet, but he'd be home in New York and that put a grin on his face.

After more wine, Jesse pulled his phone from his pocket and busied himself reading and replying to the correspondence already being funneled his way. He paused after he reached one message buried among the others, taken off guard to see the name of a man he hadn't spoken to in over six months.

Isaac.

Jesse thumbed the message open and a smile tugged at his lips.

You come to my city and don't even bother to say hello? What is wrong with you?

He stared at the words, aware of Charlotte serving his coffee and even of thanking her. But his mind stayed on Isaac Bryant, a Classics professor with whom Jesse had been involved for almost a year.

Isaac had been teaching at Fordham University when Jesse had met him through friends, and they'd formed an instant connection. The affair had run hot and cold nearly from the beginning because Isaac had wanted

K. Evan Coles and Brigham Vaughn

the one thing Jesse was unwilling to give him: monogamy.

For his part, Jesse had wanted something from Isaac, too—Isaac's coming out. The professor had been deeply closeted and only his closest friends knew his sexual identity. Jesse's frequent appearances in the society columns had made spending time in public with Isaac difficult, so they'd often stuck close to their apartments. If they'd ventured out together, they'd played the part of platonic friends. Isaac had even freaked out when he'd realized Jesse had told his brother, Kyle and Carter about the affair.

The hiding had grated on Jesse. He'd known Isaac had needed to come to terms with being out, however, and stayed largely silent on the topic. Everything had changed the night Isaac had issued an ultimatum and insisted Jesse make their relationship exclusive or lose him altogether.

An ache filled Jesse's chest. Isaac had said awful things during that last argument, biphobic insults he'd heard before but had never cut as deep. He'd steeled his heart with ice and stared Isaac down. Then he'd called him a fucking coward and let loose his poisonous thoughts about Isaac's ironclad closet.

The image of Isaac's face, heartbroken and ashamed, and the pain in his voice when he'd asked Jesse to leave were still fresh in his mind. His throat tightened. He'd had no right to demand Isaac come out before he felt ready. No one, not even Eric or Kyle or Carter, knew how badly things had ended or how much regret Jesse harbored for stooping so low. That Isaac had contacted him, despite his cruel words, made his heart thump. It took Jesse a long moment to compose a reply.

133

How the hell am I supposed to know you live in London? And since when is New York not your city?

* * * *

Three hours into the flight, many of Jesse's fellow passengers were sleeping and the cabin was silent under the plane's roar of white noise. After takeoff, he'd changed into loungewear from his bag and retrieved his laptop so he could work in earnest. He continued messaging with Isaac over breakfast until Isaac left for work, and the timekeeping app on Jesse's phone told him it was six-thirty a.m. in New York.

A pleasant warmth stole over him, and he tapped out a message to Cam. The sun had hardly risen in Brooklyn, but he knew Cam was already headed for Manhattan.

Got any plans this afternoon?

Some time passed before his phone buzzed again, and the brevity of Cam's statements spoke to a lack of coffee.

You're on a fucking plane, right? No plans 'til midnite. Working tonight.

Jesse used his laptop to alter a reservation he'd placed earlier in the week, then replied.

Yes, I'm on a fucking plane, der. Meet me outside B Flat on Church St, 3pm. I'll buy you a drink.

Playing hooky again, Big Money? Cam asked a minute later.

"Smartass," Jesse murmured.

This flight's over eight hours in duration, Red, and I clocked in while you were still sleeping. I'll be into double digits by the time I leave the office.

Cam's answer came swiftly this time.

That was shitty — my bad. I'll meet you, but I'm dressed for work sooo...

Sooo I don't care because your ass looks excellent no matter what you've got on. See you at 3.

Cam's reply popped up, the speech bubble filled with curse words and blushing emoji, and made Jesse laugh.

* * * *

He found Cam standing by the black and red façade of the B-Flat Lounge in Tribeca, still dressed for school. Cam smiled at the sleek Murtagh Media sedan that pulled up to the curb.

"Let me guess," he said when Jesse opened the door. Cam climbed in and shut it behind him. "We're not having a drink at B-Flat?"

Jesse grinned. "Not tonight, no. I'd be happy to meet you here another time, though. It's quite a decent bar."

"I'll keep that in mind," Cam replied. "Will we be flying again today?" He placed his bag and another carrier he'd told Jesse he used for transporting his records and turntables on the floor.

"No more planes today." Jesse met the driver's eyes in the rearview mirror and nodded. "I've already flown over three thousand miles," he reminded Cam. "As such, I'd prefer we stay a bit more down-to-earth this afternoon."

"That's a terrible pun," Cam scolded. His tone and touch were gentle as he took hold of Jesse's hand and the car slipped back into the flow of traffic. "But you look tired, so you're forgiven. Didn't you sleep during the flight?"

"I napped for a while," Jesse said. "I also went into the office, and it simply doesn't do to show up to meetings with sheet marks pressed into one's face."

"All part of your charm," Cam countered. His smile sent pleasure zinging up Jesse's spine. The feeling bloomed into desire as Cam pulled him close and sealed their mouths together.

Jesse's bones melted. Cam slid a hand under his suit jacket, and, Jesus, he liked those arms around him, never mind the heat on his mouth. *A guy can lose himself in these kisses*, Jesse thought lazily. He wouldn't mind doing a whole lot of that after the miles he'd logged already. He did groan when the car slowed and forced himself to pull back. He rested his forehead against Cam's.

"We're here," he said and grinned at Cam's laughter.

"Dude, we drove two blocks."

"Not even." Jesse sat up and straightened his jacket as the driver parked the car. "I have the car for the day and figured what the hell. Besides, this way you'd have no idea where we were going."

"You enjoy these games of bait and switch far too much," Cam groused, but his eyes twinkled at Jesse, and he opened the door. "I suppose I shouldn't be surprised given you do whatever the hell you want."

Jesse rolled his eyes. "Just get your ass out of the car, Cameron," he muttered.

They climbed out of the car and Cam glanced up and read the sign on the building before them. He blinked twice, his curiosity plain.

"You're taking me to a bathhouse?"

"Yes, but not the kind of bathhouse you're probably thinking of." Jesse smirked. As much as he liked the idea of seeing Cam in a gay bathhouse, he craved a different kind of vibe today.

"Aire is modeled in the tradition of the Roman and Greek bathhouses," he told Cam. "I like to come here after I fly and get a massage, do a circuit in the baths and get my head back together."

"No wonder you're so relaxed all the time."

"Please—I was born this way." Jesse waved at himself. "And I'm in the mood for extra pampering today if you'd like to join me."

He wanted Cam to accompany him into the spa, of course, but if he refused, they could always arrange to meet again another time. So the relief he experienced at Cam's nod surprised him. He'd looked forward to spending time with Cam even more than he'd realized, and what the hell was that about?

"I've never been to a spa." Cam's words broke through Jesse's uneasy thoughts. "There's a Russian place in Brooklyn my roommates rave about, but I haven't gone in."

Jesse shook himself mentally and linked their arms together. "You should check it out," he replied and led

Cam toward the spa's entrance. "Taking the waters is a time-honored practice, and I guarantee you'll be hooked in the first ten minutes."

"Are you saying I need to work on my chill?"

"Yes." Jesse chuckled at Cam's affronted expression. "Hey, you're the one who yells about surprises. I want you so relaxed that by the time we get out of here, you've forgotten your name."

"I'm all yours. But you have to promise to get me to the club tonight for my set."

"Done." Jesse let go of Cam's arm and rubbed his hands together.

Two hours later, Cam's chill had improved. He'd relaxed in the hushed silence of the bath chambers, which were illuminated chiefly by candlelight, and embraced the experience. Now, both of them were spread out on neighboring massage tables while four pairs of hands set Jesse's muscles ablaze. His lids heavy and his mind bleary, he fixed his eyes on Cam, who smiled back, his expression soft with bliss.

The next thing Jesse knew, he woke to gentle touches and whispers. He and Cam made their way to the steam room, arms linked again, and once the door was sealed, Jesse sat back and closed his eyes. He breathed in the eucalyptus-infused vapor clouds, and Cam twined their fingers together, his hold neither too loose nor tight but enough to anchor Jesse while he dozed.

"You should go home and get some rest," Cam told him another hour later. They were headed for the door to the street.

"I just spent most of the afternoon napping, Cam. I feel fresh as a New York daisy." Jesse meant to joke, but the concern he read in Cam's expression threw him off balance. "I don't have to be at Under tonight until ten or so anyway, which gives me —"

Cam cut him off. "Wait, you're going to the bar tonight?" They approached the black sedan that had returned to pick them up and he furrowed his brows.

"Y-e-es," Jesse replied slowly. "You're working tonight, too, Red, or have you forgotten?"

"No, of course not." Cam rubbed his jaw as the driver stepped out to open the door. "Seems a little weird to me you'd go in when you're exhausted."

Jesse waited until they were seated and the car door closed behind them before he spoke again. "I've been out of town all week. I need to show my face at the bar and check in with Kyle to make sure everything's running well." He raised a brow at Cam's pursed lips. "I'll be going in tomorrow night by the way, in the event you feel like giving me shit about that, too."

"No, I... That's not what I'm trying to do." Cam's face fell. Once more, he sought out Jesse's hand, his grip firm this time. "I'm not trying to make you feel bad, but if you don't give a damn about how tired you are, someone else should."

Jesse cut Cam off with a quick, chaste kiss that belied the burst of gladness that flashed through him. He liked knowing Cam gave a shit about him and not just about what Jesse could do for him. Cam had never given him reason to think otherwise, but still — he'd dealt with enough people over the years who were only out for themselves.

"I feel fine, honestly," he told Cam. "I'll even sleep in tomorrow if that makes you feel better," he said a second before Cam leaned in and kissed him back hard.

Heat gathered in Jesse's groin, and the rush of desire made his head spin. Cam cupped Jesse's jaw between his palms and uttered a low hum as their tongues slid together. Jesse shivered when Cam finally pulled back.

"Tell me we're going back to your place." Cam's gaze heated. He pushed out his lips in a pout when Jesse shook his head. "Why not?"

"There's something I need to check out first," Jesse started, then cut himself off as Cam moved a finger and rested it on Jesse's lower lip.

"Something more important than fucking me in that big bed of yours until we have to go to work?"

"Jesus, Cam." The car pulled up to the curb and Jesse gently pushed him back. "Hold that thought for a few minutes more and stop trying to destroy my sanity." Cam's laughter curled around him and he shifted in his seat.

Cam went silent once inside the Greenwich Hotel. Jesse had no doubt he was admiring their beautifully understated surroundings and trying like hell to figure out what Jesse might be up to as he checked in. In the meantime, Jesse fought to keep his hands to himself. His cock throbbed every time Cam met his glance, so he focused on the pretty blonde hotel rep, who took them to one of the hotel's penthouse suites, and her pleasant, bland words.

"What are we doing here?" Cam whispered after the rep moved away from them.

"Checking out a penthouse, duh," Jesse replied. He smiled at Cam's withering glare. "I'll explain why, I promise, so don't yell at me. We can go back to my place as soon as I'm done looking around, if you like. Or, since the place is paid for through tomorrow, we can stay and you can fuck me in a different big bed."

Cam groaned under his breath. He didn't say another word, not even when the hotel rep reappeared with her final pitch. At last, she took her leave, closing the door behind her with a loud click, and Cam pulled Jesse into a blistering kiss. Jesse moaned into his mouth. Cam shoved a hand between them and palmed Jesse through his trousers, his touch rough.

Heat flooded Jesse's body from head to toe. He hauled Cam almost off his feet and Cam wrapped his arms around Jesse's neck. Their mouths rarely parted as Jesse manhandled him up the stairs to the second level.

Both of them were panting hard by the time they staggered into the master bedroom. They undressed each other quickly and Cam lay back against the vast bed with a smile.

"Come here," he rasped. The greed in his voice made Jesse groan.

He climbed in beside Cam, his skin pebbling under Cam's grasping hands. Cam pushed him back onto the mattress and crawled over him, sucking and biting Jesse's skin. Jesse reveled in the weight of the body bearing down on him. He pressed his fingers hard into Cam's waist, and Cam gasped. Jesse's entire body coiled tight with desire.

"Need to taste you," he ground out, thankful when Cam nodded and shifted his weight backward.

Cam turned his body around to face Jesse's feet, and Jesse couldn't hold back a moan as Cam settled his tight abdomen and erection inches from his face. Cam's cock stood red and rigid and gorgeous, and simply looking at him made Jesse's mouth water.

He pressed his face into the crease between Cam's hip and groin. He breathed in the heady smell of soap and sweat and Cam, and his stomach clenched with arousal. He took Cam in hand. Cam uttered a low noise and bucked his hips gently when Jesse licked his cockhead. But the moment Cam's mouth opened over him, Jesse was gone.

They moved against each other for an unknowable time, each pulling the other close and feasting on sensation. Jesse fell into a feedback loop. His heart thundered, rendering him blind and deaf to everything but the body against his. All he knew was Cam's heated, slick skin, the inferno of Cam's mouth, the weight of Cam on his tongue.

Jesse tensed as a finger slid along the cleft of his ass, his balls drawing up tight when it breached his rim. And he came, his scream muffled by the cock in his throat. His body jerked, and the orgasm tore through him with almost painful intensity while Cam drank him down.

He floated, his body still trembling with aftershocks as his spent cock fell from Cam's lips. Dimly, he recognized Cam's needy noises. He gripped the globes of Cam's ass harder and resumed sucking, encouraging Cam to fuck his mouth without words. Cam bucked forward, and Jesse's heart lurched. He wrapped his arms around Cam's waist and held on, his hands shaking. He moaned nonstop as Cam used him, and the punishing pace made his eyes water and his jaw ache. He loved every fucking second.

Cam made a wrenching noise and came. Jesse's chest went tight. He swallowed Cam's bittersweet cum, but when Cam finally shifted and pulled out, Jesse went boneless, too wrung out to move. Helpless against the exhaustion crashing over him, Jesse turned into the strong arms that pulled him close, and a wonderful sense of comfort made it easy to allow the world to slip away.

* * * *

Jesse didn't how much time had passed the next time he surfaced, but then Cam laughed quietly and that put a smile on his face.

"Hey, sleepy. You back with me?"

A rumbling chuckle rolled through Jesse's chest. Cam was wrapped around him, but he shifted to give Jesse room to move. Jesse raised his arms over his head and stretched.

"I think so. How long was I out?"

"Maybe half an hour? Not long." Cam ran a hand over Jesse's hair.

Jesse sank against the sheets. "Huh. The jet lag and the bathhouse blitzed my brain. Not to mention you sucked my brain through my dick and almost killed me."

Cam's cheeks flushed, but he certainly looked proud of himself. "I'm not apologizing for that." He blew a raspberry against Jesse's cheek before extricating himself enough to sit up.

"I looked around while you were snoozing, by the way, and almost got lost in this fucking place."

"It's nice, isn't it?" Jesse yawned and tucked his hands behind his head.

"Nice doesn't cover it." Cam stared at him, his expression incredulous. "I'm pretty sure it's twice the size of my apartment. There's a sauna. The kitchen and dining room could seat the whole first grade class at Midtown Academy. This isn't a hotel suite—it's a house!"

Jesse shrugged. "There's a bigger penthouse down the hall that takes up half the floor. It has two gardens and a pool, but I figured it's way over the top for my needs."

"Which are what? And you promised you'd tell me why we're here, so 'fess up."

"I'm having the floors at my place refinished. I just need to decide when," Jesse said. "I'd rather set up camp somewhere while the work is done to avoid breathing fumes and tiptoeing around wet floors. You in the mood to eat, by the way? I'm about to eat my own hand, I'm so hungry."

Cam nodded. "I could eat. But what do your floors have to do with this hotel?"

Jesse sat up and threw off the bedding. "Like I said, I need somewhere to stay while the work is being done. A friend suggested the penthouses here, and I figured I'd check them out. This is nice, but I think I'll look around closer to the office before I decide."

Cam said nothing for several seconds. "Couldn't you stay with family or friends?"

"Oh, sure, but I don't want to put anybody out. A lot of my friends have partners or children or both, and dealing with me and my weird work hours would be asking a lot. Besides, with the traveling I've done recently, it's not like staying in a New York hotel will be any big deal."

Jesse stood and stretched again, and this time his head spun. He swayed in place. "Gah."

"You okay?" Cam crawled over the bed and placed a steadying hand on his elbow.

"Headrush." Jesse ran his hands through his hair, then tipped his head toward the door. "Let's get food. Shit, I should take my drugs, too."

Cam jerked to a halt, his eyes wide. "Your what now?"

Jesse laughed. "Oh, man, your face!" He tugged Cam's hand and drew him into the bathroom. He pulled a small pill case from his Dopp kit and rattled its contents with a brisk shake. "Truvada, a multivitamin, calcium and Celadrin. All deeply boring and not worth sharing. There's extra vitamins if you want one, though."

Cam smiled. He said nothing as Jesse filled a water glass and swallowed his doses down. When he turned around again, Cam wore a sober expression and Jesse quashed an internal grumble.

"The Truvada's for PrEP, in case you were wondering. I'd have told you otherwise, of course."

"Oh, I figured it was prophylactic." Cam shrugged. "I'm guessing you'd only need one pill for HIV prevention but a fuckton more to manage it. Besides, we had the STD talk already."

"Yes, we did."

Cam stepped forward and ran his hands over Jesse's chest. "What's the calcium supplement for? And what the heck is Celadrin?"

"They're for bone and joint health, respectively." Jesse reached down and patted Cam's ass. "When I'm not traveling, I try to run with Carter a couple of times a week and I need to keep my skeleton healthy because that fucker is fast."

Cam looked thoughtful. "Huh. What do you do when you are traveling?"

"Oh, I still run, but I don't have to keep up with his long-ass legs."

They washed up and continued chatting, then each pulled on a plush hotel robe. After ambling downstairs to the kitchen, they found the refrigerator stocked according to Jesse's orders when he'd made the reservation. Cam opened a bottle of Semillon, and they sat down to snack on cheese and fresh fruit while they paged through the hotel's restaurant menu.

"What about your brother?" Cam asked after they'd called in an order. "You could stay with Eric and Sara while your floors are being done, couldn't you?"

Jesse made a face. "They're getting ready for their first baby — they need all the alone time they can get. I thought about staying with my parents, but my mother would be up one side of me and down the other over my hours at the bar."

"Fair enough. And Kyle?"

"He lives in a glorified studio with barely enough space for one person, let alone two. So, no." Jesse popped a grape in his mouth. "You've been there, haven't you?" He raised a brow when Cam shook his head. "Aren't you guys gaming?"

"Oh, we are." Cam sipped his wine. "But we can do that online any time. Besides, I didn't know if things would be weird with Kyle considering, you know, the last time I saw him."

Jesse chuckled. "Dude, I told you — Kyle's fine with what happened. He'd be even more fine if things go differently sometime the three of us are together, of course. I also happen to know he'd be fucking thrilled if you ever wanted to hook up with him regardless if I'm around or not."

"Really?" Cam looked at him askance.

"Sure. It's not like Kyle's my boyfriend or anything." *And neither are you.*

The words Jesse didn't say hung between them even as he continued. "If you're both into it, don't hesitate. Kyle and I have shared partners before and never had a problem."

A knowing expression crossed Cam's face. "You guys do that a lot?"

"Occasionally. Kyle's not into women, which means there are fewer opportunities than there could be. Unfortunately." Jesse's scowl made Cam laugh.

"So, did you and Kyle do that occasionally with Carter?"

Jesse blinked, caught off guard by the conversation's left turn. Cam's ears went pink. "What do you mean?"

"Riley told me you and Carter used to be involved," Cam explained. "And that Carter and Kyle used to be involved, too. I figured maybe you, Carter and Kyle—"

"No," Jesse cut in, his voice gentle. "Kyle and I were both seeing Carter at the same time, true, but we never made it a group thing. We tried like hell to talk Car into it, mind you, but he didn't feel comfortable with the idea."

Jesse sipped his wine. In truth, Carter was dead set against threesomes, almost to the point of hostility. However, once upon a time, Carter and Riley had been very into group sex, so long as they participated together. They'd started sharing girls on a whim during their college years and stopped the threesomes only after graduation. But the spark between them had never gone out, even after they'd married other people. Carter's son, Dylan, had still been in preschool when Carter had initiated the group scenes with Riley once more, this time with a hired escort. From that moment, the secrets he and Riley had kept and the lies they'd told had slowly sabotaged their marriages and almost destroyed their friendship. With work, Carter and Riley had made it out of the turmoil, but each bore their own scars.

He schooled his expression. Carter's story wasn't his to tell, but he also didn't agree with his friend's ban on threesomes. "I'm still working on changing Carter's mind," he admitted. "I figure he can only hold out for so long if I play my cards right."

"What about Riley?" Cam rolled his eyes at the wolfish smile Jesse gave him.

"I think Riley would do many things to see his boyfriend hook up with another man, and I am more than happy to volunteer as tribute."

"You're such a hedonist."

"Out and proud. But I mean, come on, can you blame me?"

"No, I can't." Cam sighed. "They're both gorgeous. I remember meeting Carter last summer at the school's open house. He came with his ex-wife, and they told me about Riley, too. Then, I met Riley a couple of weeks later and wanted to know why the universe hated me so much."

His pout made Jesse laugh. "My poor Cam," he crooned and ran a hand over Cam's shoulders. He stilled when the door chime sounded.

"That'll be the food, thank God. Be right back." Jesse stood. "There's red wine on the counter if you want it with dinner."

A strange uneasiness wormed its way back into Jesse's head as he and Cam chatted over their dinner. He'd been surprised by Cam's questions about Kyle and Carter. And the knowledge Cam had spoken to Riley about the connections among the group of friends rankled. Jesse should have given Cam that information himself. No matter how much Jesse liked spending time with him, Cam needed to understand how he operated — that he had few boundaries and expected the same from his partners.

"What's going on this weekend?" he asked over his duck entree. "I mean, besides the club."

"Not a hell of a lot," Cam replied. "I promised my co-worker I'd meet her to shop vintage tomorrow, and I have a brunch thing in Jersey on Sunday." He grinned. "It's my dad's birthday."

Jesse picked up his glass and tapped it against Cam's. "Happy birthday to Dad. You should take the angry bartender from Ember with you — you can feed him cake to cheer him up."

"Ben?" Cam wrinkled his nose. "Yeah, that's not happening. It's not like we were even friends before we started hooking up. Besides, he's still giving me the cold shoulder. I should tell him to go fuck himself, but I don't even know why I'd bother, given we screwed around for, like, a nanosecond.

"What about you, Big Money — what's on the docket besides schmoozing at the bar?"

"I have a date with Astrid tomorrow. She's annoyed I'm not around much lately, so we set up time to do lots of terrible things together," Jesse said. "Plus, I met some people she knows while I was in London, and it turns out one of them is Astrid's arch enemy."

He held up a hand when Cam's expression shifted from curious to confused. "Don't ask. I have no idea what that means, either. Women are forever confusing."

"Yet you continue to see them," Cam countered.

"As long as they don't drag me into the drama, it's all good." Jesse sipped his wine. "And Astrid's cool. One of the reasons we get along is that we don't expect anything but fun from each other. She may be as close to a female version of me as I've ever met."

"That's mildly disturbing and disturbingly arousing." Cam slapped a hand over his eyes. "Thank you so much for putting unwanted images in my head."

Jesse cackled. "You're welcome." He poked Cam in the side with his finger and made him grunt. "Hurry up and finish your food. There's cheesecake with figs and a pine nut gelato for dessert, and I want to grope you in the shower before we have to leave. I'll have our bags brought up from the car."

"Fine, fine," Cam grumbled. He speared another piece of meat with his fork. "I take it you're not going back to your place tonight after the bar?"

"I figured I'd come back here. It's not like I've seen much beyond the bedroom and kitchen after all," Jesse joked. "Feel like meeting up after work?"

Cam's eyes lit up. "Hell yes. A four-block commute is a nice change from hauling ass back out to Brooklyn at four a.m."

"Excellent." Jesse rubbed his hands together with glee. "That means we can debauch the sauna before checkout tomorrow, too."

Chapter Ten

"I'm so fucked," Cam moaned to Taryn.

"Yep. You are."

Cam made a face and bumped shoulders with her. "Thanks."

She shrugged. "You said it. I'm agreeing with you. You are in serious, serious like for Jesse Murtagh, and there's no way for that to end well."

"Ugh. I really am." Cam flipped through the stack of vinyl without seeing them. After leaving the Greenwich Hotel, he'd met up with Taryn and they'd checked out a couple of familiar vintage shops and a new thrift store that had opened near her place. He'd also spent most of the time whining about his changing feelings for Jesse. Not that it helped. "Fuck my life."

"What did you expect, hon?"

"I don't know." Cam ran a hand through his hair and looked over at his friend. "Not this! I went into this with clear eyes. I knew what kind of guy I got involved with. He never promised me anything. I just don't know where it went...wrong. It's like my feelings fucking ran away with me."

"You've never had this problem before."

"Exactly! Fuck." Cam let out a breath. "Casual sex has always been fun, you know?"

"I know."

"I've never had a hard time compartmentalizing things. No problem getting along with and liking a guy I had a regular thing with, without getting all" — he made a face — "emotionally entangled."

"And there's some entanglement here, huh?"

Cam nodded. He felt miserable, realizing how attached he'd grown. And knowing Jesse was not on the same page. To him, Cam was someone to kill time with. One of many pleasant diversions in his life. Unfortunately, it had become a bit more on Cam's side.

"I just..." His voice came out thick. "I can't stop thinking about him. He's not like anyone I've ever met. And I don't know how to turn that off."

"Do you think it might be better to end it?" Taryn's tone was gentle, but all the same, a weird pang went through Cam's chest at the idea of not seeing Jesse again.

"Probably," he admitted. "I've thought about it. I don't know how to. Well, okay, I know how to. If I told him how I felt, he'd go running for the hills. That would be the easy part. The hard part is bringing myself to do it. I care for him. A lot. And I am royally fucked because there's no way this will end well."

"Oh, honey." Taryn rubbed his shoulder. "I'm sorry."

"Yeah. Thanks." Cam swallowed hard. "Me too."

He reached the end of the vinyl selection and stepped toward the clothing section while Taryn split off to go look at housewares. Cam welcomed the break. He'd unloaded on Taryn because he'd needed to vent, but the whole situation left him feeling weird and vulnerable, and he didn't like it at all. He wanted to hit a reset button and go back to the time before Jesse had appeared in his life. Except, the idea of undoing everything they'd done together felt fundamentally wrong. He couldn't imagine not sending texts back and forth throughout the day, sometimes flirty, sometimes funny, sometimes just checking in. He didn't want to think about never feeling the soft prickle of Jesse's beard against his mouth or trembling over Cam's body as he came with a hoarse moan. And he couldn't imagine never falling asleep again beside Jesse, exhausted and content.

Cam didn't know the precise moment when things had shifted for him, but he'd thought about the issue since the night at the club before Jesse's last trip to London.

Seeing Jesse with someone else had been very strange for Cam. He was used to Jesse's interactions with the other speakeasy guys. That didn't bother him. It didn't bother him at all when Kyle and Jesse flirted, either, even though Cam knew they fucked semi-regularly.

But seeing him with Astrid at the club had filled him with a strange emotion he couldn't shake. And he didn't understand it. Cam didn't think it was because she was a woman—he'd dated bi guys before, and it had never made any difference one way or the other to him.

He'd never been a jealous person at all, but an unreasonable flash of jealousy shot through him whenever he imagined Jesse and Astrid together. Cam couldn't quite figure out what made it different. Maybe because he knew and liked Jesse's friends, especially

Kyle, and Astrid was an unknown quantity. Not to mention beautiful and charming. Hell, Jesse had called her the female version of himself. The entire situation made Cam question what he could possibly do or say to keep Jesse's attention.

Despite his current mixed-up feelings, Cam still toyed with the idea of the threesome with Jesse and Kyle, too. Even though the suggestion he hop into bed with Kyle—independent of Jesse—made him pause. Or maybe the entire situation overwhelmed and confused him. Cam's head was a giant fucking disaster at the moment, and he couldn't sort through any of it.

Since Jesse had come back from his work trip, thoughts and worries like these had been whirling through Cam's mind. He had no claim on Jesse, but that didn't lessen the sting when he thought about him and his place in Cam's life. He didn't want Jesse to change or become someone else, but on some level, Cam wanted to know he mattered to Jesse. And that Jesse wouldn't just disappear from his life. Cam couldn't remember the last time he'd felt that way about anyone.

Jesse was the worst possible person to develop feelings for. Whether it ended now or later, Cam predicted heartbreak for himself.

"You ready to head out?" Taryn asked.

Cam turned and stared at her blankly for a moment before the words sank in. "Uh. Yeah, sure. I didn't find anything I can't live without today."

Out of necessity, Cam was a minimalist when it came to furniture and housewares. His clothes and records took up most of the limited space in his cramped bedroom, so he was careful about what he brought home.

Taryn held up the reusable tote she always carried in her purse. "I managed to get out of here without buying any large furniture for you to move," she said with satisfaction. "Just new wineglasses to replace the ones that got broken at the last party and an awesome, kitschy painting for the gallery wall in my living room."

"Nice!" Cam said. He forced a smile onto his face. "Now, how do you feel about stopping for a coffee before I head to Jersey? I need to hear all about the hot nanny you hooked up with."

A little while later, Cam shook his head at his friend. "I didn't realize the nanny was your student's nanny. I thought you met him on Tinder or something. Jesus, Taryn. Living dangerously, huh?"

"First of all, he's a man who's a nanny, so you should be referring to him as a manny. Second, I'm pretty sure the kid's mom is screwing him, too."

Cam groaned. "That doesn't make it better!"

"You worry too much. He was hot but we're over now. No harm done, I promise."

"Until you meet the next hot manny or substitute teacher!"

She grinned. "Jealous?"

Cam made a face. "No, I think I get up to enough trouble on my own. Thanks."

* * * *

Despite the jolt of caffeine, Cam dozed on the train ride from Brooklyn to Manhattan, and again on the one from Manhattan to Jersey City. Still groggy, he knocked on the door of the yellow row house where he'd grown up and pushed it open before anyone could answer. He came face to face with his father. Frank Lewis stood the same height as Cam, with graying ginger hair and a tired but content face.

"Happy birthday, Dad." Cam hugged him and passed over the vividly colored gift bag Taryn had helped him pick out at the pharmacy. He'd bought the gift a few weeks ago, but he'd blanked on the wrapping and card.

"Glad you could make it. We haven't seen you much." Frank's blue eyes twinkled and softened the chiding tone and words.

"I'm sorry." Cam offered him a smile. "Things are nuts."

"What's his name?" his mother, Maureen, asked brightly from the hallway.

Cam groaned. "And so it begins."

His father chuckled. "No one expects the Spanish Inquisition but—"

"One should always expect the Maureen Grilling." Cam finished the oft-quoted phrase in their family. "Hi, Mom."

Maureen elbowed her way in front of her husband. "Move it, Frank. I need to hug our son."

Cam smiled down at his mom, equal parts exasperated and glad to see her. She stood a foot shorter than Cam and Frank, and Cam had to stoop for a hug. Maureen had a short, curvy figure and blonde hair—a far cry from Cam's rangy build and ginger coloring—but he'd inherited her lively brown eyes.

"To answer your question, there's no one serious." That felt like a lie, but Cam didn't know what else to say. He was close to his parents, but there was no way in hell he wanted to spill about the entire complicated situation with Jesse.

His parents exchanged a look Cam remembered from his childhood. The look that said they'd let it slide for now, but not forever. *Crap.*

A thundering sound behind them announced the arrival of more of the Lewis clan.

"Cam, Cam, Cam!" A small figure weaseled between the wall and his parents to attach to his legs, followed by a second.

"Hi, guys," Cam said, crouching down. George and Lily were the youngest among the Lewis kids. His parents had gotten pregnant with Cam in their early twenties, soon after their wedding. Daniel and Arthur had come along six and eight years later, followed by an almost ten-year gap, and finally, the twins had arrived. While no one ever said as much, Cam suspected George and Lily were a welcome but unintended surprise following Frank's treatment for testicular cancer.

Maureen's pregnancy with the twins had been rough, though. She'd been over forty and considered high-risk. She'd spent much of it on bedrest, and Cam had felt guilty because he was busy taking college classes and striking out on his own. He'd still lived at home and done what he could to help out by taking care of Arthur and Daniel, but he could have done more.

The twins had held out long enough to be born slightly premature but healthy overall and, after a brief stint in the NICU, had been released. They were now rambunctious five-year-olds who kept his parents running nonstop.

"I drew a picture for you," George announced, his words overlapping with Lily's chattering about their recent trip to the zoo.

"And we saw the pandas and the camels. The two-humped ones!" Lily added.

"I can't wait to see your picture," Cam said. "And hear all about the zoo, but can I come inside first?"

"Oh!" Maureen laughed. "Yes, let your brother in the front door, you two."

Once Cam was inside the house, with his shoes and coat off, his mother offered him a drink.

"Coffee, please. I'm beat. But I can get it myself." He moved toward the kitchen, but Maureen waved him off.

"Sit down and catch up with your siblings. I'll get the coffee for you."

"Is it only the seven of us?" He hadn't seen any signs of anyone else in the family, but it was rare for his mom not to invite Frank's two brothers and their families, who also lived in the Jersey area.

"Oh, no. Everyone else will be here for dinner. I wanted you to come early so we could catch up."

"Are you sure you don't need help with anything?" he asked.

"No," she said. "Snacks are in the living room, the lasagna's about to go in the oven, the salad and garlic bread are prepped, and I picked up the German chocolate cake from the bakery around the corner last night."

Cam's mouth watered. They were his dad's favorites and some of Cam's as well. "Yum. I can't wait."

"Well, you're going to have to wait about an hour. Now, shoo."

"I'm going, I'm going."

Cam walked into the living room where two teenagers were sprawled on the loveseat, so engrossed in a video game they barely looked up at his greeting.

He got grunts and a half-hearted "hey" in response to his hello.

He took a seat on the couch near his father, and Lily clambered into his lap. She wore striped leggings, a sparkly tutu, and an Iron Man shirt, and her tangle of red-blonde curls was held back by two Day-Glo-colored bows. It was a subdued look for his little sister.

"You wanna hear about the camels now?"

"Yes." Cam settled her into a position that didn't crush parts he'd prefer not to be crushed, and George wiggled into a spot on his other side, clutching a creased piece of paper covered with crayon drawings. "Tell me all about the zoo and the two-humped camels."

* * * *

A good hour passed after dinner before Cam got a chance to sit down with his father. Lily and George had demanded most of the attention at first, and he'd gotten in a quick video game with Arthur and Daniel, too. Then the extended family had descended on the house, engulfing it in chaos until after everyone had sung 'Happy Birthday' and they'd cut and eaten the cake.

Cam's aunts, uncles and cousins had finally dispersed, and relative quiet had settled upon the house again. Maureen was attempting to get the twins down for bed, but from the intermittent sound of running feet coming from upstairs, he guessed it wasn't going well.

"So, how's work?" Cam asked his dad.

He shrugged. "Same 'ole, same ole. Hired a new apprentice a few months ago. She's working out well, so that's good. Might keep her on."

Frank was a master electrician and owned his own company. Over the years, he'd trained a number of apprentices, a few of whom he'd gone on to hire to work for him.

"Business is good then?"

His father nodded. "Yep, it's picked up in the past few months, and we've had a lot of jobs."

"That's typical for spring, isn't it?"

"It's up fifty percent from last year."

"That's great!" Cam said. The housing market crash and economic downturn had hit Frank's business hard. His mother's pay as a middle school English teacher provided steady income, but if his father hadn't inherited the house from his parents, Cam didn't know what would have happened to them. Now, with two kids in high school and two more in elementary, every bit helped.

"Yep." Frank was a man of few words. Quiet and introspective, he was hardworking, devoted to his loved ones and often overlooked in their boisterous family. "How's your work? Still teaching and DJing?"

"Of course. I talked to Mom a few days ago. I would have told you guys if I'd made any big changes."

"Hmm." His father eyed him. "I don't know. You keep things close to the vest."

Cam smirked. "And where did I get that from?"

Frank looked sheepish. "I suppose you do take after me a bit. More than the red hair, anyway."

"Yeah, a bit," Cam agreed. "But everything's great at school. I took the fifth graders on a field trip to Lincoln Center to see the philharmonic play."

"Ha. Must have been interesting wrangling them during a performance."

Cam grinned. "Thankfully, the school requires plenty of chaperones, and there are some great parents."

"Yeah, your mom always said that made all the difference for her."

"The kids have an end-of-the-year concert of their own coming up soon," Cam added. "So that's keeping me busy. And I'm still DJing. I've picked up a few extra gigs, and that's nice."

His father frowned. "You need the money?"

"No, I'm doing fine," Cam hastened to say. He didn't want his father thinking he needed help. "The gigs are fun, and the extra money gets split between savings and a few splurges." He'd bought a few nicer pieces of clothing that weren't for school so he didn't look quite so thrift-store dressed when he went out with Jesse. "But I'm being financially responsible, I promise."

"Good. Glad to hear it."

They were silent for a moment, and Frank leaned down and tweaked Daniel's foot. He scowled up from where he sprawled on the floor on a pillow and pulled his earbuds out of his ears. "What?"

"Is your homework done?"

"Um. No?"

"Then I guess you'd better do it. I warned you not to wait until the last minute. What did you do yesterday?"

"I got some of it done," Daniel said, brushing his shaggy blond hair off his forehead. "And, come on, I want to hang out with Cam. I never get to see him."

"You've been on your phone with your earbuds in all night," Frank said, sounding exasperated. "I wouldn't call that quality time with your brother."

Trying to stave off the inevitable power struggle between his teenage brother and his father, Cam intervened. "Why don't you get your work done now,

Dan? I'm nearly done teaching for the year, and I'll have extra time. You can come to Brooklyn and hang out with me for a day or two after school's out for both of us."

Dan sulked but nodded. "Yeah, okay."

Frank turned his attention to Arthur. "What about you?"

"It's mostly done."

"Same deal for you then," Cam said. "As long as Mom and Dad say you guys are keeping up on your work, you can come hang out in the city with me."

Arthur scowled. "Do I have to spend it with Dan, too?"

Cam tried not to roll his eyes. "We'll figure it out later. Night, guys."

Arthur and Dan left the room, bickering about who got to hang out with Cam first. Cam and his father exchanged wry smiles. Cam hoped he hadn't been that much of a pain in the ass during his teenaged years. He thought of saying so when Maureen walked into the living room.

"Did you get them down?" Frank asked.

"In theory. We'll see if it sticks."

"I sent Dan and Arthur off to do their homework."

"Oh, good. I don't have the energy to fight with them tonight."

"Cam offered some incentive." Frank explained Cam's plan, and Maureen gave him a grateful look.

"That would be a nice break, especially if you don't mind taking them separate days. They're at each other's throats right now."

"Of course," Cam said. "I don't mind."

In truth, he still felt guilty he didn't help out more.

"Do you want any help with the dishes?" Cam asked. Knowing his mom, she wouldn't go to bed until the kitchen was clean, and she had school in the morning. He needed to head out soon, too, but he could stay for a little longer.

"Most of them are done, but you can keep me company while I finish up." Her eyes gleamed, and Cam bit back a curse. Damn it, he'd walked right into an interrogation.

"Sure," he agreed.

He followed Maureen into the kitchen. She'd loaded the dishwasher after dinner so he worked on unloading it while she scrubbed the pans by hand.

They talked about school for a while before Maureen went in for the kill. "I know you said it's nothing serious, but who is he?"

Cam groaned and considered banging his head against the cabinet door. "I saw this bartender at the club for a while, but we called it off. And there's this guy, Jesse."

"I do read the gossip pages, you know," she huffed. "I know who Jesse Murtagh is."

Cam winced. He'd forgotten that he and Jesse had made a brief two-line mention in the society column not long ago.

She lowered her voice. "He's very good-looking."

Cam huffed out a laugh. "Yeah, he is."

"And he's treating you well?"

"He's been great," Cam said. "He flew me to Nantucket for gnocchi."

Her mouth opened in a small O of surprise. "Well, it must be getting serious then."

Cam held up a hand and stopped the train about to barrel down on him. "That was our first date." He struggled to put it into words. "He's just that kind of guy. And he has the means to make extravagant gestures. That's all."

"Even so, you're welcome to bring him home anytime," she said.

"Mom, no," Cam said, his tone firm. "Don't go looking for something that isn't there. He's not the settle-down type, and I'm not in any hurry for it, either."

A small pang went through Cam at the memory of Jesse pushing him to bring Ben to his parents' house. He looked around the small, homey kitchen and imagined Jesse in it. Like the rest of the house, it was well-loved. Frank updated it himself when he could, and Maureen had painted some of the dark, dated woodwork, but the old home had seen better days. It was a far cry from the gleaming perfection of the Greenwich Hotel or Jesse's posh loft.

And yet, Jesse wasn't a snob. He liked his luxuries, but he'd never treated Cam like he was any less because he didn't have a similar upbringing or wealth. He was a bit of a chameleon, too, seemingly able to adapt to any situation. Cam could almost picture him teasing Maureen into letting him help with dinner or asking Frank intelligent questions about his job as an electrician.

He would handle George's and Lily's craziness beautifully, and by the time he was done, he might even eke a grin or two out of Dan and Arthur. If he wanted to, he could win over the whole Lewis family the way he'd won over Cam. But there was the sticking point. Jesse didn't want that.

He turned to his mom. "Yeah, don't go getting your hopes up. There will be no meeting the family. I think maybe whatever we have has already run its course."

His mom dried her hands on a towel and frowned at him. "Are you sure you're okay with that?"

Cam offered her a wan smile. He wasn't. At all.

But he couldn't do anything about it. He couldn't change Jesse, and he wasn't about to try.

All he could do was brace himself for the inevitable heartache.

* * * *

Cam took the train home in a melancholy mood. Frank had offered to drive him to the train station, but Cam had declined. He wanted to be alone with his thoughts.

He'd shrugged off his mom's concern and wished his father a happy birthday. He'd caught a glimpse of them standing in the doorway of the house, watching him walk away. The sight of them, arm-in-arm, made his chest ache. Although he didn't want a suburban family life with five kids and home ownership, he did want...something. Something more permanent than random hookups and friends with benefits. Someone he could rely on.

But Jesse didn't want the things Cam realized he did want.

The train entered Manhattan, and Cam transferred to a direct line into Brooklyn, fighting the urge to hop in a cab and head for Jesse's place. *But that's stupid, right?* Cam needed distance instead of getting wrapped up even further. Besides, he had no idea what he'd find.

Jesse and Kyle in bed together was the best-case scenario. Cam didn't want to consider the worst.

Cam pulled his phone out after he took a seat on the deserted train to Brooklyn. The screen showed he'd missed a message from Jesse, and he drew a deep breath before he unlocked the phone and read it.

How was the day with the fam? Hope Dad had a good birthday.

Cam wanted to ignore it, but he typed a response and sent it before he could stop himself.

Good, thanks. And yes, he did.

He didn't feel up to making small talk, so he tucked his phone back in his pocket and stared at the poster on the wall in front of him without really seeing it. A guy at the other end of the car started singing under his breath, and Cam tried to block it out. He didn't have the tolerance for the musically challenged of Manhattan at the moment.

He couldn't keep doing this. Shouldn't continue with Jesse knowing he wouldn't reciprocate the way Cam wanted. It would be better for both of them if he ended it, right?

His phone buzzed in his pocket. Against his better judgment, he took it out.

You seem quiet tonight. Hope everything's okay.

Yep. Just got a lot on my mind.

Let me know if I can help.

And a moment later, *You up for brunch next Saturday with the breeders aka my brother Eric and his wife Sara?*

Cam stared at his screen, dumbfounded. According to everything he'd heard from both Jesse and his friends, Jesse didn't bring people around his family. Or, at least, not outside the speakeasy. What did it mean that he included Cam in that small circle? The hope that had dimmed in Cam's chest flared to life again.

Sure. Where and what time? he asked.

Still deciding on the restaurant. Somewhere near Rose Hill so the pregnant lady doesn't have to travel far. 11 a.m.

Cam replied with a funny lump in his throat and a stupid smile on his face.

I'll be there.

Chapter Eleven

"Who's coming today? The DJ from that club you like, right?"

"Right." Jesse offered Sara his arm. They were headed to Pineapple in Murray Hill. Eric had gone ahead over an hour before to scout out a table and save Sara and her baby bump from standing in line. "The DJ's name is Cameron, by the way."

"Okay, and what's Cameron like?" she asked.

"Eric didn't tell you what I told him?"

"Eric told me you were fooling around with the DJ at that club you like." She flashed him a smile. "So, how about you give me some useful information about the man?"

Jesse smirked. "Okay, fine. He goes by Cam, and he's funny and smart, has a good sense of humor — all that fun stuff."

"He's also extremely easy on the eyes." Sara chuckled. "I saw the paparazzi photo of you two, Jes."

"Of course you did." They paused on the curb and waited for the light to change as cars whizzed by. "In the interest of full disclosure, Cam's twenty-five and, in a strange twist of fate, knows Carter's kids." He met Sara's glance. "He's a music teacher and works at the school Sadie and Dylan attend."

"A teacher? Huh." Sara hummed. "He must be as poor as a church mouse."

Jesse burst out laughing. "Girl, that is rude."

"I didn't mean it as an insult!" Sara protested. "School teachers aren't paid all that well, even at private schools, and there's no way in hell your guy's salary could ever compete with the Murtagh money machine. That level of disparity can't be easy on a guy's ego."

"Mmm, I see your point, but we don't talk about money."

Sara arched an eyebrow at him. "At all?"

"Not explicitly, no. Cam's got two jobs, so it's not hard to infer he budgets. He also lives way the hell out in Brooklyn and has mentioned having roommates. Yes, you heard right, I used the plural of 'roommate'."

"Don't be snotty."

"I totally am not." He shrugged off Sara's teasing, and they crossed the street. "I was in college and younger than Cam the last time I had a full-time roommate, though, and I can't imagine having one now."

"Maybe they're more than roommates?"

He smiled. "I have no idea. A few of them are female, and Cam's not into women, which rules them out, and the males appear to be either involved with the females or go outside of the habitat to mate."

"You make it sound like a wilderness show on public television," Sara observed with amusement.

"That's the impression I get from Cam whenever he's talked about them, which isn't often. At any rate, I think he'd have mentioned a live-in boyfriend by now."

"Sounds like you haven't slummed with the cool kids in Brooklyn."

"Not as of yet, but I'm thinking that should change."

Sara furrowed her brow. "Oh? Why is that?"

"I've been footing the bill on dates with Cam, in part because I know he doesn't have unlimited funds. I also like nice things, good food and excellent booze and have the money to buy them." Jesse waved a hand at himself as Sara eyed him. "I know I'm a spoiled brat, Sara, and I don't mind spending the money."

"I'd imagine Cam doesn't mind, either."

"Why would he? My point is we spend all our time here in Manhattan in my habitat. Cam's met my friends and been to my place but never said anything about returning the gesture."

"Maybe he'd rather be here and doesn't want to admit it." Sara looked up at him. "You can't deny your habitat's loaded with a lot more toys, Jes. It could be Cam enjoys being a spoiled brat, too."

Jesse frowned. It seemed likely Cam appreciated his sometimes opulent lifestyle, but that didn't bother him in the least. The idea Cam might be hesitant to tell him certain things did, however.

"What's got you thinking so hard?"

"That thing you said about Cam liking the spoiled-brat lifestyle. He's pretty independent. I can see him wanting to take me out and maybe spend time in Brooklyn for a change."

Sara gave Jesse a pointed look. "You realize hanging with Cam in Brooklyn means you'll be expected to enter places frequented by twenty-somethings, right?"

"Yes. I'll also be honest and say I have no idea about such places and what one does in them." He grimaced.

"I'm sure you'll do okay, old man," Sara replied with a laugh. "Be yourself and leave your wallet in your pocket. It's not like you don't go out and do perfectly average things. We're about to gorge on comfort food in a glorified shack, for crying out loud."

"That's one of the reasons I invited Cam along with us today," Jesse admitted. "I get the feeling he thinks it's normal for me to drop a ton of cash no matter what I'm doing. Like I don't know how to just be."

"Whose fault is that, Big Money?"

"Mine. I came on kind of strong at first because I wanted to wow him." He laughed at Sara's mimed gagging. "I know it sounds gross, but fuck it, we had fun."

"I'll bet you did, honey." Sara sounded reflective. "You like this guy, don't you?"

"Sure, I do. I like everyone I date."

"Duh." Sara chuckled. "Are you sure he's not different from everyone you date? It's not as if you bring your girl and boy toys around to meet Eric and me outside of the bar, and it sounds like you're working hard to get to know him."

"I want to get to know Cam because I like him as a friend, not just a boy toy. And bringing him to meet you and Eric has as much to do with the Crockpot strapped to the front of your body as anything else." Jesse enjoyed Sara's cackling. "Your words, not mine, babe."

"And wholly apt." Sara ran the palm of her free hand over her belly through her white tunic.

Jesse grinned. His sister-in-law's odd observations about her pregnancy never failed to amuse him, especially now that she'd entered her second trimester and her baby bump was obvious. She and Eric did spend less time at Under, and he didn't feel bad at all for exploiting that as his excuse to bring Cam to meet them. In truth, Jesse wanted Cam to know more about his life because he had grown more and more curious about Cam's.

"Seriously, Cam's been to Under, but you and Eric haven't for weeks. Once the photo landed in the gossip pages, I knew I'd have to go a different route if you were going to meet each other before the arrival of your spawn."

"I'm not much in the mood for bar hopping these days, it's true." Sara frowned. "I think Eric would be, but his migraines have been pretty bad since the deal in London started."

"He mentioned that. I'm sure it has to do with keeping weird hours because I'm five hours ahead." Jesse made a mental note to check in with his brother. Eric had started experiencing migraines during college but had only recently resorted to taking medication in a bid to control them.

Sara nodded. "I'm sure you're right. I don't miss going out and we've got to get used to having a baby in the house anyway. However, there are days I'd kill for a mojito. A real mojito swimming with rum," Sara clarified when he chuckled.

"I'll bring you one as soon as you've delivered the spawn," he promised, then paused. "Or whenever it is you're all clear to drink alcohol again, anyway. You just say the word."

The crowd outside the restaurant stretched down Lexington Avenue and around the corner, and he breathed a sigh of relief to see Eric sitting on a wooden bench near the head of the line. He blinked at the realization Dylan Hamilton sat beside Eric, and the party waiting ahead of them included Carter, Riley and

Sadie, as well as Carter's ex-wife Kate and Carter's mother, Eleanor Hamilton.

"Holy crap on a cracker," Jesse muttered a second before Dylan spotted him and jumped to his feet with a yelp.

A laugh rolled out of Jesse as Dylan dashed toward him, and he bent and scooped up the little boy the moment he got close. "Dyl Pickle! What the heck are you doing here?"

"Mommy called this morning and told Dad that Grandma wanted to meet us for bruh-lunch!" Dylan told him. Jesse smiled at his careful, two-syllable mangling of 'brunch'.

"Cool! I'll bet your dad was excited to hear that."

Dylan glanced at the party waiting by the door, then turned back with a gleam in his eye. "He swore kinda loud," Dylan said in a lowered voice. "Then Ri took away Dad's coffee cup and told him to get in the shower."

Jesse fought like hell to keep a straight face while Sara disguised her laugh with a hasty cough. "It's a good thing Ri knows how to handle your old man, huh?" he asked. "Hey, you remember Sara, right? She's married to Eric over there."

"Hi." Dylan smiled at Sara, who waved. Then he spied her belly and his eyes went wide. "Whoa, you're having a baby!"

The two chatted amiably over Jesse's shoulder while he led the way to the line to join the others. He and Sara greeted everyone before she moved back and joined Eric on the bench and Jesse exchanged a high five with Sadie and one-armed hugs with Carter and Riley around Dylan. His friends looked stressed, and Riley's body language was uncharacteristically tense.

"I found something of yours," Jesse joked. He handed Dylan off, and he didn't miss the gratitude that flashed in Riley's blue eyes. Carter's parents didn't approve of Riley's part in co-parenting the Hamilton kids, and now that Jesse had the opportunity, he wanted to find a multitude of ways to subtly tell Eleanor Hamilton she and her opinion could go fuck themselves.

Dylan kissed Riley on the cheek, and Riley's entire person softened. "Hungry, buddy?"

"Starving," Dylan agreed. "Can I go talk to Sara until we eat? She told me she'd let me feel the baby kick."

Riley grinned. "Absolutely. Be gentle and don't touch unless Sara says it's okay."

"Where's Robert?" Jesse asked after Riley set Dylan down.

"Away on business, the lucky bastard," Riley replied in an undertone. He and Carter were on good terms with Kate's boyfriend, and the four socialized over regular meals with the kids. "Didn't know you'd be here today."

"Sara's got a craving for the biscuits and gravy, so here we are." Jesse pulled his phone from his pocket. "One sec while I tell Cam we're up next for seats — that woman will kill me if we get called and have to wait because he's stuck on a train somewhere."

"Cam as in Cam Lewis?" Riley asked.

Jesse sent off the message and blinked at his friend. "Do you know many Cams, Riley?"

"Several, actually, but only one of them teaches my, uh, Carter's kids." Riley's cheeks turned pink in what Jesse recognized as a fit of adorable embarrassment.

Ordinarily, he'd at least tease Riley for the "my kids" slip-up, but he thought it best to hold off, given his friend's state of mind. "Right. For the record, yes, I'm talking about Cam Lewis."

Riley licked his lips. "I hate to ask this but could you two keep from doing anything super couple-y while we're all in the same room together?"

"Sure." Jesse pursed his lips. "But, come on, man, we're having brunch with my brother and his wife — what do you think is going to happen?"

Riley gave him a sheepish grin. "Sorry. I'm on edge today." He stole a glance over his shoulder at Carter, Kate and Eleanor, who were deep in conversation. "We were surprised when Kate and Eleanor called this morning, but neither of us expected they'd invite me along," he said. "This is the first time in years I've spoken to Eleanor, and I'm not embarrassed to say I don't want to give her anything to gossip about."

The strain in Riley's expression sent a pulse of anger through Jesse. "You have every right to be here," he said. "You do a lot to parent those kids, Ri, and everyone whose opinion counts knows it."

Riley nodded. "Carter said the same thing. I'd be tempted to call it flattery if he wasn't always painfully honest about everything. The kids have started calling me 'Ri-Dad' on occasion, though, so I guess they feel the same way."

His smile, both shy and proud, leveled Jesse's irritation. Times like these, he understood what so attracted Carter to Riley. Who knew a simple portmanteau of Riley's name combined with 'dad' could reduce a man who ran a multimillion-dollar business to a blushing mess?

"That's cute," Jesse said, his tone dry. "But I'm not so sure how cute you'll find it the next time you're in my bar and I have an audience."

The hostess called the Hamiltons to their seats then, and Carter caught Jesse's eye.

"Stay afterward for a drink?" he called back and smiled at Jesse's eager nod.

"Car's pretty stressed," Riley said. "And it doesn't help that I need to go out of town again this week. Don't be surprised later if one drink turns into three, even though he's trying to limit his intake."

Riley looked past him and gestured to Dylan, who was seated beside Sara on the bench, his hand on her belly. "C'mon, kiddo, it's time for waffles!"

"Woohoo!" Dylan gently patted Sara's bump, then leaned down and put his face inches away from the buttons on her tunic. "See you soon, baby!" he hollered and scampered inside with Ri following, a wake of laughing adults behind them.

"Oh, shit, I wish I'd recorded that," Eric gasped once he'd gotten himself under control. "That kid is a scream."

"He kept telling me I needed to try the waffles," Sara said. "All he did was make me hungrier, so please tell me your DJ is on the next block, Jes."

"Well," Jesse hedged. He glanced down the block and spied Cam's tall frame moving toward them. "I can do better than that because here he comes now."

* * * *

"Hey, Cam? You're not shacked up with any of your roommates, right?"

Jesse inhaled a mouthful of his Bloody Mary and groaned as the wasabi in the drink seared into his sinuses. Cam, who'd been poised to take a bite of

French toast, lowered his fork and stared at Sara with wide eyes.

"Um. Excuse me?"

Eric covered his eyes with one hand. "Jesus, Sara," he muttered, and a broad smile spread across his lips.

Jesse exhaled noisily. They'd been having such a pleasant afternoon. Eric and Sara had liked Cam straight off the bat and he'd enjoyed meeting them, too. They'd eaten a delicious meal while the conversation flowed, and Cam had handled the unexpected presence of the Hamilton kids with aplomb. Initially, he'd seemed confused by Jesse's suggestion they dial back on affectionate gestures, but he'd seen reason when Sadie and Dylan came over to say hello. Far easier to tell the kids they were friends and leave it at that, and Cam was clearly relieved not to have to lie about how they knew each other.

Jess sniffed and wiped his eyes with his napkin. Leave it to Sara's total lack of filter to spoil the easygoing vibe.

"I'm just trying to get to know him, honey," Sara told her husband, then turned back to Cam. "I asked Jes earlier about your roommates and he said he had no idea."

"No," Jesse rasped out. "I said you'd probably have mentioned having a live-in boyfriend by now, but I acknowledge I could be wrong." Of course, now that he'd considered Cam having someone back in Brooklyn to screw on the regular, he didn't exactly love the idea of it having been kept secret.

"I don't have a boyfriend," Cam replied, "and I'm not involved with any of my roommates, either. Don't get me wrong—they're all cool people, but none of them are my type." He gave Sara a small smile, which she echoed.

"Fair enough. That may be best, considering Jesse wouldn't hesitate to poach your man, anyway."

Jesse pressed one hand to his chest with an aggrieved noise. "That is patently untrue," he protested. "I would never poach anyone's man unless they wanted me to."

Cam wrinkled his nose. "Does that happen a lot?"

"Not often enough," Jesse admitted. "But I can't complain." He winked and reached beneath the table to take hold of Cam's hand. The way Cam stiffened in his chair made Jesse chuckle.

"You're going to get us busted," Cam muttered.

"Relax yourself, Red. I've got my eye on the Hamilton table." Jesse wound their fingers together, and the apprehension on Cam's face melted into amusement. "Besides, the kids have seen Kyle and me loving up on each other and never batted an eye."

"Neither of you sees those kids three times a week for music theory and practice," Cam replied. "It's going to be weird if either of them mentions having seen me over the weekend to anyone, so let's not give them anything to talk about."

"Now you sound like Riley," Jesse grumbled. His pout sparked regret in Cam's expression, but before either of them could speak again, Sara abruptly sat up straight in her chair.

"Ow," she grunted and rubbed her sternum with one hand.

Eric leaned forward to catch her eye. "Heartburn again?"

"Uh-huh." Sara grimaced. "Motherfucker."

"Are you okay?" Jesse asked. He frowned at the way Sara grabbed for her glass with a shaky hand.

"I've had this killer heartburn," she muttered, "and son of a bitch, does it hurt."

"I have gum." Moving quickly, Cam pulled a package of chewing gum from his jacket pocket and handed it to Sara. "My mom always said chewing gum helped with her heartburn. She got pregnant when I was nineteen," he added as the others stared at him.

"Twenty years between children," Sara marveled, her eyes wide. "I can't imagine!"

"There were a couple more in between," Cam told her. "I'm the oldest of five."

"Well, thank you, oldest of five, and please thank your mother, too, because I appreciate any tips that'll make this shit better." Sara popped two pieces of gum into her mouth. "Mmm, grapefruit," she muttered and chewed. "Much better than stomach acid."

Eric laughed. "C'mon, girl, let's get you home." He aimed a rueful glance at Jesse and Cam and reached into his pocket for his wallet. "I'm afraid we've got to cut this short. Sara's got a date with a bottle of apple cider vinegar."

"Sounds kinky," Jessie joked.

"She mixes it with water," Eric explained. "Swears it works better than any antacid."

"She is right here," Sara grumbled, then winked at Eric, who stood and tossed several bills onto the table.

Jesse stood, too, as Eric held out a hand to Sara. "Do you want me to call the car service?"

"No, thanks, babe." Sara waved him off. "It's not far and being on my feet is better than sitting, anyway. Besides, the gum is definitely taking the edge off." She raised her eyebrows at Cam. "Who knew?"

Cam looked pleased. "Happy to help. I hope you feel better."

He stood and smiled through handshakes and goodbyes with Eric and Sara, but Jesse detected an undercurrent of nerves in his demeanor. Cam's gaze kept skittering away, like someone had caught him out. Which, Jesse supposed, was true. Clearly, Cam had kept things from him. Like a sibling being two decades younger than Cam himself. Jesse didn't know why Cam would keep that — or anything — from him, but he saw only one way to find out.

After Eric and Sara had gone, Jesse caught his eye. "You mind if we settle the bill and move over to the bar? Carter and Ri asked me to meet them for a drink after their family leaves."

Cam glanced to the wine bar at the far end of the room before he answered. "Oh, sure, that's fine."

Jesse said nothing more until after they'd paid the check and moved across the room, and Jesse had ordered a bottle of Jolie Folle rosé. Cam sipped his wine, his expression tight, like he was braced for an argument, and Jesse wondered what the fuck was going through his lover's head.

"I didn't know you had a five-year-old in your life." Jesse kept his tone mild, but Cam still winced.

"I have two five-year-olds in my life." His brown eyes were somber. "George and Lily are twins."

Huh.

Jesse sat back in his seat. "Okay. And the others?"

"Daniel's eighteen and Arthur will be sixteen this fall."

"Your parents must have energy by the fuckton."

Cam chuckled. "They truly do. They also joke that they're abject failures at family planning, too. I'm sure every one of us came as a surprise, in one way or another."

"Eh. Surprises are underrated." Jesse swirled the wine in his glass. "People should welcome more spontaneity in their lives."

"Easy for you to say," Cam replied. "Being spontaneous in New York is easy for a single man without dependents."

Jesse nodded. "Good point. What about Jersey? Is it easier for a single man to be spontaneous in Hoboken or wherever it is your parents live?"

Cam's grin faded. "Jersey City," he said, his voice solemn. "My parents live in Jersey City. I haven't stayed there overnight for a couple of years now, so I can't say what life is like for a single man."

"Fair enough." Jesse furrowed his brow. "Cam, does it seem weird to you that I didn't know where your parents live? Or know you have almost literal baby brothers and sisters? Because, I gotta say, it seems weird to me. Particularly since we just ate brunch with my brother and his wife, and I know I've been open with you about them and my parents."

"That's my fault." Cam blew out a breath, and his shoulders sagged. "I didn't set out not to tell you about my family, but somehow, it worked out that way."

Jesse pressed his lips into a line. "It's not only that, Cam. Most of what I know about you is in bits and pieces."

"How do you mean?"

"I know you live in Brooklyn, but I have no idea where. You have a bunch of roommates, and I remember some of their names, yet how many roommates you have in total and how you know them is a mystery. I'm obviously aware of where you work, but aside from Ben, the bartender you used to screw, I don't know anything beyond Midtown Academy and

Ember." Jesse waved a hand between them. "Do you see a pattern here?"

Cam grimaced. "Okay, that sounds bad when you lay it all out."

"I don't get it. You've been to my place and met my friends. And it's pretty fucking weird when you consider you googled me before I even got to know your first name." Jesse ran a hand over his hair while Cam looked embarrassed. "You have a private life, and that's totally understandable. But it's as if you materialize out of nowhere whenever I call and only when I call. Granted, I'm probably to blame anyway, seeing as I've been bulldozing you into going out with me from the start."

"No, that's not true." Cam paused, licked his lips. "Okay, it might have been true to a degree in the beginning, but it's not now. I'm with you because I want to be. When's the last time you had to persuade me to meet you to do anything?"

Jesse couldn't help smiling. He certainly hadn't sweet-talked Cam into the torrid night they'd spent in the penthouse at the Greenwich Hotel.

"So, what's with the secret keeping?"

"I didn't keep secrets, Jes. I just didn't give you a ton of details."

Jesse rolled his eyes. "Okay, that's a technicality, but the point remains I don't know why you're keeping things from me at all."

Cam worried his bottom lip with his teeth. "I didn't think any of it was important enough to share."

"Why not?"

"Ugh, I don't know." Cam made a helpless motion with his hands. "All of that shit seems ridiculously mundane compared to your life. My parents and their blue-collar lives, my dumpy loft with the cheap furniture—even my piece-of-shit bike that I use to get to and from the ferry because I can't afford a car." Cam shook his head. "That stuff doesn't have a place in your world, and I never once imagine you'd be interested in knowing about any of it."

Ouch.

Jesse stared at Cam for a moment before he looked away. For the first time in what felt like forever, he didn't know what to say. He also had no idea why Cam's words stung so much or why they made him feel like a first-class asshole and a shitty friend.

That was when it struck him—maybe Cam didn't consider him a friend. A lover, yes, and someone fun to spend time with, but otherwise, what did they have between them? Jesse was a diversion, someone with whom to share laughs and good sex. Cam might miss him if he stopped calling, but he'd get over it, and things in his life would continue without pause.

A weird ache worked its way through Jesse's chest at the idea of not seeing Cam. Because he did consider Cam a friend. He'd miss seeing him, and not only because they had a lot of fun fucking each other silly. Jesse liked the rangy, ginger-haired smart-ass seated beside him, and he found the idea of Cam stepping out of his life unpleasant, to say the least. But where the hell did that leave him if Cam didn't feel the same?

Well, fuck. Sara had been right. He did like this guy.

"Jes?"

Jesse blinked when a warm hand covered his where it lay on the bar. He looked up and found Cam regarding him with obvious concern.

"Hey. You okay? You don't look so good."

"Liar." Jesse cleared his throat and gave himself a mental shake. "I always look good."

"Okay, I'll grant you that," Cam said easily. He cocked his head. "You kind of zoned out there for a second."

"I'm good." Jesse made himself smile. "You're wrong, by the way—I'm interested in hearing about that mundane life of yours, if you want to tell me."

"Honestly?" Cam raised his brows.

"We've been hanging out a lot, Cam. Call me old-fashioned, but I wouldn't mind getting to know the guy I'm spending my time with."

A shy but pleased expression broke over Cam's face and told Jesse he'd said something right. Fingers crossed he could keep it up. "I thought we could spend time out in your neck of the woods for a change, too."

"Say what now?" Cam's expression went flat. "Jesse Murtagh in Brooklyn. Yeah, no. I can't see it."

"Dude, what is wrong with you?" Jesse raised a brow. "I grew up in this city and I've been all over every borough. There's a ton of good food and drink out in Brooklyn, not to mention the Widow Jane distillery where they make one of my favorite bourbons."

"I've never heard of that, but I'm down to check it out."

"Check what out?" Carter asked. He and Riley stepped up beside Jesse, and though they both looked tired and in need of a drink, their hands were wound together. Jesse smiled.

"The Widow Jane distillery, a place you introduced me to, my good man," he replied.

"We're talking about places to go in Brooklyn," Cam added. He smiled broadly. "And I'm thinking it's high time I drag Jesse off this godforsaken island he loves so much."

Jesse signaled the bartender for more glasses, and pleasure pulsed through him as Cam continued speaking.

Chapter Twelve

"So, how do you feel about thrift stores?" Cam asked. He'd been apprehensive about bringing Jesse to Brooklyn, but he'd taken it all in stride. From the ferry ride, to the walk through the neighborhood, to a late lunch at a hipster barbecue joint, he'd proved perfectly adaptable. He hadn't even blinked when Cam paid for the ferry and lunch.

"Thrift stores?" Jesse raised an eyebrow at him. "In theory or in practice?"

"Is there a distinction?"

"Well, in theory they scare me a little. In practice…" Jesse cleared his throat. "In practice, I have no idea."

Cam hazarded a guess about what he meant. "You've never been in one."

"I have not."

Cam looked skyward. "Oh, Jesse."

"What?" He sounded a touch defensive.

"You have been missing out, Big Money." Cam took hold of his hand. "Come on. Let me show you how the unwashed masses shop for home goods and clothing."

"Clothing?" Jesse's lips curled up in disdain, but he followed Cam.

"I know. It's awful. Previously worn. Off-the-rack."

"The horrors of lack of tailoring aside, it's the previously worn part that worries me. You joke about the unwashed masses but...bedbugs." Jesse's tone was pained.

"Items are cleaned before they're sold. I always wash stuff before I wear it anyway, to be on the safe side. And I've only gotten bedbugs the one time."

"Say what now?" Jesse gave him a look tinged with horror, and Cam nearly doubled over laughing.

"No. I've never in my life gotten bedbugs—from a thrift store or anywhere else," Cam said after he'd composed himself. "I did get lice once." He grimaced. "But that was the kids at school."

Jesse shuddered. "They are germy, disgusting little things."

Cam snorted. "I'd believe you meant it if I hadn't seen you interact with Dylan and Sadie."

"Guilty as charged. I do like those particular germy, disgusting little things."

Cam bumped shoulders with him. "So, I shouldn't call you to come help if my mom needs an emergency babysitter for George and Lily?"

Jesse looked at him askance. "It depends on if you're willing to throw in some bribery."

"Hmm." Cam pretended to be skeptical. "What could I bribe you with?"

Jesse's low, warm chuckle made Cam's stomach flip. "Oh, I can think of one or two things."

"I'll keep that in mind."

"Seriously, though, I can't believe I had no idea you had siblings that young."

"I'm sorry." Cam licked his lips. He didn't know how to tell Jesse he worried about getting his heart broken without giving himself away and revealing he was way more emotionally invested than he was supposed to be.

"It's okay. Tell me more about your siblings now."

"Well, Arthur and Dan are pretty typical teenagers. They're both obsessed with video games and driving our parents crazy. But Dan's also a killer soccer player and a fucking genius with computers. He got an almost full scholarship to Rutgers for computer engineering."

"That's impressive."

"We're all proud of him. Although, my parents are struggling with him right now. He's so bright, but he's kind of checking out of school in this last semester. He's refusing to turn in his homework, and I had to bribe him with a weekend in the city to get him to buckle down."

Jesse chuckled. "You know you're from Jersey when a trip to Brooklyn is a treat."

"Hey, now, no bashing my home state." It occurred to Cam he'd never asked Jesse much about his childhood. "Now as for you, I know you grew up in Manhattan."

"I did. Born and raised." There was a touch of pride in Jesse's voice.

"You know," Cam began, "you gave me shit about not telling you about my family, which is fair, but you don't talk about your parents much. You talk about Eric and Sara, but not so much your mom and dad. Is that a touchy subject?"

"Not at all. Things were tense sometimes while I grew up and tried to figure what the fuck I was doing, but we get along well now. Believe it or not, I try to keep out of trouble, mostly in deference to them. They've come to terms with my sexual orientation and my lack of interest in settling down, and are okay with the way I live my life for the most part. Still, it doesn't keep my mom from dreaming about weddings. If I told her I'd met someone and planned to propose, she'd be ecstatic."

"And you have no desire for that?"

"I have no desire for that kind of life. Marriage and monogamy don't compute for me."

"Hmm." The conversation had veered into territory Cam didn't want to explore at the moment, especially in the middle of a crowded Brooklyn street. He turned the subject back to the Lewises.

"My brother Arthur is the sixteen-year-old. He's also a pain in the ass. Very bright, too, but in different ways. He's way into music, so we have a lot in common there."

"Listening? Performing?"

"Both, but he's kind of obsessed with the rock orchestra thing."

"Lindsey Sterling-type music?"

"Yeah, exactly. Two Cellos, that sort of thing. He's composed some stuff and he's good."

"What a frighteningly accomplished clan you have," Jesse said.

Cam laughed. "Not bad for a blue-collar family from Jersey, right?"

"Not bad for anyone, but sure, it's easy to achieve great things with unlimited resources. It can't have been easy for your parents to afford music lessons and instruments and soccer gear and all that."

"No. But they managed."

"The twins are George and Lily, right?"

"Yep. George is obsessed with taking things apart and knowing how it all works. He's older by, like, twenty minutes, but second in command to Lily. He's a sweet kid and way quieter than his sister. Sweet is not the way I'd describe Lily."

"She sounds fun."

Cam chuckled. "She's something else. She's a great kid — smart as hell and tough."

"Well, what do you expect with four brothers?"

"Yeah, I'm sure that contributed. But I think Lily would be tough no matter what. She's our warrior princess. Obsessed with glitter and all things sparkly, and no doubt destined to take over the world. We all joke that once she's supreme ruler, we hope she'll think of us benevolently. Or, at least, make our deaths swift and merciful."

Jesse's laugh was loud and genuine. "I'm starting to think I'd like your sister."

"I suspect you would," Cam said, his tone dry. "Although, I have a feeling that would be terrifying for the world at large."

"No doubt."

Cam chuckled. "I'm familiar with your encouragement of Dylan's love of practical jokes. I had to have a talk with Carter and Riley about that sometime last year. After Christmas, maybe? Though I was informed his uncle, Max, had been supplying the gag gifts, and Dylan's bag would be checked every day before school in the future."

"Poor kid." Jesse snickered. "Ask Carter about the trick gum Dylan gave to his grandmother."

"Oh, God. I don't even want to know."

"It was epic."

"Okay, that confirms it. You are not meeting Lily. Ever. She does not need encouragement."

Jesse grinned. "How are they all with the gay thing?"

Cam shrugged. "Totally fine. My mom seemed marginally disappointed by the idea of no grandkids from me, but she has four other kids to get them from, which softened the blow. And my dad...well, you'd expect a union electrician from Jersey to be all macho and 'not my son' about it, but he was very low-key. Well, he's always low-key," Cam corrected. "But he kind of nodded and said he supported me, and that was the end of it. My mom switched from asking about girls I had crushes on to asking about boys, and they both welcomed my first boyfriend with open arms."

"Well done, Lewis family," Jesse said.

Cam stopped in front of Thrift Kingdom. "We have arrived at our destination."

Jesse eyed the storefront with a skeptical expression, but Cam held the door open for him, and he preceded Cam inside.

"Welcome to my world."

"It smells..."

Cam looked at him expectantly, waiting for him to finish.

"Better than I expected."

Cam snickered. "What did you expect?"

"Mildew and B.O."

"I never considered you a snob, Jes."

"Hey, I'm here, aren't I? And I'm admitting I'm wrong."

"There is that. Come on. Let's start out with my favorite section — records."

"Lead the way."

Browsing through records together proved enjoyable. Cam found a few gems that he tucked under his arm and steered Jesse toward the clothing. "Now, we have to look at clothes and try them on."

Jesse gave a long-suffering sigh.

They worked their way through the racks, and he shook his head occasionally, but he proved a good sport when Cam held shirts up against his chest to contemplate them.

"That's a good color on you," Cam said about a smoky blue sweater. It made Jesse's eyes even more vibrant than usual.

"Fine, I'll try it on."

By the time they'd hit the final racks of men's clothes, Cam had chosen several shirts and a jacket for Jesse, and a few things for himself.

They stood in a small line for the fitting rooms. When they reached the head and a room opened up, Jesse motioned for Cam to follow. "Come on, we can share."

"Uh-uh." Cam pointed to the sign proclaiming no more than six items at a time and one person per room. "I'm afraid not."

Jesse groaned. "But that was the part I looked forward to."

"I'll make it up to you later. Now go. I'll hop into the next one."

Jesse disappeared into the open fitting room and a few minutes later, his voice rose over the low hum of noise in the store. "Am I supposed to model this?"

"Obviously," Cam teased. "What's the point of taking you here if you don't get the full experience?"

"Fine, fine."

Cam, who had been poised with his camera ready, took a shot the moment Jesse stepped through the doorway.

"You're the worst," he grumbled, but he closed the distance between them and brushed his lips across Cam's. "You're sending that to the speakeasy guys, aren't you?"

"I hadn't planned on it before—the photo was for my own personal pleasure. But now that you mention it, I absolutely am." It still boggled Cam's mind that he had the personal numbers of some of New York's elite in his phone, including a state senator.

Jesse looked pained. "It's a good thing I like you, Cam. I wouldn't put up with this from just anyone."

Cam grinned, but he couldn't formulate a coherent verbal response. He'd been at such a low point last week, worrying he'd get his heart broken. But this was what kept him going—feeling like he mattered to Jesse.

"So, what about the shirt?" Jesse asked.

Cam gave him an assessing glance. "It doesn't fit very well," he admitted. "The cut is off somehow."

"That's what I thought. Okay, on to the next."

Cam waved the next person in line forward when another fitting room opened up. Over the course of the next ten minutes, Jesse modeled more shirts and a tweedy blazer for him. None seemed quite right.

Cam frowned at him. "Weird, I thought those would work on you."

"I have a hard time buying off the rack," Jesse said. "My proportions make most shirts too short, and if they fit in the shoulders, they're bulky at the waist." He smoothed the baggy fabric over his abdomen. "Anything I buy has to be tailored anyway, so I might as well order clothes made to my specifications."

"I'd say that was a convenient excuse, but I can see what you mean," Cam admitted.

"It's because I'm one of a kind." Jesse winked.

"Go, you egomaniac," Cam laughed and pushed him toward the dressing room. "If your head will fit in that tiny little box."

"I have one shirt left," Jesse said and disappeared through the door. "And see? My ego fits just fine."

A girl standing near Cam snickered. "You guys are a riot together."

"Thanks. I think."

"Oh, no, trust me, it's a good thing. It's worth the wait in line."

"Glad I could help."

"Stop flirting and tell me how I look." Cam glanced away from the young woman and saw Jesse standing in front of him in the blue sweater.

"I'm not," Cam protested. "Flirting with every human in sight is your thing, not mine."

"Focus, Cameron. How does this look?"

Cam gave him a critical glance. "Great." Despite Jesse's protestations he couldn't do off the rack, the sweater fit him beautifully. The cut showed off his build, and the color made his eyes so blue Cam felt weak in the knees.

"I'm surprised, but it does look pretty good on me." The hint of reluctant admiration in Jesse's tone made Cam grin.

"Guess we're getting it then."

"What? No. I don't need it, Cam."

"Sure you do. I mean, if you're spending the night with me for the full Brooklyn experience." Cam held his breath. They hadn't discussed how the night would end.

Jesse groaned. "Fine. But I draw the line at buying socks and underwear here. I'll stop somewhere and get new ones."

"They don't sell previously worn underwear and socks at Thrift Kingdom, Jes. You don't need new ones anyway because you can borrow some from me."

"Am I not allowed to buy new ones? Is that not done in Brooklyn? Or does it go against your rules?"

"Ha ha. When have I ever told you what to do?"

A thoughtful expression crossed Jesse's face. "Fair enough. You are remarkably undemanding."

How could I be demanding? Cam wondered. Jesse had all the power. It wasn't his money or social power but his ability to walk away. Then again, hadn't he proven he was more interested in Cam than Cam had given him credit for? He wouldn't be here slumming it if he didn't care. And he'd seemed hurt earlier after pointing out Cam was the one holding back.

All—well maybe most—of his jokes about the Brooklyn experience today had been for comedic effect. It was fun playing up the disparities in their lives. It seemed to reduce them and make them less of a looming presence.

Cam squeezed Jesse's upper arm. "Go change and I'll try on my stuff. Make sure you bring out the clothing that doesn't work and hang it on the rack there."

"I have tried on clothing before."

"At a place that requires you to lift a finger to do anything?"

"Only in cases of extreme emergency." He turned away, and Cam grinned. "And stop smirking!"

"I wasn't smirking," he argued, knowing full well he had been.

They continued to banter through the door while Jesse changed back into his own clothes. They swapped spots a few minutes later, and Cam tried on the first of the clothes he'd picked out.

"You have to model, too," Jesse called out.

Cam obliged, and by the time he'd made it through all the potential choices, he had two shirts and a pair of trousers for purchase.

"Ready?" he asked after he'd hung up the ones that hadn't worked out.

"Yep."

They encountered another line at the register, but Jesse was patient. He chatted with the people in line around them and, of course, charmed them all within the first six seconds. He had a gift, Cam mused.

"I've got this," Cam said when their turn arrived, and Jesse had reached for his wallet.

Jesse's lips twitched. "After today, I may have to start calling you Big Money."

The salesgirl finished ringing up their combined purchases. "Your total comes to twenty-three dollars and fifty-eight cents. Will that be cash, debit or credit?"

"Debit," Cam said.

"Would you like to round up and donate the remainder to children's cancer research?" she asked.

"Sure," Cam said. He swiped his card and accepted the charges for twenty-four dollars. The salesgirl handed them a plastic bag with their clothing, and Cam thanked her and headed for the door.

Cam glimpsed Jesse slip a neatly folded bill into the fishbowl beneath the crumpled one-, five- and odd ten-dollar bills and bet he'd donated at least fifty, if not a hundred dollars.

The gesture reinforced everything Cam had observed in Jesse. He was generous, with both his time and money, but understated about it. He treated himself well—and why shouldn't he?—and gave lavishly to others. Before they'd met, Cam'd held a semi-dim view of people with the kind of wealth and power Jesse possessed. He'd had a few too many encounters with entitled rich kids at clubs and demanding parents at Midtown Academy to think everyone handled privilege well. Jesse and his speakeasy crew were notable exceptions.

Cam had once overheard Jesse and Kyle discussing a charitable foundation and fundraising campaign the Murtaghs donated to. Kyle had pushed Jesse to accept an award from the foundation, and while Jesse had agreed, he wanted to do it away from the gala that had been proposed. Cam hadn't heard the whole conversation, but he'd gotten the impression Jesse didn't like getting attention for that sort of thing. Which was funny because he drew people's attention with little effort. He basked in that, but he wasn't an attention whore.

Jesse's voice pulled Cam from his thoughts. "I don't want to hijack the plans you had for the rest of the day, but how do you feel about touring the Widow Jane distillery?"

"It's whiskey, right?" Cam asked.

"Yeah, they primarily make bourbon and rye, but they have a few varietals of rum and chocolate liqueurs as well. They also share space with a fantastic chocolate factory."

"Whiskey and the like aren't my favorite, but the rest sounds fun. Any idea what times the tours run?"

Jesse brought out his phone and fiddled with it for a moment. "Hmm, there's one at four and one at six."

"Where is it?"

"Red Hook."

Cam looked at the time on his phone. "We'll never make it for four p.m. Want to do the six?"

"Sounds good to me. I'd imagine their tours are popular, so what do you think about reserving spots online?"

"Perfect. No point in heading all the way out to Red Hook today if we can't take the tour."

Jesse snagged them two spots while Cam contemplated what to do for the next two hours.

"Want to wander toward Brooklyn Heights for a bit? We can stop anywhere along the way that appeals or hop on the subway toward Red Hook."

"Sounds great."

* * * *

Cam was tipsy when he let Jesse into his apartment. He'd enjoyed touring the distillery and tasting a number of the products they offered. The rum and chocolate liqueurs were delicious, and on a fairly empty stomach, Cam was feeling them.

"S-o-o-o, this is home." Hoping for the best, he pushed open the door and waved Jesse inside. To his relief, the jackets and shoes were less of an explosion of clutter than usual. "Not much to see here, but you can leave your shoes, and I'll give you the quick tour."

Jesse set his discarded shoes neatly beside Cam's before following him down the hallway.

"I dig the raw loft vibe," he said. They'd stopped in the open living and kitchen area, and he drew closer to the floor-to-ceiling windows. "And, damn, that's a nice view." Sunset was approaching, and the low, warm light lit up the city.

"Starting to see the appeal of living with four roommates?"

Jesse shot him a grin over his shoulder. Cam's heart skipped a beat at the image of his lean, tight body silhouetted against the darkening sky. He looked both out of place and at home in Cam's apartment.

Cam closed the distance between them and leaned his right shoulder into Jesse's left. He rested his chin on Jesse's shoulder, and they stood there in silence for a moment.

"The distillery tour was fun. I'm glad we went," Cam said.

"Me too."

"I'm even rethinking my stance on non-clear liquors." He straightened, and Jesse faced him with a laugh.

"Kyle will be delighted to hear that."

"We should have invited him." Cam had considered inviting Kyle earlier but dismissed the idea without mentioning it. He'd selfishly wanted Jesse to himself today.

"Oh, he's been. Many times. Kyle's a regular with all the local distilleries. If you want a guided, guided tour, he's your man."

"Good to know."

"Don't hesitate to hang out with Kyle outside of the club or without me."

Cam contemplated his words with a furrowed brow. "That's the second time you've said that. Are you trying to push the two of us together?" The alcohol made his tongue looser than normal.

Jesse looked startled. "No. I know you guys get along well, and I like my friends to have a good time together."

"Fair enough," Cam said. "Sorry."

Jesse made a humming sound. "Why are you so quiet, Cam? What's up? You've acted a little off at times in the last couple of weeks since the attempt at the threesome happened." His tone was soft and non-judgmental, but Cam still felt guilty. "Are you sure everything's okay with you?"

"I'm okay," he reassured Jesse.

"I didn't mean to push you to let me into your life, but I realized things seemed…" Jesse appeared to search for words. "Unbalanced. But if I pushed too hard, I'm sorry."

"No, no, it's not that. I've had a great time today." Cam wet his lips. "The conversation this morning made me think about a lot of things. And, frankly, I'm feeling like a bit of an asshole."

Jesse furrowed his brow. "In what way?"

"I've been holding you at arm's length," he admitted. He'd tried so hard to keep from getting hurt that Cam hadn't let Jesse in. It was basic self-preservation but unfair. There was being realistic, and there was not giving him a chance.

Jesse's frown deepened. "I'm still not sure what you mean."

"I've been afraid of getting hurt when you get bored and decide it's time to move on, that I've kept you at a distance."

Jesse brushed his thumb across Cam's cheek. "I'd never intentionally hurt you, Cam."

"I know." He swallowed hard. God, should they be having this conversation while he was under the influence? He might blurt out a lot of things he didn't intend. "But you're who you are, and I'm worlds away. I don't mean the money or the job or even where we live. I mean... I don't know." He bit his lip. "Maybe I wanted to protect myself.

"But maybe it's not fair," Cam mused. "What's the point of getting close to someone if you don't let them see who you are?"

"It's been an honor to see what you are comfortable sharing. And whatever else you want to show me in the future. But no pressure from me, I promise."

"Then why don't I finish showing you the rest of the place?" Cam asked. "We can have dinner. You can meet whichever of my roommates are home and see what my life is like. Then spend the night. If you want."

"I'd like that," Jesse said with a smile.

Cam took a deep breath and acknowledged Jesse would break his heart. Cam would let it happen. He'd be realistic about the inevitable outcome. He'd do it with full knowledge of how awful it would be once it was over. But it was either that or let Jesse go. *Go big or go home*, he thought.

* * * *

"This is rather charming," Jesse said after they'd finished the tour, ending with Cam's bedroom. There was barely room for the two of them to stand with the door shut. "I mean, the amount of space in the bedrooms is criminally small, and I don't want to think about sharing a bathroom, but the loft has great bones."

"Thanks." Cam smiled at him. "True loft spaces are getting more and more rare. All of the great ones are getting gentrified by hipsters and turned into these horrible generic luxury lofts."

Jesse snorted. "First of all, your banjo in the living room declares your hipster status. Second, I live in a luxury loft. Third, I had no idea you had such strong feelings about urban architecture."

Cam's answering look was sheepish. "Your loft may be luxurious, but it has character. There's nothing generic about it. My strong feelings about urban architecture are because I like atmosphere. And don't badmouth my banjo, or I'll have to kill you."

"I don't think I could handle the lack of space." Jesse's gaze drifted skyward to the gap between the top of the bedroom walls and ceiling. "Or the lack of privacy. How do you fuck here?"

"Well, I don't, often," Cam admitted. "Or I'm just very quiet." He dropped back onto the bed, and Jesse grinned down at him.

"Tonight should be interesting then."

"Mm-hm," Cam agreed, shifting on the bed. A part of him looked forward to it. Hot, stealthy sex and the possibility of being overheard sent a thrill through him. "It'll be fun."

Jesse's expression turned lascivious. "Oh, Cam, you do realize that's a challenge, right?"

"What is?" Cam licked his lips.

Jesse knelt on the bed between his legs and knee-walked until he hovered over Cam. "Making you moan." He pressed his lips to Cam's throat and licked a path up toward his ear. "Making you scream when you're trying hard to be silent."

Jesse bit his neck, and Cam's whimper became a yelp. He grabbed Jesse's hips and pulled him down on top of him. "I think we're alone right now," he said, his voice going husky. "You could fuck me now." *And later*, he thought.

"You're not actually here alone," Louise called out from the bedroom next to his. "Just so you know. But your guest sounds pretty hot, Cam, so you can keep going if you want."

"Damn it," Cam muttered. Jesse landed on top of him, his body shaking with laughter. "Oof."

"Thanks, Cam's roommate," Jesse called back. "I'll keep that in mind."

"It's Louise."

"Nice to meet you, Louise. I'm Jesse."

"Can I keep calling you Mr. Hot Voice instead?" she yelled.

"Yes, you may!"

"Oh, Christ. I hate you both," Cam muttered.

Jesse managed to stop laughing long enough to kiss Cam's neck. "I take it that's a no, then? We're not having sex right now?"

"Correct." Cam gently pushed Jesse off him. It was one thing to fool around while everyone else slept and try to be quiet. But he didn't want to put on a show for Louise.

"So, what are we going to do?"

"I vote we see if my roommates have had dinner, order a shitload of Thai food and spend an evening drinking with whoever is home."

"Sounds good to me." Jesse drew him in for a lingering kiss before he whispered in Cam's ear, "There's always tonight."

Chapter Thirteen

Someone was using a buzzsaw. No. That wasn't right. Someone was snoring, loudly enough to peel paint.

Jesse checked his watch. Six-thirty a.m. *This is why I live alone*, he thought with an internal sigh. He blinked at the concrete ceiling high above him and felt a mixture of exasperation at being woken and pity for the snorer's sinuses — noises like that couldn't be healthy.

Turning his head, he stared at Cam, who lay sprawled on his stomach with his face smashed into his pillow, sleeping like the dead. Clearly, he'd become immune to the snoring and the host of other noises Jesse now heard echoing through the loft — someone else snoring more softly, a faucet dripping, pipes banging, a whirring portable fan, perhaps.

"Fuck a duck," he murmured. He sat up, mindful of Cam beside him. He needn't have bothered, though, because Cam didn't even twitch.

Jesse smirked. Maybe the drinks he'd mixed the night before were the reason he had his very own life-sized Comatose Cam action figure this morning. Said cocktails were to blame for the slight pain knocking around between his temples, and they'd definitely contributed to the overall hilarity of their evening.

They'd thrown an impromptu party after Cam introduced Jesse around to the horde he came to think of as the DUMBO babes. They called for the takeout Cam promised, and Jesse secretly placed a booze order with Minibar. Cheers erupted when both deliveries arrived at the same time, and Cam's smile warmed Jesse from head to toe. From there, things had gone pretty much as he'd expected, including Cam organizing an aptly named Drunken Noodle Slurping Contest that went straight to sloppy and very giggly hell.

Stifling a yawn, Jesse climbed out of bed. He stretched languorously, relishing the pleasant ache in his muscles, but stopped short after catching sight of himself in the mirror on the back of Cam's door. He stepped closer, staring in the dim light, and his mouth fell open a bit. Half a dozen purple hickeys marked his skin.

Jesse ran a hand over his chest. "Holy shit," he whispered to himself. Cam snorted loudly in his sleep then and made Jesse jump. He clapped a hand over his mouth to stifle his laughter.

Was this real life? Had he really woken up, hungover and in a borough not his own? Surrounded by kids who were at least ten years younger than him? With fucking hickeys on his chest, for Christ's sake?

Jesse went to the old chair in the corner where he'd draped his shirt and trousers, in the process stepping over Cam's clothes, which were strewn over the floor. Once dressed, he grabbed a paper bag from the top of Cam's dresser and quietly let himself out into the large, open area of the loft. He picked his way along the floor, grimacing at the sensation of raw concrete and crumbs on his bare feet. Served him right for not finding his goddamned socks.

Once in the bathroom, he eyed the shower for a long moment before he decided against using it. Somehow, in the cold light of day without a drink in one hand, he understood much more clearly how many people used these facilities. He washed his face and hands at the sink, all the while fighting a strong sense of squeamishness. He finger-combed his hair and felt immensely thankful he'd bought a toothbrush and travel-sized toothpaste after leaving the thrift shop.

"This is why I love living alone," he muttered.

Or maybe you're too old for this shit, a small, sly voice in his head told him. Jesse frowned. He hated that voice during moments like this because it sounded way too much like Will Martin, always the last person to cut Jesse slack for anything. It wasn't like the voice was wrong, either. Maybe the problem wasn't Cam and his slovenly roommates, but Jesse and his money, expectations and, yes, age.

Jesse found the loft quieter when he emerged from the bathroom, either because the snorer had rolled over or because someone had smothered them with a pillow. He went to the kitchen, intent on a cup of coffee, and paused when he saw a petite gray and white striped cat sitting in the middle of the floor.

Funny—he didn't remember seeing the animal the night before. Then again, the combined noise of the DUMBO babes would have sent any animal into hiding. Jesse cocked his head at the cat and grinned at the way it mirrored his movements.

"Hey, you," he said in a low voice. He stepped forward and squatted while the cat uttered a tiny meow, and he ran a hand over its head. While small, the cat appeared clean and well fed. It closed its eyes and leaned into his touch and uttered a low noise when he scritched behind its ears.

"Buy you a cup of coffee?" he offered. "Or maybe you're more a milk type of feline, hm?"

When he stood, the cat's eyes popped open again, and it trotted beside Jesse as he crossed the kitchen. He opened the refrigerator while the cat wound itself around his ankles. He pawed through the leftover takeout boxes looking for a container of mildly spiced khao pad, and the cat meowed again.

"I'll bet you like fried rice, huh?" he asked the cat. "Ooh, yeah. Lots of shrimp and chicken and pieces of egg." He hummed for effect and carried the box to the counter beside the sink, his furry new friend at his heels.

Jesse pulled a saucer and small bowl from the strainer, then reached over the small pile of unwashed dishes and turned on the faucet. He scooped several pieces of meat out of the rice box and quickly rinsed each under the stream of water while the cat rubbed against his shins. It issued a stream of complaining noises as Jesse placed the pieces on the saucer and was nearly frantic by the time he placed the plate and water bowl on the floor. Chewing sounds filled the air, and Jesse turned back to the task of coffee making with a smile.

An hour passed before Jesse heard stirring in the loft. By then, the sun had risen, and he'd started his third cup of coffee. He'd seated himself in a chair by one of the big windows, his feet up on a second chair while the cat—which he'd confirmed was female—purred in his lap. Ten or so minutes after the first signs of life, bare feet padded closer, and he glanced up when Cam ambled in.

Cam was clad only in sweatpants and sporting a spectacular case of bedhead, his thick red hair standing almost entirely up on end. Though his eyes were still half-closed, his expression brightened after he spied Jesse, and he made his way over. Jesse held out his coffee cup, and Cam took it and lifted it to his lips without hesitation. He sighed after he'd swallowed a mouthful.

"Good?" Jesse asked.

Cam lowered the cup and nodded. "Fucking delicious." He stared at its contents. "Did you make this with coffee pods?"

"The only coffee pods I saw are hazelnut flavored. So, no." Jesse wrinkled his nose. "I did find an espresso pot and a can of Cafe Bustelo in the freezer, however. Please, don't tell me how old the can is," he added hastily.

Cam grinned. "You're in luck. Myron's the one who uses the pot, and he goes through a can every couple of weeks."

"Oh, good." Jesse made zero effort to hide his relief, and Cam patted his head. "I mixed the espresso with hot water for Caffe Americano, and there's still a couple of shots left."

Cam glanced at the pot on the stove. "You want me to fix you another cup?"

"No thanks." Jesse ran his fingers over the cat's somnolent body. "Two and a half cups are enough."

Cam furrowed his brows. "How long have you been up?"

"Long enough."

"Couldn't sleep?"

"There was snoring," Jesse replied. "And water dripping, pipes banging, a partridge in a pear tree, and, no, I couldn't sleep."

"Gah, that sucks." Cam leaned down and pressed a kiss against Jesse's lips. "I forget how noisy this place must sound to the uninitiated." The tenderness in his expression sent a shiver of delight through Jesse. "Especially someone who lives alone."

"One person's noises don't bother me," Jesse mused. "Six people, however..."

"Yeah, that's a whole other beast. It took me a while to get used to it, too, and they still wake me up on occasion." Cam straightened up and moved toward the stove with the cup. "I used to sleep with earplugs in, but I don't need to anymore."

Jesse gave him a sly smile. "I'll bet. Four cocktails on top of whiskey probably helps, too."

"Mmm, well, yes." Cam snickered. "What the hell were you making last night anyway?"

"Oh, you mean the drinks you asked me about twice and told me were 'fucking delicious'?" Jesse made wide eyes at Cam, who pursed his lips together against obvious amusement. "Kyle makes them to go with Asian food. Bourbon, gin, citrus juice and ginger beer. I'm not sure he ever named it but I'm thinking of calling it DUMBO Juice."

Cam tipped his head back and laughed. "Please tell me you'll add it to Under's menu," he urged once he'd calmed down.

"With your picture right fucking next to it, Red," Jesse promised. "Oh, before I forget, David messaged. He's doing some fundraising with Carter at Corp Equality next Friday, so he and Will are staying over in the city. They want to go out on Friday night. You wanna come?"

"Can't. I'm spinning Friday and Saturday." Cam went quiet for a moment and poured coffee. "You guys could come by Ember," he suggested. "Carter mentioned you've been pestering him to check it out with you."

"Did he actually use the word 'pester'?" Jesse paused as the cat stretched and uttered a curse when it sank its claws through his trousers and into the meat of his thigh. "Ow-w-w. God. Why are cats such fickle motherfuckers?" He rubbed the fingers of one hand under the cat's chin, and it cuddled in closer again.

"I dunno." Cam rubbed his hand over his hair. "I meant to ask—where'd the cat come from?"

Jesse stared. "Isn't it yours?"

Cam raised his brows. "No. We don't have a cat, Jes. Or didn't when I left yesterday morning. I wondered if maybe you ordered it along with the booze."

"Ha ha." The irritation that surged up inside Jesse surprised him, but he didn't need yet another reminder of the size of his fucking bankroll. "Pretty sure that wouldn't be legal, even for a big money guy like me."

"Oh, jeez." Cam clucked his tongue. "I was kidding, dude. Don't be salty."

"Yeah, okay." Jesse turned his frown on the cat in his lap and met its sleepy green gaze. "So, who the fuck are you?"

* * * *

"And whose cat was it?" David asked.

Almost a week had passed since Jesse's visit to Brooklyn. He'd taken Cam's suggestion and brought his friends to Ember, minus Riley, who'd gone to Munich on business. They were sitting at a VIP table while he told them about the DUMBO loft, and David's eyes gleamed with mirth as he waited for an answer about the origin of the mystery cat. Will and Malcolm were still laughing, along with Kyle, who'd already heard the tale. Carter simply stared at Jesse, one eyebrow cocked high, and the corners of his mouth turned up.

"No one knows." Jesse looked around at his friends. "Best anyone could tell, it climbed in an open window. Cam and his roommates asked around and hung up flyers, but so far, nothing."

"Well, it sounds like you had fun, at any rate," Malcolm observed.

Jesse nodded. "Oh, I did. Despite the redundant hipster vibe."

He'd found DUMBO a blast, actually. He'd mixed drinks while Cam's roommates entertained him with stories, and they'd patiently corrected him the few times he got their names muddled. Louise had suggested Jesse judge the noodle-slurping contest, a privilege he'd accepted in an effort to keep his clothes clean. Naturally, he'd checked out each of the roommates as well. They were all very appealing in their own way, particularly the girl called Bernice, who'd flirted back just as hard. But, with Cam around, Jesse'd had no trouble behaving himself, and Cam had pounced on him after the roommates went out to a neighborhood bar.

He'd practically shimmied up Jesse's body, and they'd hardly managed to peel off each other's clothes before they fell laughing into Cam's bed. Their laughter had devolved into moans as Jesse had tortured Cam, using his mouth and fingers and cock to repeatedly bring Cam to the edge, only to back off before he could reach his peak. Both of them were panting, sweaty wrecks by the time Cam started begging, and Jesse thought it would be a long time before he forgot the way Cam had sounded when he came.

"What happened with the cat?"

Jesse snapped back to the present at Malcolm's question. "I took her home with me because Kevin is allergic to cats."

Malcolm nodded. "Kevin is one of the roommates?"

"Yes," Jesse replied. "I'm the one who found the cat, so I offered to keep her at home until we find the owner."

"Wait a second." Kyle frowned. "I had dinner at your place on Wednesday and didn't see a cat."

"That's because it's now at my place," Carter told him. He narrowed his eyes at Jesse. "Someone decided to come by with their lost cat on Tuesday, a night I had Sadie and Dylan because my ex had a late meeting. The goddamned cat was riding on Jesse's shoulder for crying out loud. You can imagine what happened next."

Malcolm's laughter made his eyes crinkle at the corners. "You adopted a cat, clearly."

"So it would seem. She made herself at home on my shoulder about five minutes in." Carter's wan smile sent guilt coursing through Jesse.

"I didn't know Sadie and Dylan would be there," he explained. "Carter and Ri had them over the weekend, and I figured it was safe!"

"Ding dong, you were wrong," Carter chided. "Anyway, the kids played with her for the rest of the night, and Sadie was in love by the time Kate picked them up. Jesse travels too much to own a pet, so I promised we'd foster the kitty until her owners are found."

"This assumes her owners will be found at all, darlin'," Kyle replied. He patted Carter's arm over the table. "What's Ri say about it?"

"Nothing polite at the moment. He's pissed at me for quasi-adopting a cat without checking with him first, especially since he's out of town until tomorrow." Carter groaned. "But given Miss Zebra doesn't require walking, and Jes had already bought all her supplies, I'm sure Ri will get over it once he meets her."

Jesse couldn't hold back his grin. "Miss Zebra?"

"That's the name she's been given by Lady Sadie." This time, Carter's eyes warmed. "You're lucky I love you, Jes, because, otherwise, I would cheerfully wring that pretty neck of yours."

"You have a way with people, Mr. Murtagh."

Everyone turned to look at Cam, who'd appeared out of nowhere and now stood smiling at the end of their table. He met Jesse's gaze over the others' greetings.

"Hey, Red! I was telling the guys about the cat I found. I don't suppose you've heard from any of your neighbors about her?"

Cam winced. "No. I will absolutely let you know if I do, though."

Carter raised a hand. "You can tell me, too," he said. "The kitty is staying at my place for the time being."

"Oh." Cam looked from Carter to Jesse. "I didn't know she'd moved again."

"It's a long story and all my fault, as usual," Jesse told him. He gestured to the empty seat across the table from him and beside Carter. "Sit down and we can tell you all about it."

Cam shook his head. "I'm on in five, but I'll send one of the waitresses over with a round for you guys. What'll it be?"

Carter waved him off with a smile. "Nothing for me, thanks. More than a drink or two fucks with the medication I take," he said when Cam appeared about to protest. "I'm sure the rest of these degenerates will be happy to take you up on your offer."

Cam collected orders from the table. He'd gone almost silent again after the Brooklyn weekend, leaving messages largely unanswered unless they had to do with the cat now known as Miss Zebra. Whether Cam had been busy or decided he'd distance himself again, Jesse didn't know. He knew one thing, though – the hot-and-cold behavior didn't sit well with him.

"What about you, Jes?" Cam asked, snagging his attention again.

"I'll take a Redhead in Bed." Jesse stared at Cam until Cam rolled his eyes. "Kyle can help the bartenders with the recipe if necessary –"

"I'm sure they'll manage," Cam replied, his tone droll. He turned to go. "Adriana is working your area tonight, and she's a nice girl, so please behave when she comes by."

A chorus of low laughter rang out after Cam moved on, and Jesse found Carter watching him with raised brows.

"What was that?"

Jesse shrugged. "Cam being Cam."

"And are things with Cam being Cam okay?"

"Depends on the week, I guess. Most of the time, we have a lot of fun."

"What about the rest of the time?" David asked.

"Turns out he's moody and kind of shuts down. Said he needs distance to make sure I don't hurt his feelings. Whatever that means." Jesse ran his fingers over his lips. "Not that I plan to, either, but he does what he wants."

"Have you told him about your non-plan to hurt his feelings?" Carter asked.

The sympathetic expression in his friend's big eyes made something in Jesse rebel. He'd gambled bringing his friends here with Cam in a mood. Now he was going to have to fucking talk about it, and he had no desire to do that.

"Yes, I have," he replied and willed himself not to get defensive. "Doesn't stop Cam from giving me the silent treatment if he feels like it."

"You sound put out," Will observed.

"I despise it," Jesse agreed. "I don't know what I'm doing to piss him off in the first place, and, frankly, I don't like walking on eggshells around my friends. It sucks."

"I see." Will smiled. "So, you and Cam are friends?"

"Err, yes." Jesse made a face at him. "Why wouldn't we be?"

"Well, I always assumed your friendships with Carter and Kyle were an exception and not the rule, but then I met Astrid and realized you truly enjoy making friends with the people you fuck."

Jesse stared, mystified by Will's words. "Yes, Will, I suppose I do. Don't you?"

"Sure, but I only sleep with one person at a time," Will replied. Jesse immediately bristled, and Will held up a hand. "That is in no way a slam against you."

"Okay. What is it then?"

"My way of saying you are the shittiest libertine ever. You've got this reputation as the guy leaving a trail of broken hearts all over Manhattan, but I know you well enough now to see that's bullshit." Will cocked his head. "I know you're a decent person. Oddly enough, I think the people you share your bed with would say the same, too."

"Maybe not all those people," Jesse demurred. It was true that not everyone appreciated his unconventional approach to sex.

"I'd wager there'd be more than you'd find with any regular Joe who says he's looking for true love."

"Well, for God's sake, keep your voice down." Jesse sniffed. "It's bad enough you know, never mind blabbing that big mouth of yours all over the city."

Will smirked and the others laughed. Carter rested his foot over Jesse's, providing him with a simple, grounding touch, and Jesse smiled. He'd made the same gesture to Carter many times, and his heart hurt in a wonderful way at the seeming role reversal.

The light in the club changed then, shifting darker and tingeing with red and purple. At the same time, the tempo of the beats pulsing through Ember's speakers changed, too, the bass going deeper and dirtier. It curled in Jesse's gut like a living thing. A dull roar went up from the crowd, and when he glanced at his friends, they were watching the DJ booth. Cam's set had started.

Jesse caught Carter's eye. "You wanna dance, handsome?"

"Oh, God." Carter grimaced. "Six-foot-five is too tall for dancing—you know this."

"I know it's all in your head," Jesse replied. "You dance just fine."

Kyle reached over and tapped Carter's arm again. "Yeah, c'mon, big man. Time to shake your ass." Kyle stopped speaking when an attractive, dark-haired waitress appeared with a tray of drinks.

"Hello, boys," she said with a grin. "Cam told me you're friends of his, so I won't bore you with the usual spiel about accepting drinks with his compliments and yadda-yadda-yadda."

"Thank you, Adriana." Jesse flashed her a smile and pulled out his wallet.

Adriana's expression warmed at his use of her name. "All right, I've got a Sidecar for the politician and a Last Word for the professor."

She turned to David and Will, who rubbed his hands together in anticipation. Next, she set a rocks glass filled with an intensely green cocktail in front of Malcolm.

"Uncle Jalapeño for the cutie with the bright eyes," she said, "and a Maine Maple Lemonade for the corporate guy."

Carter looked at the tall glass garnished with lemon with furrowed brows.

"It's my go-to when I'm on duty and can't have booze," Adriana explained. "They're totally delicious."

She turned to Jesse and Kyle then, and her eyes shone with mischief. "Last but not least, something for the playboy and his partner in crime." The drink she placed between them had been mixed in what Jesse guessed was a mini fish bowl. The vessel held at least twenty ounces and was filled with a beautiful red cocktail and garnished with lime slices.

He raised a brow at Adriana. "And this is?"

"A Redhead in Bed," Adriana said with a grin, then popped two straws into the bowl. "To share."

Jesse met Kyle's eye and the two exchanged a smile over the others' amused laughter. He tipped Adriana but didn't bother telling her the order she'd delivered was slightly wrong. Kyle had requested a French 75. It seemed unlikely Cam had made a mistake, however. He'd obviously been careful with the order and given Adriana a few details about everyone at the table.

No, it appeared Cam had purposely ignored Kyle's drink request in favor of sending Jesse and him a message. And Jesse very much looked forward to following it up.

* * * *

After Cam's set wrapped, he reappeared to join the larger group, and his mood seemed much improved. They ordered another round of drinks and danced some more until Carter, Malcolm, Will and David called it a night. Jesse took Kyle and Cam back to his place for a nightcap, where Kyle mixed up a round of mint juleps in an effort to exploit Cam's newfound appreciation for dark liquors.

Cam eyed the half-empty highball glass in his hand with a pensive expression. "Do either of you ever wonder what might have happened if you'd talked Carter into a threesome?"

Jesse went still at Cam's question. He knew without checking that Kyle had done the same.

Kyle lowered the Boston shaker he'd been agitating and set it down. "No," he replied, his tone wary. "I'm sure we'd have had a hell of a time, but we understood why he didn't want that from us."

"I feel the same," Jesse said. He raised a brow at Cam. "Where are you going with this?"

Cam shrugged. He stepped up and threaded his arms around Jesse's neck. Jesse looped an arm around his waist.

"I watched you both dancing with Carter tonight," Cam said. "And so did everyone else in the club. You were unbelievably erotic together. I mean, you even kept things clean for the most part, but the three of you caught every eye in the place." He licked his lips. "It got to the point I wanted to change places with Carter. To feel what he did with the both of you."

Jesse smiled. He'd noticed Cam watching him dance with Kyle and Carter. Jesse had kept Carter out on the floor for that very reason. "You don't have to change places with anyone, Cam. You're here with us now, and you can do whatever you want."

After a loaded pause, Cam nodded. He held a hand out, and Kyle stepped closer, his eyes locked on Cam's. Cam brought the hand up and traced Kyle's cheekbone with his thumb before he leaned in to kiss him. The first touch of their lips was gentle, but the kiss deepened in a flash, and Kyle's eyes fluttered closed. A low noise rumbled through his chest and that sound made Jesse's cock pay attention.

Cam's grip on Jesse's waist tightened. He watched Cam and Kyle, heat racing under his skin. His breath caught when Cam broke away from Kyle and seized Jesse's mouth with his own. Jesse opened eagerly. He stretched one hand toward Kyle and pulled Cam in tight with the other. His skin prickled at the brush of Kyle's along his jaw. He knew Kyle was licking his way along Cam's neck when Cam moaned into Jesse's mouth.

Kyle curled an arm around Jesse, and the fire burning inside him leaped higher. He tilted his head back and shivered as two hard, eager bodies boxed him in against the counter. Kyle thrust his tongue into Cam's mouth again.

"Oh, fuck." Jesse's cock jerked. Cam broke the kiss and turned to look at him, his eyes ablaze. "You okay with this, Cam?"

"Hell, yes," Cam bit out. "I'm done wanting to know what it feels like to be with both of you."

"Good man." Kyle chuckled. He reached up and ran a hand over Cam's hair before he looked to Jesse. "You okay with this, babe? Because I really am."

"Mm-hm." Jesse leaned in and pressed a kiss against Kyle's lips. "So much more than okay."

The three stayed close as they headed for the bedroom. Jesse fell back to allow Cam to lead the way, but Cam slung his arms around Jesse's and Kyle's waists. Once they were by the bed, Jesse opened his arms and Cam stepped into the embrace while Kyle pressed in close on Cam's other side. They took turns exchanging kisses and pulled at each other's clothes, their breaths growing ragged.

When they were nude, Jesse yanked back again to breathe and watch. The hickeys on his chest were fading, but he suspected they'd all have a few before the night ended. Cam turned his head and kissed Kyle, and the sight sent a bolt of lust straight to Jesse's balls. Jesus fuck, watching Cam kiss another man made him feel like he'd implode.

Kyle wrenched his lips free. He bent and mouthed at Cam's neck, his stare locked on to Jesse's. Cam lolled his head against Kyle's shoulder, his eyes closed and his expression almost desperate. Blindly, he pulled at Jesse's hip with one hand and made a strangled noise as Jesse lowered a hand and palmed him.

"Jes," he whined.

Jesse dropped his arms and scooped Cam up against him, the globes of Cam's ass hot against his palms. He deposited Cam onto the bed, but Cam's back had hardly hit the mattress before Kyle's arms were around Jesse. Kyle kissed him deep and slow. He dug his fingers into Jesse's skin and ground their erections together until Jesse's bones seemed to melt.

"Baby," he moaned against Kyle's mouth.

Cam let out a low curse. "Oh, my God, you two."

Kyle turned Jesse loose, and they climbed onto the bed with Cam. Jesse's body buzzed. He surrendered to the two pairs of hands that manhandled him and quickly found himself sitting on his heels with Cam behind him, his chest pressed to Jesse's back. Kyle settled in between Jesse's spread knees, his big palms grasping Jesse's thighs.

Cam kissed the nape of Jesse's neck, then brought his mouth to his ear. "What do you want, Jes?"

Jesse's chest tightened painfully. "Need you in me." His words ran together in his haste, but Cam understood. Jesse was bursting with the urge to touch and suck and come. With the urge to be filled.

A haze of need settled over him. Kyle scooted backward, freeing up the space in front of Jesse, and together, he and Cam guided Jesse forward onto his hands and knees. Jesse hung his head low and bit his lip in an effort to get hold of himself while Kyle leaned over the bed and opened the nightstand drawer.

Jesse closed his eyes when the bottle of lube clicked open, and his breath wavered at the touch of a cool, slick finger along the crease of his ass. Cam pushed the finger inside him, and the strength ran out of Jesse's arms in a rush, leaving him to drop his forehead down onto his folded hands. A hand rubbed circles into his back, and he moaned under the soothing touch that provided a direct counterpoint to the stretching burn in his ass.

"C'mere, darlin'," Kyle murmured. He lay back against the pillows and guided Jesse down beside him until he lay on his stomach and half on top of Kyle. Jesse held on to his friend, his grip tight.

Kyle kissed him, swallowing Jesse's noises while Cam worked him open. Jesse rutted helplessly against Kyle's thigh until Cam withdrew his fingers, and he wrenched his mouth free with a grunt.

"Cameron."

A condom wrapper crinkled, and Jesse panted, aware of Kyle's thrusts against his hip. At some point, Kyle had slicked himself with lube. Cam nudged at Jesse with the head of his cock, then breached him, and Jesse held his breath through the push. He pressed his face into Kyle's neck and sweat sprang out over his body. Cam began the slow slide home, splitting him in two. All the while, Cam and Kyle held him, anchoring him even as he came apart.

Jesse's mind and body overloaded with sensation. He recognized his own breathless voice asking for more and gasped at the feeling of Cam's body over his own. Cam slid one arm under Jesse's chest and rocked, holding him close. The pain razoring through Jesse bloomed into a delicious ache. Cam's movements ground him harder into Kyle, and Kyle groaned. Blindly, Jesse moved his head, intending to kiss Kyle, and he gasped as two pairs of lips met his. Kyle slipped a hand between them and took Jesse's cock against his own in one slick fist.

Jesse had no idea how long they lay entwined like that, Cam fucking him while Kyle frotted them both. Jesse's body was liquid, and his senses filled with the men surrounding him — the salty taste of Cam's sweat, the sweet smell of Kyle's almond soap, their hot, damp skins and tender-rough touches. God, he was so close.

Kyle stretched his free arm around Jesse's body, searching with slick, unsteady fingers. They came to rest on Cam's cock where it slid in and out of Jesse, drawing a moan from all three men.

"Oh, God. I fucking love this," Cam ground out. The fierce triumph in his voice made Jesse's balls tighten.

He loved it, too. He wanted more. Wanted more of Cam, any way he could get him, and Jesse shivered at the realization. In the next moment, his orgasm screamed through him, knocking both his mind and his body for a loop. Waves of bliss took hold of Jesse, and his back arched hard. The moment stretched and stretched until Jesse thrashed. He held on to his friends for dear life.

He was still dizzy with pleasure when Cam yelled, his grip on Jesse like iron. He pressed his mouth against Jesse's neck and came, panting hard while his movements stuttered and slowed. Kyle gave a great shudder. Jesse forced his eyes open. He caught Kyle's gaze, dark and wild and filled with fire, and reached down to cup his balls. Kyle pressed his head back into the pillow with a moan, Jesse's name on his lips. He came, his mouth going slack and his hips jerking lazily as his cock pulsed. His eyes never left Jesse's.

"Fuck, you two are gonna kill me," Kyle slurred at last. He closed his eyes and let out a low noise when Cam straightened up and pulled him in for a kiss.

Eventually, Cam's and Kyle's movements ceased. Kyle broke away from Cam, his eyes still closed, and nuzzled Jesse's hair with his lips. He wiped his hand on the sheet and gave Jesse a squeeze before going still, his breaths evening out almost at once. Cam roused then, and he shifted back enough to slide out of Jesse. He worked off the condom with a hiss.

Jesse lay quiet, floating on hormones and the lust still simmering inside him. Lazy delight lapped through him when Cam returned and draped his body over Jesse. Kyle snuggled closer. Jesse thought suddenly of the drink order that kicked off this encounter and huffed out a laugh against Kyle's chest.

Cam smiled against his shoulder. "What's so funny?"

"I'm gonna order the Redhead in Bed around you every chance I get," Jesse told him.

Cam gave a dry chuckle. "You get what you want, huh?"

Jesse hummed and closed his eyes. "Always do, Cam. Always do."

Chapter Fourteen

Jesse was sprawled on his stomach, sleeping hard, when Cam awoke. Kyle had left sometime before dawn with a kiss for both of them, and Jesse and Cam had passed out not long after. Cam wasn't sure why he'd woken so early. Maybe his full bladder demanding he do something about it. He slipped out of bed to relieve it, then returned to the bedroom.

He stood in the door for a moment, watching Jesse sleep. He lay with one arm stretched out toward the half of the bed Cam had vacated, and a bolt of panic shot through Cam.

What the fuck was he doing? It wasn't the scattered condom wrappers around the bed that freaked him out or the flashes of images from the night before. He'd loved every fucking second of being in bed with Jesse and Kyle. Having a third hadn't diminished Cam's closeness to Jesse. If anything, it had strengthened it. He'd loved watching Jesse kissing someone else. He'd loved the extra set of hands roaming his body and the feel of another set of lips on his.

But now, in the cold light of day, the need to run crawled across Cam's skin and urged his feet to move. He retrieved his discarded clothing from where he'd dropped them the night before, grabbed his bag and gear and bolted.

Outside of the building, the bright morning sun sent pain shooting through his head, and he squinted. He fumbled in his bag for sunglasses, groping blindly before he closed a hand on the case. He jammed the glasses on his face as fast as he could and let out a small sigh of relief. He'd forgotten his phone charger yesterday, but at least he'd packed sunglasses. He wasn't sure he could face the world without them at the moment.

He was too tired and hungover to walk fast, but he set out for the nearest subway station. He needed the safety of Brooklyn and to figure out what to do next.

* * * *

Later that afternoon, Cam stood in his kitchen, poking around the refrigerator and looking for edible substances, when a sharp rap sounded on the door. He was closest, so he grunted, shut the fridge and walked to the entrance of the loft. He peered through the peephole, expecting a delivery person or the building super on the other side, and was totally unprepared to glimpse Jesse scowling at the door.

"Fuck," Cam muttered under his breath. His heart took off, pounding in his chest. A part of him wanted to walk away and ignore Jesse until the mess swirling around in his head made a lot more sense. But that was childish, and he'd already avoided this conversation once today.

Reluctantly, Cam pulled open the door. Jesse looked so good it made his chest hurt. "Hey," he said. The tightness in his throat made him strain to get the word out.

"You're alive then. I wasn't sure." Jesse's tone was short. "Can we talk?"

"Um, there's no privacy. Several of the roommates are home." Cam stepped into the hall and pulled the door shut behind him. "Let's talk out here."

Jesse swore under his breath. "We would have had plenty of privacy at my place if you'd stayed."

"Sorry. I, uh, had a lot of end of the year stuff to do for school." While technically true, Cam's workload had nothing to do with why he'd left. From the look on Jesse's face, he didn't believe a word of it.

"Is that why your phone's been off and you haven't returned my calls?" Jesse crossed his arms over his chest. The sleeves of his gray button-down shirt were rolled up and showed off his forearms. They were lean and sinewy, and Cam had a sudden vivid flash of those arms braced next to his head as Jesse had fucked him.

He cleared his throat. "Dead battery. It's charging."

Also true, but…

"Oh, come on, Cam. If you needed to get work done, you would have kissed me goodbye or at least left a fucking note." Jesse pressed his lips together into a thin line. "Answer me honestly. Was the threesome with Kyle last night a problem?"

"No!" Cam protested, but his conscience prodded him to be honest. "Maybe."

"Fuck."

"Not the way you think," he argued. "Look, it was hot as hell. I have zero regrets about getting naked with you and Kyle. It just… It made me think about things."

"What kind of things?"

Cam's stomach lurched. Now that he'd had a little time to think, he'd realized a few things. It hadn't been Kyle specifically that had sent the intensity of the night through the roof, although he'd been the perfect third. It had been exploring it with Jesse, the feeling they'd done something significant together, that shook Cam. Because he wanted more. More time with Jesse, a bigger place in his life. But if Cam was realistic, Jesse wasn't on the same path.

There'd be another person in Cam's place at some point. It would be Kyle, or Astrid, or some other new shiny person Jesse hadn't even met yet. Cam would be at Ember or Under, watching him flirt with and take home someone who wasn't Cam. And Jesse wouldn't understand why it would hurt Cam so much.

Cam bit his lip. They were just too different. All of Cam's bravado about risking his heart felt like stupid bullshit in the face of imagining what it would feel like when Jesse walked away for good.

"What things, Cam?" Jesse prompted.

"The kind of things you don't like to talk about. Feelings. What we both want. I don't know."

"You're not making any damn sense, Cam."

"I know." He dragged his hand through his hair. "I'm sorry I took off without saying anything, but I'm struggling right now. I'm not sure I can keep doing this."

"Doing what?"

"Whatever it is you and I have been doing." Cam looked away. "I'm not saying we can't see each other at all, but maybe a cooling-off period is called for."

"What does that even mean?"

"I mean, maybe we should focus on being friends for right now."

Jesse stared at him for a long, silent moment. "Is that really what you want, Cam?"

No, he thought. "Yes," he said aloud.

"Okay." Jesse cleared his throat. "Well, I don't understand a damn thing about what's going on with you right now. And I fucking wish you'd talk to me about it, but I won't force you. If you want to cool off, fine. I won't push you to do anything. If you need space, I'll respect that."

Cam swallowed hard. That was the thing with Jesse. He wouldn't force Cam to do anything. Chasing him down in Brooklyn was more than Cam would have expected. If Cam sent him on his way, that was it. He didn't want to, but he didn't know what else he could do. Because he knew if he spilled everything on his mind, Jesse would run. And friendship would be off the table. At least this way, Jesse wouldn't be totally gone from his life.

"I'm sorry," he said, his tone lame. "I think it's for the best."

"Right." Jesse nodded once, sounding baffled and more than a little irritated. "You set the boundaries from here on out. You know you're welcome at Under anytime, and I'm sure we'll see each other around."

Without another word, he turned on his heel and strode down the hall. Cam's eyes pricked with tears.

He'd done the right thing, though, hadn't he?

* * * *

"Pretty sure I fucked up," Cam said, morose. He stared down into his coffee. He hadn't been able to bring himself to get his usual order of a tall, hot blonde. He'd gone with an Americano. Taryn's pointed look hadn't gone unnoticed, but he'd tried to ignore it.

"I'm gonna need you to back the bus up," she said.

He glanced up at her. "How far back?"

"Somewhere around the place where you had a threesome last night with Jesse Murtagh then bolted. Then he chased your ass down and you said you only wanted to be friends."

"Keep your fucking voice down." Several people at nearby tables gave them sidelong glances. Cam had made a mistake meeting Taryn in a cafe instead of somewhere more private. "I don't want this shit in the gossip column."

"Sorry." She lowered her voice and leaned forward. "What happened? Was it sharing him with someone?"

"No," Cam said slowly. "You would think so, right? But I liked it. I didn't like that I have no idea where my place is in Jesse's life. It's all so tenuous."

"You're not making sense, Cam."

"Don't I know it?"

"So make sense!" Taryn sounded exasperated. "You've never been this wishy-washy about dudes."

"He's not just any dude."

"Yeah, I get that." She sighed. "But I'm starting to think you don't have two brain cells to rub together. You ended things with a beautiful, amazing, rich guy after getting it on with him and his beautiful, amazing, rich friend. Something you enjoyed the hell out of."

"Kyle's not rich," he corrected. "And I'm not into Jes for the money. You know that."

"What the fuck ever. You know what I mean."

Cam swirled the cooling coffee in his cup. "Kyle's not the problem. Group sex isn't the problem. The fact that

Jesse and I want different things in the end is." His throat seized and, for a moment, he couldn't continue. He finally forced the words out. "I think he's strictly looking for fun, and I'm not. I want more."

"You didn't before you met him."

"No, I didn't," Cam admitted. "I just wanted fun, too. But sometimes...sometimes you meet someone who makes you question if you aren't looking for something different. He makes me want more. Someone who is mine. I don't even give a shit if I share him with someone else. I want to know at the end of the day he won't just fucking disappear." Cam's voice cracked and he paused. "I get it. He's not the right guy for me if he doesn't want what I want. And Jesse will never be that guy. He's told me so himself enough times. But I don't know how to stop wanting him to be."

"Well, shit," Taryn said. "Here I thought I'd get all the dirty details of what you three did."

Cam cracked a smile. "Sorry to be a downer."

"Nah, I get it. I'll just imagine myself in your place." She looked off in the distance, a dreamy expression on her face.

"Kyle's not bi," Cam pointed out.

"Shush!" She waved at him. "You're ruining this."

Cam managed a genuine snort of laughter.

"I suppose Jesse is available now, isn't he?" Taryn said a moment a later.

Cam breathed through a sharp stab of pain. "Sure. But he always has been, right? I'm just not in the picture anymore."

* * * *

"Great job tonight, guys!" Cam called after his students. "Don't forget to take home what you left in the classroom! Backpacks, lunch boxes — anything like that."

Two of the kids raced toward his room, disappeared for an instant, then streaked out and down the hall to catch up with their friends. Cam didn't bother to try to get them to walk. With a week left in the school year, the children's spirits were high and Cam couldn't do much to contain them.

Besides, he'd been trying hard not to let his shitty mood infect the kids. He hadn't seen Jesse for several weeks. He would have liked to say it had gotten easier, but it hadn't. He still missed Jesse like hell, and although his head knew this was for the best, his heart wasn't convinced.

Cam had gotten a few texts from the other guys and been glad to realize he wouldn't lose those friendships, too. He and Kyle had even played *Fallout* until Cam was convinced he might hallucinate from lack of sleep. He wanted to reach out to Jesse, suggest they grab lunch or drinks, but he couldn't. Other than a few brief and stilted texts, they hadn't interacted at all.

Yet, Cam wasn't surprised to step through the door of his classroom and see a familiar figure on the far side of the room, examining the photos and biographies of composers plastered on the wall. June's focus had been female composers, primarily women of color. Cam made it a point to explore beyond the usual bunch of old, dead white guys.

"Jesse," he said. He wished his voice didn't sound so strained.

Jesse turned to face him. "Great concert."

"Thanks." He wet his lips.

Jesse looked amazing in a striking soft blue suit with a white shirt, open at the collar. It picked up the silver in his beard, but his usual at-the-ready, charming smile was nowhere to be seen.

Cam couldn't smile either. He'd wondered if Jesse would show up tonight. Cam hadn't seen him during the concert—thankfully—but suspected he'd been there. Of course Jesse would want to support Sadie and Dylan. And here was what Cam had feared would happen before they'd gotten involved. Thank God, the school year was about to end and Cam could take the summer to get over Jesse before he had to do this again.

"I hope you don't mind me being here. Sadie and Dylan invited me, and I didn't want to let them down," Jesse said.

"Of course not," Cam assured him. "It's fine."

Jesse stepped a few feet closer, and the skin on Cam's arms prickled. He wanted to throw himself into Jesse's arms and tell him he'd made a stupid mistake. Instead, he jammed his hands in the pressed trousers he'd put on earlier. Had he subconsciously dressed with care because he'd known Jesse would be here tonight?

"I hate this," Jesse said. "I don't like this awkwardness between us."

"I know." Cam looked away and stared out of the window of his classroom. Although evening, at this time in June, it was still light out.

"I know you're still talking to the other guys, and I'm glad. I don't want whatever happened between us to get in the way of that. But what the fuck, Cameron?" The frustration in Jesse's voice and the use of his full name pulled Cam's attention back to him. "I would like to understand what the hell happened." He stepped closer again. "One minute we were having a great time and the next, you were just gone. You said you wanted a cooling-off period and to be friends, but that's not what this is. This feels like you're done with me. Totally."

Cam swallowed hard. "I know. And I'm sorry."

"Jesus. Stop saying that and talk to me."

"I don't know what to say," he admitted.

"I don't care what you say!" Jesse's voice rose before he looked around and seemed to remember where they were.

Cam strode to the door and closed it. The school was nearly empty, but on the off chance someone walked by, he didn't want them to overhear. He returned to his spot in front of Jesse, and Jesse looked Cam in the eye.

"It doesn't matter what you say. I just want you to say something."

Cam wet his lips. "I'm sorry."

"I don't want another fucking apology," Jesse snapped. "I want to know what's going on. You said you enjoyed what happened with Kyle but that it made you question things. Please explain because I don't have a clue why you're running all of a sudden. I'm making an effort here, but you're not giving me any information. And I feel like an idiot because I don't understand what happened, and you won't tell me."

"Who would have thought I'd be the one to pull a runner, huh?" Cam joked. "I'm sure everyone's money would be on you, under the circumstances."

"Under what circumstances?"

Cam swallowed hard. As much as he didn't want to have this conversation, it would happen anyway. "I...I care about you, Jesse. A lot more than I ever planned on. I wasn't looking for anything beyond a hookup when we met, but things have changed for me."

Jesse regarded him in silence for a moment, clearly absorbing that information. "Okay. And the threesome with Kyle made you realize that?"

"To some degree, yeah. You've told me where you stand on relationships. I didn't expect to have feelings for you and it freaked me out. I couldn't handle the idea of getting my heart broken, and it made sense for me to end it before it got worse, you know?"

"Sure." Jesse's expression was serious. Far more serious than Cam had ever seen him. "I understand that."

"I'm sorry. I know that was never part of the plan."

"It wasn't, no," Jesse said slowly. "I wish you'd told me what was happening, though. I would have liked to have had a conversation about it instead of chasing you around half the boroughs to talk."

"Shit." Cam rubbed his head. "You're right. I've acted immaturely. I kinda panicked."

"Yeah, you did." Jesse sounded tired and frustrated. Pain ran through Cam to know he'd been the one to hurt Jesse in the process. "So, let me be sure I understand what's going on. What do you want from me, Cam? Commitment?"

"I guess. I'm not sure what I want, but I know I can't be one of a number of random people you pick from when you feel like it." The conversation made Cam feel more and more ill by the second. "I know how you feel about being tied down. You don't want anything like what your brother and Sara have, and I get it, Jes. The last thing I want is to ask you for things you can't give me. Or that you might regret down the road." Cam pulled in a deep breath, struggling to keep the emotion out of his voice. "I don't want you to be anyone but yourself."

"I don't know what to say."

"I know." Cam's throat tightened again. "I veered off-script here, and I didn't mean to. But I don't see how I can keep doing this. Not when I want something you can't give me. It'll be too hard."

Jesse nodded. His sad expression made Cam's chest ache.

"Give me some time," he said. "I don't want to lose you as a friend, Jes, but right now it's hard to see you and not want to be with you. I'll be at Under next Thursday night, and we can hang out that way. I need a little space until then. Maybe that'll make being friends a bit easier."

All Cam could do was hope.

"Okay." Jesse gave him a small smile that held none of its usual warmth. "Take care of yourself in the meantime, Cameron."

Chapter Fifteen

Despite his reputation as a careless rogue, Jesse was acutely aware of the emotions of those around him. From a young age, he'd been able to step into a room and gauge the emotional temperature of most of its inhabitants. He also possessed an innate understanding of the energies flowing between people and himself, and how to manage them to achieve his own and others' goals.

These skills made Jesse successful at school and in business, and had also helped him build the personal life he wanted. Because while he didn't put stock in the typical normative alignments of sexual and gender identities, he understood and respected why most people clung to them.

That's why he couldn't wrap his head around why things went so terribly wrong with Cam. Where had their signals crossed?

"I don't want you to be anyone but yourself."

Jesse's stomach curled, like it did every time he remembered their last conversation. He wasn't like most people. He'd been comfortable with that knowledge for a long time, and he never hesitated to be himself. So why did Cam's words hurt so much?

Because you started feeling like there might be more between you than fucking around, Jesse thought. That was true. Things with Cam had started to feel bigger and deeper, and Jesse hadn't known how to handle any of it. Not that it mattered, of course—before he'd had a chance to start figuring it out, Cam was gone.

Jesse pushed away from the desk in Under's office and got to his feet. He paced, and God knows how many circuits he made of the room before the speakeasy's passphrase phone chimed and stopped him in his tracks.

Fuck.

Jesse straightened the heavy black frames of his glasses with one hand. Under's monthly private party had started almost forty minutes ago, and he needed to quit sulking and get out there. He and Kyle were celebrating the bar's first anniversary tonight with the friends and family who'd been there from the beginning. This night—this whole year at the speakeasy—meant a great deal to both of them, especially Kyle. Jesse didn't want to spoil that for him.

He took a moment to throw away the uneaten sandwich Kyle had forced on him earlier and made his way out onto the floor. He moved among the familiar faces, greeting people with all the warmth he could muster. All Under's staff were present, whether on duty or off. Malcolm and his brother Jackson were there, along with Carter's sister and her husband. Astrid had come with Jarrod and Gale, and Eric stood near the bar with Jesse's parents. Eric hugged him and gave him a kiss from Sara, who'd decided to keep the baby bump at home to watch Netflix. Harry and Ellen Murtagh hugged Jesse, too, after practically tearing themselves away from a conversation with Will and David.

"Sorry to interrupt." Jesse chuckled at his parents' wide-eyed expressions. Hot damn if they didn't appear star-struck by Senator Mori.

"Oh, honey." Ellen Murtagh laid a gentle hand on his cheek. Affection warmed her clear gray eyes. "We've been waiting twenty minutes for you to emerge from that office! Although, maybe you were out here all along—I almost didn't recognize you with those glasses hiding your face."

Will's lips twitched in amusement, and Jesse fought off a groan. Ellen had been saying almost those exact words about Jesse's glasses for fifteen years, no matter what kind of frames he wore.

"Eh, my eyes are too dry for contacts. Nothing I can't handle. I see you've met the senator," he added with a knowing grin for David. "Mom and Dad have been asking about you for ages."

"Because we were surprised our liberal son and his friends actually let you in the door," Harry told David. "We assumed they'd mistaken you for someone else."

"I take it your political views run more conservative?" David asked. He raised his brows when all four Murtaghs burst out laughing.

"Harry and Ellen here are so far left they're almost full circle," Eric replied. "They've been registered Democrats for over forty years."

Harry shrugged. His blue eyes, so like Jesse's, gleamed at Eric. "As if you haven't."

"I'm thirty-eight, Dad. So, no, I literally haven't."

Jesse snickered at the way his father flapped a hand in their direction.

"What about you, Jes?" Will furrowed his brow. "I assume you vote blue, but it's not as if we've ever discussed it."

"You're not allowed to discuss politics in polite company, William, or have you forgotten?" Jesse asked, his tone droll. "I vote the best way I see fit, but I'm currently between political parties." He watched Will's expression go flat.

"Of course you are."

"Undeclared. Well, that figures, I suppose." David sniffed. "You certainly do march to the beat of your own drum, don't you?" Amused admiration crossed his face, but Jesse couldn't find it in himself to smile back.

"You're one to talk, babe," he replied. "And it's not hard, with the current crop of presidential candidates."

Regret pulsed through Jesse when David's face fell. Like many Republican moderates, David felt intensely conflicted about the turmoil evident within the GOP. Jesse suspected his friend struggled to envision his future in the party, and that was a sobering idea indeed, particularly during a night meant to be about celebration.

He slipped an arm over David's shoulders. "Time for a drink and a topic change," he declared. Jesse sought out Will's gaze, and they shared a smile. "I'll send a round of trouble over while Will tells everyone all about Senator Sexy's fantastic dance moves."

David's cheeks flushed red. "I hate you so much," he muttered over Will's laughter, but he was chuckling when Jesse let him go.

At the bar, Jesse found Carter and Riley seated with someone he didn't recognize. They were watching Kyle at work with Masen, his second in command. Masen was agitating a shaker while Kyle addressed a line of tulip glasses. As always, he looked both beautiful and capable, but the line of Kyle's shoulders seemed tense under his black shirt, and a slight frown marred his face. Jesse's chest tightened. Kyle looked stressed, and that just would not do.

He glanced up when Jesse drew close and his expression lightened, especially the shadows in his deep brown eyes. He stood straight, his fingers around the neck of a clear bottle filled with deep red liqueur, and smiled when Jesse extended a hand.

"Need a hand, gorgeous?" Jesse asked.

"I'd love one. I wondered if I'd see your handsome face," Kyle replied. He handed Jesse the bottle and gestured to the tulips. "Three or four tablespoons in each, if you wouldn't mind."

Working together, they turned out a half-dozen Kir Royale cocktails, lighting up Kyle's homemade Crème de Cassis with pale gold champagne and fresh raspberries. They handed out the glasses, and the act lessened Jesse's burden, as did the kiss Carter planted on his cheek and Riley's pat on his shoulder.

Kyle handed him a tulip. "I'm glad you're here," he said, his tone gentle. He tapped his glass to Jesse's.

"Not half as glad as I am that you are, too." Jesse smiled. He was immensely grateful for Kyle and their friends, the two men grinning at him on the other side of the bar in particular.

Make that three men on the other side of the bar because the stranger beside Riley was grinning, too. Jesse thought he also looked familiar with his dark hair and attractive features. Particularly his brown eyes, which were dark and framed by long, sooty lashes and strong brows.

Jesse glanced at Kyle, who curled an arm around his waist. His friend looked excited, and Jesse abruptly noticed the man seated beside Riley looked a lot like…

"Whoa." Jesse's mouth fell open, and the men around him burst into laughter.

"Jes, this is my brother, Oliver," Kyle said over the noise. He beamed as Jesse and Oliver shook hands. "Ollie, this is Jesse, my business partner—"

"And partner in crime," Oliver said at the same time as Jesse, prompting more amusement from the group.

Jesse dropped Oliver's hand and glanced between him and Kyle with genuine delight. He'd never met any of the McKees. Kyle's father had passed away years ago, and his interactions with his mother were civil at best. He hadn't been back to his tiny hometown of Swanton, Vermont in the almost two years Jesse had known him either, even during their trips to Eric and Sara's second home near Burlington. However, Kyle spoke often with Oliver, who taught English as a Second Language in schools around the East Coast.

Jesse poked Kyle in the ribs. "Dude, you should have told me your brother was coming."

"He didn't know," Oliver threw in. "He invited me, but I've been in North Carolina since April, and my schedule's super hectic. I didn't know if I'd get up here at all until yesterday."

"Then you're a rock star for making it," Jesse replied. "Especially since I take that to mean you drove eight hours?"

"I took a bus, and it sucked." Oliver nodded as the others groaned in sympathy.

Jesse patted Oliver's hand where it rested on the bar. "You definitely need another drink, my friend. And a hug, a good steak and maybe a session in a decon shower."

"I can help you with one of those things right now," Kyle declared. He set down his glass and moved toward the racks of bottles, his eyes shining bright.

* * * *

Jesse's mood mellowed as the evening went on. He wasn't happy, exactly — there were too many jumbled-up feelings in his head to allow him to let go and enjoy himself. But it felt amazingly right to look around the speakeasy and recognize the fruits of his and Kyle's work and allow the good spirits of his friends to buoy him along.

He didn't fool everyone, however. He'd caught Eric frowning at him a few times. And Carter gave him a searching kind of look when they joined Malcolm and Jackson in one of the seating areas. Kyle had been watching Jesse like a hawk, too. No surprise there. Cam's disappearing act had left Jesse feeling unbalanced. His sleep had suffered and his appetite had disappeared, and being around other people's drama made him feel more than a little stabby.

At least I don't have to deal with other people's drama tonight, he thought, then immediately wanted to kick his own ass. Because that was the moment Cam showed his face again, and goddamn if he didn't look fantastic in that stupid gray leather jacket he insisted on wearing despite the summer heat. Cam had a friend with him, too. A pretty red-haired girl with nice legs and what appeared to be a smoking body under her little black dress. Jesse could have sworn the king and queen of a Goth prom had rolled in the door, but he knew better.

"Fuck a duck," he muttered.

"Oh boy." Carter eyed Cam and his friend, who were chatting up Kyle at the bar. "She works at Midtown Academy, too, by the way. She's the art teacher."

"Of course." Jesse barked out a laugh. "What the hell kind of school do you send your kids to, man?"

"One that belongs in a soap opera on the CW, apparently." Carter swirled his limeade. Kyle had dressed it up with ginger and blackberries, and Carter appeared to be enjoying it very much.

"You really watch that station?" Jesse asked.

"I do when Sadie is in the house and *Supergirl* is on, yes." Carter knocked shoulders with Jesse and tilted his head toward the bar. "You want me to run interference for you?"

Jesse blew out a weary breath that did nothing to lessen the way his insides twisted. "Nah. Cam's got every right to be here. He's friends with Kyle and you and the other guys. He's still my friend even if we're not what I'd call friendly right now."

"Friends call each other," Carter replied in a dry tone. "Sometimes, they check in to make sure everyone's okay. Like, say, after they've been shouting at each other behind closed doors." He lifted a brow at Jesse's snort of laughter.

"You know, you're adorable when you're playing Mama Bear." Jesse patted his friend's hand. "I did the shouting that day, and shame on me for losing my temper. Cam asked me to back off and give him space, so I did. We both needed time to cool off anyway."

Carter nodded. "Do you feel better now that you've cooled off?"

"Nope." Jesse swallowed a healthy sip of the Rusty Nail he'd been nursing and watched Cam and his friend approach.

"Hey, guys." Cam's manner seemed a touch hesitant, and his gaze skipped over Jesse, as if trying to avoid direct eye contact. The same couldn't be said of his friend, who stared at Jesse with undisguised curiosity.

He showed them both a smile. "Hey, Red. Long time, no see."

"Uh, yeah." Cam cleared his throat. "Kyle told me tonight was more than the usual get-together and I didn't want to miss it. Congratulations on your first year," he added. He finally met Jesse's eye and the sincerity in his expression eased the knots inside Jesse a little.

"Thanks. It's nice to be able to celebrate Kyle's hard work." Jesse stood and offered his hand to the girl at Cam's side. "I'm Jesse Murtagh. Welcome to Under."

The girl smiled and shook his hand, and Cam's face flushed a hectic shade of red. "Oh, jeez, my bad," he said. "Jesse, this is my friend Taryn Guillory."

"It's nice to meet you," Taryn said. "I hope it's all right I crashed your party," she added. "I sort of forced myself on Cam when he told me about the party tonight."

"Cam's friends are welcome, of course," Jesse replied.

Cam licked his lips. "Taryn and I work together at Midtown Academy," he said.

"Yes, Carter mentioned that." Jesse watched with interest as Cam grew even more flustered. Taryn turned a grin Carter's way without missing a beat.

"Hi, Mr. Hamilton."

"Hello, Miss Guillory," Carter replied with a wave. "Ri — er, Mr. Porter-Wright should be along soon if you haven't seen him yet." Carter then introduced Taryn to Malcolm and his brother, which left Jesse and Cam staring at each other.

Jesse stepped away from the sofa and waved Taryn toward his seat. He raised his eyebrows at Cam then pointed at an empty table nearby, hoping to give them some privacy and keep things minimally awkward.

"How are you, Jes?" Cam's expression became somber. "I like… I didn't know you wore glasses."

Okay, things were actually maximally awkward.

"I don't wear them unless the mood strikes me or my eyes are dry," Jesse replied. "And I'm well, thanks. How've you been?"

"I've been okay. Busy wrapping up the school year and figuring out how much I can work over the summer."

"Oh, yeah? What are your options — summer school and that kind of thing?"

"Mmm, no." Cam propped his elbows on the tabletop. "Elementary school students can't fail music unless they make zero effort or are disruptive. Some people aren't wired to be musically inclined in any way, and it's not fair to punish them because they're literally unable to make music. So there's not much in the way of remedial lessons. I've been thinking of offering music tutoring services, though."

"Makes sense. And you'll be spinning a lot?"

"That's the plan." Cam smiled. "The gig at Ember is steady, and I'd like to pick up another one maybe two nights a week. What's been going on with you? Traveling a lot?"

"I'm flying to London again tomorrow night to start finalizing the internet radio acquisition. I'll be back and forth for the next several weeks." Jesse swirled his drink. "Living out of a suitcase is a pain in the ass, but London's nice, and I have friends there."

"Right. Friends of Astrid's." Cam's features shifted into a smirk that made Jesse want to groan. He hadn't seen that pinched, fake expression on Cam's face in a long time.

"Mina and Niall and a few others are friends of Astrid's, yes. I reconnected with an old friend from New York, too. His name is Isaac. He moved to London earlier this year, and we've messaged back and forth for a while now. Finally made plans for dinner."

Cam cocked his head, his expression considering. "Isaac, huh? I don't think you ever mentioned him."

Jesse blew a breath out through his nose. "We lost touch for a bit. Which sucked because I missed him." He raised a brow at the doubt that crossed Cam's face. "What? I'm capable of missing people I care about, Cam. Isaac and I went out together for almost a year, for Christ's sake — it'd be crazy if I didn't miss him."

Cam's jaw dropped. "A year? You" — he pointed at Jesse — "were in a relationship with another person? For a year? But you don't do relationships!"

"Obviously, I don't do them well," Jesse muttered. "I saw other people, too, but yeah, we were together. Isaac was always good at getting me to try new things. That asshole."

"So, what happened?"

I hurt him, Jesse thought grimly. *I broke Isaac's heart and he broke mine right back.* He uttered a rough laugh and shoved his glasses higher onto his nose.

"What you'd expect," he told Cam. "I fucked up. Isaac called it off, and we didn't talk for a while. So, yeah, I missed him." That description didn't even scratch the surface of what had gone down between Isaac and himself, but that was beside the point. And Jesse wasn't in the mood for a therapy session.

A piercing whistle split the air, halting Cam's reply and every other conversation in the bar, too. Jesse wheeled around and almost dropped his drink when he saw the normally reserved Kyle at his usual station behind the bar but somehow standing head and shoulders over everyone else in the room.

"What the fuck?" Jesse asked himself.

Kyle spotted him and broke out in an enormous smile. He gestured at Jesse with his glass. "Jes! Come up here, man. I'm in the mood to say a few words!"

"Oh, boy, I can't wait!" Jesse called back. He crossed the room, his obvious surprise prompting a wave of laughter. He joined in after he realized Kyle was standing on a cooler he used to store liqueurs in progress. Quickly, he reached up and grabbed Kyle by the waist to keep him steady.

"I started planning to open a bar even before I moved to New York," Kyle told the crowd. "But I was broke, of course, and the more I worked, the less time I had to move the plan out of my head and off the ground. Before I knew it, I'd been here a couple of years and I wasn't any closer to getting my bar. One night, Jes and I got together for pizza and beer, and he asked me what I wanted to be when I grew up."

Jesse groaned. "Dude, you're drunk."

"Only a little!" Kyle ran his free hand over Jesse's hair. "Doesn't change the fact I love you, Big Money."

"And I love you back, babe," Jesse replied without hesitation.

Kyle turned to the crowd. "I told Jes about my idea for a bar, and he somehow convinced me to take him on as a partner. A year ago, we opened Under. He'll be the first person to tell you that I do all the hard work, by the way."

"That's because it's true!" Eric hollered. Jesse rolled his eyes at his brother, and raucous laughter rang out, but Kyle held up a quelling hand.

"I do a lot of the work out here, sure, where all of you can see me," he said. "I have the freedom to do that because Jes is holed up out back, using his big brain to grow the business and make it better. Plus, he handles the press, the lawyers and the accountants, and I hate all that shit."

Jesse gasped theatrically. "You love the press!"

"You know, that's true, but I'm almost done, so hold your horses." Kyle squeezed Jesse's shoulder.

"Under wouldn't be the place it is without the two of us, Jes, but it wouldn't exist at all if you hadn't helped me turn my idea into something real. For that, and everyone here tonight, I am very, very grateful."

Kyle raised his glass to Jesse and the people gathered around them, his eyes aglow. "To paraphrase a toast my dad's family has used for generations, 'May this bar always be too small to hold all our friends.'"

Jesse raised his glass, and their loved ones did the same, and his whole being filled with pride. He swallowed a mouthful of whiskey under the cacophony of good wishes that tumbled over them, and Kyle hopped off the cooler and pulled Jesse into a hug. For a moment, Jesse forgot about the words and thoughts and feelings that had dogged him for weeks.

He shared a kiss with his friend instead and counted himself a lucky man indeed.

* * * *

An hour after Kyle's toast, Jesse slipped back inside Under's office. The party was in full swing but he struggled to ignore the keen, brown-eyed stare that seemed to follow him everywhere, and he needed a moment to regroup.

Jesse moved to the small bar cart he and Kyle kept stocked and picked up a bottle of Glenmorangie single malt. He'd unscrewed the cap when the door snicked open again, and the buzz of house music and many conversations filled the room. Jesse hauled in a breath. He waited for the door to close again and shut out the party noises and pasted an easy expression on his face before he turned around. However, he didn't bother hiding his surprise when he spotted Taryn by the door, a drink in one hand while the other rested on the doorknob.

"Whoops." Her eyes were wide. "I totally thought this was the restroom."

Jesse raised a brow. "The restrooms are totally in the hallway behind the bar," he said, his tone light. "Go left past the coatroom, and you can't miss the signs."

"Ah, thanks."

Taryn held his stare for a long moment before she glanced at the room around her. Jesse looked her up and down without shame. He hadn't spoken with her outside of welcoming her to the bar, but he'd certainly noticed her loveliness. Now, as he watched her in the low light, a bland amusement filtered through him. He didn't know what she wanted, but he thought it obvious she wasn't in the office by accident.

"Cam's been talking up this bar since the spring. I can see why, too — it's fantastic." Taryn stepped away from the door. "Not that I don't see PR online, too, of course. By the way, is it a requirement that everyone who drinks here be gorgeous?"

"Thank you." Jesse turned back to the task of making his drink. "A gorgeous face isn't a requirement, but no one here's going to complain about it, either." He poured two fingers of Scotch into a rocks glass while Taryn moved around the room, and his skin prickled with awareness when she drew near. She stood close enough that he could smell the tantalizing mix of vanilla and amber in her perfume.

Jesse looked up and found Taryn's eyes on him. He nodded at the tulip in her hand. "I'd offer you a drink, but I see you've got that covered."

She grinned. "I'm okay, yeah. I'm not much of a Scotch drinker, anyway. Too much smoke and wood for my palate."

"It's an acquired taste for some," Jesse agreed. "But that's all right. Makes sharing a good bottle with someone you like even more pleasurable."

"I see." Taryn inclined her head toward the leather sofa on the opposite side of the room. "You mind if I sit down? These heels are higher than I should have worn tonight."

Jesse waved her on. "Of course, make yourself comfortable." He followed her across the room, his eyes on her ass while a prickle of irritation grew in his chest. This girl was very attractive, all sparkling eyes and creamy skin, not to mention that tight body. Sadly for

Jesse, his head and heart weren't on board with her seduction routine.

Taryn set her drink on the side table as they sat and pulled the evening bag she carried over her shoulder onto her lap.

"What are you doing in here, Jesse?" She bent forward and massaged one ankle with her fingers. "Shouldn't you be out playing the good host?"

Jesse hummed. "They won't miss me for a bit. People come here for the drinks and the bartenders have that covered. Besides, you heard Kyle earlier—it's not unusual for me to spend time in here during business hours."

"Even at your own anniversary party?" Taryn cocked a brow. "I find that hard to believe. Maybe you need a distraction to take your mind off whatever's got you hiding out."

"I'm hardly hiding."

"Mmm, I think maybe you are." Taryn straightened back up and opened her bag. She pulled out a cigarette case and opened it to expose several thick joints. "Care to smoke? I have some Molly if you're not into weed."

"No, thank you, and please put that away." He gave her a tight smile. "Under has a strict no-drugs policy."

"Oh?" She frowned down at the case. "Cam never mentioned that."

"He shouldn't have had to." Jesse set his glass on the table. "You seem like a smart girl—every nightclub and bar in this city has policies against illegal substances. Under is no different."

"Not even in the co-owner's office?"

A chill fell over Jesse at her knowing expression. "Especially in this office."

"Oh, fine," Taryn grumbled. She dropped the case into her lap and brought one hand up to his shirt collar. "I still say you need a distraction."

"I'm good, thanks." Jesse drew a deep breath in through his nose and tried not to tense at the touch of her fingers along his collarbone. He just wasn't in the right state of mind for games tonight. Not to mention Taryn and Cam were friends, and something was off in the way things were going down.

It felt wrong.

"I need to get back out there," he said and gently stayed Taryn's hand with his own.

"Oh, come on, sit with me for another minute." She slid closer. "I can cheer you up if you'd let me, you know. Plus, I'll owe Cam twenty-five bucks if I go out there admitting defeat."

Ice flooded Jesse's body. "What did you say?"

"Cam and I made a bet I could put a smile on your face before the end of the night. Well, I bet that I could, and Cam bet I couldn't." Taryn moved close enough to press her hip against his. "It was a friendly wager — no need to look so shocked."

The words "Cam and I made a bet" were still processing in Jesse's brain when the door to the office swung open again and noise from the party spilled over them. He turned to see Cam step inside, and his thunderous expression didn't do a thing to melt the cold in Jesse's veins. The air practically buzzed with energy as Cam shut the door behind him.

"What the fuck is this?"

Jesse remained silent while Taryn pulled her wrist from his grasp and straightened against him.

"Hey, Cam. Jesse and I were just talking."

Jesse tore his focus from Cam and focused on Taryn. Despite her smile, the warmth didn't reach her eyes. She sobered at Cam's harsh laugh.

"Yeah, I can see that. Talking is how it starts, right, Jesse?" Jesse met Cam's hard gaze. "A couple of drinks, some easy conversation, no pressure and no promises." He shook his head. "I don't even know why I'm surprised."

"Cam," Taryn started, but Cam cut her off.

"You know what, scratch that." He glared at her. "I am surprised you're here. Jesse was always going to pull the rug out from under me sooner or later. God knows he's screwed half the people out in that bar, so the odds are he'd screw one of my friends, too. But I expected more from you, Taryn. You know better. I expected you to at least respect our friendship enough to not let this happen."

Something in Jesse's chest cracked as Cam's scrutiny returned to him again. It was all he could do to not wrap an arm around himself and soothe the hollow ache inside him. Anger and sadness mingled in Cam's expression, but the raw hurt in his eyes made Jesse's throat tighten. Cam might be mistaken about what he'd walked in on, but, in the end, it didn't matter. He thought Jesse didn't care about him at all, not as a friend or as a lover. Fuck, Cam didn't even think he was a good person.

Jesse did care about Cam, far more than he'd expected to. But maybe Cam had a point. Because a good person didn't hurt his friends the way Jesse had hurt both Isaac and Cam.

Jesse stood and pulled his phone from his pocket, dimly aware of Cam and Taryn arguing. He focused on keeping his breaths even while he tapped at the phone's screen to call a Lyft. Next, he sent a message to Jim, Under's head of security. He'd just tucked his phone away before the office door opened, and Cam and Taryn fell silent.

"What can I do for you, Mr. Murtagh?"

Jim's Boston accent sounded unusually sharp. He almost never called Jesse by his full name, and, though his expression remained neutral, Jim's light brown eyes held real concern when Jesse faced him. And for good reason. Jesse had never summoned security to the office before.

"Jim, Miss Guillory needs a ride home. Please escort her upstairs and wait with her for the Lyft that should be here in six minutes. And please use the back exits— we need to avoid disrupting Kyle's party as much as possible."

Taryn got to her feet. She exchanged a wide-eyed glance with Cam, who appeared even more stunned.

"I'd appreciate it if you didn't come back here, Taryn." The color drained from her face, and she fumbled with her cigarette case and bag. He turned his back on her and Cam even as Cam said Jesse's name.

"You may not have noticed," he continued, "but there's a security camera over the door. We store that footage to ensure no one misinterprets the actions of Under's staff when they're in this room, particularly Kyle's and my own."

"Jesse," Cam said again, and this time the strain in his voice forced Jesse to face him. Cam's face had paled, and he appeared completely shell-shocked.

Shit. No surprise there. These days, Cam never looked happy around him.

"You should go, Cam." Jesse tried on a smile so he could show Cam he wasn't angry at him, but the muscles in his face wouldn't cooperate. "You can share the Lyft with Taryn, or I'll call another if you have plans. Whatever you like."

Cam stared at him for a long moment before his whole body seemed to droop. "Okay."

Jesse fought off a wave of nausea at the turmoil in Cam's face. Jesus, he was tired. He met Jim's eye as Taryn slung her bag over her shoulder, and they exchanged a nod. Jim led Taryn and Cam out, but Jesse turned away before the door closed behind them.

He felt heartsick. Whatever Cam and Taryn had been up to tonight, he blamed himself and not them. He spoiled everything eventually, like he had with Isaac and now Cam. It didn't matter that Jesse still didn't know how he'd fucked things up with Cam. Just that he had.

Now he'd spoiled Under. It was just another place where he'd fucked up and caused people he cared about pain.

He lifted a hand and rubbed his burning eyes beneath his glasses.

Yeah. It had only been a matter of time before Jesse spoiled Under, too.

Chapter Sixteen

"Want a ride?" Taryn asked quietly. Cam shook his head. He didn't know what to make of what he'd seen in Jesse's office.

"C'mon, talk to me," she pleaded. She tugged at his sleeve while the bouncer, Jim, stood silent and watchful nearby.

"Not right now, Taryn." He shrugged her off and kept walking. At the moment, Cam couldn't stand to look at her. Rather than hop on the 1 train at the One Hundred Sixteenth Street station, he walked for a while, moving downtown along Broadway. He needed to burn off the restless energy and hurt boiling up inside him. It was difficult enough to think of Jesse hooking up with someone else, but Taryn of all people? Worse, Cam had seen them together. The sight was more painful than any physical blow.

Truthfully, he'd expected better of both of them. He'd expected Jesse to not rub any new hookups in Cam's face at Under and assumed Taryn knew how much it would hurt him. He'd been wrong.

The walk did nothing to soothe Cam. By the time he'd gone several miles and reached the far border of Central Park and Columbus Circle, he was still as hurt and angry as he'd been when he left Under.

For almost a week after the debacle, Cam felt numb. He went through all the normal motions of his day-to-day life, but it was a blur. He packed up his classroom for the summer, did a gig at Ember, then didn't get out of bed for a few days except to shuffle to the kitchen or bathroom. Myron gave Cam a wide berth, no doubt assuming he was sick, but the rest of them offered sympathy he couldn't stand to hear after he told them he and Jesse weren't seeing each other anymore.

In between sleeping, he listened to music, grimly amused by the fact that he'd compiled the perfect breakup playlist in his head.

Since then, Taryn had left him a handful of texts, but he hadn't been able to bring himself to talk to her.

He'd had no messages from Jesse.

That silence wasn't surprising, but it still made Cam's heart hurt. Despite his anger with Jesse, Cam missed him like hell.

Cam tried hard to put together the pieces of what had happened that night, but none of it made sense. His brain whirled with images of Jesse and Taryn pressed together on the sofa, her hand on his chest, his hand covering hers. Jesse's hurt expression when Cam accused him of pulling the rug out from under him. The strain in Jesse's voice as he'd asked Taryn to leave. The tight smile when he'd asked Cam to do the same.

Eventually, he admitted to himself he needed to read Taryn's texts. He'd only get half the story, but maybe it would clear up some of his questions.

Cam took a few deep breaths, then steeled himself to read the messages. They were apologetic, and Taryn claimed Cam had misinterpreted what he'd seen. He scoffed at the idea, but the thought nagged at him while he did laundry and went to the grocery store instead of ordering takeout again. Questions dogged him until he texted her back.

They exchanged a few messages, and Cam agreed to meet her the following afternoon so they could talk, on the condition of complete privacy.

He'd never dreaded a conversation more in his life and almost turned back at least three times on the way to Taryn's apartment. He knocked on the door with a churning in his stomach. Taryn looked subdued when she answered. She'd dressed far more simply than usual, and the only other time Cam had seen her without her signature red lipstick was the time she'd come down with a nasty, lingering cold and he'd dropped off meds he'd picked up from the pharmacy and chicken soup from the deli next door.

"Thanks for coming over," she said. "Coffee?"

"Please."

Taryn poured coffee into mugs and Cam sat at the little table by the window with a charming view of an alley with a dumpster. "Are the roommates gone?" he asked, fiddling with a pair of vintage owl salt and pepper shakers.

"Yeah, I asked them to clear out." She set a mug in front of him and took a seat across the table.

"Thanks," Cam said. "I didn't want to risk someone overhearing."

"Isn't it a little late to be worried about Jesse's privacy? We talked about you hooking up with him and Kyle in a cafe."

"That was a mistake. Being pissed and hurt doesn't mean I've stopped caring about him."

Taryn winced. "That's why I wanted to talk to you." She wrapped her hands around her mug and stared down into it. "You misunderstood what happened."

"Okay." Cam rubbed his head, not quite sure how to process that statement. "But why did you have to come on to him, Taryn? Of all people."

"Come on, you knew I thought he was hot," she said, sounding defensive. "And you told me he was free to see anyone."

Cam recalled their conversation at the cafe a few weeks ago. "Fuck, I did. I thought you were joking, though. If I'd known you were serious…"

Taryn let out a small, brittle-sounding laugh. "You're also the one who took me to meet him."

Cam closed his eyes, realizing he'd brought on much of what happened. Taryn and Jesse were both flirtatious people. What had he expected, putting them in the same room together? He wasn't happy with either of them, but he should have known better. "Yeah, well, you hounded me for days to take you, and I agreed because I needed a buffer," he explained. "I didn't think I could handle seeing Jesse without someone there who was on my side. Everyone else there started out as his friend."

"I didn't think it through." She was silent for a moment, staring down into her coffee. "I think maybe I wanted a shot at him so bad I didn't see what was actually happening. I'm sorry, Cam. You shouldn't blame Jesse for any of this."

"I get that you feel bad, but you don't have to defend him. He's all about the conquest. And I should have seen this coming."

"No, you don't get it. Jesse didn't do anything. I initiated it all, and he wasn't having any of it. I followed him in there, Cam. What you saw when you came in was Jesse, well, turning me down."

Cam stared at Taryn, open-mouthed.

"It gets worse." She looked miserable. "I kinda led him to believe you knew I went in there and that we'd made a bet to cheer him up."

Cam listened intently while Taryn described what happened. "A bet to cheer him up? God, what the hell? I would never —"

"I know. I was just trying to lighten the mood. I — I had no idea he'd take me at my word."

"Right," Cam said, stunned and still trying to absorb what he'd learned. "I don't even know what to say. Jesse's had people use him before to get what they want. He must have thought you were doing the same. Maybe that *we* were doing the same... Fuck!"

Taryn winced. "Look, it's shitty I tried to poach your friend with benefits, but I had no idea it would set off this chain of events."

"You threw a metaphorical grenade in what was already a fucking disaster. That part was my fault," Cam said, his tone bitter. "I'd already done plenty to fuck things up."

Taryn twisted a lock of hair around her finger. "I hope you know how sorry I am."

"I know you are," Cam said. Taryn was selfish and thoughtless — more so than he'd ever realized — but he wouldn't call her deliberately cruel.

"I guess it was my turn to make bad choices." Her tone was joking, but it fell a bit flat.

"Yeah, okay. But I'm still baffled about the way everything went down."

"I feel terrible." Taryn wiped at the corners of her eyes. "I'm so embarrassed about the way I behaved. I can't believe I got both of us kicked out."

"That surprised me. I've never seen Jesse have someone escorted out," Cam admitted. "Even if he was upset because he thought we'd made a bet, it seemed over the top."

Taryn looked up at the ceiling. "I, um, offered him drugs."

"Seriously? What the fuck?"

"It was just pot and Molly, Cam. Christ. And it's a fucking bar! How could I have known he'd be the kind of owner with a stick up his ass about that sort of thing?" She sounded defensive again.

Cam had dropped Molly a few times, but he wasn't crazy about the way it made him feel, and he'd never done it while spinning. The presence of drugs at Under wasn't a small thing in Jesse's and Kyle's eyes. What part about that did Taryn not get?

"Jesse and Kyle could get into serious shit if drugs were found on the premises, Taryn."

"I'm not saying it was the best choice, but they've got more money and power than they know what to do with. They'd be fine."

"Jesse might, sure. But Kyle doesn't have his kind of wealth or power," Cam snapped. "And neither do the bartenders and other people who work there. Sure, they're paid well, and Jesse would do whatever he could to protect them, but I'm not surprised he was angry. Jesus. Under is his sanctuary. You brought in something that could threaten it. His reaction makes perfect sense now."

"I think you're both making way too big a deal out of it," Taryn protested.

A thought occurred to Cam, and he felt ill. "Please tell me you're not bringing shit like that into the school."

"What? No! Don't be insane, Cam. I miscalculated things with Jesse and the speakeasy, but I'm not a total idiot. What if the kids got into it?" She shuddered. "Besides, I love my job. I don't want to lose it."

"Yeah, well, that's how Jesse and Kyle feel about Under. Did you stop and think about that?"

"Fuck." A look of remorse crossed Taryn's face. "No, I didn't, and that was stupid of me."

Some of Cam's residual anger at her leached out of him at her troubled expression. "Like I said, things were already complicated," he admitted. "This just made it worse."

"I'm so sorry," she said.

"I know. I believe you, and you've apologized enough. But I need you to do one more thing."

"What's that?"

"Promise me nothing to do with any of this has been leaked to the press or could be in the future."

Taryn shook her head vehemently. "No. I haven't said anything to anyone, I swear. And I won't. Promise."

Cam didn't stick around much longer. He told Taryn he'd call her when he wanted to hang out again, but he didn't think that would be anytime soon. It would be a while before he could totally forgive and forget. Perhaps the other teachers at Midtown had been right about her all along. Cam had just been blind to it.

The first thing Cam did after leaving Taryn's place was text Kyle.

I think I fucked up.

It didn't take long for him to get a response.

I think you and Jesse both need to be better at communicating.

To say the least. I don't want to put you in the middle of this but is it out of line to ask for advice on how to fix shit?

He wanted to message Jesse, but he also wanted to be sure he wasn't going to fuck things up even more.

Nope. I'd like to help. Come by Under anytime after 4 today.

Not sure I can face Jesse right now.

He's still in London.

Okay, I'll be there.

Cam hopped on the ferry to Manhattan, the words echoing through his head. London. Still in London. How long was Jesse going to be away? Cam had gotten the impression he'd be traveling back and forth. He'd be gone long enough to handle the internet radio deal. Then he'd be back home except for the occasional trip to London for meetings. But now Cam feared Jesse had stayed away because of him. The idea made him sick.

Cam had brought drama and stress to Jesse's place of refuge. Who could blame him for wanting to stay gone?

* * * *

"Hey, man. Glad you came." Kyle met Cam at the door and pulled him in for a huge hug. For a moment, Cam sagged against him and let himself be held.

"You're being awfully nice to me, considering the circumstances," Cam muttered against Kyle's shoulder.

"Hey, you're my friend, too." Kyle gave Cam a squeeze before he let go. "Plus, I feel bad because I'm pretty sure the threesome with me set all of this in motion."

Cam shrugged. "Yes and no. Jesse and I were always going to get to this point. And it's not your fault we're doing such a shit job at communicating."

"There is that." Kyle tilted his head toward the bar. "Come on. It's early for booze, but how would you feel about some mint lemonade? I'm trying to expand my selection of mocktails."

"Sounds good."

Cam followed him across the room and settled on a barstool.

"So, you said he's still in London?" Kyle nodded and pulled out a pitcher filled with a pale yellow-green concoction. The sweet, pungent scent filled the air. "I thought he'd be flying back and forth for the acquisition?"

"That was the original plan. To be honest, I think he stayed to lick his wounds as much as to avoid any additional drama with Taryn. He's concerned rumors about what happened will land in the gossip rags and the possibility of blackmail or legal action."

"Shit." Cam dropped his head into his hands. "I screwed this up. I should call him."

"Jesse's both pissed off and hurt. I hate to say it, but he doesn't want to talk to you right now."

"Fuck!"

Kyle patted his shoulder. "He doesn't get his feelings hurt too often, so when he does, he's not particularly well-equipped to handle it."

Cam raised his head. "What about Isaac?"

"Jesse's ex?" Kyle looked surprised. "What about him?"

"Does Jesse still have feelings for him?"

"Oh. That's hard for me to answer, but I'll do my best. Did their relationship leave Jesse with scars? Sure. Does he want Isaac back? No. They struggled because Isaac wasn't out. But they had other issues, too. Jesse's lack of interest in monogamy being one of them."

"So, you don't think he's staying in London because of Isaac?"

"What? No. Isaac is quite happy with someone else. He's not trying to get Jesse back." Kyle slid a glass of lemonade toward him.

"Oh." Cam accepted the drink, relief filtering through him. "I had this whole nightmare scenario built up in my head that he was in love with Jesse and Jesse was in love with him and—"

Kyle waved a hand to stop him. "I do think they loved each other actually, but no, there isn't going to be any kind of reunion like that. Jesse will come back, and the two of you can get things straightened out."

Cam shook his head. "You know, it's funny. The last time I was here, you and Jesse made those speeches, and it hit me that you two love each other, too."

Kyle winced. "Yeah, but not—"

"No, I get it. It doesn't sound like the same thing Jesse had with Isaac, but come on. There's more there than he admits. He doesn't recognize that you two are in a relationship, but you are." It came out more bitter than

Cam intended, but Jesse's and Kyle's "I love yous" to each other at the party had stung.

To his surprise, Kyle laughed. "Yeah, I've been telling him that for a while."

Cam stared at him. "Wait, what?"

"Don't misinterpret me. I'm not saying I want Jes to be any more than what he is to me right now. I love the fucking guy, and I hope he's in my life for a damn long time, but I don't want more than that. Jes and I, we're great like this. It may seem casual to a lot of people, but we are in a relationship."

"I think I get what you mean," Cam said. "Jesse doesn't see it that way, though, does he?"

"No. He's hung up on that word and all the baggage that comes with it. He's hung up on the idea that relationships always lead to marriage, too, or always mean monogamy. He's so set on being a non-conformist he winds up being more rigid than he needs to be." Kyle sniffed. "Me, I'm flexible. I want someone who will build a day-to-day life with me. Ideally, I'd like him to be open-minded enough to hop into bed with me and another guy if the mood strikes us. But if I fall head-over-heels for someone who can't handle that…" He shrugged. "I'll be fine."

"Jesse needs more freedom," Cam said slowly. The pieces were starting to come together for him.

"Yes." Kyle leaned forward. "Can I ask you a few questions?"

"Sure." Cam took a sip of his lemonade. Damn, it was delicious.

"Don't think about what you think Jesse wants or if you can give it to him. What do you want?"

"It's not so far off from what you want," Cam said. A thoughtful expression crossed Kyle's face, and Cam jumped in to clarify. "Um, don't take that to mean I want to start up with you. You're great and all but—"

Kyle smiled. "I didn't think you were going there. I'm in agreement. And, despite some shit Riley gave me the other night, I don't think either you or Jesse is looking for a permanent triad sort of thing. Nor am I, for that matter."

"Yeah, exactly." Cam laughed in relief. "I do want someone to share my life with, though. My future doesn't have to include a ring or kids—I don't want those things. But I have to be a priority to the guy I'm with, you know? I don't give a shit if we hook up with other people sometimes. I just need to be sure at the end of the day he's going to come home to me."

"That's not so far off from what Jesse wants, either," Kyle said, his voice gentle. "I know things are hard right now, but once he's home, you two need to sit down and talk. And I mean really talk. Not this bullshit you've been doing where he chases you around and you don't tell him anything. That's been driving him crazy, by the way. You need to lay it all out on the table and see if there's some kind of compromise that works for both of you."

"I hate asking him to be someone he's not."

"That's why I think you two can make this work," Kyle said. "Look, man, letting him know how you feel and what you want isn't asking him to be someone he's not. Both of you making a few small compromises is totally reasonable. If no one made any, relationships wouldn't even exist. It would be fucking anarchy."

"Yeah, I get what you mean."

"So, you're gonna do this?"

Cam nodded. "As soon as Jesse gets home, yes."

Kyle grinned at him. "Then it's time I drop some hints to him to get his ass back here. I'm sure he'll be back in a couple of weeks. You guys can talk then."

Cam's throat tightened at the thought of working things out with Jesse. And with gratitude for Kyle's reassurance and help. "I can't thank you enough," he managed. He hated to wait to speak to Jesse, but he was the one who needed space now. Cam would give it to him.

Kyle reached out and squeezed his shoulder. "Hey, you're my friend, and I love the shit out of Jes. I want him to find someone who makes him happy. I think you're it. And if I can help you two be together, then that makes me happy."

Cam cleared his throat and straightened. "That brings me to my next point."

"Okay?" Kyle raised an eyebrow at him.

"Apologizing for what happened with Taryn."

"Ah."

"And I want to clear some things up." Cam fidgeted with his glass. "I don't know how much Jesse told you, but I assume it was everything. Apparently, she claimed we'd made a bet to 'cheer him up'. I assure you I never made any kind of bet with her."

Kyle nodded, his expression grave. "It seemed out of character for you."

"Yeah. I get why Jesse freaked out. Taryn also clarified that she initiated everything and he turned her down. I need to apologize for flying off the handle at him."

"Okay."

"And the drugs." Cam cleared his throat. "I am pissed at her for that. It was out of line, and I think I got through to her about what a shitty decision she made. She feels bad."

"Well, Jesse's livid," Kyle admitted. "And so am I. Frankly, Taryn's not welcome here. We won't risk this place."

"You'll get no arguments from me there," Cam said. "That's fair. There's one thing I'd like you to tell Jesse, though, if you don't mind." Cam wet his lips. "I talked to Taryn and made sure there was zero chance of any of this ending up in the papers. I didn't think it was likely, and she's the one who would come out of this looking bad, but I wanted to be sure. I don't want him worrying about it."

"Thank you. I'll pass that on because he'll be relieved to hear it. I'm glad he has someone in his life who's protective of him."

Cam managed a faint smile. He wasn't in Jesse's life. But God, did he want to be. And he would do whatever it took to get him back.

Chapter Seventeen

Jesse glanced up as the woman seated across from him at the conference table made a grumbling noise. He caught her eye, and she set down a sheaf of papers with a rueful smile.

"This is the part of the job I've always hated," she said. "It's like death by a thousand paper cuts."

Nicola Parkman was CEO of Clash Radio, and she'd worked side by side with Jesse since the initial stages of Murtagh Media's acquisition of the company. Currently, they were reviewing contract edits at Clash's corporate headquarters, in the conference room where Jesse set up shop every time he came to town. They'd been at it for most of the day, and as the hour neared seven p.m., the words on the pages were beginning to swim before his eyes.

"You do not have a paper cut," he challenged, grateful for distraction. He went silent when Nicola held up a bandaged index finger.

"I beg to differ."

Jesse reached out and grasped her wrist. "Holy shit." He examined the bandage, which showed the word POW in bright blue letters against a fiery explosion. "Where did you get this fantastic Band-Aid?"

Nicola sniffed at him. "I'm fine, by the way, thanks very much. My assistant keeps a fraudulent first aid box in her desk. It's stocked with things like silly bandages, fake blood, a flask of whiskey and emergency chocolate. There are bacon strip bandages, but I am partial to these comic strips. There's one that says *AAARGH,* and I laugh every time I look at it."

"I need these in my life." Jesse leveled a stare at Nicola. "Will you be very angry if I take what's left of them?" He grinned at her chuckling and let go of her hand.

"No need to steal anything—I'll ask Lucie to pick up a box for you next week, and you can have your own stash."

"Ask her to pick up two, if you wouldn't mind? I'm putting stuff together for friends back in New York," Jesse explained. "And now that I'm thinking about it, I have another friend who'd appreciate the comic strips, too. So, maybe three boxes." He chuckled. "I'll leave some money in Lucie's desk before we leave tonight."

Nicola's gray eyes twinkled. "Are these friends under the age of ten or overgrown children like yourself?"

"Don't be mean," he chided. "Two of them are indeed children, but one is not. My friend David is more of a secret man-child. He's incredibly responsible in his day-to-day life, but an undercover comic book nerd with an ever-expanding collection."

"That you've enjoyed, I take it?"

"Every time I'm in his home. I'll tell you about him some time," Jesse offered, then glanced down at the piles of documents in front of them. "When we're not swimming in stacks of dead trees, that is."

Nicola huffed out a groan. She sat up straight and combed her long blonde hair back over her shoulders with both hands. "I say we give it one more hour, then go eat steak and get blotto."

"I'm down with that, sister," Jesse said and leaned forward to resume reading.

The mind-numbing aspects of contracts review aside, he enjoyed working with Nicola. She was smart as hell and tenacious in the boardroom, but funny and engaging out of it, like her brothers, James and Philip, whom Jesse had met several times. The Parkman brothers sat on Clash Radio's board but mostly focused on other branches of the family's business dealings. They left Nicola alone to run the show at Clash, which she did with great enthusiasm alongside her partner, Ellen Kaes, Chief of Operations. Jesse and his brother and father planned to let Nicola and Ellen continue on with minimal intervention after the acquisition, too.

When the hour ended, Jesse happily packed it in, and they walked through the deserted office to the exit.

"Do you have plans for the weekend?" Nicola asked.

"Nothing crazy," he replied. "I'm having dinner with a friend tomorrow night, but otherwise, I'll probably do a fair bit of work."

Nicola made a tsking kind of noise. "You should take time off to relax, you know. You've been like a machine since flying in this trip. All work and no play doesn't make Jesse a dull boy, but it certainly makes him look like he's not having very much fun."

Jesse shrugged. He didn't mind having dinner or drinks with the Clash Radio personnel for business purposes, but he hadn't been in any kind of mood to socialize on this trip. Outside of his morning runs, he stayed focused on his job and keeping up with Kyle and Under, which all equaled out to more than a full-time job with the time zones involved. However, if Jesse was being honest, his funk had started well before he left New York and immediately after Cam had kicked him to the curb.

"Haven't had much time for play," he replied. "I need to keep up with the New York staff, which sometimes makes for late nights. Not to mention my business partner at the speakeasy keeps restaurant hours."

"Ah, right. He's no doubt starting work while you should be sleeping."

"Basically. By the way, I'm talking with Eric tomorrow morning and we'll go over the notes you forwarded."

Nicola snorted. "Your brother's as big a workaholic as you, then?"

"It's a family occupation," Jesse quipped. He and Nicola boarded the elevator. "Eric and his wife are having a baby in October, though, so we'll be catching up on non-business things, too."

"Oh, that's lovely. Do they know the baby's gender?"

"Not that they're admitting, no. My sister-in-law says she can 'feel' that it's a girl, but Eric's convinced of the opposite."

"How fun!" Nicola smiled. "There are so few real surprises left to us in this world of instant gratification. I think it's wonderful they've decided to wait to find out."

"Wonderful except for the part where not knowing is driving my mother crazy," Jesse confided. They headed out into Leicester Square where the sky was still sunny and the summer air warm. "I get the feeling Mom thinks Eric and Sara do know the baby's gender and are withholding it from us. She keeps trying to trick them into admitting it."

Nicola burst out laughing. "What a kerfuffle. At least you'll be home in plenty of time to meet the baby."

We'll see, Jesse mused. He immediately felt guilty. He would go back to New York to meet his new niece or nephew. He didn't plan on leaving London anytime soon, however. He'd be free to go anywhere he liked after the acquisition completed, and he wasn't keen to head home. Being back in New York meant dealing with people he didn't want to focus on right now.

* * * *

The next morning, Eric got up early to web conference over breakfast while Jesse ate lunch in his room at the Connaught Hotel. Eric was still sporting major bedhead as they finished reviewing Nicola's notes, and the dark smudges under his eyes spoke toward another recent headache. Eventually, their talk turned to Taryn Guillory, who topped the list of people Jesse wanted to avoid.

"Have you heard anything from her?" Eric asked, his expression somber.

A knot formed in Jesse's stomach. He'd told Eric and Kyle what had transpired in Under's office with Taryn, of course, and given each of them copies of the footage from the security camera showing his interactions with her.

"No. Nothing even before Cam spoke with Kyle to clear things up." Jesse set down the fork he'd been using to pick at a room service salad. Even thinking about the situation with Cam and Taryn made him queasy.

Some of the tension in Eric's posture fell away at the confirmation, but Jesse didn't feel any less conflicted. Hearing Cam's side of things through Kyle had eased some of his hurt. The Cameron Lewis he knew wasn't a cruel person, and there had obviously been a tremendous amount of misunderstanding among all parties. Jesse didn't know Taryn at all, however, and he wasn't convinced he'd heard the last of her. Even now, he was braced for the other shoe to drop. Whether or not Cam had known Taryn's intentions that night at Under, he'd put Jesse in her sights.

Eric set down his coffee. "How are you feeling about the whole thing?"

"Better than I did a couple of weeks ago. I think Cam told Kyle the truth—he didn't know about the drugs. He never did anything stronger than booze around me. Or not that I saw, anyway." Jesse grimaced. "For what it's worth, I don't think he ever brought anything into the bar, either."

A line appeared between Eric's eyebrows. "It wouldn't be on you even if he had, Jes. You know that, right?"

"Sure, I know." Jesse licked his lips. Kyle had said almost the same thing, but he felt driven to reassure them he hadn't knowingly put Under's reputation at risk.

Eric exhaled through his nose. "At this point, I'd say we don't need to worry. Taryn would have talked to the gossip rags or a lawyer or even the fucking police by now if that's the route she wanted to go. Besides, you told her about the security footage, and she knows it proves nothing happened."

"We'll see." Jesse ignored the heat splashing across his cheeks. He wasn't that guy — he would never force himself on anyone, and the people he cared about knew it. He fucking hated feeling compelled to defend himself. He hated feeling so uncertain about everything just as much.

His appetite faded completely and he pushed his plate away. "I'm done talking about that. How's Sara feeling?"

"Hungry." Eric grinned. "Aside from the heartburn, she feels good. She muttered something on July Fourth about you not being around to make her Pregnant Lady Mocktails, by the way. I told her I'd get a recipe from you."

"I'll send the ones I've got and get a couple more from Kyle today," Jesse promised. "If his face isn't attached to his gaming console, that is."

"I don't know who the bigger kid is, you or Kyle. I'm surprised you don't game, too."

"No way. The last thing I need is Kyle and his dweeb friends wiping the floor with my sorry carcass."

"I don't understand," Eric mused. "You have good hand–eye coordination — how can you suck so hard at every game?"

"Honestly, it's tough staying focused on virtual worlds around Kyle because I'd rather be sucking something else."

Eric tipped his head back and laughed, hard. His eyes were sparkling when he met Jesse's gaze again. "There you are. It's been way too long since I saw my devil-may-care brother. I miss you, y'know. We all do."

Jesse sighed. He spoke with Kyle and Carter often and messaged with the other guys from the speakeasy.

He'd chosen not to break the silence between Cam and himself, however.

At first, he'd been too angry and frustrated to reach out to Cam—any conversation between them in those first few days would have quickly devolved into arguing. Now, with time and distance between them, he just felt worn out and unsure about...everything. Jesse didn't know what to say to Cam. While Cam now knew he'd turned Taryn down, that didn't mean he'd changed his mind about Jesse being a good person and a decent friend. Cam's first impulse had been to blame him for coming on to Taryn. He'd actually expected Jesse to fuck him over.

Maybe that's what hurts so much, Jesse thought. *Cam and I got to know each other, and he still expected the worst from me.*

He cleared his throat. "I miss you, too."

"So, come home."

"I'm kind of digging the vibe here, Eric. I'd like to stay a while after the Clash deal is done, maybe do some traveling. I could use a break," Jesse added. Eric's eyes went wide. "Provided you and Dad agree, of course."

"Sure, if that's what you need," Eric said, his voice gentle. He worried his lips with his teeth. "Don't stay away too long, all right? At the risk of sounding unbelievably selfish, I want you here when the baby is born. It wouldn't be the same without you, Jes."

He frowned at his brother. "Hey. Of course I'll be back. Don't think for a second I'd miss it, okay?" He waited for Eric's nod. "What do you and the little woman have going on tonight?"

"Dinner and board games with friends. Sara's out cold by ten p.m. these days, but she doesn't mind if the rest of us hang out and make a bunch of noise. What about you?"

"Dinner with Isaac."

Eric beamed. "Get out."

"Yup. We've been trying to get together since I got here, but he went out of town and I'm always buried under paper. We finally arranged to have dinner at Isaac's and I get to meet the boyfriend."

"That's great! What's the boyfriend like?"

Jesse smiled at his brother's obvious enthusiasm. "English, attractive, a sommelier for a four-star restaurant. I googled him, and he's beautiful—like Bollywood movie star beautiful, ugh. So, way to go, Isaac. He seems happy being out."

"Good for him. Are you up to that level of happy homemaking?"

"Definitely. I'm looking forward to it. The wine's bound to be good, and you know how Isaac is in the kitchen. This city has amazing food, but it'll be nice to get a home-cooked meal."

"You could get those back here, you know." Eric arched a brow at him.

"Fair point." Jesse ran his fingers over his lips. "I don't care what we eat. It'll just be nice to see him. I know he and I butted heads a lot, but Isaac's a good man. I'm glad things worked out for him."

"Me too. I always liked that guy."

"He liked you, too."

Eric's expression softened. "Isaac would say the same about you, by the way—that you're a good man."

"Mmm. I don't know if he would. At least, not yet." Jesse studied his hands where they rested on the desk. "But that's okay. He seems ready to be friends again and that works for me."

"Okay, kid," Eric said, his tone gentle. "Give him my best, will you?"

"I will." Jesse managed a genuine smile for his brother.

* * * *

Prior to meeting Isaac, Jesse visited a spa near his hotel. He emerged massaged and groomed to within an inch of his life, his hair cut short and his face clean-shaven for the first time in over a year. He felt good and more refreshed than he had since leaving New York. However, the relaxed vibe fell away as he climbed the steps of the brick-terraced building in Clapton where Isaac lived. Jesse had enjoyed reconnecting with Isaac through speech bubbles on his phone and email messages, but seeing him in person was another thing altogether.

He rang the bell and smiled when the gleaming black door swung open, and there was Isaac, tall and broad-shouldered, his big gray-green eyes bright and his grin wide. He looked amazing, exactly as Jesse remembered. Even better, he appeared happy to see Jesse.

Isaac waved him inside. "Hoshit, you shaved off the beard!" he exclaimed.

"Yeah, well, I needed a change," Jesse replied a second before Isaac grabbed him in a bear hug that made his heart squeeze. Isaac's hugs were a full-body experience. He stood an inch taller than Jesse and broader through the chest, and anyone he decided to hang on to had little hope of escaping. Not that Jesse tried to get away. Weeks had passed since anyone had really touched him, and the simple act of being held felt so good his eyes stung.

Great.

"It's so good to see you, Jes," Isaac said. The fondness in his voice showed in his gaze when he pulled back enough to get a look at Jesse. "You're too skinny, though. Don't they feed you at that hotel?"

Jesse's melancholy disappeared. He dug his fingers into Isaac's shoulders with a laugh. "Eh, they do okay, I guess. But, whatever, I fucking missed you!"

"Yeah, yeah, we missed each other enough to not talk for a dog's age, like a couple of idiots." Isaac rolled his eyes, but his tone held only warmth. "Come in, please. Darsh is in the kitchen opening a bottle of wine and no doubt messing with my curry."

"Curry?" Jesse noticed a wonderful savory aroma then, and his mouth watered at the idea Isaac might have cooked Japanese curry rice, a dish he adored. "Did you make kare?"

"Why, yes, I did!"

Jesse went to rub his hands in anticipation and remembered the bag he'd been carrying. He held it up. "I almost forgot—booze and chocolates from the Big Apple."

Isaac's eyes widened. "Oh, no, you didn't." Eagerly, he grabbed hold of the bag and peered in at the gift boxes of whiskey and chocolate. He beamed.

"Man, you are my favorite New Yorker ever. I told Darsh all about this stuff, and I'm damned sorry he got called into work tonight. You know how it is with restaurants—no matter how carefully you plan, it can go to hell in a heartbeat." Isaac shrugged. "Darsh has time for a drink before he leaves, though, and he's looking forward to meeting you."

Isaac led Jesse through the chic flat decorated in warm tones and blonde wood. The open floorplan led to a kitchen set at the rear of the space, and Jesse glimpsed a small garden through a windowed door. Darshan, Isaac's boyfriend, was carrying wineglasses to the counter, and he glanced up as Jesse and Isaac drew near.

"Jesse, this is Darshan Raj." Isaac looked at Darshan, and his smile lit him up like a Christmas tree. "Darsh, this is Jes."

Soft affection washed over Darshan's face and warmed his deep brown eyes. He set the glasses down and turned to Jesse with an outstretched hand. "A pleasure. Isaac's told me so much about you I feel as though I know you already."

Jesse grumbled playfully and shook Darshan's hand. "I'm not sure if that's a good thing or bad, but it's great to meet you, Darshan."

Darshan smiled. He let go of Jesse and immediately gestured to the glasses and open bottle of white wine.

"Would you care for a glass of wine? I got it into my head to mix cocktails tonight, but then Isaac reminded me of your speakeasy venture, and I decided to quit while still ahead." He raised his brows. "Unless you'd like to mix some up yourself?"

"Oh, wow, that's very flattering, but I'm completely okay with wine." Jesse held up both hands. "Mixing drinks at the bar is more a hobby for me. Under's real mixologist is my business partner, Kyle."

"How is Kyle?" Isaac placed the gift boxes on the counter, a safe distance from where Darshan was pouring. "And how did the two of you hit on this idea to open a blind pig in the Bronx?"

Jesse murmured his thanks as Darshan handed him a glass, then looked back to Isaac. "Under is in Morningside Heights, dude. That's Manhattan."

"Barely," Isaac teased. He gestured toward the door that led to the garden. "Let's go out so Darsh can show off his honeyberry bushes."

Jesse sat with Isaac and Darshan in the quiet shade of their outdoor space, and the last of his nerves slipped away. Their conversation flowed smoothly, punctuated with banter and laughter instead of awkward pauses, and set him at ease. When the time came for Darshan to leave, Isaac walked him out and left Jesse in the garden, feeling oddly content. Guilt edged his happy buzz, however, and a sense of loss fell over him. He and Isaac had spent too much time hiding from each other.

Jesse frowned. He'd chosen not to bridge the gap that had opened between them after Isaac had called things off, which was unlike him. He should have made an effort to keep their friendship intact instead of allowing his injured feelings to get in the way.

You're letting your feelings get in the way of making things right with Cam.

He sipped his wine. His inner voice had a point. Yes, Cam had hurt him, but, from what Kyle said, Cam was hurting, too. As a friend, Jesse owed it to Cam to hear him out. Hell, Jesse owed it to himself. He just needed to get over himself and take that first step.

"You look shell-shocked."

Jesse glanced back up at Isaac's drawl and stood. "I think I might be, yeah. After the way you and I parted, I guess I anticipated more strife, maybe?"

"You do love the drama." Isaac crossed the garden toward Jesse, his face stern, but the tips of his ears turned red, a telltale sign of embarrassment. "I fed into it, too. I blamed you after we split and talked about it to anyone who would listen."

Jesse grunted. "I get it, but way to be a dick, Isaac."

"I know. Carter got the brunt of it, the poor man." He winced when Jesse's mouth fell open. "I hope you understand how much he cares about you because anyone who puts up with that level of self-pitying bullshit from their friend's ex is a damned good friend."

"I had no idea," Jesse admitted. He'd known Carter and Isaac had stayed in touch after the breakup but not how deep their communications had gone. "Carter never said a thing."

"I'm not surprised—I'm sure he thought I'd regret spilling my guts after things settled down. Which I did." Isaac pursed his lips. "But I was just as much to blame for things going bad. Maybe more so. I spent so much time lying to everyone about who I was I didn't know where the truth ended and the lies began. I turned my guilt about it on you, and that wasn't fair."

Jesse furrowed his brows. "I think you're being too hard on yourself. No one should be forced to come out, and I know I didn't always deal well with having to hide."

"You were only being yourself." Isaac gave him a crooked smile. "I used to envy you that ability. You're so sure about who you are."

"Yeah, well. Unfortunately, it makes it easy for me to hurt people. I try hard to avoid it, but I make mistakes."

"Did that happen with me?"

"Yeah." Jesse swallowed. "And for what it's worth, I hurt myself, too."

Isaac stayed silent for a long moment. "I know," he said at last. "That's one of the reasons I couldn't keep hating you. Maybe our timing was off, or maybe we just weren't meant to be more than friends with benefits. It's obvious now you and I were never going to work long term. I think we both wanted it to work, though, right?"

Jesse's throat tightened up. He nodded without speaking, and Isaac's face filled with sympathy.

"It took a while for me to be ready to let go being angry and hurt, Jes, but once I did – "

"You got past it," Jesse finished. They shared a knowing glance. "You may find this hard to believe, but I understand where you're coming from."

Isaac shook his head slowly. "I don't find that hard to believe at all."

They carried their drinks inside then, and Isaac forced Jesse to sit at the dining table while he plated up their curry. It tasted delicious, exactly as Jesse remembered and even more comforting. The hominess of the meal and Isaac's company pinged the buttons in him that missed New York.

"So, the radio acquisition thing should be finished this week, right?" Isaac asked after they'd cleared the table and prepared dessert and coffee.

"Barring anything catastrophic, yes."

Jesse carried their coffee cups to the table while Isaac plucked two spoons from a drawer. He went to the freezer for what he'd already promised would be an amazing ice cream experience. He slid back into his seat and placed a bowl in front of Jesse.

"Honeyberry ice cream," he said. "I learned how to make it after Darsh got obsessed with those damned bushes."

Jesse groaned around the explosion of vanilla bean and intense fruit flavors in his mouth. "Bless you both because damn. This is like the best blueberry ice cream I've ever had, times one thousand."

"Glad you like it." Isaac chuckled. "Anyway, I expect you'll be going back to New York soon, but do you have time to get together before then? I would love you and Darsh to get to know each other better."

"Sure, no problem. I don't have a firm return date," Jesse explained. "I talked to Eric about taking a break following the radio deal. I haven't traveled in Europe for pleasure in forever, and it'd be good for me to do it before Sara has the baby and Eric disappears into a black hole of parenthood."

"Your brother's going to love being a dad, I'm sure. But is that the only reason you're sticking around?" Isaac gave Jesse a searching look. "You seem… I'm not sure. Wistful, I think. I'm not conceited enough to think it's about me, so am I wrong in thinking you're putting off going back?"

"Eh." Jesse examined his ice cream. "You're not wrong. Some stuff went down before I flew out here to close the deal. Part of me thinks staying away is better for everyone involved."

"Boy trouble, huh?"

Jesse snapped his gaze up to meet Isaac's. "Mostly, yeah. How'd you guess?"

Isaac smiled. "When we were dating, I noticed you'd get a lot closer to your male lovers than female. As much as you love women, you give a lot more of yourself — of your heart — to the men in your life. What happened?" he asked. "You got close to someone, and it didn't work out?"

"It wasn't supposed to go that far," Jesse replied slowly. "The guy, Cam, and I talked about it a lot at the beginning. We both wanted something fun and light.

Nothing heavy, nothing serious. That worked for a while. Until it changed and started feeling serious. And I didn't mind."

Isaac took his hand over the table, but Jesse saw nothing but kindness in his handsome face. His chest went tight. "I don't know how to feel about this, Isaac."

"Have you told him?"

Jesse bit out a hard laugh. "No."

"I think you should."

"I'm not sure I can. Cam told me he didn't want to see me anymore because he thought I'd hurt him. Which I would because I'm me, right? Everyone knows I'm not the guy you take home to meet your parents." Jesse's gut dropped at the idea of what Cam's parents would think if they ever met him.

"The problem is, I don't know how to be Cam's friend without wanting more. And I do want more, even though I know I shouldn't."

Isaac's expression grew troubled. "What makes you say that?"

Jesse narrowed his eyes at his friend. "Come on, man. You're the last person I should have to explain this to. I'm terrible at relationships. I don't even want them!"

"Are you sure? Because for a man so determined to be an emotional island, you have a lot of up close and personal friends."

"Friends and lovers are two separate things," Jesse scoffed. "I don't sleep with all my friends, and I'm sure as fuck not friends with everyone I sleep with."

"Now that is a lie," Isaac fired back. He frowned. "You absolutely make friends with everyone you sleep with on the regular, Jes. That's one of the reasons no one's strangled you with their bare hands by now, you know. Everyone likes you too goddamned much to stay mad at you!"

"That is patently untrue, and, again, you of all people would know." Jesse's laughter faded. "Cam wasn't only my friend. For me, there was more between us. Maybe for him, too. Like…like the way things were with you and me, but even bigger." He swallowed as Isaac pressed his lips together in a grim line.

"We both know how well that turned out between you and me, Isaac," he said, his voice gentle. "I couldn't give you a ring or a white wedding or a house in the 'burbs, and I hated disappointing you. I don't want to disappoint Cam, too."

Isaac watched him, and the pain that flashed in his eyes eased. "You sound awfully sure you're going to fail, but I don't understand why. Did Cam ever ask you for a ring or a wedding or a country life?"

"Not in so many words, no. But he made it clear that what we've been doing doesn't work for him anymore. He wants commitment. Things I can't give him. Those were his exact words." Jesse shrugged. "Any fool could make the inference."

"I don't think you should infer anything." Isaac squeezed his fingers. "So, Cam wants more from you than a casual fuck. Why can't the two of you work that out? You make it work with Kyle. You made it work with Carter, too, when you two were fooling around, and he's still one of your closest friends."

"What I have with Kyle and had with Carter is different from what I had with you."

"No, sweetheart, it isn't." Isaac gave him a gentle look. "You have deep, loving connections with them that go beyond sex. You love them. Maybe that love isn't conventionally romantic, but the emotions are true. I got to know Kyle pretty well when you and I were together, and from the things he said, he doesn't expect anything from you that you're not willing to give. He'd never ask, either. He's happy with you as you are. So is Carter. His heart belonged to Riley, and it didn't hurt him to share you with other people. You helped him figure out how to be happy with a new life and let him go when the time came because you wanted the best for him."

Isaac's face shifted into a frown. "I didn't know how to handle my connection with you. How to handle you, if I'm being totally truthful. How to live and love in the moment and be happy with that. And that's down to me, Jes. I didn't want to admit it back then, but we both know you and I weren't right for each other."

Jesse nudged his ice cream away. Isaac's words actually hurt his heart. They were true, however.

"You're right. But I'm not sure I'm right for Cam, either. I don't know what he wants from me anymore."

"You never will unless you talk to him." Isaac patted Jesse's hand before he let go. "Tell me what happened."

* * * *

In the days following his dinner with Isaac, Jesse moved through the world with renewed energy. Talking everything over with his ex had left him both drained and relieved in the best way. They'd put the last of their ghosts to rest and could truly be friends without regret. He still wasn't sure how to deal with Cam or even if he wanted to face Cam yet. However, Jesse knew for certain he didn't want to lose the connection between them.

On Friday afternoon, Murtagh Media finalized its acquisition of Radio Clash. Jesse set up a web conference so the staff in New York could be part of the final signing, and he shared a smile with his father and brother once the documents were notarized.

After a celebratory dinner with the Clash staff, Jesse returned to the conference room for his things. He spied the fraudulent first aid box Nicola's assistant had put together for him on the table and opened it eagerly. Inside, he found various boxes of goofy bandages, both plastic and confectionary. There were pairs of plastic spectacles, sugar-encrusted tongue depressors, chocolate buttons in every color and other packets of sweets. Jesse sifted through it all, struck by an immediate impulse to share them with Dylan and Sadie, and missed home so much, his breath caught.

His phone rang, the White Stripes' *Seven Nation Army* ringing through the deserted office, and Jesse set the box down. He connected the call with a grin.

"Hey, Sara!"

"Jes? Where are you right now?"

He frowned. His sister-in-law didn't sound right. "At the office. I'm about to head back to the hotel. Are you okay?"

"No. No, I'm not. How soon can you get back to New York?"

The hairs on the back of his neck rose at the waver in Sara's voice. "What's going on? Are you and the baby okay?"

"We're both fine, but Eric isn't. We're at the Emergency Department in NewYork–Presbyterian."

Oh, God.

Jesse started gathering his things, his heart in his throat. "What happened?"

"He felt a migraine coming on and left work early, but when I went to check on him, he couldn't get up. He's numb on one side, and his words are all mixed up."

Sara sobbed once, and the sound made Jesse's stomach lurch.

"He's scared, Jes," she murmured. "I am, too, and I know you're busy in London, but you should be here. I'm sorry to call you like this —"

"I'll be there, sweetheart," Jesse cut in gently. He hustled toward the door with his things. "I'm leaving right now, I'll get my stuff, and I'll be in the air as soon as I can, okay? Are Mom and Dad with you?"

"No, they left for Los Angeles after your big meeting. I, um, talked to them a little while ago, and they'll turn around as soon as they can get a flight out of LAX."

Shit. Sara and Eric were alone. Jesse's thoughts immediately turned to his friends.

He made a dash for the elevator. "I'm coming, Sara, and I'll send someone to keep you company."

"Okay," she said, her voice soft. "My folks are driving up from Baltimore, too."

Jesse pressed his lips thin. Sara's meek acquiescence signaled her extreme stress, and he kept talking as he boarded the elevator. He still didn't feel at all ready to think about what had happened to Eric, so Jesse shifted all his focus on getting his ass home.

Chapter Eighteen

"Oh, you are so dead!" Cam yelled. "So dead, you asshole. I am going to beat you to within an inch of your life and—"

Kyle's cackle was cut off by the sounds of *You're So Vain* coming from his phone.

Jesse's ringtone.

Cam froze and Kyle hit pause. "Give me a sec, Cam."

"Sure." Cam set his controller aside and tried to look anywhere but at Kyle.

"Hey, Jes. What's up?" Kyle sat up straight. "What? Of course. Which hospital?"

Hospital? Cam turned to look at Kyle. *Shit. But who? Jesse? Oh, fuck, what if something's happened to him?* But Cam didn't think he'd come back to New York yet. *Plus, if he's the one calling, it couldn't be that bad, right? Sara? Maybe she's gone into labor early.* It was mid-July, and Cam felt sure she wasn't due until October. Jesus, he hoped she and the baby were all right.

Kyle fell silent for several moments and just listened. A deep frown furrowed his brow and he sounded grave when he spoke again. "Yes. I'll head out right away."

"Before you freak out, Jesse's okay," Kyle said and lowered the phone.

"Sara?" Cam asked. He'd been worried about Jesse, but the idea of his sister-in-law and her baby being in trouble was nearly as concerning.

"No. Eric." Kyle stood and reached for his wallet where it sat on the coffee table. "He's in the hospital. New York–Presbyterian. Sara's with him, but Jesse asked if I'd go sit with her."

"Yeah, of course," Cam said, standing too. "Do you think I should come?"

"Yes," Kyle said. "Come on. I'll tell you more on the way. He's at their Weill Cornell Medical Center campus in Lennox Hill, and that'll take time on a Friday afternoon."

Cam nodded. "Public transit will take forever."

"I'm thinking a Lyft will be the fastest way to get there."

"Sounds good."

It took a few minutes to find a nearby Lyft, and once they were in the car, Cam turned to Kyle. "What happened to Eric?"

"They don't know," Kyle said grimly. "He came home from work with a migraine, but now his speech is all mixed up and he's numb on one side."

Cam blinked. He'd figured Eric had been in an accident. "That's crazy. It sounds like a stroke, but he's young and healthy."

"Yeah, they don't know what's going on. Jes is on his way to the airport now, but it's going to take a while," Kyle said. "Sara's there. Her parents are on the way from Baltimore. The Murtaghs were going to

California, but they're flying back as soon as they can. And Jes said he'd call Carter, too."

"He must be going crazy not being here," Cam said.

"He is."

"You're sure I'm not overstepping by showing up, too? My first instinct was to go and do what I can to help but..."

"Trust me," Kyle said. "You and Jesse have shit to work out, but there's no better way to show him you care about him than by supporting his family."

Cam nodded. Kyle's logic made sense. They were mostly silent for the rest of the ride to the hospital. Every time traffic slowed, Cam wanted to scream with frustration, and he couldn't imagine how Jesse was faring, trapped at an airport, waiting for a plane to take him home.

The moment the car pulled up at the main emergency department entrance, Kyle tipped the driver and opened the door. He made a beeline for the check-in desk with Cam following close behind. "We're here for Eric Murtagh," he said.

The woman raised an eyebrow. "Are you family?"

"Yes," Kyle said. "We are."

It turned out Eric was in the Radiology Department for testing, but eventually, one of the admissions staff led Cam and Kyle back to a waiting area where Sara sat, staring at the wedding ring on her finger and twisting it around and around.

"Sara?" Kyle said. "Jesse called and asked us to come."

"Oh!" Sara wiped at her eyes and stood. Cam grabbed her elbow when she seemed to struggle out of her chair. She smiled and hugged him around her belly. "I can't believe you guys came so fast."

"Of course we did." Kyle hugged her and kissed the top of her head. "Now, what can we do to help?"

She shrugged. "Distract me? They're running a bunch of tests on Eric right now, so all we can do is wait."

"Can I get you a drink?"

Sara laughed weakly. "I mean, if I wasn't pregnant and you had booze stashed on you, I could go for a margarita."

Kyle grinned. "I meant coffee or tea from the cafeteria or whatever."

"Herbal tea would be nice."

"Okay. I'll go hunt some down and be right back, okay?" He glanced at Cam.

"I'll stay with you, if that's all right," Cam said to Sara.

She nodded. "Thanks."

"Do you want anything, Cam?" Kyle asked.

He shook his head. "I'm fine, thanks."

Sara settled into the chair and rubbed her belly.

"How are you feeling?" Cam asked.

"Other than scared shitless my husband's had a stroke?"

Cam offered her a rueful smile. "Yeah. I figured that's a given. I meant with the mini Murtagh."

Sara chuckled. "Mini Murtagh, I like it. The spawn is fine. I'm trying to stay calm so I don't stress out and wind up in labor."

Cam winced. "Yeah, no kidding. How have you been feeling? Is the heartburn better?"

"It's been manageable, thanks. You're the pregnant lady whisperer."

"That's what happens when you're nineteen years old and your mom gets pregnant with twins."

"The gum tip helped so much. It's been a lifesaver."

"Good," Cam replied. "I figure it's the least I can do to help the people doing all the work to continue the species."

Sara chuckled. "God, I'm glad you guys came. I thought about calling my best friend and decided against it. I love her to death, but she is not calm in a crisis. And she doesn't know how to deal with my sarcasm and dark humor during one."

"Trust me, I get it."

"I keep telling her this is how descendants of the Irish handle stress—booze and black humor. Can't have the booze right now so…"

"I'm familiar," Cam said drily. "My grandma's surname was O'Shea."

Sara took his hand. "I'm glad you're going to be here for Jes, too. He's going to need it."

Cam looked away, but he squeezed Sara's hand. "Assuming he wants me to be. Things are fucked up right now."

"Oh, I know. But I also know this is only a blip for you guys."

"You think so?"

"I do," she said. "You're good for him, Cam. I've known him for years, and this is the first time I am sure he's met someone who is the right fit."

"Then I have a lot of work cut out for me to fix it."

Sara opened her mouth to answer, but Carter's appearance in the lounge cut their conversation short.

"How's Eric doing?" he asked before he'd even reached them.

"They're running tests now," she said.

"No, don't get up," Carter protested when Sara moved to stand. "I'll come to you."

"So I am beginning to resemble a beached whale then?" she joked. "I was afraid of that."

Carter leaned down to hug her. "Nothing of the sort." He held a hand a few inches from her belly, and he waited until she nodded to pat her stomach. "How's this one doing?"

"Sleeping at the moment, I think. For future reference, we're now going to be referring to it as the Mini Murtagh." She winked at Cam.

"I like it," Carter said. He held a hand out to Cam. "Glad you could be here, too."

"I came with Kyle," Cam explained and shook it. "He's hunting down tea for Sara at the moment."

"He has found tea for Sara," Kyle said from the doorway. He crossed the room with a hot cup in his hand.

"Oh, perfect." Sara smiled. "You guys are the best."

* * * *

Several hours later, there was still no news. Sara spent time with Eric between tests, but there were more to be run. Jesse was on a plane over the Atlantic.

A notification on Cam's phone reminded him that he needed to be at work in a few hours.

"I don't know what to do," Cam said to Kyle. "I don't want to leave, but I've got a gig tonight."

"It'll be hours before they know anything, I'm sure," Kyle said. "And hours before Jesse gets here."

"I want to be here when he arrives," Cam admitted.

Kyle smiled faintly. "I get that. Well, would your boss care if someone filled in for you?"

"He won't be thrilled on such short notice," Cam said. "But maybe if I got someone lined up before I told him, he'd be okay with it."

"Worth a shot, right?"

"Yeah, agreed." Cam fired off a few texts to some other DJs with regular rotations at Ember, but his phone remained silent.

"It's not looking good," he said, half an hour later. "I think I'm going to have to go in."

He remembered then that all his equipment was back at the loft. "Fuck, and I'm going to have to go to Brooklyn before the club. I need my gear."

"You have a couple of roommates, right?" Kyle asked, stretching out his long legs. "Can't one of them grab your stuff and meet you?"

Cam shrugged. "Guess I'll find out."

He sent texts to Myron and Louise. Kevin and Bernice were already upstate with her family, looking at wedding venues.

Louise responded within a few minutes.

Sorry, Cam. I'm stuck at work until 11 tonight. Hope you find someone.

Myron texted back shortly after.

I would, but I'm going into work in half an hour.

Fuck. Who else could he ask? Taryn, maybe, but they hadn't talked much lately. *Fuck it*, he decided. *I'll ask anyway. The worst she can say is no.*

Cam fired off a quick note. *I know we haven't talked much, but I could use a big favor. You free right now?*

Taryn responded a few minutes later. *What do you need?*

* * * *

Cam was beat by the time he returned to the hospital around one a.m. Thankfully, Taryn had pulled through for him. Myron had let her into their apartment to pick up Cam's things, and she'd met him at the club. He'd also heard from Jeff, another DJ who'd agreed to fill in. Jerry had given him the okay to do half a set and hand it over to Jeff, so he'd been able to get back to the hospital sooner than expected.

The security guard in the Emergency Department let him through. Eric hadn't been admitted yet and was still in the emergency observation area. Since it was well after visiting hours, and Cam, Kyle and Carter weren't actually family, Cam suspected someone had pulled strings to allow them all to wait there. Harry Murtagh, perhaps, or maybe Jesse himself.

Kyle and Carter were both in the waiting area.

"Any news?" Cam asked. He dropped his overnight bag on the floor. He'd left his gear at the club with Jerry's permission, but Taryn had also brought a change of clothes and some toiletries.

Kyle shook his head. "Not yet. It sounds like he's got a hell of a headache on top of everything else, but at the moment, he's sleeping. They're going to do more tests in the morning. Sara's with him."

"Okay."

"Jesse landed and cleared customs, and he's on his way now. It shouldn't be long. His parents are still a few more hours behind."

"Good."

"Riley said hi," Carter added. "He stopped by for a bit while Audrey watched the kids, but he headed home to be with them for the night."

"Oh, of course," Cam said. "Tell him hi back."

Cam took a seat, but he couldn't stop fidgeting, and several times, Kyle laid a hand on his jiggling knee to stop his movement. "Sorry," he muttered.

Kyle simply nodded. Cam felt profound gratitude for their friendship at the moment. Kyle was an oasis of calm in the midst of the stress and anxiety.

A short while later, Kyle glanced up from his phone and looked at him. "He's here. He's talking with Eric and Sara now. He'll come by here when he's done."

"Okay."

That did nothing to calm Cam's nerves. He kept his gaze trained on the door, and the moment Jesse stepped through it, Cam was on his feet. Jesse looked exhausted and worried, and Cam desperately wanted to gather him close.

He held his breath, expecting Jesse to go to Kyle, but he strode straight toward Cam. Without thinking twice, he pulled Jesse into his arms. Jesse sagged against him and buried his head against Cam's neck.

"God, I'm glad to see you." His words sounded muffled against Cam's shoulder. "I didn't know if you would come."

"Of course." Cam stroked his back. "If there was any chance you needed me—"

"I did." Jesse straightened, but he didn't let go. Instead, he rested his forehead against Cam's. "I do."

They stood there for several long moments, just breathing. Cam soaked in the feel of Jesse's body against his, wishing he could give Jes any strength he needed. Eventually, Jesse stepped away to hug Kyle and Carter. He returned to Cam's side almost at once, and Cam guided him toward a small loveseat. Jesse sank onto it and leaned against Cam's side, entwining their hands.

"Eric's still in a lot of pain, but they're expecting results soon. Some of his symptoms are improving at least, like his speech. And my parents should be landing within the hour. Thank you guys for being here for Sara."

Carter and Kyle both nodded. They made light conversation until Jesse lapsed into silence. His usually vibrant spark was dim at the moment, but Cam couldn't blame him. Cam didn't know what to say, but Jesse squeezed his hand occasionally, and Cam decided maybe being there was enough. He hoped so anyway.

They sat quietly until Ellen and Harry Murtagh arrived. Jesse went to join his family in Eric's room and Cam dozed while they were gone. An hour later, Jesse returned, followed by his parents and Sara and her parents.

Sara seemed to be scolding him. "You should go home. We know Eric's out of the woods, and there's nothing more you can do here tonight."

"Are you sure?"

"Yes." Sara's tone was gentle but firm. "You have been up for an unreasonable number of hours and are running on fumes. Go home, sleep and come back tomorrow."

He frowned and came over to stand by Cam. Cam agreed with Sara. Jesse looked wrecked, and he needed sleep.

Sara raised her voice slightly. "The doctors spoke with us. It looks like Eric didn't have a stroke. There's no evidence of one on the MRI, and all signs point toward something called a hemiplegic migraine."

"What does that mean?" Carter asked.

"Basically, it's a type of severe migraine with symptoms that mimic those common to stroke," Sara replied. "The muscle weakness, vertigo and confused speech are all rooted in what started out as a regular migraine."

"Jesus." Cam ran a hand over his head. "That's super fucked up."

Sara smiled. "Well, you know these Murtaghs — they're special in a lot of ways." Jesse scowled and poked her gently in the ribs, and Sara chuckled. "Anyway, the migraine isn't life-threatening, and the symptoms should be gone in a few days. Eric's being admitted so they can keep an eye on him, and there will be follow-up testing tomorrow."

A collective sigh of relief went up from everyone.

"Now, although I appreciate everyone coming, everyone should go home and get some rest."

Jesse frowned. "What about you? Shouldn't you go home?"

"Before they came to the hospital, my parents stopped by our place and got me a change of clothes. I'll sleep in the reclining chair in Eric's room tonight. Trust me, with the added bulk of the Mini Murtagh, not to mention the heartburn, that chair is going to be a hundred percent more comfortable than my bed at home right now." She patted her stomach.

Jesse relented. "Okay, okay, I'll go get some sleep."

Cam pulled out his phone.

"What are you doing?" Jesse asked. He rubbed at his eyes.

"Ordering us a Lyft," Cam said.

"Why don't we use the family car?"

"Sure. Tell me who to call. I'll take care of it."

Jesse dug his phone out of his pocket, fiddled with it a moment then handed it to Cam.

The call went through after the first ring. "How can we help you, Mr. Murtagh?"

Cam cleared his throat. "I'm calling on behalf of Mr. Murtagh. Can I get a car to pick him up at NewYork–Presbyterian Hospital, the Weill Cornell Medical Center Emergency Department, to take him home?"

"Certainly, sir. I'm in the area and can be at the main entrance in ten minutes."

"Thank you," Cam said. He said goodbye, hung up and handed the phone back to Jesse. He started slightly, as if he'd been spacing out.

"The car should be here in ten minutes. I'm taking you home," Cam said.

"My home or your home?"

"Yours. Madison Square Park is a hell of a lot closer than Brooklyn."

"Are you coming with me?"

"Yes." For the first time, doubt stirred inside Cam. "Unless you don't want me to."

"I want you to. I didn't know if you wanted to, in light of" — Jesse made a vague gesture — "things."

"Right now, 'things' don't matter. Once you've had some sleep and this crisis is over, we can talk and hash it all out. But unless you tell me otherwise, I'm taking care of you," Cam said firmly. He wrapped an arm around Jesse's shoulders.

Jesse leaned against him with a tired grunt. "I like the sound of that."

* * * *

Jesse dozed on Cam's shoulder for the better part of the ride to his place in NoMad. Cam dragged him into the elevator in his building, then his loft. Jesse let out a sigh after they were inside, and he'd punched the security code into the alarm panel.

"'S good to be home. Not just here, but New York."

"I'm glad to hear it," Cam said, his voice soft. "You were missed."

"Yeah?" Jesse gave him a sleepy smile. "So were you."

Cam wanted to say a lot more, but Jesse was crashing, and Cam suspected he didn't have the energy for more than a quick shower. "Come on." He coaxed Jesse toward the bedroom. "Let's get you cleaned up and into bed."

Jesse didn't protest when Cam led him into the bathroom, stripped him and pulled him into the shower. He leaned on Cam like he was the only thing keeping him upright — which Cam suspected might be the case — and moaned with appreciation when Cam scrubbed his hair and body.

Cam toweled him dry and dressed him in a pair of boxer briefs. Cam changed into his own clean pair of boxers, then maneuvered Jesse into bed.

Jesse tugged the covers up and held out an arm. "Sleep with me?"

Even if Cam had planned to refuse, he never would have managed it after a request like that. "Yes, I'm just going to make sure the lights are out and our phones are plugged in," he said.

"Good." Jesse flipped onto his side and burrowed under the covers. "I'll be waiting."

Of course, by the time Cam returned, he was snoring. But even in his sleep, when Cam spooned behind him and draped an arm around Jesse's waist, pulling their bodies close, he made a contented sound.

Smiling, Cam pressed his lips to Jesse's shoulder, closed his eyes and fell asleep, too.

* * * *

Jesse was still out cold when Cam awoke after eleven a.m., but he had no inclination to wake him. They hadn't gotten to sleep until after four a.m. Cam slipped out of bed without disturbing him, dressed in sweats and a long-sleeved tee and ventured into the kitchen to make coffee.

While it brewed, he checked his phone to make sure there were no urgent messages from any of the guys or Sara regarding Eric. Everything was quiet, which he took as a positive sign.

An hour or so later, Cam heard the toilet flush. He poured a cup of coffee, fixed it the way Jesse liked and carried it into the bedroom. Jesse stepped out of the walk-in closet dressed in sleep pants and a T-shirt.

"Hey there." His voice sounded raspy, and he was still a bit bleary-eyed, but he looked much less wrung-out than the night before. "I was coming to find you."

"Coffee?"

"Please." But after Jesse took the mug from Cam, he set it on the nearby dresser rather than drink it. He stepped forward so their bodies brushed. "Thank you for last night."

"Of course," Cam replied. "I'm glad I could help."

Jesse smoothed his hands over Cam's shoulders. "You really stepped up for me. I'm not sure you know how much that means to me."

Cam didn't know how to respond. Jesse stood even closer now, and Cam realized their bodies fit together like nothing had changed between them. God, it made his heart ache. Cam had missed this so much.

"I want to kiss you," Jesse said, his voice husky.

"Then kiss me," Cam said.

Jesse raised an eyebrow and leaned in to press their lips together. It was sweet and tender, with an undercurrent of need snaking through it. They kissed for several long moments. It was hello, and I've missed you, and I'm sorry all wrapped into one. Cam's chest felt very full when they pulled apart.

Jesse rubbed his stubble against Cam's cheek, and Cam held him tighter. "I want to talk soon," Jesse said, his voice soft. "There's a lot to clear up."

"Yeah, me too," Cam said.

"But I need to call Sara and see if there's any news."

"I haven't heard anything, so I suspect no news is good news," Cam said and shushed Jesse, who drew breath to speak. "I'm not saying we need to talk before you check with them. I just wanted you to know."

"Thanks."

"Even if we can't talk for a few days or a week, or however long you need to deal with this crisis, it doesn't matter. I'm not going anywhere," Cam said. "I'm here for you and your family. We'll figure out the rest later."

"Thank you." Jesse leaned in for another kiss. "Give me a few?"

"Of course."

Cam returned to the kitchen while Jesse made his call. Cam could hear the gentle rise and fall of his voice. It was too faint to make out the words, but Cam felt reassured knowing he was close.

Jesse appeared in the doorway a short while later.

"I spoke to my mom and Eric. They told me in no uncertain terms I am not to come to the hospital yet." Jesse looked vaguely grumpy. "But Eric said we could visit later. Also, I asked him if he was okay, and he said, and I quote, 'Slow your roll, kid, or you'll give me another migraine.'"

"That sounds promising," Cam said.

Jesse nodded. "The head pain is gone and the speech issues have cleared up. A sense of humor is always a good thing. In fact—" A growl from his stomach cut him off, loud enough for Cam to hear. He held a hand over his abdomen. "Scratch that. I need food before I do anything else."

"I had breakfast delivered," Cam said. "Bagels and cream cheese arrived while you were still asleep."

Jesse grabbed Cam's face in his hands and pressed a smacking kiss to his lips. "You are a prince among men."

"I try."

Cam fetched the refrigerated ingredients and assembled a plate. Jesse liked lox on bagels, so he'd ordered that with all the accompaniments, but Jesse's expression became pensive while Cam worked.

"Shall we talk?" Jesse asked after he'd eaten half of his food. Cam had devoured his own breakfast earlier.

"If you're ready," Cam said.

"I am." Jesse wet his lips. "And I want to say I'm sorry I stayed away for so long," he said. "But that's not precisely true."

Cal swallowed hard, reeling a little from the statement. "Okay."

"Being in London gave me time to think. And to see Isaac."

A sliver of worry worked its way in and lodged in Cam's chest. "He's your ex, right?"

"Yes." Jesse wiped his mouth. "But if you're thinking it's because I wanted to reconcile with him, you'd be wrong."

Cam blinked. "Did Kyle tell you I was worried?"

Jesse gave him a rueful, sad smile. "Yes. But I also know what your face looks like when you're hurt and concerned, and that's exactly what it looks like at the moment."

Cam nodded. Jesse wasn't wrong. Even though Kyle had assured Cam there was nothing between him and Isaac, he'd needed to hear it from Jesse. "If you didn't want to reconcile with Isaac…"

"I met him and his boyfriend at their place for drinks and dinner. Isaac and I had an opportunity to clear up some lingering things. It made me realize you and I have a lot to talk about."

"Yeah, we do," Cam agreed.

"You know Kyle brought me up to date on the situation with Taryn." Jesse rubbed at his stubble, and Cam wondered if he missed his beard. Cam did, although Jesse looked handsome no matter what. "That you had no knowledge of the drugs, and she'd made up the thing about the bet."

Cam worried his bottom lip with his teeth. "I still feel terrible about that night. I never imagined she'd do either of those things. I know Under is your sanctuary, and I hate that I brought her there and—"

"It's okay, Cam. I don't blame you. But it hurt knowing you immediately assumed I'd sleep with her," Jesse said, his tone raw.

"I know," Cam said. "I shouldn't have leapt to conclusions."

"And I hate that I wind up hurting people I care about." Jesse's frown deepened.

"While you were in London, I realized some things, too. I've kind of had one foot out the door because I expected you to move on. For you to find your next shiny, pretty new thing that caught your attention."

Jesse winced.

"I knew when you did, it would hurt."

"I know. I can't blame you, given my history." Jesse looked remorseful. "In the past, that's what I've done. I pushed people away before things got too serious."

Cam stayed silent for a moment. "Can I ask you something?"

"Of course."

"When I said I wanted more with you, what did you think that meant?"

"Oh, God. I don't know." Jesse tilted his head back and stared up at the ceiling. "You talked about what Eric and Sara have, and you said you didn't want to tie me down. You made it clear what we were doing didn't work for you anymore. And that you wanted commitment. I inferred you wanted the whole heteronormative deal. Marriage. A family. Whatever it is most people are so desperate to find." He swallowed. "I'm not, Cam. I've never wanted that. Most of the time, I'm very, very happy to not be like everyone else. But sometimes, in the process of being me, I hurt people. And the last person I wanted to hurt was you. I'm sorry for that."

"I know. And I don't think I was clear," Cam admitted. "I said I wanted a relationship, but I didn't mean you had to sacrifice your freedom completely, Jes. Or change who you are."

"What do you mean?"

"Using Sara and Eric was a bad example. Maybe it's because I don't know any couples who have what I want," he explained. "So, I don't have anyone to compare it to."

Jesse rubbed his forehead. "I feel like we're talking in circles again, Cam. Be candid with me. Tell me what would make you happy."

Cam took a deep breath. "Knowing that at the end of the day, I'm the person you come home to. If something happens with your family, I'm the one you call. I'm the one you rely on."

Jesse nodded. "I'd expect that from you, too, Cam."

"Of course."

"Are you suggesting living together?"

"Yeah. At some point. It wouldn't have to be right away. But I'd want to eventually." Cam held his breath, unsure if Jesse could be on board with that.

"Rings?"

Cam shook his head. "No. I don't want kids, either. I had plenty of that living at home after my mom had the twins. God knows, I get enough kid time at work, too."

"And there's Carter's kids," Jesse offered.

"Yes. And you're about to have a niece or nephew," Cam added. "We could play uncle whenever we want, but I don't want to raise a family."

"Good. I don't either," Jesse said. "But I need you to be clear about what you're looking for."

"I don't know," Cam said, feeling frustrated. "I do know I've never felt this way about anyone before. You matter to me, Jes. I don't want to lose you."

"You matter to me, too, Cam, and I don't want to lose you, either. But I can't agree to something if I don't know what it is."

"I know. I'm struggling to explain what I'm looking for."

"So, let's go over what we do agree on. We'd live together. Someday," Jesse said. Cam nodded. "And we'd be what to each other?"

"Partners?" Cam supplied. "People who care about each other and want to make each other happy."

Jesse breathed in and out. "Yeah. Okay. I can live with that."

"It sounds like there's a 'but' there."

"Yeah, a big one. You say you want me to come home to you, but I don't think I'm wired to be with one person for the rest of my life, Cam. Even if I wanted to, I—"

"No, that's what I've been trying to say. I don't need monogamy," Cam said.

Jesse's brow furrowed. "You're sure?"

"Yes. I've thought about it a lot." Cam licked his lips, trying to figure out how to explain it. "I don't think you fucking someone else means you care about me less."

"Okay." Jesse rubbed his chin. "This isn't you sacrificing your needs to be with me, right?"

"No, it's not. Hell, I like the idea of still being able to hook up with someone else. Like we did with Kyle. That was great. When we hooked up with Kyle, I felt closer to you, not further apart."

"Okay. We'd only do it together then?" Jesse asked. "Because it sounds like that's what you would prefer." He frowned.

"No. We could keep doing stuff on our own as well. I do want to talk about how to make that work, though. Because I need to know when push comes to shove, I'm your priority."

Cam stared at Jesse, hoping he understood what Cam was trying to say. He didn't care if he shared him with other people. But he had to know where he stood with Jesse. That was the deal breaker for him.

"I don't want you to doubt you're a priority to me," Jesse said. "But the idea of anything outside of sex between us being restricted to one particular box completely goes against who I am."

"I know. And I swear I'm not trying to change you. I just want to figure out a way you can still be you and yet we can be together."

"But anyone else I got involved with would be just sex then, right?"

"I doubt it. Not with everyone you got involved with." Cam shrugged. "I don't think that's the way you operate. A lot of the people you have sex with are your friends. Hell, I know you love Kyle, so that means it would be more than sex with him. I'm fine with that."

"Will and Isaac said nearly the same thing to me." Jesse sounded annoyed they'd discovered something about him he hadn't known himself.

"What I'm trying to say is that if Kyle hops into bed with us sometimes, great," Cam continued. "If you want to blow him at the bar, go for it. If you meet some hot guy you want to go home with, I'm on board. Hell, I don't want to stop you from being with women, if that's what you want."

Jesse blinked at him. "You're not attracted to women. How would that even work?"

"I don't know. I'm not sleeping with them, so that's up to you, I guess." Cam smiled. "But if you wanted to make it a group thing, maybe we could find a couple. You could fuck the woman while I fuck her boyfriend.

Honestly, I haven't worked out every detail yet. I'm still trying to figure this out in my head."

"You're sure you can handle me fucking someone without you there?"

"Yes." Jesse looked relieved, but there were several more things Cam wanted to clear up. "Would you be okay with agreeing to come home to me after?"

"I could do that. Would you want to know about it? I mean, if I'm staying out late with someone, I'd let you know, but would you want details after?"

Cam bit his lip. The thought was unexpectedly hot. "I think I would. And who knows? We both know I'll meet someone I'd want to hook up with. I suspect I'd be doing that less often than you, but I'm not ruling it out. At all."

Jesse sat back, a little of the tension in his shoulders disappearing. "Knowing you'd go off with someone else on your own is a relief to me."

"Because it feels more equal?"

"Sure, but also because it makes me feel sure you're doing this because you want to and not trying to change yourself just to be with me."

"I can understand that. But, Jesse, you're the first guy I've wanted any kind of long-term partnership with. The idea of still having freedom and flexibility as part of that is a relief, not a concession." Cam hesitated. "Having said that, there's one more thing I want to ask. What do you think about putting any solo hookups on hold for a little while so we can work on straightening things out between us first? We've done a terrible job communicating up until now, and I just think maybe it wouldn't hurt to focus on us for a little bit while we figure all of this out."

Jesse stayed silent for a moment, obviously mulling over the idea, before he slowly nodded. "Yeah, I think that makes a lot of sense. Make sure we're solid, first."

"Exactly," Cam said, feeling relieved. "We're not going to have a relationship like the rest of the world. We can make the rules up as we go. And find things that will satisfy both of us. I need to be sure where I stand with you. I can't have doubts about your feelings for me. Or that you want a future with me."

Chapter Nineteen

Jesse took Cam's hand, his heart hammering wildly. Jesus, he was terrified, and for so many reasons.

"Don't doubt that I have feelings for you, Cam. I do. Big, Hollywood-sign-sized fucking feelings, to tell you the truth, and I'm not embarrassed to admit it." Of course, his words made Cam smile. Heat flooded Jesse's face, and he barely managed not to roll his eyes at himself.

"I also have no idea what I'm doing." He worried his bottom lip between his teeth for a moment. "And I'm a little scared right now."

Cam's expression softened. "Why? What are you afraid of?"

"That I'll fuck up. That I'll do something wrong and let you down. It wouldn't be the first time." Jesse's voice caught, and he cut his gaze away from Cam's. "You keep telling me to be me, but I'm not sure I know how to do that but also be the man you want."

"Hey, you didn't let me down." Cam tugged his hand free and raised it to Jesse's cheek. "I was being pig-headed and hiding things, and that didn't help. You're already the man I want. I like you the way you are, and I don't want you to change."

"Yeah, you say that now, and the next time I bang a cocktail waitress, you'll be ready to smother me in my sleep with my pillow," Jesse muttered. He smiled at Cam's burst of laughter, but his nerves were still getting the best of him. "Seriously, man, I'm kind of flying blind here."

"I know. So am I." Cam slipped his arms around his shoulders in a loose hug. Jesse leaned in, grateful for the contact, and slid his hands under the hem of Cam's T-shirt.

"I know this is new territory for you — it is for both of us. The guys I've dated were great and all, but I never pursued anything like a real partnership with any of them," Cam said. Now he sounded abashed, but his pretty eyes were filled with warmth.

"And you've decided you want that with me, huh?" Jesse meant to tease, but he grimaced for real and gave Cam a gentle squeeze. "I hope you know what you're getting into — this is going to be one hell of a work in progress."

"I think it'll take both of us time to figure out how it all fits together," Cam replied. "And I'm okay with that."

"Well, then I think I should warn you there will be days you hate me."

"I don't think that's possible," Cam started but fell silent when Jesse shook his head.

"Unfortunately, I have some experience with this. Isaac and I tried to make things work, and when we couldn't, it got ugly. He became bitter and angry, and I know for a fact there were days he hated me. By the end, I'm sure it was a relief for him to break things off."

Cam's expression grew troubled. "I'm not Isaac."

Despite the heavy vibe of their conversation, that made Jesse grin. "I know. But I'm still me, and I will get things wrong. I need to know you'll have patience enough to at least try to see past the fuckups and know I'm trying to get it right. I need you to stick around to work on the problems with me."

He leaned forward until his forehead met Cam's. "Keep talking to me, Cam, even if only to tell me I'm the biggest bonehead in the city. I don't think I'm up to chasing you down and being pushed away again," he said, his voice low.

Cam exhaled through his nose. "I wouldn't do that to you. I promise not to take off, either." He brushed his lips over Jesse's. "I'll keep talking if you do the same."

Jesse pulled back enough to raise a brow. "You're encouraging me to talk more than I already do?"

"About how you feel, yes," Cam got out over a snort of laughter. "You're not the only one who's bound to screw up, and I need you to clue me in if you don't like the way something's gone down. You called me out for being flighty a couple of times this summer, but I had no idea you were having big, scary feelings. I might have done things differently if I'd known. Instead, I thought for sure I was a blip on your radar. Suddenly, you were standing in my classroom yelling at me, and I didn't know where any of it was even coming from."

"I wasn't supposed to be having big, scary feelings," Jesse replied. "Neither of us was. I didn't even know if I could bring them up, never mind how. Plus, I'd just started to figure things the fuck out when you ghosted."

Cam wrinkled his nose, but Jesse's phone chimed then, and Jack Black's wailing guitar filled the air. Jesse's anxiety levels jumped.

"That's Sara," he said.

Cam kissed him quickly and let him go. "Go on—we can talk more later." He stood and started clearing away the breakfast remains.

Jesse connected the call. "Hey, girl."

"Hey. You still thinking of coming down here?" Sara's voice sounded steady, but also thick with emotion, and Jesse had to force himself to stay seated and calm.

"Of course. Everything okay? You're not alone, are you?"

"No, I'm not. Your mom and dad are here, and my parents are on their way from my place now. Eric is so much better today. His motor issues are mostly gone, and the physical therapist has him out of bed. He's been walking around the halls with only a little help." Sara chuckled. "Your brother's looking damned proud of himself, Jes. I'm guessing he likes being vertical again!"

Jesse got to his feet. He smiled so wide his cheeks hurt, but the relief he experienced was so intense he thought his chest might cave in. He covered his sternum with his free hand and uttered a strangled laugh. "Of course he does. The big lug's never gotten over the fact I'm taller than him by an inch—no way would he stay down any longer than he had to."

Sara laughed, too, but Jesse could hear tears in her voice.

"Sara—"

"It's okay," she said. "I'm just...shit, I'm so pumped up I don't know what to do with myself right now."

"Well, sit down, for God's sake—you need to keep your blood pressure in check!" Jesse immediately started for the bedroom but made sure he aimed a smile Cam's way. "I'll get dressed and be there as soon as I can. Should I bring anything?"

"No, we're good. Eric'll need to crash for a while after we get him back to his room. This is all so exhausting for him, but his neurologist says it's normal—his body's recovering and needs sleep."

Jesse paused outside his closet and blinked against the sting of tears. His roller-coaster emotions over the last several weeks had left him raw, and the last two days had pushed his limits almost to breaking point. He'd never forget the terror he'd glimpsed in his brother's eyes the night before.

"Maybe you could stay until dinner?" Sara asked. "I think Eric would like that. He's missed you, and he worried about you the whole time you were gone. He's so glad you're back and patching things up with Cam. Wait—the two of you are patching things up, right?"

"Yes, we absolutely are." Quickly, Jesse shook himself and stepped into the closet to pull jeans, a T-shirt and underwear from various drawers. "Tell you what—there're a couple of delis near the hospital, so how about I pick up food for everyone on my way, and we can have a picnic dinner kind of thing?"

"Oh, I love that idea."

"Should I bring food for Eric, too, or—?"

"I think that'd be okay. They've put some restrictions on his diet to help us start narrowing down his migraine triggers, but I'll send you a couple of suggestions. Um. An avocado smoothie would be great."

Jesse racked his brain for a place to buy smoothies. "Avocados are okay?"

"The smoothie is for me. So, yes."

He laughed. "Sounds good. I'll call if I have any questions or feel like geeking out, okay?"

"Okay. Hey, Jes?"

He stepped out of the closet and walked to the bed with the bundle of clothes under his arm. "Yeah?"

"Thank you for coming home."

A long moment passed before he trusted his voice enough to speak, but Sara didn't press. "Tell Eric I'll see you both soon, okay?" he managed before he and Sara said their goodbyes.

The moment he ended the call, another jolt of relief hit Jesse, and the tears he'd fought off welled in his eyes again. In an effort to regain control, he flipped through the apps on his phone only to find over a dozen new messages checking on him and his family from Kyle, Carter and Riley, as well as Nicola Parkman at Clash Radio. A lump rose in Jesse's throat, and the words on the phone screen blurred. Carefully, he set his clothes down on the bed and took a seat. He propped his elbows on his knees so he could drop his head forward and concentrate on not falling to pieces.

Jesse didn't know how long he sat there, his body and mind buzzing with a weird mix of near hysteria and fatigue while the occasional stray tear slid down his cheeks. He knew he must have made quite a picture when Cam found him, but Cam didn't comment. He took a seat beside Jesse instead and brought a hand to rest on the back of his neck. Jesse hummed in appreciation of the broad palm that warmed his skin. He finally straightened up and shared a watery grin with Cam.

"That sounded like a good conversation with Sara from where I stood. You okay?" Cam asked.

Jesse dashed at the moisture in his eyes with his fingers. "Yeah, for the most part. Eric's up and around, and Sara sounds about one thousand times better than she has since she asked me to come back to New York. On the other hand, I'm kind of a mess."

"Well, you're a hot mess at least." Cam knocked shoulders with Jesse and made him laugh.

"Duh. It's like my brain and body have never met, and neither one knows if they're coming or going."

Cam nodded. "Your body clock is still jacked from all the stress and travel and time zones. I'm tired, and I never left New York." He looked Jesse over carefully, his gaze sharp. "Are you really okay?"

"I'm getting there. Seeing Eric like that scared me." Jesse licked his lips. "From what the doctors can tell, he's going to be fine, but I'm still waiting for my head to catch up and realize I don't need to freak out anymore."

"Why don't you get some more sleep?"

"Mmm, I can't. I need to head over there again. I told Sara I'd pick up food for everybody, and I can tell she and Eric need someone who is not a parent around."

Jesse pressed a quick kiss against Cam's lips. "I apologize, but I have to take off on you again. It sounds like Eric will be released tomorrow, and things can start getting back to normal-ish."

That includes things between us, Jesse thought with determination. He gathered his clothes, then glanced at Cam, who stood.

"I'll come with you."

"Are you sure?"

Cam held out his hand and hauled Jesse to his feet. "Absolutely. But I'm working midnight to three a.m., so I'll need to head to Ember from the hospital." He laughed at Jesse's groan. "I can come back here afterward, if you like?"

"You'd better." Jesse planted another kiss on Cam's mouth. "Leave your stuff here. I'll do laundry, and you can borrow some of my clothes if you need to. Now get the fuck in the shower so I can find a place to order food, and we can get out of here."

"You could shower with me and save water," Cam suggested, his expression sly. He pushed his lips into a pout when Jesse pointed to the bathroom door instead.

"Uh-uh. We will never get out of here if you get wet and naked around me, and the last thing I want to do is piss off the pregnant lady."

Jesse smacked Cam's ass lightly, but even that fleeting touch was enough to interest his cock. He shivered as Cam headed for the bathroom. It had been far too long since he'd enjoyed that toned body, and he looked forward to some quality, uninterrupted time with his man.

Your man, huh?

Jesse grinned. His man, yeah.

* * * *

With the food pickup included, it took almost two hours for Jesse and Cam to make their way uptown to the hospital. Eric was asleep when they stepped into his suite, his skin still somewhat pale but his face relaxed in slumber, and the elder Murtaghs were home resting before dinner. While Jesse tried to project outward calm, he felt frazzled. He'd hardly set down the bags of takeout before Cam pushed him toward the couch by Eric's bed. The next thing Jesse knew, he was seated next to Sara with a bottle of water in one hand and an apple in the other while Cam unpacked the food with Sara's mom and dad.

"Who knew your boyfriend could be so charmingly bossy?" Sara asked. She took a quiet slurp of the avocado smoothie.

"Not me," Jesse muttered around a mouthful of fruit. "I kind of dig it." He sat back, his eyes trained on Cam until Sara's laugh caught his attention. When Jesse turned back to her, she grinned. "What?"

"I called Cam your boyfriend, and you didn't correct me. What's up, Buttercup?"

"I'm feeling chill, Daffodil," Jesse quipped back with a wink.

"Uh-huh. Clearly, you and Cam worked out a bunch of stuff?"

"We're in a better place than we were a week ago." He took another bite of his apple, then gave it to Sara when she held out her hand. "But don't get carried away with the 'boyfriend' thing. We're still working through stuff, including mundane details like titles."

"You guys will be fine. Trust me on this, Jes. I could tell things were different for you from the beginning." Sara bit into the fruit with a loud crunching noise.

"Yeah?" Jesse cocked his head at Sara, and she handed back the apple. "How?"

"The first time Eric mentioned Ember, you got quiet. You quit moving, quit talking, almost like you didn't want us to notice you thinking about it. But then you mentioned meeting Cam, and you were super casual about it, so I knew things didn't add up. You've never hidden stuff from us before, and I figured that whatever you and Cam had going fell outside the norm."

Jesse tried to protest he hadn't been hiding but closed his mouth when Sara also handed him the smoothie cup and got to her feet. She flashed him a sheepish smile and excused herself with a muttered, "Gotta pee." She high-fived Cam as they crossed paths.

Cam dropped into Sara's vacated seat. "This suite is bigger than Kyle's entire apartment," he said. The awe in his expression made Jesse chuckle.

"Sara says the maternity suites are even bigger. But, c'mon, let's be real — Kyle's apartment is a tiny, crappy hole."

"It's not that bad."

"I suppose. It suits him, at any rate." Jesse remembered the messages from his friends on his phone then and groaned. "Damn. I forgot to text him and the others on our way over here."

Cam nudged him with his shoulder. "Do it now. They won't hold it against you. Besides, I'm sure they think you're still sleeping."

"I wish I was." Jesse smothered a yawn behind one hand. He moved to rub his eyes under his glasses and frowned at his full hands. Cam's amused expression caught his attention. "What?"

"I'm still getting used to you without the beard. What made you shave it off?"

"I needed a change. And maybe to let go of some old baggage I didn't even know I'd been carrying around." Jesse set the cup and apple on Eric's bedside table. He rubbed his fingers over his chin. "I like it, but I still find it strange, too. It's been a long time since I had a naked face."

"The beard was hot, but I like this, too." Cam ran the backs of his fingers along Jesse's cheek. "You look—"

"If you say younger, I am going to thump you so hard."

Cam grinned wickedly. "I meant to say less impish and more sweet. Almost like a little boy. Combined with the glasses, it's like I'm talking to a whole different person."

Jesse snorted. "Don't worry. I'm still the same pain in the ass who drives you crazy."

Cam's expression gentled. "Good. I kind of like your brand of pain in the ass."

* * * *

After Eric woke from his nap and the Murtaghs returned, the collective family ate a light dinner. Jesse and Cam then accompanied Eric while he took a couple of laps around the hospital floor, and the last of Jesse's most intense anxiety over his brother eased. Nearly all Eric's symptoms had resolved and, with the exception of being slightly off balance and fatigued, he felt like himself again. There were lifestyle changes in his future, including medications and altering his diet and work hours. Jesse and his father were ready to do whatever Eric needed to help him get there. In their minds, Eric's continued health easily outweighed any temporary wrinkles those changes might cause in their lives or business.

The remains of Jesse's jet lag left him both tired and keyed up when he let himself into his loft after eleven p.m. that evening. Despite his body's impression it was still five hours ahead, he unpacked his suitcase and carried a load of his and Cam's dirty clothes to the laundry room off the kitchen.

With the low hum of the washing machine providing background noise, he started to relax. He sat at the island in his kitchen with his tablet, reading through the new migraine treatment regimens Eric and Sara had shared with him earlier in the evening.

Jesse slipped into a lazy autopilot mode after the wash cycle finished. He loaded the wet clothes into the dryer, then moved around his home and simply enjoyed being there again. The work on the floors had been done in his absence, and he smiled at the idea of the Hamilton kids sliding over the softly gleaming redwood planks in their socks. He paused in the act of arranging throw pillows on the couch when his phone buzzed in his pocket and wasn't surprised to see a message from Cam.

Something tells me you're puttering around your place right now like an old man.

Jesse bit back a laugh. *Wrong,* he replied and took a seat. *I hired a troupe of exotic dancers to entertain me. I'm setting out Gatorade so no one gets parched.*

LOL.

You on a break? Jesse asked.

Yep, back on in 5. Been talking to Ben, aka the angry bartender who hates you.

"Oh, man." It warmed Jesse immeasurably to see Cam back to his playful, teasing ways.

I hear that guy is a jealous douche.

He is, Cam replied, *but he's got a new guy and seems a lot less ragey.*

Good for hjim, Jes replied. He only noticed the typo after yawning so hard his jaw cracked.

Go to bed, Jes. You know you're tired.

Yeah, okay. Jesse waited a moment before he tapped out another message. *I put a key and the alarm code in your bag so you don't have to bother the doorman.*

A long pause followed, and Jesse suspected Cam was actually searching for the key and code. The reply that eventually popped up made Jesse grin.

You're crazy if you think you're getting these back, Big Money.

After Cam's break ended, Jesse folded the load of laundry and turned off most of the lights. Things were a bit hazy by the time he brushed his teeth, and he let out a satisfied groan once he stretched out in bed. His exhaustion claimed him so quickly he didn't even manage to turn off the bedside lamp.

He surfaced to find the light still burning when Cam slipped into bed beside him, and the clock read close to five a.m. Cam had stripped to his boxer briefs, and Jesse admired the play of shadows and light over his fair skin. He smiled when their eyes met, even as Cam raised his brows.

"Damn, I didn't mean to wake you."

"Glad you did," Jesse rasped out. He put one hand over Cam's to keep him from turning out the lamp.

The apology in Cam's expression faded. After a beat, he leaned over and covered Jesse's lips with his own and slipped farther down into the bed. Jesse closed his eyes, luxuriating in the sensation of Cam's tongue in his mouth and those long limbs against his.

They peeled each other's underwear off and spent a long time just touching and kissing. Jesse pulled Cam in as tight as he dared until their skin met from lips to toes. Cam shivered against him, and Jesse's body was ablaze when they finally broke apart. Lust pulsed deep in his groin, but he found the mere sight of Cam enough in that moment. The realization made his heart hurt in the best possible way.

"I love you, you know," he murmured, and the roar of his heartbeat almost drowned out Cam's sharp inhale. Jesse raised a hand and ran his fingers over Cam's lips. Looking at him was almost too much to take. "It's okay if you don't feel the same way. We're making this up as we go along, right?"

Cam nodded, stars in his eyes. "That's right. I do feel the same, though," he said, his voice steady. He pressed one hand over Jesse's sternum. "I think I have for a while."

Jesse couldn't stifle his moan. "Fuck, that's unbelievably hot."

Cam skimmed his hand down Jesse's torso, then lower to palm his cock. He smiled at Jesse's shudder and kissed him. They were both panting when Cam pulled away. He shifted back and trailed kisses along Jesse's body.

Jesse grunted as Cam nosed along his pelvic bones. "Holy shit, you are going to kill me."

"Not intentionally." Cam chuckled.

Cam sat back again and reached toward the nightstand. He found the bottle of lube and some condoms from the drawer, Jesse's hand on him the whole time. Jesse loved it when Cam put on a show, but right now, he needed to touch and be touched. He shuddered at the warm, wet hand Cam wrapped around him.

"Oh, God."

"I know," Cam agreed.

"Don't...gah, don't tease me," Jesse gritted out. "It's been a while since I did this, and I am about to blow just from you touching me."

Cam bit his lip. He worked a condom over Jesse with a light touch, but Jesse's balls tightened anyway. He closed his eyes and fisted the sheets to keep hold of himself, then opened them again when Cam's hand fell away. Goosebumps sprang out over his skin at the sight that met him.

Cam had come up on to his knees. His cheeks were flushed red and his lips swollen, and he stared down at Jesse with heavy-lidded eyes. Sweat sheened Cam's skin. His cock stood hard, bouncing lightly against his abdomen as he rocked his hips forward with gentle motions. Cam splayed one hand over Jesse's belly and reached back behind himself with the other. He uttered a deep groan. Jesse eyed the way Cam's muscles flexed as he moved and went still upon realizing Cam was working himself open with his own fingers.

"Gorgeous," Jesse whispered. The simple utterance made Cam gasp.

"God, Jes."

The tension in Cam's voice told Jesse he was close. He reached for him immediately, and Cam's eyes filled with fire. He lifted a knee and straddled Jesse's body, his stare unwavering, and Jesse guided him down.

Jesse's heart thundered as Cam rode him. He gripped Cam's hips with bruising force, firm in his belief that Cam anchored him to earth. His breath got caught up in a growl when Cam closed his eyes, and his head fell back. A long moan rumbled through Cam, and that debauched noise sent lust jolting through Jesse's body.

"Shit." A deep, sweet ache pooled in his groin. His hand trembled as he took Cam in hand. "I'm close, Cam."

Cam leaned forward, caging Jesse's head in between his arms. Jesse thrust up hard and cupped Cam's balls with his other hand. Pride surged through him at Cam's cry.

"Fuck!"

Cam's whole body shook. Jesse thrust hard again, and Cam lit up like a firework. His eyes went wide, and he came hard with another cry, streaking Jesse's torso with his cum. He collapsed down on top of Jesse, his cock still pulsing and his lips pressed close to Jesse's ear.

"Love you," he got out, his voice harsh, and Jesse came, too, the orgasm tearing through him like wildfire.

The pleasure spun out longer and longer, so intense Jesse nearly sobbed. He lay limp and stunned in its aftermath, his breaths still coming fast when Cam pulled off. He tried to rouse himself as Cam cleaned them up with what he guessed was a T-shirt, but his eyelids refused to cooperate.

"Sorry," he muttered. He managed a dopey chuckle, and Cam shushed him.

"Let's sleep," Cam whispered. He drew the sheets up around them and turned out the lamp, and they held each other close while dawn broke over the world outside Jesse's window.

I could get used to this, he thought, before he slipped back under into sleep with a smile on his face.

Chapter Twenty

"He's very charming," Maureen said with a sigh. "But in such a genuine way."

Cam smiled at his mom. He dried the last pan and hung it on the rack. "Yeah, he is. Jesse never says anything he doesn't mean."

"I see why you care for him so much."

There was a roar from the living room that sounded suspiciously like Jesse. Last Cam knew, he'd been playing with Lily and George. It was a terrifying but entertaining prospect that made Cam grin so wide his cheeks hurt.

"I'm glad you brought him to dinner. It seemed like he enjoyed himself."

"He did," Cam said without hesitation. As Cam expected, Jesse got along beautifully with the loud and chaotic Lewis clan. He'd only been subjected to Cam's parents and siblings, but Cam thought they were more than enough for the first meeting.

Of course, it was no surprise he'd impressed Cam's family. He'd brought a bouquet of flowers for Maureen and a six-pack of Frank's favorite microbrew to start, but from the eldest to the youngest Lewis, he'd won them over. He'd even offered to help Maureen with the dishes after dinner, but Lily and George clamored for his attention, and he'd given in to their demands with a smile.

If Cam hadn't already been smitten, he would be now.

"Let's go see what they're up to," Maureen suggested. She tucked a hand into the crook of Cam's elbow, and they walked toward the living room together. Cam paused in the doorway, taking in the scene in front of him.

The tabloids might have dubbed Jesse the Playboy of Manhattan, but two months after he and Cam had become a couple, he was roughhousing with kindergarteners. And appearing to be having the time of his life.

Jesse was under attack from Lily and George, and his arms flailed as he died a horrible and dramatic death, complete with gurgling noises. Lily and George cheered after the final death rattle, and Lily planted a small rainbow-striped sock on his chest.

Cam glanced at his father, who offered him an amused smile.

"The knights have vanquished the dragon who held the villagers hostage." Frank nodded toward the array of stuffed animals arranged in a small fort of chairs.

"Ah," Cam said, then clapped. "Well done, Sir George and Sir Lily!"

Lily gave him a withering glare. "I'm a lady. Ladies can be knights, too, Cam."

"Of course," he said in a grave tone. "Thank you for informing me of the proper title."

Jesse glanced up at him from the floor. "Well, Lady Lily and Sir George vanquished this dragon most thoroughly. I have learned my lesson and will go forth and bother no more villagers."

"If you promise to be good, I'll make you a knight too," Lily said, brandishing her cardboard sword. She just missed whacking Jesse in the face as he sat up.

He deftly avoided the sword and smiled at her. "I promise no more villagers will be harmed on my watch."

Maureen leaned her head against Cam's arm. "He's lovely, Cam. Are you sure you two won't want kids someday?"

Cam gave her a stern look. "I'm sure. We are sure."

"Well, all right. I was just asking." She gave him an impish smile. "He's good with George and Lily. Your brothers have been hanging on his every word, too. You know you're not getting out of here until they play a video game with him."

"I know." Cam grinned. "But that's how he is. He's good with everyone."

"Hard to believe he's so wealthy and powerful," she said under her breath. Jesse's hair was disheveled, and his shirt creased in a few places. He was gorgeous. Ignoring the fact that the shirt was bespoke and his haircut had cost a small fortune, he didn't seem out of place in the suburban New Jersey living room at all.

"I forget sometimes," Cam admitted. "Or as much as I can when we're spending time at his loft near Madison Square Park, anyway."

"I'm sure he likes that," Maureen said. "That the money doesn't matter much to you."

"I think so. I know a lot of people have been into Jesse for what they can get from him. He knows I want him for, well, him. Although when those storms came through the other day, I didn't argue when he suggested I use one of the Murtaghs' cars to get to and from the club. I don't take him up on an offer like that often but…"

"That shows he wants to take care of you," Maureen said. "He simply has more means to do it than most."

Cam nodded. He suspected part of the reason Jesse warmed to the Lewises was that they treated him exactly like any other guy Cam ever brought home.

They had been surprised when Jesse mentioned Cam had applied for a passport so he could join Jesse on some of his trips in the future. With the school year about to start, they'd have to wait for the holidays, but Cam looked forward to it, and his parents seemed excited for him.

"Wanna play again?" Lily pleaded. She tugged Jesse's arm, and he shot a "help me" glance in Cam's direction.

Cam strode into the room. "Well, it looks like I missed all the fun!"

"You did," Jesse said. "I've been vanquished and knighted."

"Busy night," Cam quipped. "But we have about an hour before we have to leave. You want to get in a game with Dan and Arthur?"

"Sounds good." Jesse stood and attempted to straighten his rumpled clothes.

Lily let out a wail of protest, but Cam crouched down beside her. "Hey, Lily-Bug, remember, you and George got your turn playing with Jesse. You'd be mad if Dan and Arthur hogged all the time with him and you didn't get any, right?"

Lily's lips quivered but she nodded. "Yeah."

"Then is it fair for you to do that?"

She shook her head. Cam smiled at her. "I know I'm not quite as awesome as Jesse, but would you maybe play with me for a while?"

"I s'pose," Lily muttered. But her face quickly brightened. "Oh! I need to show you my doll. I gave her the measles!"

Cam glanced over at his mother, who gave him a helpless shrug. "Don't ask," she mouthed at him.

Lily returned a few minutes later, brandishing a doll covered in hideous green spots. "See!"

"I don't think the measles are usually green, Lil." It appeared she'd used marker to make them.

She gave him a scornful look. "It's a new kind of measles. And I'm a scientist searching for the cure! You can help."

Cam took a seat on the floor while Lily dumped out a bin filled with various toys. "What are these for?" he asked.

"Research."

"Got it."

Lily chattered away about the best way to research a cure for the green measles, and Cam glanced around. Cam's parents were curled up in an oversized chair together, surveying the room with contented smiles on their faces. Jesse sat on the couch between Arthur and Dan, with George on the floor by his knee.

A lump rose in Cam's throat. He hadn't been searching for someone to build a life with. Or to fit in with his family so well. He'd never expected to find it with Jesse. But he'd found it nonetheless. And Cam knew exactly how lucky that made him.

Forty-five minutes later, Cam encouraged Lily to put away her toys. She did so with a mournful noise but didn't put up too much fuss.

Cam leaned over the back of the couch and rested his chin on Jesse's shoulder. "We should head out, babe." They had time before they needed to leave, but goodbyes took a while in the Lewis house.

"Sure." Jesse glanced at Cam's brothers. "Sorry, guys."

"Aw, man," Arthur said. But he saved the game and set down his controller.

"Thanks, Arthur." Cam pressed a loud, smacking kiss to Jesse's cheek.

"Gross," Dan muttered.

"You're jealous because you're not dating anyone," Arthur sneered.

Dan tossed his controller on the couch next to him. "Meh, there's a guy on my soccer team who's pretty cute. I think I might ask him out."

The entire room fell silent.

"Anything you want to tell us, Dan?" Maureen asked.

"No," Dan said. "Just that there's a guy I might ask out. So, bite me, Arthur, I might not be single for long. And it was my brother's PDA that grossed me out."

Cam remembered a girl Dan had dated the year before and the various crushes he'd had throughout the years. "Are you bi, Dan?" he asked.

"Duh."

"Oh," Maureen said. "We had no idea."

"Well, now you know." Dan shrugged. "Besides, Arthur knew."

All eyes turned to Arthur, who stared back like he couldn't figure out why anything happening qualified as a big deal. "What? His news. Not mine."

"I hope asking him out goes well," Jesse said. "As a fellow bi dude, I wish you luck."

They bumped fists, and the lump that had been in Cam's throat returned full force.

"Well, you'll have to tell us all about him!" Maureen said.

Dan groaned. "This is why I don't tell you guys anything. Everyone in this family is so nosy."

"You get used to it eventually." Cam patted him on the shoulder. "But we should head out."

Jesse stood and they said their goodbyes, and Maureen and Frank followed them out.

"Do you want any leftovers?" Maureen asked at the door.

"I think we're fine," Cam said.

But Jesse nodded. "If you can spare some blueberry cobbler, I could go for that. It's the best I've ever eaten."

Maureen beamed. "I'm so glad you liked it! I'll send some home with you." She hustled toward the kitchen. "You wait right here, and I'll be back."

"You made her day, you know." Frank held a hand out to Jesse.

Jesse shook it. "It was delicious. There's a strong possibility it won't last until tomorrow morning."

Frank gave him a broad smile and patted him on the shoulder.

"Here you go," Maureen said a few moments later, holding out a massive container of blueberry cobbler. "Now give me a hug."

Jesse hugged her, but when he pulled back, Lily and George each latched on to a leg. He looked down with a grin. "Err. I seem to have growths." He gently tried to shake them off, but they clung tighter. "Barnacles, maybe."

"You can't leave!" Lily wailed. "We were having fun!"

"Ouch." Cam pouted. "I've been ousted as their favorite."

His mom offered him a sympathetic smile.

Frank crouched down and looked at Lily and George. "Now, we've talked about this. I know you want to play more, but Cam and Jesse have plans tonight. It was nice of them to come all this way to see us. If you ask nicely, they might come over again. But if you're rude and demanding, they might be less excited about coming back."

Lily's small shoulders heaved, but she let go and so did George. "Okay."

Jesse crouched down, too. "I would love to come back. And maybe sometime Cam and I can have all you guys over for dinner at my place," he said. "How does that sound?"

Lily's despondent expression shifted. "Do you have toys at your place?"

Cam covered his snort with a laugh. The toys Jesse owned were extremely adult in nature. Jesse glared up at him, no doubt guessing what Cam was thinking. It had only been two days since he'd slipped a ring over Cam's cock and balls, then tortured him with a vibrating prostate massager and a blow job until Cam had begged to come. How could he think of anything else?

"I'll make sure there're things you could play with," Jesse said. Which Cam suspected meant he'd go out and buy something outlandish and wildly fun to have on hand for Lewis family visits. Thank God, Jesse's loft had fancy climate-controlled storage units in the basement of the building because kids' toys did not mesh with Jesse's home décor aesthetic.

Lily wrapped her arms around Jesse's neck. "Bye, dragon man. Remember you're a knight now, so you have to behave."

"I'll try," Jesse said. He dropped his voice to a whisper. "I'm not always very good at that."

Lily sighed. "Me neither."

"We'll have to keep working at it then."

Cam's lips twitched at their exchange. He was still smiling when he and Jesse extricated themselves from his family's grasp and made it out to the Range Rover.

After Jesse started the vehicle, he turned to look at Cam. "You look happy."

"I am." Cam reached over and squeezed his thigh. "Thanks for coming today."

"I had a nice time." Jesse smiled at him. "They're great."

"They're nuts, but I like them."

"That's kinda how I feel about you." Jesse pulled away from the curb.

"Hey!" Cam protested with a laugh.

"So, Dan, huh?"

"Yeah, didn't expect that," Cam admitted, shaking his head. "Never a dull moment."

Jesse chuckled. "I suspect that's an understatement. But I love the way they handled it."

"Pretty low-key, huh?"

"Well, I'm sure it helped you'd already come out."

"Sure. But they didn't have a much bigger reaction with me," Cam said. "We make a big deal out of some things, but not the ones most people do."

"I can see that."

They were silent while Jesse focused on the GPS's directions to the Holland Tunnel.

Cam was lost in his own thoughts when Jesse spoke again. "What do you think about moving in together?" Jesse's tone was casual, but the topic was anything but.

Move in together? Cam twisted in his seat and looked at Jesse, wondering if he'd heard right. "Well, we've talked about the idea before. In a 'someday' sort of way," he said and kept his voice as neutral as he could manage.

"I know." Jesse glanced at the rearview mirror. "I think maybe someday is approaching. You spend most of your time at my place, anyway."

"I do," Cam agreed. "But there's a huge-ass difference between me having a place I don't use much and me moving in on a permanent basis."

"There is. And I never expected to feel this, much less say it aloud, but I miss you when you're not there, Cam."

His heart felt like it was suddenly too large for his chest. "I miss you, too."

"And I like knowing I'll be coming home to you," Jesse said.

Truthfully, his place already felt like home to Cam. Though he loved Brooklyn, both of his jobs were in Manhattan. It was a relief to take a short train ride to Jesse's place rather than the time-consuming trek via ferry and train to DUMBO. But the hassle of commuting between boroughs wasn't the reason Cam wanted to move.

It wasn't the snoring roommate and water dripping that made it hard to sleep when he was at his loft. Jesse wasn't there. Cam would move to Albuquerque if Jesse wanted it. And he felt genuine surprise that he'd brought up the idea of cohabitation so soon.

"Well, we've got a couple of options," Cam said. "My lease is up in a few months. I could wait and move into your place then. Or I could start moving my stuff into your place and look for someone to sublet."

"I'll start clearing out closet space," Jesse said. "Think you'll miss Brooklyn?"

"A bit," Cam said. Just like that, they were going to move in together. Surreal. "But it's worth the trade-off." And Cam meant a hell of a lot more than the short commute and cushy digs.

"There are a couple of things we should talk about first," Cam said while he mulled over what living together would mean for their relationship. "You own your place, right?"

"I do."

"So, I'm guessing you won't be charging me rent."

Jesse grimaced. "I hadn't planned on it. Please don't tell me you want me to out of some misguided sense of pride."

"No, I don't. I would like to contribute to utilities and groceries, though."

Jesse opened his mouth, then closed it. "Sure. And I'd like to splurge on you occasionally. Like when we take a trip to London, I'll cover your travel expenses."

"Keep it to a dull roar, and you've got a deal, Big Money."

Jesse snorted. "This is not the kind of shit I ever pictured when I thought about relationships."

"Well, you've never been in a relationship with me before," Cam teased.

"True."

The Holland Tunnel spit them out onto Lower Manhattan's streets. Cam glanced at the GPS and realized Jesse was on the way to his place in NoMad.

Our place, he corrected himself. "Aren't we going to Under tonight?"

"We are," Jesse said. "But I want to change first. Lily did a number on my shirt."

Cam chuckled. "The first rule of hanging out with the Lewis family is always bring a spare set of clothes."

"Noted."

"Don't you keep a change of clothes at the bar?"

"I did." Jesse shot a quick glance over at Cam. "But there's less need for it these days."

Since Jesse hadn't hooked up with Kyle at Under lately, that made sense.

"Are you freaking out at all?" Cam asked. "At the way your life has changed since we've been together?"

Jesse fell silent for a moment. "No." His tone was thoughtful. "I'm not. For a long time, I was afraid anyone I tried to be with would try to change me into someone I didn't recognize. You aren't trying to change me, though. Sure, I've changed some of my behavior, but I'm still me. And pretty fucking happy."

* * * *

A couple of hours later, Jesse cleared his throat, and the assembled crowd at Under fell silent. "I have a small announcement to make. Make sure you're all sitting down." He waited until everyone was. "Cam and I are moving in together."

Dead silence rang out for a moment followed by cheering. A babble of congratulations followed, punctuated by people clinking glasses. *We'll have to let Eric and Sara know, along with both sets of parents*, Cam mused. He'd talk to Jesse about that.

"Am I to assume you're leaving Brooklyn then?" Carter toasted Cam with his drink.

"You are correct," Cam said. "I'm not going to try to drag Jesse out of Manhattan. He loves me, but there is a limit to what I'll ask."

Carter nodded. "That's why you two work."

"You know, Kyle, it looks like you and Malcolm are the only single guys now," Riley observed. "There seems to be an epidemic of coupledom going around."

The crowd hooted with laughter.

"No guys in uniform strike your fancy?" Carter asked.

Kyle shrugged. "Saw one a couple of weeks ago. I went across the street to the burger joint for lunch, and a couple of firefighters came in to grab a takeout order. One was downright stunning, and we chatted for a bit before he had a call."

"Any sparks?" Will asked.

Everyone groaned. "Punalty!" Carter called out. "You're an author, Will. You should know better."

Kyle smiled. "Eh, not sure if there were any sparks or not. He could have just been a friendly guy."

"What'd he look like?"

"You heard the man. Stunning!" Cam joked. "Isn't that enough?"

Kyle smirked at him. "Tall, like David. Brown skin, gorgeous blue eyes. Biceps the size of my head. Looked great in his turnout gear." Kyle's cheeks were a little pink.

Carter snickered. "Such a uniform whore."

"Did you get his name and number?" Riley asked.

"Name yes. It's Luka. But not his number."

"Why the hell not?" Jesse asked.

"I didn't know if the interest was mutual. Even if it were, what if he's not out to the firehouse? I'm not about to out a guy who could get killed if his coworkers decide they aren't cool with it."

"Yeah, good point," Riley said. "Still, you could have discreetly slipped him your number."

"It's not like I'd planned on picking up a guy during lunch. I wasn't prepared. I'm not saying I haven't eaten at the place more often," Kyle said with a small, wry grin. "On the off-chance of seeing him again."

"What about you, Malcolm?" Riley asked. "Anything new with you?"

Malcolm shook his head. "Just work and family stuff."

Riley looked as though he wanted to say more, but Carter nudged Riley with his foot in what looked like a signal to back off.

Malcolm was still an enigma to Cam. He came to Under regularly, and always seemed to enjoy himself, but rarely volunteered anything personal. Cam wondered if he should make an effort to get to know him better. He wasn't sure how to go about that though.

The conversation veered away from relationships and toward current events. When it shifted to politics, David stood. "Hold on. I'm going to need a drink before we get into this."

Laughing, the group split up to refresh their drinks, and Jesse pulled Kyle aside. "Hey, can I talk with you in the office for a minute?"

"Sure." Kyle looked puzzled but he followed Jesse. "What's up?"

"I just wanted to go over a few papers."

Cam took a seat on the couch and sipped a glass of the mint-ginger caipiroska Kyle mixed up by the pitcher, a tweak on the traditional vodka and lime drink. He watched Jesse and Kyle walk away, and his gaze lingered on both of their asses. Damn, that was a nice view. It made Cam's mind wander to the time the three of them hooked up. He looked forward to doing it again.

At Cam's request, he and Jesse had gone to a bathhouse a couple of weeks ago. Not the kind where they'd gotten massages and relaxed in the steam room, but the very gay and very sexual type. It had been an eye-opening experience for Cam and though he and Jesse hadn't played with anyone else, they'd both enjoyed it immensely. They liked watching other men having sex. And they'd loved other men watching Jesse fuck Cam. They'd made plans to explore that again in the future.

When they'd first discussed their partnership, they'd put casual hookups on hold until they were sure it was solid. Neither of them had been with anyone else — together or apart — since. Cam thought it was about time they did.

Who better to do it with than Kyle?

Cam set his drink on the table at his elbow, excused himself and followed Jesse to the office. He knocked on the door, then poked his head in. "Mind if I interrupt for a sec?"

Kyle eyeballed him from where he leaned against the desk. Jesse was seated on the couch. "You're not interrupting, babe. Jesse used work as a tactic to get me alone and interrogate me about the firefighter and why I didn't bring him up before."

Cam chuckled. "And why didn't you?"

"Because all of you are a bunch of busybodies. Besides, nothing happened. I will probably never see him again." Kyle rolled his eyes. "Anyway, what's up?"

"Well," Cam smirked at him. "I have a proposition to run by you both."

Jesse raised an eyebrow. "I do like being propositioned."

"You'll like this, then. If you don't have plans tonight, Kyle, what do you think about coming home with Jesse and me?"

A flicker of surprise crossed Kyle's face. "I assume you aren't talking about gaming."

"You are correct. I was thinking threesome."

Jesse looked surprised. "Really?"

"Yeah." Cam sat beside Jesse and laid a hand on his thigh. "The idea popped into my head, and I figured I'd come in and throw out the suggestion."

"Want me to give you guys a few minutes to discuss?" Kyle asked.

"That's not a bad idea," Jesse said. "Thanks, darlin'."

"Sure." Kyle made a beeline for the door, but before he stepped through it, he turned back. "For the record, if you're both in, I am, too." He winked and closed the door behind him.

Cam turned to face Jesse.

"You sure you're ready for this?" Jesse's expression was very intent. "We had a great time at the bathhouse, but it could be different with Kyle. Especially after what happened last time."

"I'm sure." Cam brought a hand up and stroked his cheek. His stubble rasped against Cam's fingers. "I feel secure about where we are now."

"Okay." Jesse grasped Cam's hand. "I don't want to rush anything, that's all."

"Neither do I."

"You're not just trying to prove a point, are you?"

"Maybe a little. I appreciate how you've pushed yourself out of your comfort zone in the past few months. Letting me into your life, meeting my family, talking about moving in together..." Cam shrugged. "It's not all one-sided. You know I'm okay with you being with someone else. We both want an open partnership, and who better to start with than Kyle? Besides, I couldn't keep my eyes off his ass when he walked away. Trust me, I want this." He took Jesse's hand and pressed it to the fly of his pants where his cock was already half-hard at the thought of going to bed with Jesse and Kyle again.

Jesse leaned in and kissed him hard. "God, I love you, Cameron."

"I love you, too, Jesse." Cam leaned his forehead against Jesse's. "And while I didn't plan for tonight, I have been thinking about this in general. Imagining the three of us in bed again."

"Yeah?" Was it his imagination or did Jesse sound breathless? *Good.*

"Yep. I'm picturing Kyle fucking me while you suck me."

Jesse let out a small groan. "Fuck. I'm convinced."

"Should I ask Kyle to come back in?"

"Yes." But Jesse didn't let go. Instead, he looked Cam straight in the eye. "But if you need more time, we pause it, okay? No hard feelings. We can talk and work it out."

"Agreed. I don't want to rush it either, Jesse. I want to be sure we're both getting everything we want out of this."

Jesse's kiss was answer enough.

"So, what do you say?" Cam asked Kyle when they were all in the room together again. "Want to help us celebrate our plans to move in together?"

Kyle laughed. "That would be a difficult invitation to turn down."

"If you need extra incentive," Jesse said, "Cam put forth the idea of you fucking him while I suck his cock."

"That is quite an incentive," Kyle leered. "But you don't have to convince me. Since both of you are sure you're good with this—"

"We are," Cam said. He squeezed Jesse's hand.

"Then so am I."

* * * *

Later that night, after Kyle kissed them both goodbye and let himself out of their loft, Cam turned on his side and looked over at Jesse. Cam was spent and so sated his bones seemed liquefied.

Cam smiled at him. "Did you ever think you'd be in this position?"

Jesse stretched and let out a contented-sounding noise. "Moving in with a man who is very enthusiastic about exploring new things in the bedroom and fucking other guys? No, I can't say I did. I assumed they were mutually exclusive, pun not intended, and I've never been happier to be proven wrong."

"Who'd have thought we could make something like this work?"

"You, Cam." Jesse's voice sounded a little thick. "You showed me this was an option."

Cam pressed his lips to Jesse's. "You know, when I started falling for you, I thought for sure you'd break my heart," he said after he'd drawn back.

"Nah," Jesse said. "I love you too much for that. And when I put my mind to something, I almost always succeed."

Jesse made his declaration with the kind of certainty only a man like him could have. But Cam knew he meant it. Jesse's single-minded determination got him what he wanted in life, but the touch of humility was new. He'd made up his mind about wanting a life with Cam, and Cam knew he'd do whatever it took to make it happen.

Cam's upbringing was worlds apart from Jesse's, but he was every bit as determined to make their life together work. Maybe they didn't have the kind of partnership many people were looking for. But it worked for them. Nothing else mattered.

The Speakeasy: Behind the Stick
K. Evan Coles and Brigham Vaughn

Excerpt

September 2015

Kyle McKee set down his gym bag and yoga mat and pulled up a seat at his gym's juice bar. The class he'd taken had warmed his skin and stretched his muscles and joints to their limits. He felt like the world's most relaxed slab of single New York man, which was good for Kyle's state of mind. He'd been stressed lately, about his love life in particular. Because damn if every guy he'd been out with in the last two months hadn't turned out to be a shitheel of epic proportions. So much so, Kyle had decided to stop dating entirely.

Eyes closed, Kyle forced away thoughts of dating catastrophes. He rolled his neck from side to side but peeled his lids open again when the chair on his left slid back and his friend Malcolm Elliot dropped into the seat. Malcolm gave Kyle a lazy grin. At six-three, he stood a few inches taller than Kyle, and he looked rosy-cheeked and loose limbed, his blue-gray eyes shining.

"I am a man-sized untwisted pretzel," Malcolm said. "I'm not sure what that means, so don't ask."

"You're yoga-stoned, dude." Kyle smiled at Malcolm's laugh.

"Is that a thing?"

"Totally a thing."

Malcolm narrowed his eyes at Kyle. "You're the one with the bloodshot eyes—what did you do after class?"

"Ugh, nothing but itch from allergies. Ragweed is my kryptonite." Kyle pinched the bridge of his nose between his fingers, then nodded at the menu on the wall behind the counter. "What are you drinking?"

"I'll do a Kale Storm with protein," Malcolm said.

Kyle held up a hand when Malcolm reached for his wallet. "I'll grab these—you paid last week." He smiled at the barista who'd stepped up to take their order. "A Kale Storm with a protein powder shot and a Peanut Butter Baby with chia, please. You headed home after this?" he asked Malcolm.

Malcolm shook his head. "I've got errands to run. My kitchen has mysteriously emptied itself of food since my brother and his girlfriend came back to town. What about you?"

"I'm opening tonight, so I'll just head to the bar. I have extra clothes at the office I can change into." Kyle co-owned a speakeasy called Under with his friend Jesse Murtagh and, while he loved his job, the commute uptown from Chelsea to Morningside Heights could be a pain in the ass. He welcomed the option to skip extra stops when he could.

Malcolm ran his gaze over Kyle's gray Henley and dark jeans. "You could always serve in what you're wearing, you know. You'd blow Jesse's mind."

Kyle covered a theatrical gasp with one hand. "I would never!" His preference for black or dark gray clothing while working was a source of gentle teasing among his friends. "Seriously, I don't feel like I'm working unless I've got my blacks on. I've done it for so long it's just part of how I do my job."

A thoughtful expression fell over Malcolm's face. "I think I get it," he said. "The black clothes are your uniform. I've got one too, though it's a lot less hipster bartender." He grinned at Kyle's snicker. "When I worked in advertising, I wore a suit or a good jacket with dress trousers. It took me a while after I started at Corp Equality to feel okay about not dressing formally." Malcolm waved at his hoodie and joggers. "I wouldn't go into the office dressed like this unless I was working on a weekend even now."

Kyle nodded. Malcolm worked as a social organizer at the headquarters of Corporate Equality Campaign, an organization dedicated to defending the rights of LGBTQ people in the workplace. While a non-profit, the CEC maintained a business-casual culture, and Malcolm always dressed with understated chic.

"Did you start wearing black at work on purpose?" Malcolm asked him. "Definitely seems like a smart idea given you mix drinks all night and could get splashed with booze."

"I only get splashed when Jesse is mixing drinks," Kyle replied, his tone dry. "But it was more an accidental habit. I got a job at a nightclub right after I moved to New York, and everyone on staff wore black," he explained. "Not like that's out of the ordinary—unless a club has a gimmick, staff usually wear black so they don't stand out. Can't have the clientele feeling like they're not as pretty as the guy schlepping booze behind the bar."

The barista appeared with their smoothies, and Malcolm quirked an eyebrow at Kyle.

"I get what you're saying, but that doesn't work, does it? I mean…it's not like anyone forgets you're a good-looking guy whether you're wearing black or not."

Kyle shrugged. "It's more about fading into the background than anything else. Staff in any bar or club are supposed to keep the customers happy without their noticing the hard work going on."

He sipped his smoothie and let out a satisfied sigh. He'd need something more substantial to eat before he started his shift at Under, but for now, his taste buds and stomach were happy with the combination of banana, peanut butter and chocolate almond milk.

Kyle ran a thumb over the moisture on his cup. He'd given Malcolm a pat answer, and though he could leave it at that, he didn't want to. Compared with other friends in their shared circle, Malcolm was reserved to the point of appearing introverted. He'd become very close with another of their mutual friends, Carter Hamilton, who also worked at the CEC, and he'd also formed a connection with Kyle in the last several months.

Initially, being single among so many coupled-up friends had brought Kyle and Malcolm together, but Kyle had found he liked hanging out with Malcolm. Malcolm had introduced him to Sunday afternoon yoga classes, and Kyle had ushered Malcolm into the world of Fallout, an event Malcolm sometimes rued, particularly after an all-nighter of playing hard. Malcolm had listened while Kyle grumbled about men, and Kyle had taught him to mix killer drinks and cook fish tacos, and now, as the weather turned autumnal, Malcolm shared the occasional personal detail. Kyle knew those overtures were a sign of Malcolm's trust, and he wanted Malcolm to know he trusted him in return.

"The real reason I stuck with the black clothes at work is because I was broke," he said. "I moved here with fifteen hundred dollars total and a bus ticket back to Vermont, and I kept the ticket and most of the money in a safe deposit box at a bank in Midtown. Jesse jokes that I had more interest in buying food than clothes back then but he's not wrong. Even if I'd spent my cash on clothes, I didn't have a place to store them." Kyle gave his friend an easy smile, but Malcolm's expression sobered.

"You stayed with friends, right?" he asked.

"Friends and acquaintances, yeah. Guys I dated if they were okay with it. I'd kick in with extra food and I'd cook to help out, and people were cool about it. Sometimes, I'd take over a room if someone left, and if that wasn't an option, I moved every couple of weeks to keep from wearing out my welcome."

Kyle ran a hand over his dark hair. "Couch surfing meant keeping my stuff in one duffel bag so I could pick up and move at a moment's notice. I bought three changes of blacks for work, and I'd do laundry every couple of days to make sure I had something clean. The pattern worked for what I needed at the time, but the habit stuck even after I got my own place and unpacked my duffel bag."

Malcolm smiled. "Did you burn the bag?"

"No way, babe. I kept it! What do you think I used the last time we went to Southampton and stayed with Carter and Riley?"

Malcolm furrowed his eyebrows as he considered Kyle's words, then his eyes went wide. "Your big green bag is the bag? Where the frock did you even buy that thing?"

"It belonged to my dad," Kyle replied. "He served in the army and the sea bag is standard issue." He wrinkled his nose. "Topic change, dude, because what is up with the 'frocks' and the 'darns' and the 'back that truck ups'? Why are you talking like a summer camp counselor all of a sudden?"

A flush crept up Malcolm's neck. "I might have let loose a bunch of f-bombs in front of Carter's kids." He held his hands up when Kyle's jaw dropped. "Before you give me crap, I didn't know Sadie and Dylan were within earshot. Carter's ex brought them by on her way out of town with her boyfriend, and the kids set up a fort in the closet in Car's office. They were supposed to be in the employee lounge, though, so Astrid and I didn't check when we ducked into the office to talk about an event that started going pear-shaped."

Too late, Kyle tried to smother his laugh and failed. It bubbled up out of him even as Malcolm's expression shifted from contrite to aggrieved.

"It's not funny, Kyle."

"Oh, yes, it is."

Malcolm scrubbed his forehead with one hand. "I swear a lot when I'm stressed."

"You know, I'd never have guessed that about you."

"That's because I don't usually do it out loud in front of people!" Malcolm exclaimed. "I was in the middle of a full-on rant when the kids started laughing, and of course, Carter walked in at that moment. Sadie told him I have an 'even bigger potty mouth than Jesse,'" he grumbled, and the air quotes he drew with his fingers made Kyle laugh harder.

"Oh, man," Kyle got out. "Car wasn't mad, right?"

"I don't think so. He told the kids they weren't allowed to use the grown-up words, but I could tell he was having trouble keeping a straight face. I didn't dare ask about it because I want him to forget it ever happened."

Kyle leaned over and ruffled Malcolm's light brown hair, still damp from the shower. Malcolm normally wore it cropped short, but he'd been growing it out, and his hair spiked up in soft peaks under the playful touch.

"No offense, but I'm pretty sure Carter won't forget if you keep up with the soft swearing. He knows you didn't mean it, and he'd have told you by now if he had a problem with it. Just be yourself and don't worry about it." Kyle sipped his smoothie. "Maybe keep the 'what the frock,' though. That shit is funny."

Malcolm's lips twitched up into a smile. "Okay."

PUBLISHING

Sign up for our newsletter and find out about all our
romance book releases, eBook sales and promotions,
sneak peeks and FREE romance books!

About the Authors

K. Evan Coles is a mother and tech pirate by day and a writer by night. She is a dreamer who, with a little hard work and a lot of good coffee, coaxes words out of her head and onto paper.

K. lives in the northeast United States, where she complains bitterly about the winters, but truly loves the region and its diverse, tenacious and deceptively compassionate people. You'll usually find K. nerding out over books, movies and television with friends and family. She's especially proud to be raising her son as part of a new generation of unabashed geeks.

Brigham Vaughn is starting the adventure of a lifetime as a full-time writer. She devours books at an alarming rate and hasn't let her short arms and long torso stop her from doing yoga. She makes a killer key lime pie, hates green peppers and loves wine tasting tours. A collector of vintage Nancy Drew books and green glassware, she enjoys poking around in antique shops and refinishing thrift store furniture. An avid photographer, she dreams of traveling the world and she can't wait to discover everything else life has to offer her.

K. and Brigham love to hear from readers. You can find their contact information, website details and author profile page at https://www.pride-publishing.com